A

CURSE

OF

SALT

A CURSE OF SALT

OF

SALT

SARAH STREET

HODDER

HODDER CHILDREN'S BOOKS

First published in Great Britain in 2023 by Hodder & Stoughton

1 3 5 7 9 10 8 6 4 2

A CIP catalogue record for this book is available from the British Library.

ISBN 978 1 444 96766 1

Typeset in Perpetua by Avon DataSet Ltd, Alcester, Warwickshire

Printed and bound in Great Britain by Clays Ltd, Elcograf S.p.A.

The paper and board used in this book are made from wood from responsible sources.

Hodder Children's Books
An imprint of
Hachette Children's Group
Part of Hodder & Stoughton Limited
Carmelite House
50 Victoria Embankment
London EC4Y 0DZ

An Hachette UK Company
www.hachette.co.uk

www.hachettechildrens.co.uk

For the girl who I was when I wrote this book.

1

The tide rolled in.

I stepped closer to the edge, drawn by the lick of salt on the breeze. In one breath, the wind tugged back my briny curls and swept blue into the black lung of the cliffs. Sea spray flecked my cheeks, and the knot in my chest tightened.

Down below, waves tossed a broken body against jagged rocks, leaching old blood into the tidepools. Another day, another dead.

Gods — don't be him.

Villagers trudged the shoreline, fishermen in waterlogged slacks braving the shallows. They waded towards the homebound corpse, superstition snapping at their heels. My heart thrummed an anxious rhythm, waiting.

Their families hung back, a crowd gathering at the water's edge. I watched from above, pretending I didn't long to push my way past them, to feel the bite of the ocean through my worn boots. Safer up here, letting the wind whip my heart's tug of longing into submission.

All I could see were the man's thin arms and dark hair, a grimy shirt plastered to his pale flesh. I'd seen enough bodies in the past weeks not to fear the death in his hollow cheeks, but my pulse still raced. Terrified that the body the fishermen lugged between them belonged to my father. And if not today, then tomorrow.

Seawater scattered beneath wading boots as the villagers laid the body ashore. The crowd scrambled forward, their steps swallowed by sand. Still, I hung back. I'd have my answer soon.

Sure enough, a cry cut through the dusk.

I scanned the cluster of figures, spotting a woman as she sank to her knees, head cradled in her hands – as though they could hold the weight of her grief. She was the village blacksmith, her husband one of my father's crew. One of the few who'd returned at all.

My fingernails bit into my palms, hot tears welling at the anguish that filled the air. It was getting harder and harder to cling to old hopes when each day presented a horrifying new truth. It would've taken a miracle for Father to leave those waters with his life.

I shut my stinging eyes and turned back to the sea, listening to the blacksmith's cries echo through the bay like the call of a gull. Clouds descended to the clifftops, obsidian crags glistening with fading sunlight. I inhaled, smelling the brewing storm as it whispered through the forest towards us. Not long now.

'Ria!'

I glanced over my shoulder. Aberdeen marched down the hill towards me, lilac skirts whipping about her legs. She halted at the edge of the dead grass, eyes sharp and quizzical.

Strangled sobs rose from the shoreline below and I saw a sigh of relief escape her. I didn't need words to tell her what we both already knew.

'Get inside,' was all she said, her gaze flickering to the heavy horizon before she spun around and stalked back up to the house. Any slower and I might've caught a glimpse of fear in her moonstone eyes. But no, that wouldn't be my sister.

I threw one last glance at the sea, bit down on my lip and hurried after her.

Aberdeen snaked up the path with brisk steps, her raven hair pulled back in a tight braid, safe from the wind as it swept twilight into the bay.

Our cottage sat in the crescent of two hills, its backyard spilling into the woodlands beyond. Gnarled ivy overtook the crumbling stone walls and little arched doorway, but gardening had long ago lost its place on our list of priorities.

'How is she?' I asked, stepping over the threshold.

Aberdeen shoved a lukewarm bowl of broth into my hands and ushered me towards the stairwell. 'Take this up to her.'

I stared down at the bowl, its watery contents stirring the hunger in my belly. We lived on the stuff in winter, but the leaves had only just turned and our cupboards were near barren already.

Worry nipped at my stomach as I took the broth upstairs, nudging my way into our bedroom. The stale air hit my nose, the small room cloying with the scent of sickness. Felicie lay with the covers shoved down to her ankles, nightdress sticking to her pale skin.

My expression tipped softly into a smile. 'Are you awake?' I whispered, kneeling by the side of her bed.

My older sister's eyes slid open and a returning smile tugged at her tired lips. 'Hi.'

'I brought your supper,' I offered, gesturing for her to sit up. Felicie's head wavered as she pulled herself upright and I settled the bowl into her lap, brushing a hand over her damp forehead. 'Bad day?'

She nodded mutely, leaning into my touch. We'd passed countless hours this way, with me wiping her fever-ridden brow, whispering stories into her gold-spun hair. Being two years younger had never stopped me from trying to take care of her.

Felicie lifted the bowl to her mouth, taking a delicate sip. Then she frowned. 'Did Aberdeen make this?'

I tried to swallow my laugh, but failed. 'Yes.'

'I like the way you make it better,' she said.

'I know. I'm sorry, I was in the village.'

Felicie's brows creased. 'Was it . . . ?'

'It wasn't Father,' I assured her, offering what I hoped was a fortifying smile. I didn't tell her who it was, or that he was the third washed home in just a week. I didn't tell her a lot of things. 'But yes, he was dead.'

When she shuddered, I felt it in my bones.

'And the sea?' Felicie murmured into the wooden lip of the bowl.

My fingers danced over her back, tracing a pattern of the purling waves across the cotton of her shift. If she were anyone else, I'd have lied. 'Like magic,' I answered.

I wasn't supposed to love the sea, not the way I did – not when it only ever brought us ruin. Gods knew, nobody else did. But no amount of blood could ever taint that endless, ferocious blue. It lingered: saltwater pearls on my cheeks, my lips, my lashes. Flecks of the ocean's ache followed me everywhere I went. Begging me to do the same. To follow.

Rain thrummed against the windows, lifting my gaze to the world outside. The storm had arrived.

When she was finished, I pressed a kiss to Felicie's temple, took her empty bowl and left her to rest, occupying myself with chores as the sun sank and silvery light filled the kitchen. But as usual, keeping my hands busy did little to distract me from my thoughts.

Our father's absence haunted this house more with each voyage, a shadow that lengthened in his wake. We'd come to whisper his name like a curse, as if prayers would ever be enough to bring him home. Northbay echoed with the truth of what had killed Father's crew. *Who.*

It'd been centuries since any god's name had been whispered with a shard of the reverence that the Heartless King's demanded. I prayed to only one of those gods; believed in her only so far as she crashed against my cliffs. It was the Heartless King, his pirates, who loomed over us all, casting darkness down the coast and inspiring the stories we'd begged to hear as children. Back then, that was all they'd been – stories.

The dull thud of ceramic on wood broke the silence that stretched between Aberdeen and me at dinner. The sound was hollow, like most of our days here. Like my lungs, seizing every time I thought of the future that faced us.

How many nights have we spent like this? I wondered, glancing up at my eldest sister from across the table. Only four years apart in age, but there was an infinity between us, this valley of silence and cold looks that I'd never been able to cross. The fact that we came from different mothers didn't seem to mean a thing; we'd never been even half the same.

Her silence grated on me, now more than ever. Her stoicism might've kept us alive in the hardest months, but with the world outside turning to frost, I couldn't help craving a little warmth.

'What're we going to do?' I ventured, braving the quiet. 'What if he's really gone?'

The words clogged my throat long after I'd forced them out. It was a struggle not to picture the stark reality ahead, not to imagine what our lives would become without Father.

Aberdeen didn't even glance up when she spoke. 'We'll survive. We always do.'

Have, I wanted to say. We always *had*. Things were different this time. I could still smell the rot, still see the glassy eyes of those whose bones had rattled home to families just like ours. Ones with little chance of making it through the encroaching winter. But when Aberdeen said it, it sounded almost possible. Almost real.

I stared at her from across the table. Her dark, pointed features were shadowed. Impassive. Felicie and I shared our mother's eyes; Aberdeen had our father's. But her almost-black hair and sharp jaw – they must've come from *her* mother. Tall and angular, she was as far from Felicie's soft, honeyed appearance as possible.

I blinked, scraping up the last dregs of soup with my spoon. Aberdeen was right, of course. We'd done it before, tiding over the weeks during Father's voyages. I balanced the ledgers, cleaned the house, cared for Felicie when her lungs failed her. Aberdeen took whatever little we had to bargain with into the village. It took an iron will to refuse her; I always settled for the fairest price.

It was Father's blood that drew us together on the coldest, hungriest days. An unspoken agreement that we'd grit our teeth and do what it took. *Whatever* it took. For Felicie, if not for ourselves.

The storm whistled through the broken windowpanes, shaking the timber of the cottage. The howl of the tempest masked the clang of our bowls as I tossed them into the sink, shoving the hair back from my face with a sigh.

Come home, I whispered to the wind. I didn't know how much longer we'd last alone in a house so cold, in a land so close to dust.

Rain battered the thatched roof, the sea calling to me

from above. I ignored it, scrubbed the dishes clean and retired upstairs, my restless mind soothed by the harmony of my sisters' snores.

It wasn't much of a life, but it was what we had. I'd do what I could to hold on to it.

I woke in the dead of the night, jolted into the cold, moonlit room. Voices shouted somewhere below, their words indistinguishable from the squall. Fists pounded against wood, against the roar of wind and rain whipping at the cottage walls.

I knew the voices, gruff and male, and growing louder. I glanced hesitantly between Aberdeen and Felicie, their faces peaceful in sleep, before tossing my covers aside and darting from the room. I hurtled down the stairs and raced for the door, throwing it open with my heart in my throat.

The storm ripped inside. Three rain-soaked figures clambered over the threshold, chased by the night. I knew two of them from the village, their gaunt faces sending panic ringing through me.

Water surged across the floorboards as they staggered in, supporting a third man between them. His head drooped against his chest, dark hair slick to his pale scalp.

The air swept from my lungs. Every nightmare from the past weeks collided, blooming into the very thing I'd feared and hoped for most. *Father.*

A cry escaped my lips as the villagers dragged his unconscious form into the living room. I hovered nervously as they lowered him into an armchair, his tattered clothes soaking through the upholstery.

Gods, I prayed, *don't let him be dead.*

'What happened?' I finally choked out.

The taller of the two men shrugged. 'Ship washed up in the

storm. She's seen better days, but yer father took the worst, by the looks o' it.'

I glanced down at his slumped form, taking small comfort in the slow rise and fall of his chest. *He's alive. He's alive.* But no matter how many times I repeated it, I couldn't shake the thought that followed – *How many aren't?*

An image of the blacksmith's husband flashed before my eyes, shirt bloodied and torn, his body broken on the shore. 'And the rest of the crew?' I asked, dreading the answer.

The second man ran a hand over his balding head, scattering raindrops to the ground. His lips thinned. 'Nuthin'.'

'Damn pirates,' his companion grunted.

A chill sluiced down my spine. *Leviathan* had left port with a crew of seventeen sailors. Five would be buried in dirt graves on a cliff east of the bay, and those were the lucky ones.

'Take him up to the bedroom.' Aberdeen appeared in the doorway, her face grave. She led the way as the two men hauled Father upstairs, no questions needed. Her footsteps were steady as the rain, unfazed by the horrors that had my heart and mind racing.

I hurried in tow, fingers gripping the banister in an attempt to stop the world falling out from under me.

The men settled Father on to his bed, the colour swept from his fair skin by some ungodly tide. They withdrew with a solemn bow of their heads, leaving Aberdeen and me standing wordlessly over his unconscious body.

The room swirled with stories we'd whispered in the dark as children, stories I'd prayed would never come true. Black-hearted pirates who sailed the raging tides, men and monsters alike at their mercy. Creatures with shark teeth and serpent tongues, and water so thick with blood it tasted of steel.

One figure loomed in all of them. A man, in some tales,

a tentacled beast in others. Here in Northbay, the stories gave him eyes like an abyss, scaled skin and the fangs of an anglerfish. In Bray, his tentacles were made from shadows, his eyes gleaming red and hands like hooks of bone. No matter where we went, the moniker of the Heartless King meant one thing: monster.

Some said the cities of the north were free from King Oren's reign because of him. Because of *pirates* who ravaged and pillaged and plundered. Our village knew better – the Heartless King's fleet did not rail against King Oren in support of anyone but themselves. They did it because they could. They sank ship after ship of soldiers and sailors alike only because they were too proud to share an *ocean*.

I sank on to the side of the mattress and drew one of Father's hands into mine, frightened by how cold it felt. I brushed the damp hair back from his forehead and shivered.

As if he could sense my touch, Father's eyes flew open. Wide and startlingly blue, the horrors they'd witnessed were drowned in terror.

'*Felicie*,' he gasped.

2

'Soup isn't going to bring him back from the dead.'

Warm morning light trickled across Father's sunken face as I set the bowl of broth in my lap with a sigh, ignoring Aberdeen's snide remark. We were both on edge; it had been a restless night, overshadowed by a sense of doom that thickened with each passing hour. Father had barely been able to string a sentence together since he'd woken last night, let alone explain what had happened to his beloved *Leviathan* and crew.

He lay beneath the coarse white sheets, hair still damp from the sea. The smell of salt only sharpened the dread gnawing at my stomach. I could've woven together a thousand stories from what I already knew, but each was as violent and harrowing as the last. I was only surprised – and grateful – he was alive at all. Pirates weren't known for their mercy.

I returned the bowl to the table by Father's bed as he lifted his head to offer me a weak smile. There was colour in his cheeks despite the unnerving emptiness of his eyes and I forced out a sigh of relief.

At least he's here.

Aberdeen stepped closer, her pale green dress crisp against her almond skin. 'What happened?' she demanded, at the same time I asked, 'How do you feel?'

Father struggled to pull himself upright, his thin arms shaking. 'My dears,' he rasped, soft blue eyes hollowed by a fear I'd never seen before. 'We're in greater danger than I feared.'

Greater? We'd always known the perils that lurked beyond the bay, but Father had escaped. He was free. What other kind of safety was there, in this world?

Aberdeen's brows creased, mirroring my concern. 'What are you talking about?' she asked, low, cautious.

'Didn't I always say I'd someday return to regale you with tales of my daring escape from the Heartless King?'

His humourless laugh was undercut by the dark rings that guarded his eyes.

'So it's true?' I pressed, leaning in. 'It was really him?'

Father bowed his head with a slow sigh. 'We were just days from home when they found us,' he began. Brown-and-grey speckled hair fell across his face, but he didn't bother to sweep it back. 'A single ship. His fleet was nowhere in sight, only the mightiest vessel I've ever seen. She towered over us, made *Leviathan* seem a child's toy in comparison. But she was beautiful, too, bedecked with vines of roses that bloomed along the railings.'

His eyes were distant, fixed upon something faraway, something dark.

'The *Blood Rose*,' Aberdeen murmured. She'd come closer, perching stiffly on the edge of the bed.

I shuddered at the sound of the ship's name. Every story

I'd ever heard of it had ended in horror.

'There was time to surrender,' Father continued, suddenly sharper. 'We watched them approach, just waiting. Seeing death sail towards you like that, just knowing . . . I should've surrendered. It was so foolish, I—'

He choked, angry tears tracking the valleys of his weathered cheeks. I squeezed his palm, willing us both the strength to go on.

'Did you see him?' Aberdeen urged.

Father shook his head, hands trembling under mine. 'He never showed his face, only . . .' He swallowed. 'We *felt* him. Like some great, smothering shadow that fell over us all. I half expected the sky to collapse with the weight of it.'

A shadow: that was exactly what the Heartless King was. A darkness that stalked every life he'd ever touched. A looming threat to anything his fleet was yet to destroy. He had no kingdom, no crown, but the sea was his to reign. I couldn't think of a power more absolute than that.

I leaned closer, terrified by what I was hearing yet not wanting to miss a word.

'That ship was the last thing your mother ever gave me, besides you.' Father's grasp tightened around my hand. 'I thought I would never see your faces again and *Leviathan* was the last piece of home I had. I clung to her. Some part of me just couldn't let go – couldn't see her destroyed. I'd heard that even the Heartless King's pirates wouldn't kill an unarmed opponent, but . . . still, I couldn't lay down my sword. Couldn't let go. My crew stood by me, and they paid the price.'

I blew out a breath. I didn't want to hear the rest, didn't want to picture the carnage that had followed. But Father went on, stirring a new kind of dread in the rift of my chest.

'I'm a coward . . .' he said, pulling his hands from my grasp.

12

'I didn't want to die, but I should have. I *wish* I had died before he saw me. We'd all be safer if I had.'

'Who saw you?' I pressed, my heart thudding against my ribs. 'The Heartless King?'

Father shook his head. 'Not him, no. One of his crew. A man I knew long ago, in another life. He spared me.'

I frowned. In what life had Father known pirates?

He never spoke of much before Bray – of life at King Oren's court and his marriage to Aberdeen's mother, nor the things that had chased him from her. Who my parents had been, all those years ago, I'd never truly known.

'He was like a brother to me, once,' Father went on, picking at the fraying threads of his nightshirt. 'We grew up together in the capital. If it weren't for him, I'd never have made it out. He convinced his companions to stay their swords, but as soon as they did . . . he asked about Estelle.'

I winced at the dull pang of grief that shot through me. He spoke of my and Felicie's mother more than he ever had Aberdeen's. Spoke of her laughter, her kindness, her sunshine eyes.

'*Dead*, I told him.' Father's words came out flat, pained. '*And the child?* he asked next. He wanted to know about Felicie.'

Aberdeen's back straightened, and I shot her a sharp look. *Does she know something I don't?*

'I don't understand,' I said, glancing between the two of them. 'How does this pirate know about Felicie? What does she have to do with anything?'

'Estelle and I fled Forea the day Felicie was born,' Father explained to me. 'This man, Mors . . . he helped us escape. He wasn't exactly a pirate back then.'

Fled. Escape. My head spun. He'd never used those words before. What had they been fleeing from?

'What does this mean?' Aberdeen asked tersely. Her face was grave, hands clasped white-knuckled in her lap. 'What do they want?'

'They wanted a trade.' The words fell from his lips like stones, his tongue stumbling over their jagged edges. 'My life, in exchange for the child.'

A shiver tore through me. A pirate's mercy, indeed.

'That makes no sense,' I said. 'What do they want with her?' What could one young woman do for them that they couldn't find, or steal, for themselves?

'I said no, of course,' Father continued, brushing aside my question. 'But they...there was this one pirate, staring down at me like I'd be her next meal. She said I was mistaken if I thought I had a choice. Told me to go home, to send...well, Felicie. Or we'd all pay the price.'

'And your friend didn't try to stop this?' The mattress sank as I shifted my weight, my brows furrowed tightly. *Some friend*, I thought. *Some pirates, too.* This deal they'd made – a girl, for... what? A little blood spared? It made no sense.

Father shrugged. 'I don't think he had much say in the matter. The man I knew never would've let this happen, not to Estelle's daughter. But here we are.'

I released a breath, letting my shoulders slump forward. I thought I'd have given anything to see my father safely home. But if I'd known it would lead to this – to pirates demanding the one thing I could never give up...

'They don't call their king heartless for nothing,' Father muttered darkly.

'But she's ill,' I said, as if it would make any difference. 'We can't just hand her over.'

'We aren't handing her over,' Aberdeen snapped.

'No,' Father agreed. Not for the first time that morning,

I could tell the two of them knew more than they were letting on. 'She'll stay here with the two of you. I know you'll protect her; you always have.'

I bit my lip. 'I still don't understand.'

'I only came home to say goodbye.'

No.

Father's long fingers smoothed the oaken tendrils back from my face. 'I leave again at first light,' he said. 'If I don't return, they'll come looking, for all of us. I can't hide any longer.'

I shook my head again, wiping the smudge of tears from my cheeks. *Hide?* Since when had he been hiding? From what?

'You can't,' I pleaded. 'Don't leave us again.'

'We don't have a choice.'

I stared at my father, trying to swallow the hurt that threatened to consume me. He was keeping something from me, I could tell. And now he wanted to leave all over again, in a way I couldn't see him coming back from. Leave us in pieces to fight through the winter, and every winter to come, without him.

'Go now,' my father told me gently. 'I need to speak to your sister.'

Aberdeen sat back in resignation, rubbing her brows, and I had to swallow to stop the flare of anger inside me from igniting. I cast a look between them, their identical blue eyes deflated with a shared understanding. How long had there been secrets there? How had I never noticed?

I rose begrudgingly from the bed and left with a wary backwards glance, my mind tripping over a tangle of new information. A pirate's trade. My sister's life caught in the balance . . .

The door snapped shut behind me and I stood, dumbfounded, on the landing.

He's going to die, I realised. *And we're all going to starve.*

Slick peel slipped through my fingers and into the sink. I rinsed the potato and reached for another, deftly carving the dirt-caked skin from its green-tinged flesh.

Felicie's figure wavered in the glass windows as she moved through the damp yellow grass out front, scattering seed for the chickens and soaking up the weak afternoon sun. Scrawny, half-feathered things, the hens were all that remained of the livestock Father had bought with the cottage four years ago. Pitiful now, like us.

Felicie seemed better today, livened by the relief of Father's return last night. Still, her health was fickle. Some days she was filled with the strength of a hurricane, others she could barely lift her own smile.

A familiar tightness rose in my chest. What price rested on her head without her knowing? What could the Heartless King's crew possibly seek from a girl who had nothing? Was it the monster himself who wanted her, or was this about something else – something Father and Aberdeen understood, and I didn't?

More than that, what was to stop them from killing Father and coming after us still? My fingers trembled, the knife slipping from the potato's hard skin. If they really wanted Felicie, what made him think he could stop them?

I knew there was more to it, that he wasn't telling me everything, but it didn't change the facts. The *truth* wouldn't fill our stomachs, and if we didn't find a source of income to replace Father's trade before the month was out, nothing would.

The clouds sat heavy against the fringe of the sky, dark and looming as my thoughts. The storm hadn't quite passed, but it had abated for now. There was salt on the breeze that blew in through the open windows and the cool air filled my nostrils, caressing my bare arms as waves crashed against the distant cliffs. I set down my knife with a sigh, trying to remember something more than longing.

I didn't miss the city the way my sisters did. Didn't miss the cold nights and tight dresses and the smell of manure that edged the cobblestones. The dancing, perhaps, but not the endless hours of empty conversation, not the flushed cheeks and creeping hands of over-eager suitors. I was only fourteen when we'd left Bray, but that had never stopped them.

Here in Northbay, I was free to lose myself among the pages of my novels, to walk the bluffs that arched alongside the ocean and let the wind sweep my problems behind me. I didn't love the cottage, for it wasn't our home, but I had books, and the sea. That had always been enough for me.

Footsteps descended the stairs and I glanced up to see Aberdeen enter the kitchen, silk skirts brushing over the worn floorboards. Her long hair was pulled taut in its usual braid, but her eyes were weary, her cheeks wan.

'What's for dinner?'

I tried to fix her with a hard stare. 'Are you going to tell me what's going on?'

She sighed. 'Better you don't know.'

I let my knife fall into the sink with a clatter and drew myself up to my full height. I was tall, but Aberdeen was taller. I scowled.

'Lie to Felicie,' I said. 'We both know this world's darker than she can bear. But don't lie to me.'

'As if you need another reason to be better than me,' Aberdeen muttered.

'What's that supposed to mean?'

'Nothing.' Her hard eyes pierced my indignation. 'Don't pretend you know half the things Father's done to protect you, too.'

I faltered. My sister had never worn the word *love* well. She draped herself in clothes we could no longer afford and kept her emotions buried somewhere beneath. I'd never dared ask for more than Aberdeen gave, not when it had cost her childhood to become the mother none of us ever had. But I wasn't a child any more. I didn't need protecting.

I gritted my teeth, torn between my waning anger and hurt at the spite that pinched her words.

'Just tell me the truth,' I said, wondering how many secrets that silver tongue guarded.

Aberdeen's eyes narrowed. 'There's a reason we fester in this godsforsaken village, Aurelia,' she said harshly. I flinched at her use of my full name – the name my mother had given me. The one only Aberdeen used to scold me. 'You never wondered why Father cast us out to the brink of the world?'

I hesitated. 'It's right on the trade route between Bray and Prynn. And the sea air ...' Father had always said the city smog would be the death of Felicie, that her lungs needed to breathe. But the seaside was no place for anyone any more. With pirates honing in on the last dregs of wealth clinging to the weather-beaten coasts and scouring the Channel between our continent and the wastelands to the west, it would've been foolish to think we'd be safe for long.

Why *were* we here?

'We're right at the edge of the world,' Aberdeen remarked. 'Nobody asks questions here because nobody wants to know what their neighbours are running from. What could chase them so close to the brink of danger.'

I folded my arms across my chest, suppressing a shiver.

'Bray was on the water, too,' I tried to argue. 'Northbay is no more dangerous—'

'Try telling that to Father's crew.'

'So what're you saying?' I snapped. 'That we're hiding here?'

'It's *what* we're hiding.' Aberdeen raised her brows. 'Who.'

My mind whirled. 'You mean Felicie?'

I glanced through the windows again as our sister picked her way back towards the cottage, taking Aberdeen's silence as confirmation. But it still explained nothing. What was so special about Felicie that Father had fled cities to shield her? From pirates and the gods only knew who else . . .

'Why?' I asked. *What other lies have you kept buried all these years?* It felt as though the boards beneath my feet were being ripped away, one by one, exposing a pit of lies beneath.

'Don't ask me,' Aberdeen said shortly. She retreated to the doorway, silhouetted by the sombre hues of the sinking sun. 'I wasn't the one who decided you couldn't handle the truth.'

3

The door creaked as I nudged it open and peered inside. Father sat propped up in his bed, sheaves of parchment spread across his lap, lit by the flickering glow of a candle. The smell of him, of ink and cotton and wood, was so familiar, so comforting, I almost forgot my anger at the door.

Wrinkled hands skimmed across his papers, stilling when I entered. He glanced up, a warm smile falling short of his cornflower eyes.

'How're you feeling, child?'

Eighteen years old and the way he called me *child* made me want to curl up beside him and beg for a story. I ignored his greeting, heart loud in my chest as I crossed the room to sit in the armchair by his bed.

I gripped the worn upholstery with clammy fingers and stared at him, trying to discern my father – my softly spoken guardian, my patient teacher, my favourite person in the world – from the man who'd staggered home in the night.

Age had softened his handsome face, threading his dark brown hair with grey. He usually wore it tied back with a ribbon as a nobleman would, though it had been years since he'd deserved the title. Today it sat straggled about his shoulders, frizzy and dried with salt.

I swallowed thickly. He'd always been more a scholar than a sailor, his slim body built for knowledge, not battle. He didn't have a chance of surviving the Heartless King a second time, especially not alone and empty-handed.

'You've done well with these,' Father spoke, nodding to the documents in his hands.

Any other day, I'd have flushed with pleasure at his praise. *Not today.*

Heat spilled into my cheeks, my hands curling into fists on the armrests. 'What aren't you telling me?'

Father's bewildered expression wavered. 'I know you must be scared,' he started slowly. 'Terrible things are happening, but we've always known a sea merchant like me wouldn't be safe forever.'

His hand reached for mine but I drew back. He really planned to leave. 'I can't let you go when I don't understand why it's happening,' I pressed.

'Dreadful people do dreadful things,' Father insisted, his half-smile threaded with worry. 'This is a pirate's promise – stoking fear into the hearts of those their swords cannot reach. Soldiers couldn't keep them out of Bray fifty years ago, and there's nobody here to even stand a chance against them now. I can't let them find you here; I must return to the *Blood Rose*.'

But you can't, the child in me wanted to cry. *You can't leave me again.* 'What does Felicie have to do with this?' I asked instead.

'I know you're hiding something, Aberdeen told me.'

His eyes narrowed. 'What did your sister tell you?'

A lump clogged my throat, an angry heat clawing at my eyes. They really had been hiding things, all this time. 'She said you don't think I could handle it. You think I'm weak.'

The sigh that escaped him told me everything I needed to know. *She's right.*

Hot tears threatened to burn through my composure. There we sat, like strangers – the father I loved lost in a fog of lies. When did he decide I wasn't good enough? When did he stop believing I'd do anything to protect us?

'I thought you trusted me,' I whispered.

Father's jaw tensed. I could see the pity clear as day in his frown. I didn't want it – hated it almost as much as what faced us. *How did we end up like this?*

'I do trust you,' he insisted, setting the parchment aside to fix me with a look that stirred guilt in my belly. *It's his life on the line here, not mine*, I reminded myself. 'I trust that you'll look after your sisters. You always have. But if you knew the truth behind all this . . . I know you too well, child. You'd do something foolish.'

His words cut like a knife. So I was a fool, too. No wonder they didn't tell me anything.

'Your mother and I swore we'd do everything we could to make sure the three of you were safe and happy,' Father said.

Happy. I stared at him blankly. Did he honestly think I was happy here?

'You think we'd be safe without you?' I fired back.

'Safer here than in the hands of pirates.'

I sank into the armchair, arms wrapped around myself. This couldn't be real. *Pirates.* The mere mention of those unwashed mercenaries and their pointed blades made my heart stutter in fear. The thought of Father facing them in the flesh again turned my blood to ice.

How had it come to this?

He could refuse to tell me what the Heartless King's crew wanted with my sister, but whatever it was, I couldn't let him die for it.

I glanced up, seeing my anguish mirrored in Father's watery gaze. A tear slipped from my eye and I let it fall.

'Just don't go,' I pleaded through trembling lips. 'Please.'

'Forgive me,' he whispered. I knew what that really meant. *Don't cry. Stay here. Be happy*. But I couldn't. The world wasn't made for women like us – young and poor and hungry. I couldn't let him go, because I couldn't protect my sisters without him.

Forgive me, then, I thought, leaning forward to press a kiss to his temple. My lips were wet and all I could taste was salt. It made me ache for the sea, made my heart throb to be far from here, to be free.

'I leave at first light,' Father said.

I nodded, stepping back and wiping my cheeks. 'Then you should rest,' I told him, retreating slowly. 'I'll be here when you wake.'

The lie sat heavy in my throat as I left the room and descended the stairs, knowing what I had to do.

I'd find out exactly what these monsters wanted with my sister. Her blood was my blood, too. How would they know the difference?

Rain lashed against the cottage windows, muffling the sound of my footsteps as I entered the dark kitchen. I grabbed a knitted shawl from the hook on the wall, draping it around my shoulders, and slipped an apple into my dress pocket. I'd find everything else I needed on the ship.

'What are you doing?'

Aberdeen stood silhouetted in the doorway, moonlight glancing off her sea-glass eyes.

My stomach sank. 'I thought you were asleep.'

She rounded the counter slowly, eyeing my laced-up boots, the bulge in my pocket. My heart fluttered, seeing the same question that was buzzing through my mind reflected in her gaze.

What *was* I doing?

'Will you tell me the truth?' I ventured, knowing there was no use lying. She'd see through me, like always.

Aberdeen's thick brows inched upwards. 'About what?'

I suppressed a growl of irritation. 'You know what.'

'There's nothing to tell,' she said shortly.

'So you'd just let him leave?' I spluttered. 'We can't hide from the winter, Aberdeen. How do you expect us to survive?'

'What else can we do?'

My gaze darted to the window. A few hours yet until first light. Enough time for me to –

'No.'

I glanced back at my sister. Her hair danced like ink, eyes shining in the silver-blue light. I'd never seen her look so ethereal, so vivid.

'This isn't some story from your books, Aurelia. This is our lives you're playing with.'

'I'm not *playing*,' I snapped. 'I'm trying to protect us.'

'Those pirates will *kill* you,' Aberdeen said. 'If the monsters of the deep don't get to you first. What makes you think you'll get anywhere alone?'

Monsters or not, I'd rather face death on the water than let it stalk my family here. 'I have to try.'

Aberdeen reached out, hesitating for a moment before she laid a hand on my arm. I stared down at her slender brown fingers, firm on my sleeve.

'You're just a girl. I know you think you can save us, but you'll never survive the beasts beyond the bay, human or otherwise. And what then – what if you're dead and the pirates come looking?'

I glanced away, my eyes burning. How many different ways could she call me weak?

'Stay,' my sister said, almost pleading. Almost. 'Wait until tomorrow. We can work this out, find a way to save them both.' Aberdeen held my gaze, blue eyes piercing, seeing into me like glass.

'Just tell me why,' I countered, wishing I could see into her, for once. See *something*. 'Tell me what they want with Felicie. Or why you're keeping it from me, at least.'

It was futile, I knew; we were as stubborn as each other. Our stand-offs could last hours, even days. But we didn't have the luxury of time any more.

Aberdeen knew as well as I did that we'd get nowhere like this. She shook her head, jaw set as she retreated for the door.

'Please,' I choked out.

She hesitated, making my heart trip over a beat. Her eyes bore into mine, reading my last, silent plea.

'Tomorrow,' she said quietly. 'Stay, and I'll tell you tomorrow.'

I blinked, the world slipping in and out of focus for a moment. 'All right.'

Aberdeen nodded. The darkness of the hall swallowed her, footsteps fading up the stairs.

So that was it. I supposed an empty promise was as good a farewell as any.

*

Mist curled around the wooden docks, seeping into the shoreline.

Shadows swarmed me as I descended the hill towards the village, passing ramshackle timber houses, the lights of candles and oil lamps leaking veins of fire into the street.

What was left of *Leviathan* rocked gently against the current, docked at the edge of the bay. Beside her bobbed Father's second vessel: smaller, and in far better condition. I paused before their hulls with my feet planted on the shoreline, blood pounding in my ears. *Leviathan* looked like she might fall apart on the waves, but my chances of survival already felt slim — I couldn't leave my family with a near wreck as their only means of trade.

I wasn't sure I'd ever feel the safety of land underfoot again, but it wasn't a difficult step that carried me from the water's edge. Even in her condition, *Leviathan*'s gangway felt just as stalwart beneath the soles of my threadbare boots.

Father had never let us sail beyond the bay, but I'd shadowed him diligently as he prepared for each voyage, learning my way around the ship. Even for a small brig, *Leviathan* would be almost impossible to sail alone. Almost.

I knew enough to rig the sails and steer myself from the cliffs, but after that, I'd be at the mercy of the wind. Still, it felt a far safer mercy than the one I was sailing towards.

If Father and Aberdeen refused to give me answers, I'd find them for myself. I'd protect my family, even if it killed me.

It probably would.

I picked my way across the deck, stomach lurching at the dark stains that spattered the tired wood. I shivered, unable to shake the echoes of death that draped the shrouds above.

I paused at the ship's helm with a grimace. I'd stood in the same spot countless times, Father's hands guiding mine on the wheel, elation brimming in my chest. There was nothing as captivating as watching the ocean unfold before me, knowing I was about to be out there for the first time, a part of it. But it dawned on me rapidly that I had no idea where I was going. I could navigate – at least, I'd read enough books to know what was to be done – but I was beginning to realise how little good that would do when I didn't have a clue where to go.

Foolish, I thought, my heart sinking. Father had been right. I was doing exactly what he'd tried to prevent. I wasn't going to save anyone like this.

Just then, the ship began to move.

I stumbled, mystified by the way the deck lurched into motion. I rushed to the starboard rail and peered down at the waves as *Leviathan* pulled away from the docks. A current churned below, roiling beneath the hull.

I squinted through the darkness. The rest of the ocean lay flat – but something was moving in the dark water. Something almost *alive* in the way its waves wove in and around one another, like children splashing in a stream, their faces sculpted from sea foam.

I braced my hands on the rail to peer closer, but it was too dark to be sure. Too dark to know whether this magic that turned the ship, unbidden, was anything more than the sea itself, sweeping me into its embrace.

Aberdeen had warned me I'd be lucky to even make it out of the bay, but somehow I knew these spirits weren't the kind I needed to fear. I stepped back from the edge, watching in disbelief as the forepeak rotated west. The lines tightened, sails blossoming like lily petals at night.

Leviathan glided from the cradle of Northbay's crags, out into the unknown with only the moon's rippling reflection to guide her. I didn't know how she'd fare on the open waters, but it seemed the hands of the ocean wind were there to carry me where I needed to go.

Clear of the bight, I slumped down at the base of the mizzenmast, looking up at the star-flecked sky, the infinite darkness that had somehow swallowed my life. I pulled my shawl tighter around my shoulders, wondering if it was the last night sky I'd ever know.

4

When the darkness lifted, my lips tasted of salt. Weak sunlight grazed my face through the sea vapour, the endless white world blanketed in fog. It was impossible to see much beyond the shimmering waves that lapped at *Leviathan*'s hull — until the bowsprit of another ship speared the haar.

My entire body froze over. Sleek and streamlined, the *Blood Rose* ghosted through the mist towards me. She towered over *Leviathan*, figurehead carved in the form of a beautiful, naked woman, arms stretched out along the forepeak. From her fingers flowed a cascade of climbing rose tresses, their buds blooming against the burnished wood. A black pennant flew proudly at the height of the mainmast, emblazoned with a rose-wreathed skull: the promise of a crimson death.

Blood-red sails stood stark against the white-domed world, but it wasn't just the splendour of the colossal warship that had my heart quivering in my chest. It was the force – the dark power radiating from within. My nerves screamed for me to flee, screamed that there was something more than a heartless man aboard that magnificent vessel.

Swallowing my instincts, I strode to *Leviathan*'s bow, my fear blown back by the wind.

He's only a man, I reasoned with myself. His crew had spared Father's life. Perhaps they would spare mine. But I knew it'd take more than bargaining to leave these waters with my life.

Ropes flew over the sides of the *Blood Rose* and iron hooks hurtled through the air, lashing around the yardarms above me. I stumbled back, the breath catching in my throat as a horde of bodies descended. They swarmed *Leviathan* like insects scuttling over the bones of a carcass, bringing with them the stench of rum and rust. Rotting teeth, dirt-caked flesh and unwashed faces; they were exactly as I'd imagined them, only so much more feral and frightening up close.

Pirates.

They crowded around me, strident laughter and raucous jeers filling the morning air.

'Look what we have here . . .'

'Pretty thing, ain't she?'

'A princess, eh?'

Princess. I couldn't tell if it was supposed to be a compliment or an insult. Leering faces swam across my vision, grubby hands restless and reaching. Their putrid stench and vulgar words brought bile to my throat as I stumbled back, dodging their advances.

Rough fingers wrapped around my arm, tugging me sideways. A man's face blurred before me as he crowed to his companions in glee, ignoring the way I squirmed in his grasp.

'A'ight, enough.'

A voice broke through the din and the pirates stilled. One man swaggered forth from the crowd and the grip on my arm slackened. I tugged myself free, turning to face the newcomer with a mixture of belligerence and fear.

The pirate slouched before me, his lean body shrouded in fabrics as filthy as he was, his bearded face leathery and wrinkled from a lifetime of sun. I met his grey eyes, surprised by what I found there – the glimmer of something dangerous yet bright.

My knees didn't buckle beneath the weight of his gaze, nor did my heart thrill in anticipation of its final beat and I knew this wasn't the Heartless King. Because I didn't see death in him, only curiosity.

A woman lolled on his left flank, clothed in the same breeches and grimy blouse as her crew-mates, a sabre glinting tauntingly at her side. Jet-black hair hung about her shoulders, shadowing gaunt features and dark eyes. I shifted on my feet, toes curling in my boots at the distaste in her bloodthirsty gaze.

'Gotta say, I'm surprised ye showed up,' the bearded pirate said, lips twitching. 'Lucroy's daughter, are ye?'

I swallowed. 'Y-yes.' Someone scoffed behind me and I straightened, fists curling at my sides. 'You summoned me, so here I am,' I forced out, bolder.

'Don't look like much,' grunted the woman.

'Well, I'm here,' I said stiffly, lifting my chin. Even the gods would've laughed at my attempts to seem brave then, with those pirates' prickling gazes turning my skin inwards, my heart hammering so loud I could scarcely hear. 'What is it you want with me?'

The two pirates in front of me exchanged a look.

'Mors, what d'ye think?' asked the bearded one, his bright grey eyes sparkling.

A third figure emerged from the crowd behind me, steps slow and measured. White hair grazed his narrow shoulders, but there was a sturdiness to his fair features that told me he wasn't nearly as frail as he looked.

Mors. I knew instantly who he was. The man who'd known my father, who'd saved his life and tried to surrender my sister's in the process. I quashed the simmering tempest in my chest, the rising tide of dread. I didn't know whether to hate him or to fall to my knees and thank him. Thank him, because if things went to plan, my sisters would live to see the summer.

I kept quiet, watching warily as he approached. The entire crew's attention fixed on me as Mors studied my face, my simple blue dress and long, tangled hair. I met his gaze levelly, praying I would give nothing away.

Mors stared into my eyes for a long time and I couldn't tell if he was lost in them or his thoughts. They were my mother's eyes – Felicie's, too. Large, round, gold as the setting sun. What was he looking for?

'Estelle . . .' he said eventually, his gaze never leaving mine. 'She looks just like her.'

I wondered how my mother's name tasted on his lips, if his tongue was poisoned by guilt. His voice was almost tender, his accent polished, and if it hadn't been for his loose-fitting shirt, his unkempt mop of hair and the small gold hoop dangling from his left ear, I'd have thought him a gentleman.

The breath of relief on my lips evaporated as Mors stepped closer. I swallowed, fighting the urge to back away as I struggled to still my pounding heart. Another step and he'd be able to hear it, I was sure.

No way he can know, I repeated to myself. *I'm my mother's daughter as much as Felicie is, there's no way—*

Mors leaned in, body angled to shield his words from the rest of the crew. He smelled of soap and salt, of sweat clinging to sun-kissed skin.

'So, where is she?'

My eyes cut to him, a glance so full of fear that if he hadn't been sure before, he would be now. My heart plummeted. *No.*

'Estelle is dead. My mother, she—'

'Not her,' Mors murmured, still quiet enough that only I could hear. His lips twisted into a smile. Smug, perhaps, that he'd guessed right: I wasn't the sister they'd sent for. 'There's too much of your father in you. You're a terrible liar.'

'I – I . . .' I stammered, but without lies I had nothing left to say. *He knows.*

Mors' smile faded. 'How many of you are there?' he asked, his gentle features suddenly sharpening, voice urgent. 'Estelle's children, I mean.'

'Just two,' I whispered, knowing there was no use lying. I'd failed.

Mors nodded, looking appeased. Why did he care? Who was this man to play puppeteer with our lives?

My chin came up as I folded my arms and glared at him, trying to cover the panic swelling in my chest, wrapping around my heart. To my chagrin, Mors smirked.

He stepped back with a nod, turning to his companions who were watching intently. 'It's her.'

I stared at the old man, trying to decipher the look on his face. But his amusement had vanished and his amber eyes were inscrutable. He knew I wasn't the daughter they'd bargained for, but he was covering for me. Like it mattered that I was the eldest – that I was her.

Gods, what are they going to do with me?

The dread in my throat thickened, dredging up the sickening realisation of just how powerless I was. Mired in something I had walked willingly into, yet hardly understood, surrounded by the deadliest pirates in the world. Now I was lying to them, too.

I blinked, cursing the fear that clawed at the backs of my eyes, pushing me to the verge of tears. *It's too late to be weak now.*

The female pirate stepped forward, boots thudding against the deck as her eyes pinned me in place. They travelled disdainfully over my flushed cheeks, my rumpled dress and unkempt hair, her fingers moving silently to the blade at her hip.

'Golde.' The woman's name sounded like a warning on her bearded companion's lips, like a master beckoning a hound to heel – only, I had a feeling it was the hound who gave the orders around here, not him.

Golde glared at me. I was half a head taller than she was, but still I cowered back, more wary of those hands than the steel that gleamed between them.

'No use killin' her,' the bearded man went on.

'Aron.' Golde's retort came out in a growl. 'Lemme have this one. We'll get Bane wi'out her.'

The man – Aron – shrugged. 'In the next few months? Doubt it.'

I didn't have time to wonder who or what they were talking about, because the woman cast another look over me and gritted out, 'If he kills us fer this, I'll murder ye.'

Aron rolled his eyes at me. 'Don't mind her. Been a while since we've seen any action round here,' he said with a laugh. As though that was a justifiable reason to *kill* me.

I stared incredulously after him as he strode to the edge of the ship, gesturing for me to follow. I glanced sideways at Mors for approval, unsure when a part of me had decided I could trust him.

He might've been a traitor — now a liar, too — but I doubted I'd find a soul around here who wasn't. Mors nodded.

I followed tentatively as the three pirates reached a rope ladder hanging from the *Blood Rose*'s starboard. The two younger-looking pirates went first, stepping from *Leviathan*'s deck and scaling with practised ease. Mors lingered behind.

'Is anyone going to tell me what I'm doing here?' I asked him in an urgent whisper.

He approached my shoulder, gazing at me with a contemplative look, softened by something almost like pity. 'How old are you, lass?'

I hesitated a moment too long. 'Twenty.' When Mors arched a brow, I sighed. 'Fine, eighteen.'

The old man nodded, shooting me a wan smile. 'Secret's safe with me.'

I gazed up at the hull of the *Blood Rose* with clenched teeth. 'So, why are you helping me? What do they want with my sister?'

'You really don't know?' he mused, those tawny eyes darkening.

'Know what?' Why was I always the one left in the dark?

'Oi!'

A shout from above made our heads snap up.

'Climb,' Mors instructed, pushing me gently towards the ladder.

Panic fluttered in my chest as my fingers closed around the coarse ropes. *I chose this*, I reminded myself. It might've been the last choice I'd ever make, but it was mine.

I set my foot on the first rung, feeling it wobble beneath my weight. A hand reached out and grasped the ladder, holding it steady.

I glanced sharply at Mors, feeling my resolve hitch at the gesture.

'Trust me, lass,' he said in my ear. 'You have nothing to fear from us.'

I fought back a laugh. *Nothing to fear. Just death — possibly dismemberment.*

With an incredulous huff, I began to climb, passing grimy, almost opaque windows that revealed glimpses of an interior as grand as the ship's façade; rooms built for more than just pirates.

In the stories, it had sounded more like a shadow than a ship — planks pieced from black clouds and broken bones, nailed through with the screams of the dying. It wasn't that. It was wood, and dully gleaming glass, and *roses*.

My fingers tightened around the next rung as I forced myself onwards. Nothing about this was like the stories. Stories couldn't kill me.

You really don't know? Mors' words rang through my mind for the rest of my ascent. I'd come seeking truth, but all I had were more questions. More secrets to make me doubt the people I loved most. How much had they been hiding from me?

At the top, Aron hauled me over the railing, his hands firm on my waist. I stepped away the second my feet met the deck, brushing down my skirts, flustered by his closeness.

My gaze drifted upwards and I marvelled at the grandeur of the great man-of-war. Rose vines snaked up soaring masts, towards sails scarlet as their buds, their haunting beauty luring me closer to the danger beyond. Tall ships were graceful by nature, but this . . . I'd never seen such magnificence, not even in pictures, in stories. My heart stumbled, terror tripping over an inexplicable beat of excitement.

Mors appeared behind me a moment later and the three pirates led me up a flight of steps to the quarterdeck, heading for a pair of ornate doors set into the sterncastle.

My feet hesitated, the urge to flee growing stronger with each step. If it weren't for the sound of the crew returning to the deck behind me, I might've taken my chances.

'Wait here,' Golde grunted, disappearing inside.

I stared at the doorway, the engraved wood carved into patterns of swirling thorns and roses. All too elegant to align with those images I'd pieced together from stories. The *Blood Rose* was a graveyard for lost and hungry souls, sailing on shadows more than wind. Not this – not . . . beautiful.

It began to rain.

I looked up at the darkened world above, drinking in the strangely mesmerising sight. Droplets cascaded down my cheeks, soft and saltless. It was a small comfort knowing that if this sky was the last thing I ever saw, it would at least be one that wept for me.

I glanced sideways at Aron, resisting the urge to ask what we were waiting for. I was fairly certain I knew the answer. Fear knifed its way between my ribs, so sharp it suddenly hurt to breathe. I kept my mouth shut, not wanting to rouse whatever lay dormant beyond those doors.

Then I felt it – a surge of power rumbling slowly through the reverberant stillness. The ship trembled, as if waking from a timeless slumber. Icy hands clutched at my lungs, halting the breath on my lips.

Run, said every nerve in my body. *Run*.

Shadows bled out from within, leaking on to the deck and pooling before my boots. Just when I thought the blood in my ears might drown me, the grand doors creaked open. Their hinges groaned, masking my gasp of fear as the pirates shunted me inside.

It was a navigation room, furnished with a large round table where I imagined the Heartless King took counsel, deciding whose blood should next blacken the coasts. Despite the windows that lined the walls, the cabin was dark, muted, and it took my eyes a moment to make out what lay beyond.

Another door stood open at the end of the chamber, emanating an almost tangible shadow. It was impossible to see past where the female pirate stood, staring into the darkness, but words rumbled from within.

'What is this?'

The room rang with his voice. It wound through me like vines of lead, rooting me to the spot. My shoulders tightened, pulse quickening. He was close – too close. I had the overwhelming sensation of someone standing behind me, but when I turned my head, heart dancing in my ribs, I saw nothing. Shadows played on the walls. The hairs on the back of my neck stood on end.

'Brought ye a lass,' said Golde, her tone dripping with derision. 'Aron seems to think we should keep her.'

'She's Estelle's daughter,' Mors added. He slid me a fleeting glance. 'The princess.'

Princess? There was that word again. Only . . . he meant *Felicie*. My racing heart faltered, mind ticking over the possibilities. He was lying again. He had to be.

I remembered Father's words: *Estelle and I fled Forea the day Felicie was born.* Our mother's firstborn, smuggled from the capital . . . Did King Oren have a wife? No – he'd never married. But he'd had a sister . . . If I'd paid more attention to gossip in Bray, maybe I'd have remembered what happened to her.

Mors stared back at me, a grimace painting his lips. *You really don't know?*

I frowned at him, desperate for an answer of some kind, but I couldn't say a thing. Couldn't expose myself in the presence of the Heartless King.

That deep voice spoke again, wrenching me back to reality. 'I asked for Bane, not some girl,' the Heartless King growled. Like Mors, his speech was refined, regal, but his tongue was rough, his words scored by an unfamiliar accent. 'I told you to forget this –

to focus on finding the bastard.'

'This is yer chance,' Aron said, sounding impatient. 'Think how quick he'll come fer her.'

Whoever Bane was, he couldn't have been more dangerous than the people around me. Couldn't have been more *anything* than the voice that rumbled from the shadows. Whatever this stranger wanted with Felicie – with me – it couldn't be worse than what I'd face if the Heartless King decided I was dispensable.

Golde turned to glare over her shoulder at Aron and Mors. 'Bane's business wi' Oren don't concern us. Told ye I'd hunt the traitor down – just need a little more time.'

'Time we don't have,' Mors replied, shaking his head. 'Aron's right. Bane's too focused on his vendetta against Oren – he won't spare us a second unless we make it worth his while, and this lass might just be Oren's one weak spot. With Estelle dead and their brother . . . missing—'

Aron flashed him a grin that made my stomach turn. Gods only knew what they'd had to do with that.

'—she remains the sole heir to the throne. Bane's a smart man; he wouldn't throw away a chance like this.'

The sole heir.

My heart was pounding in my throat. As far as they knew, I was the last living descendant of a king – the only true king the continent had. But they had to be wrong. They *had* to be.

I'd never set foot in Forea, where King Oren ruled from his gilded throne. I was no more familiar with the world of court than with that of pirates, but I knew enough to put the pieces together.

King Oren had never had children, but he'd had a sister. Dead now, as Mors said – and he'd called her Estelle. My mother. But he had to be mistaken, somehow. How could *I* be King Oren's . . . *niece*?

I glanced down at my wrist, at the blue veins that snaked beneath my skin. Mors tilted his head, eyeing my reaction as I did my best to conceal the turmoil raging within. Unless these pirates were delusional — and I wasn't entirely convinced they weren't — then *somehow*, my sister and I were in line for the throne.

The realisation twisted through me like a blade to the gut. Father and Aberdeen . . . They'd shielded me from the cities as much as they had Felicie. After everything I'd done, everything I thought I was doing to protect our family, they'd never trusted me with the truth. Never thought I was strong enough to handle it.

A princess. I wanted to turn on my heel and race home, to laugh at these misguided pirates and whatever absurd scheme they spoke of. Luring some man to his death and using me as bait, it seemed.

I shivered. *You have nothing to fear from us.* Mors' words echoed on. How could I believe a thing from the mouth of a pirate?

As if I'm innocent of deceit, another voice retorted, one uncannily like Aberdeen's. I thought of my family, waking at the first hint of dawn to find my bed empty and *Leviathan* gone. I thought of Felicie, whose name I might well be wearing to my grave.

I swallowed my guilt thickly. I had more pressing concerns. Said grave, for one.

'That sea dog will get what he deserves,' the shadows spoke. Each syllable was twined with the promise of destruction, of pain. 'I don't need tricks to make him bleed.'

The stories could not have captured it, his voice — like the moon, breaking over the sea, only it was darkness that spilled forth. Pure, endless dark.

'Aye, and this is the quickest way, Your Majesty,' Mors insisted. He twisted gold rings around his wrinkled fingers, brow furrowed.

Why were they pushing this? If their own king wanted nothing to do with me, then why was I here?

'After everythin' he's done,' Aron said. 'If ye're gonna make him bleed, let it be over the planks he betrayed us on.'

'You think that's what this is about? I said no.'

'But Yer Majesty—'

'*Enough.*'

The lamps guttered in their gilded brackets.

'Forget Bane,' said Golde, turning to face me with brazen eagerness written across her sallow features. 'May I do the honours?'

The screech of metal sliced through the air as she drew her sword.

'No.'

The word broke the pregnant silence. Golde rounded on Aron, bristling like an animal. 'Think ye can tell me no?'

Aron turned to the wall of shadows that cloaked their king, brushing her rage aside. 'The crew are restless, Yer Majesty. Give 'em somethin' to hope fer. The lass could change ev—'

My blood turned to ice as the Heartless King spoke again, his voice coming from directly behind me.

'Kill her.'

5

I spun around with a jolt.

The Heartless King stood before me, a towering mass of muscle and pure, unrestrained power. His face was hidden beneath a heavy black hood, blending into the dark, untamed locks of his head. Shivers rippled through my veins.

It was him.

A thick beard covered his jaw so that only a stretch of skin was visible, the rest of his features cast in impenetrable shadow. My eyes fell to his unsmiling mouth, blood pounding in my ears. What that cloak hid I could only guess – fanged fury and hooks for hands, scarlet skin or scaly hide. Terror clogged my throat, drowning my lungs.

I knew that if I was wise, I'd bow. But his words hung heavy in the air. If I was to die at his hands, I wouldn't do it on my knees.

The King's full lips didn't so much as twitch. '*Kill her,*' he repeated, his guttural voice rattling my bones.

I turned just in time to see Golde advance, sabre unsheathed.

'She's unarmed,' Aron spoke up, stepping between us.

The woman scoffed. *Magnanimous*, I thought, but it seemed Father was right: even pirates lived by laws. Golde halted in her tracks.

I glanced between the four of them – the three pirates and their fabled king, his shadows so thick I could barely breathe.

'So give her a sword.'

My vision blurred, the world around me dipping out of focus. This couldn't be real.

Rain lashed against the windows, the only sound in the dark, spinning room. This room, filled with strangers and shadows. *I can't die here.*

With a smirk, Golde drew a second blade from the sheath strapped to her back and tossed it at my feet. I stumbled back as the cutlass clattered to the ground. Aron and Mors exchanged a look of concern, but they said nothing, turning their gazes on me. Golde watched me with a look of cruel delight, pacing ever-so-slowly closer.

My breathing hitched. I knew if I raised that weapon against her, I'd face the same fate as so many before me. I'd die for nothing. So I did the only thing I could think of. I swallowed through my desert-dry throat and told her, 'You can't make me pick that up.'

If they were going to kill me, they'd have to do it in cold blood.

Laughter split through the tension in the room. Golde's eyes danced with fury, but Aron strolled to my side, swinging an arm around my shoulders with a snicker. I flushed, not knowing how to respond, but his presence was warm and steady, almost reassuring.

'That solves that,' he said with a chuckle.

Golde's glare sharpened, fixing on him. 'Stop tryin' to make this somethin' it ain't,' she ground out.

The shadows in the room seemed to thicken, the air growing taut once more. I swallowed again, overly conscious of the hooded King looming in the corner.

Aron's arm slipped from my shoulders, his hand moving to the hilt of his cutlass as he stared down his crew-mate. 'Given up, have ye?'

Before I knew what was happening, Golde lunged. Aron's forearm lashed out, shoving me back as he threw himself into Golde's path, parrying her lightning-quick blows. Their blades flashed, locked in a ferocious battle.

A hand tugged me backwards and I whirled around with my fist raised to strike, before I realised it was Mors, pulling me behind him. The room brimmed with chaos, limbs flailing, blood spattering. Until the Heartless King's roar erupted, tearing through my body like claws.

'*Enough!*'

The windows shattered, sending a storm of glass into the air. Wind and rain whipped inside, scattering diamond-like shards across the floor. I dove beneath the table with a shriek, feeling a tidal wave of power sweep overhead. Bodies thudded against wood, followed by a door slamming, then nothing.

When the room stilled, I raised my head and peered tentatively out from my hiding place. The crew were gone, the door at the end fixed shut. I was alone, surrounded by ringing silence and broken glass. I scrambled to my feet and gazed around, the rain spraying my face and arms through the broken windows.

The urge to run kicked at my heels, spurring me to escape. But the tug of the Heartless King's shadows from the next room kept me where I was. I stood alone on a ship brimming with blood-starved pirates and whoever – *what*ever – their king was. I wasn't going to make it far.

I forced out a long breath and turned instead to the grand table beside me, its surface littered with parchment. I brushed aside the clutter and broken glass to reveal a large map laid flat across it. A map of the realm: a whole world I'd never get to see. It was a landscape I knew well, illustrated on parchment so old I was afraid it might crumble beneath my touch.

I trailed a finger over the contours of the continent, from the tip where Northbay's cliffs stretched into the sky, right down to the cityscapes of the south.

Only at the very crest of the continent did I notice something I'd never seen before. It was a cluster of islands, small ridges of land caught between the tides of the Channel. The writing beneath them was too faded to read, but I was sure I could see the marking of a settlement there, some forgotten citadel erased by time and the sea. The maps in Father's study had never shown such a place.

My hand lingered on the old chart until I heard the faint rumbling of voices from the dark chamber beyond. I crept towards the closed door, straining to make out muffled words.

'. . . doomed . . . no point in tryin' . . .' It was Golde, my would-be murderer.

Aron spoke next, a gentle murmur. 'Revenge . . . do it fer them.'

'You think I'm stupid?' The Heartless King's growl was unmistakable.

'She doesn't need to know why . . . think about . . .'

'You said this was just about Bane.'

'The sea is growing impatient,' came Mors' voice. 'Even if you can't . . . this is our last chance.'

'. . . less than three months.'

'It's enough.'

'I know what you're playing at.'

Shouts rose in protest before the clamour broke in a deafening crash. The King's voice thundered like a sky torn in two. 'GET OUT!'

I jumped, stumbling back towards the door. My heart stuttered. *Now or never.*

But before I could make another foolish mistake, the doors burst open and the three pirates reappeared, strolling out with unhurried footsteps. Looking far too calm, considering the cloud of anger that rolled along after them.

Aron met my gaze as he passed, blood trickling from a cut along his cheek. He'd caught the brunt of the fight, but it didn't seem to have dampened his spirits in the slightest. He winked, pulled the doors open and disappeared out on to the deck. Sable-haired Golde didn't so much as glance my way as she snatched up her discarded blade and stalked outside.

Mors lingered in the doorway, a frown tugging at his whiskered lips. 'I'm sorry for this, lass. Truly,' he said, before turning and letting the door shut in his wake.

There was a beat of silence, a second of peace and rain, before the shadows at the end of the room shifted and the Heartless King re-emerged. His hulking figure took shape from the darkness and I fell back a step, talons of fear raking through me.

I didn't know if Mors had been apologising for getting me into this mess or for leaving me in the hands of his monstrous king, but right then I'd have given just about anything not to be alone with him. To have someone – even Golde – beside me, her blade at my neck or not.

Wind howled through the glass teeth of the broken windows,

blowing the King's cloak out around him as he strode towards me. It was the walk of a man with the whole world at his feet, and it made me shiver.

'So.' He stopped a few paces away, his words bleeding from blackness. 'You're Oren's heir.'

No, I wanted to whimper. *I'm no one. I'm just a girl.*

But more lives than my own hung in the balance, so I lowered my head, half in assent and half because I didn't think I could look at him any longer without my knees buckling. I wasn't even sure I could speak, or if my voice had burrowed too deep inside me, along with my last shreds of courage.

The Heartless King stepped closer. 'I've always wondered how it would feel to watch that fool's blood run between my fingers.'

I looked at him then. Looked, because it was instinctive to want to see the face of one's killer, but the shadows gave nothing away. My heart pounded against the brackets of my ribs, begging for release.

'Please,' I whispered, because it was the most I could manage. *Pathetic*, I scolded myself, heat creeping into my cheeks. But it took everything I had just to face him, to breathe when the air tasted so strongly of steel.

The King stared at me for a long time, his hand resting on the hilt of the sword hidden in the folds of his cloak. His indecision pulsed through us both, stilling the air in my lungs.

'Give me one reason why I should let you live.'

Blind panic seized me as I scoured the recesses of my mind, unable to conjure a response, a single reason. *Because I'm a princess*, I could've said, but I knew the words would sound like a lie. *Because my family needs me*, I wanted to cry. But he wouldn't have cared one bit, and I wasn't even sure it was true.

I swallowed down my swimming fear, forcing my chin up.

Because I had to; because I was *angry*. This was the man who sent hungry sailors to seabed graves, who was responsible for my whole life being ripped apart. No — *man* was the wrong word. I wasn't going to bow in the face of a monster.

'I can't,' I told him, the realisation filling me with bile-tasting dread. My eyes burned, but I refused to let him know just how close I was to crumbling. I was no one, with nothing to offer but the tattered shoes on my feet and the coward's heart quivering in my chest.

There we stood, two shadowy figures encircled by glass and wind and the whisper of rain. Disquiet drummed between us, both his and mine.

The Heartless King cleared his throat. 'A ringing endorsement,' he said at last. Then he turned his back and stalked towards the door he'd come from. It burst open without so much as a raise of his hand. 'Consider yourself my crew's problem, and keep out of my sight.'

The door slammed shut behind him. A sweeping emptiness washed over me, like a heavy blanket torn from my body. It was him – his power – relinquishing its hold.

He was gone.

The silence that surrounded me in the Heartless King's wake was deafening. I let myself breathe a sigh of relief at the fact that I was still standing, at the very least. Unsure what to do or where to go, I picked my way across the glass-strewn floor and cracked open the doors I'd entered through, peering out at the rain-slicked deck.

'Still alive, then.'

I glanced sideways to see Aron, the pirate who'd fought for my life, leaning against the ship's rail. He ambled over to me, hands shoved in his frayed trouser pockets, grinning.

I nodded mutely, inching out on to the deck, eager to distance myself from the darkness swirling within those walls. The rain had eased to a sprinkling that my anxious mind barely registered and the sky had lightened, almost blue.

What now? I wondered.

Aron seemed to read the uncertainty in my gaze. 'C'mon,' he said, jerking his head to indicate I should follow.

I glanced hesitantly around at the pirates who bustled to and fro, casting curious looks up at where we stood. Then, warily, I shuffled after him, down the steps and across the main deck.

Aron headed for a door set into the forecastle and pushed his way inside.

The hallway within was empty, burnished wood shining in the glow of golden oil lamps. We walked in silence, Aron's posture easy as he strolled a few steps ahead. My mind burned with questions, but I hardly knew how to ask, how to speak to a man like him: a pirate.

We passed two more sets of doors inlaid with swirling floral motifs and a staircase that spilled downwards, deep into the bowels of the ship.

It was silent up here, telling me that most of the crew lay burrowed beneath, likely in the berths where they slept. The only signs of life were the winding briar tresses that somehow flourished along the edges of the ceiling and around the hand railings. The word *magic* hissed through the back of my mind but I shoved it away. I had enough to fear.

That was what magic was — wasn't it? Something to fear? A whisper in the deep and dark parts of the world, something that ripped and tore and lurked.

Dust stirred in the wake of our footsteps, making me wonder just how desolate my new dungeon home would be.

'Not much fer a princess,' Aron said at last, pausing before a heavy door at the end of the wide hall. 'But ye'll be left alone in this part o' the ship.'

I nodded hesitantly by way of thanks, creeping closer as he swung the door open.

What lay beyond was no cell.

The room was overgrown with thorns and bathed in rippling azure light that filtered through the large windows, playing across deep blue walls. Roses garlanded the four-poster bed, circling the space above the sleek vanity table where a mirror should have stood, their stray petals littering the surface of a giant claw-footed bathtub. An elaborately carved wardrobe stood by the window, smooth wood glowing in the sheen of morning light.

I slunk forward to admire the bed, its silken sheets piled with a mound of pillows and fur pelts. I glanced back at Aron, seeking confirmation that all this was really meant for me. This muted opulence, fit for a real princess. What was it doing on a pirate ship?

Aron gave a gracious nod and retreated, letting the door close after him. The moment I was alone, hunger and exhaustion rushed to my head and I sank readily into the soft furs.

So this was it. I had become a bargaining chip, chattel for kings. It seemed whatever enmity this man, Bane, held for King Oren, the crew of the *Blood Rose* held the same for him. What kind of crime had he committed to earn such ire? And what kind of man was he to have escaped their wrath this long?

My head ached. Whether I could believe it or not, they all thought me a princess. Aside from Mors, they believed me to be King Oren's *sole* heir. And I had to keep it that way; had to let them lure Bane to whatever fate they thought he deserved. I didn't know why and I didn't like it one bit, but for my sisters, I'd do it.

Like I had a choice.

I buried my face in the light grey pelts and let out a sigh.

My future felt as lifeless as the creatures they'd once belonged to. I could almost feel their hungry claws digging into my mind. *Slaughter*, they seemed to say. *That's all you're good for now.*

Shivering, I closed my eyes and let the darkness claim me.

6

The wafting smell of warm bread stirred me awake. A gleaming silver tray sat at the foot of the bed, piled with sweet-scented cakes and fruits. The rest of the room was empty, no sign of whoever had delivered it.

My mouth watered as I stared down at the glazed shell of a pastry. What the hell was this place?

I'd slept unnervingly well, given my situation. The soft mattress and cerulean silk sheets were more luxury than I'd ever known, and it roused guilt in the pit of my stomach. What kind of sacrifice was this? A warm bed and fresh food, while my family back home would be rationing scraps until Father could drum up some new trade?

Father . . . The thought of his kind face brought up too many feelings, most of which I wasn't ready to face.

Aside from Mors, my captors seemed satisfied that I was who they needed me to be – a princess, the *heir to the throne*. But I'd lived eighteen years as a merchant's daughter; I'd spent my childhood dodging beneath the feet of sailors, reading books by candlelight while my family slept. I'd passed most of the last four years barefoot and hungry, and thinking about the sea. If I ever found my way to King Oren's court, I'd be as far from where I was supposed to be as possible. There was no way I could ever belong to a place like that.

There must have been more to it. Must have been a reason Father hid this from us.

From me, I amended. Aberdeen had known. How much, I wasn't sure, but enough. *As if you need another reason to be better than me.* I hadn't understood her words, just two nights ago, but there it was. A spectral crown ringing my head from the day I was born – perhaps *that* was the reason she'd never loved me quite the way I wanted.

Too hungry to think about anything but the food in front of me, I slid the tray into my lap and bit into the crisp, sticky shell of a pastry. The sweet flavour spilled across my tongue, a mixture of soft cream and ripe fruit. I groaned, taking another bite before it struck me where the food had come from.

My stomach turned. This was a *pirate* ship. I was probably eating food stolen from hungry people. *My* people. I threw the pastry back on to the tray in disgust, ignoring my body's cries of protest.

I grabbed the tray and returned it to the end of the bed, feeling a jolt of tenderness in my hip as I moved. Pressing a hand to my side, I could feel a bruise forming. I found the culprit in my skirts: the apple I'd taken from the cottage. Its green and brown skin didn't exactly look appetising, especially compared to the blood-red ones that glistened on the tray, but I bit into it stubbornly, telling myself the dull flavour was better than I had any right to ask for.

When I was finished, I set the wilted core atop the tray and gazed around the room, still unsure how I fitted into it all.

It was certainly no prison cell, but that didn't stop me feeling like a caged animal.

I crossed the room and tried the door handle. It turned without complaint and the door creaked open. Startled, I slammed it shut again.

So I wasn't a prisoner. Not to this chamber, at least. But the world at my disposal began and ended with the wooden hull of the deadliest ship I'd ever seen. Not to mention it was plagued with pirates. A bitter kind of freedom, indeed.

Still dressed in my clothes from yesterday, smelling of salt and wind and sweat, I took a deep breath and crept out into the hall, bare footsteps muffled by the layer of dust that blanketed the floor.

I sneezed. Luckily, the corridor was empty and I managed to tiptoe across to one of the two sets of ornate doors without being seen. I pressed my ear to the wood, listening for the sound of voices on the other side. Nothing. The whole forecastle felt deserted, left unlived-in for too long.

I opened the doors and slipped inside. A vaulted ceiling arched above me, the space filled with a single table, long enough to seat a dozen or more, and an empty hearth. An unlit chandelier sparked hollow light against the walls, filling the cavernous room with a dull glow.

Like my bedchamber, the room was vast and untouched by anything but time, whose passage had eaten away at the heavy curtains and strewn dust across the varnished wood, dripping waxen from candelabra stubs.

The fireplace was inset below a grand marble mantelpiece, on which rested a shattered mirror, its surface reduced to a few remaining fragments of glass. The sight unnerved me – as did the thought of lighting a fire below deck. But I supposed that whatever magic gave the shadows texture and kept the roses in bloom ensured that no fire overcame the bow of the ship.

I was retreating the way I'd come when the sound of distant voices made me pause. I lingered with my hand on the doorknob, listening. Three sets of footsteps were ascending the staircase outside.

'He's angry,' came a woman's voice, one I didn't recognise.

'Are you surprised?' Mors countered. I knew it was him from the way he spoke, a gentleman in a pirate's guise.

'Thought he migh' at least try,' grumbled another. Aron.

'And the lass?'

'She's so like Estelle.' Mors' words grew more distinct as they passed the doors behind which I hovered, breathing as shallowly as I could. 'If anyone can . . . Well. We can only hope now.'

Aron made a noise of assent. 'We've already sent word to Bray. Bane's got ears in more places than he's got enemies – won't be long.'

'That's really all ye're thinkin' about?' The woman sounded impatient.

'Ye know what they say,' Aron replied. 'Two fish, one net. All that.'

'Ye think it'll work?'

There came a long pause. Mors' voice was faint by the time he responded. 'It has to. Otherwise I've doomed her with the rest of us for nothing.'

Their steps faded as they went out on deck and I waited for the sound of the door shutting after them before I released a long sigh. Something heavy sat in the centre of my chest. Dread.

I was the catalyst to some plan I still didn't understand, caught in the centre of a powerful web. Pirates, traitors, kings. I was yet to grasp what any of them really wanted with me.

I hurried back to my room, heart racing.

He's angry.

They were talking about the King. What did he have to be angry about? Why were his crew planning things he wanted nothing to do with?

Doomed, Mors had said. If I wasn't already, I didn't want to know what that meant.

*

I didn't leave my room again for a week, terrified that I'd find out.

I had nothing to guide me but the rise and fall of the sun, waiting for a man somewhere far away to hear of me and come looking. I ate as little as I could to get by – mostly bread and fruits – and begrudged every delicious mouthful. My guilt turned to sediment in the bottom of my stomach, growing heavier with each bite, each reminder of the empty hands my meals had no doubt been snatched from.

I drifted through a gloomy routine, picking at the trays of food that appeared at my door twice a day. I spent hours at a time stretched out on the bed, wallowing in my thoughts, and wandering lazily around my room, writing half-remembered poems in the condensation on the windows.

I didn't want to face what I knew. The things those pirates had said made sense. About me – about King Oren. Letting that impossible truth sink in meant other things were true, too. That Father had kept it from me my entire life, lied to me about who I was. That he believed, for whatever reason, the cliff's edge of the continent was safer for us than a king's court. It meant that I had to see this through now. Because if I didn't, if word of a rightful heir ever reached the continent . . . People – soldiers, nobles, dissidents – would come looking. King Oren's enemies and allies alike would war over the last vestige of his bloodline. Felicie would never be free again, and I'd have given myself over for nothing.

What I did want, besides freedom, and food that hadn't been pilfered, was a book to read. I doubted pirates had much use for such things, but if I got desperate, I'd seen a few dusty volumes stacked in the navigation room – though I'd do my best to avoid the place that had almost marked my grave for as long as I could.

Still, the loneliness crept up on me. The nights grew longer and sleep drew further from my reach. I knew I'd never be more than a jewel to stud my captors' stolen crowns, but that didn't mean I couldn't at least speak to them – maybe even get some answers.

One evening, all but maddened by the nothingness, I opened my door. The hallway sang with a cold draft, scattering goosebumps over my skin. I stepped out, my feet meeting the cool floorboards, and I welcomed the discomfort.

Shadows spilled from the door leading to the deck at the far end of the corridor. A mounting darkness wrapped around me as I wandered, wraith-like, towards it. The lamps winked at me as I passed. It wasn't yet nightfall, but the light that reached me through the crack beneath the door was muffled, as if the sun itself had to fight to withstand what lay beyond. The Heartless King was out there, I knew.

My instincts told me to bolt myself back in my room and stay there another week, a month, however long it took, but my feet disobeyed. It had already been too long since I'd laid eyes on another human, even if he was barely that. I didn't want to speak to him, nor even alert him to my presence, but I couldn't help my curiosity. Each step grew easier and, by the time I reached the door, I'd almost forgotten to fear what awaited me on the other side. Almost.

I cracked the door open, leaving a gap just wide enough to peer out. The waning sunlight bathed the deck in gold and my eyes alighted immediately upon the hulking silhouette on the other side of the ship, shadows splayed out around him.

The Heartless King's power jolted through me like a bolt of black lightning. He stood at the starboard rail, his back turned as he stared out at the waves. That hood was pulled up over his broad shoulders and I couldn't help but wonder once more what it hid.

Keep out of my sight, he'd said.

I couldn't stop myself. I crept out on deck, letting the King's presence envelop me as the door snapped shut in my wake.

Shivers raced through my body, the icy wood biting my toes. Everything in me told me to run, to cling to what little safety I had left, yet something drew me on. Maybe it was that I hardly had any life to preserve, alone in that room, cowering from all the things I didn't know. Maybe it was that being afraid made me angry – made me hate him even more than I had every other day of my life. Calm seas and solitude were privileges the Heartless King didn't deserve. *What right does* he *have to hide?*

He didn't turn as I'd expected him to. That dark hood remained facing the water to the west. I watched him, curious. His silhouette was stamped against the sky, the colour of clouds before a storm. It was wrong, seeing such stark brutality haloed by the lilac gild of sunset. Such a thing shouldn't have been so pretty.

I watched him, perhaps a moment longer than I should've. Stars stirred in the descending haze of dusk, and I could've sworn they quaked when the King's voice broke through the silence.

'You aren't trying to sneak up and kill me, I hope.'

Try to kill him? What kind of fool did he take me for?

'I don't actually have a death wish,' I retorted. 'I'm only here because you threatened my father's life.'

'I had nothing to do with that.' His reply was abrupt, but he spoke again after a beat, voice rumbling right through me. 'Why did you come out here, then? I thought I told you to stay away from me.'

I hovered on the brink of another step closer. His question stumped me. I hadn't meant to approach him at all, to be risking everything for nothing. Yet there I stood, a meagre few paces from the Heartless King himself.

Not afraid, I reminded myself.

'I don't know,' I answered truthfully. What did it matter? 'Are you going to kill me?'

The King laughed, cold and dark as the coming night. 'Not tonight.'

I swallowed, my throat constricting as he turned, the top half of his face still cast in shadow. His invisible gaze traced my hollow features, like a cool sweep of sea mist that withstood the wind.

His words came out stilted, icy. 'You haven't been eating.'

I looked up into the infinite blackness of his hood. It took all the strength I had just to face him, my heart feeble and frantic inside the vacuum of my chest. Still, I didn't blink.

'I won't eat that which a tyrant steals from hungry people.' My traitorous voice trembled, giving me away.

'I steal riches,' the Heartless King retorted. 'I steal gold and weapons and ships. I don't steal food; there are some things the sea provides me that I don't need to take for myself.'

It took me a moment to understand what he meant. I'd seen it: the way the ship reacted to his presence, the candles that blinked awake each night, the doors that had burst open without a touch of his hand. Apparently the lavish meals that appeared before me twice a day were the products of no cook.

The ship was magic. Was its King, too?

I stared up at him, wondering. Remembering stories of his twisted countenance, of tentacles and gleaming eyes and gills. Were those gifts from the sea – bestowed upon him by some divinity of the waves?

But with all the mouths that keened in hunger, what god would decide *him* worthy of their gifts?

The quiet anger in me swelled, tamping down my fear.

'You'd feed your ego over innocent people, then,' I said, summoning strength from somewhere deep inside me. If he really did have magic on his side, there was no limit to the good he could do. Instead, he chose destruction. 'People are starving across the continent. Don't you know how bad the famine is? And the villagers will hardly touch the fish in the sea for fear of your wrath!'

'They *should* fear me,' the King bit out, taking a step towards me.

Shadows slid across my skin, making my body beg to curl into itself. I was a fool for provoking him, but I couldn't back down now. He might not have robbed food directly from anyone's mouth, but there wasn't a soul in Northbay who didn't live in fear of the tides for the simple fact that he reigned them.

'Is that what it means to be powerful?' I challenged. My cheeks felt hot, flushed with rage. 'Having everything you could possibly need and still taking from others? Does it make you feel bigger?'

The King exhaled sharply, a huff of frustration that only made me angrier. But when he spoke, his voice was a menacing kind of calm. 'If you won't eat alone, then eat with me.'

'Eat with you?' I echoed. He phrased it like an offer, but his tone was a command.

Why in the gods' names would I ever eat with him? I almost laughed at the absurdity. That he was even capable of caring whether I starved, his crew's scheming about Bane aside. He'd been so adamant I stay out of his sight – now this?

He said nothing, so I added, 'I don't want or need your concern, *Your Majesty*.' The title was bitter on my tongue. Unearned.

The King folded his arms, leaning back against the railing. 'Then what do you want?'

Once again, he'd caught me off guard. *What game is he playing?* I wanted nothing from him. Nothing, except maybe the truth.

'Answers,' I said eventually. 'I want to know what's going to happen to me. Why I'm here. All of it.'

He nodded slowly. 'Very well. One dinner in exchange for one answer.'

I arched a brow at him. I couldn't imagine a single question worth an entire evening of his company. Nor a single reason why he'd want mine. He was a murderer, a tyrant, a monster – did he honestly expect me to dine with him?

'That hardly seems fair,' I said.

'Then don't come,' he retorted.

'Fine.'

'*Fine.*'

Despite the anger that guarded his tone, the King seemed to hesitate, shadows stirring. I could almost feel them, like a soft wind curling around my exposed neck. I stared into the raging darkness beneath his hood, a cold chill erupting over my skin.

He's just testing me, I told myself, but my racing heart wouldn't listen. It accelerated in my chest, so fast I was afraid it might burst free and abandon me here, alone with him.

I tilted my chin, angling my head to try and catch a glimpse of his eyes, but the darkness gave nothing away. 'I'm trapped here anyway. Why not just tell me what's going on?'

'I will,' he ground out, his impatience almost tangible. 'At dinner.'

I scowled. So that was how it was going to be.

The King stepped closer, his proximity knocking the breath from my lungs. He extended his arm between us and I stared at it, perplexed. Of all the ways the day could have gone, I hadn't seen it ending up here. With the Heartless King offering me a handshake. A bargain.

What he had to gain from it, I didn't know, but at least I'd have a way to find out.

I stared down at his hand – *seeing* it for the first time. Realising, with a hungry kind of curiosity, that it was a human one. Long, light brown fingers, short nails; knuckles ridged with skin, not the spines of a lionfish. There was nothing to suggest he was anything more than a man, not much older than I was. Nowhere near old enough to have earned the destruction to his name.

I reached out tentatively, sliding my fingers into his large, rough ones. A jolt of something hot and dark pierced through me and I tried not to flinch, snatching my hand back as soon as I could.

'Tomorrow night, then,' he said, turning his back on me and disappearing into the quarterdeck. I expelled a breath, the tension in my body dissipating as the lingering weight of his shadows lifted.

I hurried back the way I'd come, trying and failing to shake the ghost of his bloodstained hand from mine.

7

I woke in the stark grey hours of morning.

The room was still but for the slow rustle of rose vines and shadows as the ship rocked gently against the waves. I rolled on to my back, sifting through the echoes of my dream. The salt, the sand, the deep eternal dark . . . the scales of something monstrous flashing silver along the seafloor.

Amidst it all, I couldn't forget the Heartless King's fingers, wrapped around mine. I should've been repulsed, touching hands like his. *Killing hands.* Something thick and shadowy churned in my stomach at the thought.

I pressed my face into a pillow, clutching the silk sheets to my chest. Then, for the first time since my arrival, I cried. I cried for myself, for my tired bones and aching heart. I cried for the dark waters that separated me from my old life, from the cottage and the cliffs and the arms of my father.

I cried because I might never know what became of my family:

when they'd last eaten a proper meal, if Father had managed to scare up some trade, if Felicie's latest bout of illness had passed. If they had anything at all, other than grief.

My heart clenched. What if this was all for nothing? What if I had doomed myself in vain, and wouldn't even live long enough to know it? But I'd saved Felicie from the hands of hungry men — that *had* to be enough. Whatever the crew were plotting, it was at least my fate now, not hers.

When the sun crested the horizon and the needling shadows slunk back, I wiped my eyes and pulled myself out of bed, venturing towards the grand wardrobe. The wooden closet overflowed with soft petticoats, supple leather corsets to be laced over silk shirts and richly coloured overskirts that would've turned my sisters green with envy.

I sighed contentedly despite myself. I didn't particularly care for jewellery or heeled shoes, but there was something about pretty dresses that made life feel somehow simpler, even when it wasn't. As I slipped into layers of silk-soft cotton and pink skirts that matched the hazy sunrise, I almost caught myself smiling.

Among the shoes was a pair of boots not unlike my own, only sturdier, more reliable. Better for running, if it came to that. I pulled them on and fastened the laces with a newfound sense of determination. I retrieved my breakfast tray from the door, bit into a warm bread roll and left my room, resolved to find something to pass the time until dinner.

I headed straight for the doors across from the dining hall. The heavy wood wouldn't budge at first, so I took a step back and threw my entire weight against them. The doors jolted and sprang open, sending me stumbling into the most beautiful library I'd ever seen.

I gasped, delight splitting my face into a grin. It looked like something to be found in King Oren's palace, not a pirate ship.

Breathtaking murals bathed the domed ceiling, depicting raging tides, marble spires and fallen kings. Ornate bookcases lined the walls, brimming with dusty volumes that made my fingers itch with excitement.

I paced the room slowly, trailing a finger over the aged spines that filled the shelves, my heart swelling in my chest. A mahogany table took up the centre of the room, set beneath a gleaming chandelier. Instantly, I knew I'd spend as many nights as I could cradled in its ring of light.

The day slipped away without me realising, one leather-bound journey spilling into the next. I was so absorbed in reading that I almost forgot to dread the evening ahead, until the world around me dipped into dusk and the chandelier flared to life.

I glanced up to see the rust-coloured sun seep through the clouds, suffusing the room with an ethereal glow. My heartbeat picked up, goosebumps prickling down my arms. The thought of dining with the Heartless King turned my stomach, but I couldn't see a way out. This Bane they'd spoken of – I knew nothing about him, only that my life might well end up in his hands. And if that was the case, I couldn't go in blind. Couldn't waste any more of my numbered days in the dark.

Night sank over the water, streaks of moonlight snaking across the walls, and I knew my time was up. I had somewhere to be.

Apprehension filled my steps as I paced the hall outside the dining room. My heart pounded, ready to burst free at the first sign of danger. I could feel his presence within, swelling like a great shadow in my chest, caging my breath in its grip.

Not afraid. Not afraid. My hand clasped the gold door handle and I kicked up my chin before pushing my way inside. *Not afraid.*

The only light came from the chandelier and the burning hearth, its flames shadowed by the mountainous silhouette of the King. Just a week ago, the room had been filled with dust; but tonight, the wooden floors shone, the furniture gleaming in the golden cast of fire.

'Sit,' the King rumbled, not bothering to look up as I entered.

Two place settings had been laid at opposite ends of the giant table and I took my seat hesitantly, relieved by the distance that would separate us.

The table was piled high with a banquet that roused the hunger in my belly. I inhaled the aroma of roasted meats, of steamed vegetables and richly spiced soups. Saliva pooled on my tongue, but I sat stubbornly in my steepled chair, waiting to see whether the King would make good on his end of the bargain. I wasn't going to take the word of a pirate.

'Eat,' he said after a minute, his head still angled to the flames, apparently deep in thought.

Irritation flared in my chest. He wasn't even going to join me? I crossed my arms, strangely insulted. I should've been glad, but his lingering presence while I ate felt more patronising than obliging.

I looked over at the King and raised a brow. 'Aren't you at least going to sit down?'

He lifted his head, considering me for a moment before he retreated from the fireplace and took the seat opposite, enough dishes to feed an army stretching between us. He reached forward without a word, impaled a hunk of lamb on his fork and began piling meat on to his plate.

Perhaps if no man can kill him, his diet will, I thought sourly, grabbing a bowl of vegetables bathed in butter and rosemary. I scooped up a single potato and dropped it on to my plate. It might not have been stolen food, but I wasn't about to give him the satisfaction of seeing me indulge in a feast he'd practically forced me into.

I could feel the King's gaze like a hot poker on my skin, branding my cheeks until they flushed under his stare. Pretending to be unperturbed, I bit into the potato, savouring its perfect, fluffy texture. The home-grown ones I'd been living off for months had tasted like stones in comparison.

We ate in silence, the only sounds coming from the crackling fireplace and the meat tearing between the tyrant's teeth. He ate exactly as I'd imagined he would – with no regard for anything beyond slaking his hunger.

Pirates.

I watched as he ripped into his food with bare hands, studying the strong curve of his shadowed jaw, the dark hair that curled its way beneath, wondering, as always, which of the stories were true. Whatever inhuman horrors he was hiding under that hood had to mean something; had to explain why he was so determined to wreak havoc against our world.

Unable to stand the silence any longer, I set down my fork and cleared my throat. Monster or not, I couldn't play taciturn forever, and I'd waited long enough for the truths he'd promised.

'I'm ready for my answer,' I said.

The King reclined in his chair, wiping his mouth with the back of his hand. He said nothing, but I took his silence as acquiescence and folded my arms neatly on the tabletop.

'Who is Bane? And what does he want with me?'

'You think I'm going to answer that when you can't even eat a proper meal?' he drawled. 'One question, that was the deal.'

'Fine, then. Who is Bane?'

The King sighed. I waited with bated breath, resisting the urge to drum my fingers on the table in anticipation.

'A traitor,' he explained eventually, sounding reluctant. When I raised a brow, he went on. 'Used to be one of our crew but he led a mutiny, few years back – roused half my damn fleet into open revolt against Oren. Now he's living on borrowed time, and I intend to collect.'

'And what does that have to do with me?' I pressed.

The King clicked his tongue. 'One question, that was the deal,' he repeated.

I clenched my jaw. That was the deal – didn't mean I had to like it. I stood, brushed down my skirts, and headed for the door.

'I didn't say you could leave.'

'Didn't say you'd be such miserable company, either,' I shot back. Forgetting, for a second, who I was talking to.

The Heartless King growled a warning, but before I could say something to make things worse, he stiffened, as though he'd caught a scent on the breeze. He rose swiftly, cloak swirling as he crossed the room and burst through the doors, brushing past me as he went.

'Where are you going?' I called after him, put out that he'd robbed me of the chance to storm off.

'Someone's here.'

A mixture of anticipation and fear twined through my veins. I didn't know where exactly we were, but I'd been gone long enough for word of my existence to have reached the coast, even a port city like Bray. And if so . . .

I hurried anxiously after the Heartless King. If I was going to have the slightest chance of escape, this was it. If all Bane had done was rebel against a tyrant – two, if King Oren could be called one – then how bad could he be? Even a traitor's ship, surely, couldn't be worse than this one?

I followed the King through the maze of pirates who thronged outside, weapons clanking, their excitement almost tangible in the sharp night air. I hovered where I stood, not wanting to be caught in the midst of a battle. If I had to risk something foolish like jumping ship, I'd have to do it without them noticing. A feat that didn't seem particularly possible, but I was yet to see another way out.

Aron brushed past me, catching sight of my expression. 'A'ight, lass?'

'What's going on?' I asked, noting the cutlass in his hand, the daggers that wreathed his baldric.

'There's a ship wi' Bane's flag approachin'.'

Aron jerked his head for me to follow as the King strode to the ship's helm. Golde was already there, armed to the teeth with weapons, her face turned eagerly towards the horizon.

A slow, deadly fear snaked through my veins and my feet refused to move, even as Aron beckoned for me to join them. A clammy sweat was breaking out over my body. Whatever was about to happen, it was too soon – I wasn't ready.

'C'mon,' the King grunted, sounding impatient as he belted a broadsword around his waist.

Heart hammering in my throat, I trailed behind Aron to the edge of the upper deck. Ready or not, this was the path I'd chosen. *For Felicie.* Whatever I was about to face, there was no backing out now.

The crew buzzed with anticipation. Golde moved to the bow, watching calmly as a solitary frigate approached. Its pennant bore a sigil I'd never seen before: a mermaid clutching a pointed dagger, her eyes burning red with fury.

'It ain't him,' Aron remarked, sounding disappointed. He glanced over at me with a look I guessed was meant to be reassuring. 'Just one o' his crews, come to see if ye're real, no doubt.'

I hardly felt real. I stared out at the oncoming vessel, pulse quickening with every passing beat. *Not him*. This was good. It meant more time, more opportunity for answers. It meant a chance, however faint, of escape.

The King and his crew waited patiently, still as masts, until the sky rained down upon us. Ropes and grappling irons flew through the air, shattering the peace as they latched on to the side of the *Blood Rose*. The crew on the deck below drew their blades and a raucous baying filled the wind. Chills swept down my spine – it was a war cry.

Soon, three dozen or more waxen-faced pirates appeared over the side, weapons slashing viciously as they clambered aboard.

I glanced around me, panic swelling in my chest. I didn't belong here, but my only way out was through the gathering tide of eager blades. I needed to get below before I saw something I couldn't unsee. But Aron nudged me forward gently as the Heartless King descended the steps to meet the interlopers' captain, a weasel of a man with eyes that drooped into his cheeks and more gold teeth than white.

'Lass.' Aron beckoned, his hand on my elbow.

I nodded, my throat dry. My knees trembled as I forced myself to follow the King to the centre of the deck, feeling only slightly less petrified knowing Aron was a step behind me. Golde stood close on my right, though her presence only set me further on edge.

'Cullen,' the King greeted, his voice drenched in disdain.

'Yer Majesty.' The pirate fell into a great, sweeping bow, bloodshot eyes dancing with mockery.

The crew behind me bristled at Cullen's show of disrespect. Tension hummed in the air, turning it static.

The captain's leering gaze slipped around the King, landing on me. His tongue slid greedily along his bottom lip and I shuddered. Aron's grip on my elbow tightened.

Swallowing the disgust that clogged my throat, I turned my gaze out to the water, praying the crew would at least keep me from those dirt-caked hands. It was obvious my death wasn't the first thing on Cullen's mind.

'This is the bitch everyone's fussin' about, eh?'

I fell back a step, blood turning to ice. All my instincts told me to flee, but Golde's fingers closed around my wrist, cold and firm as iron. 'Not so fast,' she growled.

I stilled, sure the entire ship could hear my deafening pulse.

'She can't be worth much if Bane sent you in his place,' the King said, his voice spearing the night.

The other captain's mouth thinned. 'I think ye'll find he's willin' to pay a fair price.'

'Tell the coward to come, then,' Aron spoke. 'We'll deal wi' him directly.'

'He's no coward, but he ain't no fool either,' Cullen hissed. 'Hand 'er over.'

Golde's hand left my arm, darting to the hilt of her sabre. I glanced around, noticing the way the crew encircled us like standing stones, except I wasn't sure if they were trying to keep me in, or the other pirates out.

'My only problem,' the King mused, turning his sword over in his hands, 'is how Bane will know to come if there's no one left to tell him?'

Hesitation darted across Cullen's gaze.

No, I thought. They couldn't kill them – they were supposed to take word of me to Bane. Gods only knew how long it would take for him to come looking for me himself, which made these newcomers my surest means of escape, yet . . .

I shuddered, looking over at Cullen's crew, their faces painted in shades of bloodlust. Instinctively, I inched closer to Aron.

'Ye wonder why we all left ye?' Cullen spat, his reedy voice soaked in spite. 'We got sick o' fightin' fer a cap'n who wouldn't fight fer us. Got sick o' bein' ignored by a coward—'

A shriek punctured the air as Golde lunged forward and pitched her sword straight through the captain's chest.

Chaos erupted.

8

Cries filled the salty night air as pirates from both sides collided in a roar of clashing steel and crimson mist. I flinched at the uproar as the crew barrelled past me, their bodies blocking my way as they jostled towards the impending bloodbath.

I glanced over at the King, desperate for an escape and knowing I'd find none. I could've sworn he met my gaze for a moment, wiping spattered blood from his chin. His sword hung loose in his palm as he waited, patiently, for his first victim. I was frozen in place, nose wrinkling at the metallic scent that painted the breeze, my veins coursing with a mixture of fear and curiosity.

Only when there were ten men upon him did the Heartless King finally move – and he moved like the sea.

He was ferocious, inhuman, almost graceful. He wore power like waves wore the cliffs, shattering rocks and dragging them under. I couldn't tear my eyes away, terrified and in awe.

It wasn't a fight; it was slaughter.

A dozen men met their fates right before my eyes. Their faces blanched with fear and blood loss, souls quaking as they fell to their knees and took their final, shuddering breaths. With every ruthless blow, every sweep of his blade, I could see the strength that rippled beneath the King's heavy cloak, his weapon a pure extension of himself. All the while, his hood never slipped; never revealed a fraction more of the face beneath. Even as he tossed his enemies back, splintered their bones and impaled them upon their own swords. What was he hiding? More importantly—

What was I waiting for?

Heart pressed against the brackets of my ribs, I scanned the deck for a chance of escape. But I was beginning to realise that even if I could leap across the divide and make it to the other ship, there would hardly be anyone left alive to save me. The air was thick with dying breaths, each prayer slicing through me as keenly as a sword.

A rough hand yanked me backwards. I yelped, smelling the rancid breath of my captor, the festering stench of a man living on nothing but ale and plunder. And a knife, pressed to my throat.

'Gotcha,' he snarled.

I felt the prick of his blade as it dug into my skin, my heart thrilling in fear as his muscles went taut around me. A build-up to the strike that could end my life before I'd even begun to live it. I tensed, ready to fight back – though I hardly knew how – but before I could, his body slackened and the man collapsed to the ground. My stomach lurched at the sickening sound of tearing flesh as blood spurted from a gash in his neck.

I spun around to meet the reproachful glare of Golde as she tugged her dagger free from my assailant's limp body.

'Th— thank you,' I stuttered.

The pirate raised her blade, still dripping with gore. 'Don't thank me,' she hissed, wild eyes glittering. 'I'd cut out yer heart if it wouldn't cost me mine.'

She didn't hesitate a moment longer before turning back to the fray and plunging her dagger through the chest of another man.

Anger bubbled up over the stir of relief and revulsion in my gut. I pushed my way through the thicket of bodies, heat clawing at my eyes, my boots tracking through pools of blood. I dodged fists and swinging blades, shoving aside pirates twice my size – but before I could reach the safety of the forecastle, the night sky erupted in barbaric cheers.

It was over. A hundred pirates tipped their heads back and cried praise to their tyrant king, a rolling thunder of celebration.

Bile rose in my throat. I'd read stories of battle for so long, thinking I'd never see it with my own eyes, not understanding what it really meant. Now it was over and I was left choking on the coppery air, caught in the mire of a blood-red boneyard.

The crew worked fast to clear the deck, tossing fallen sailors to the deep, their blades and boots smearing crimson across the wood. I watched two men lift the body of a boy no older than I was, his once-white shirt stained with blood.

'Not exactly a pretty sight, is it?'

I blinked, the crowd of bodies moving around me. Mors stood in front of me, a crisp navy shirt tucked neatly into his trousers, looking like he'd had the sense to stay away from the chaos. I gave him a weak smile, still unnerved by what I'd witnessed. This was just another day for them.

Mors beckoned for me to follow him back on to the main deck. I hesitated, but my desire to talk to him outweighed the call of my bed, of safety, and I trailed along the starboard behind him.

He rested an elbow on the rail overlooking the water, holding out his other hand. 'I don't believe I've properly introduced myself,' he said, amber eyes twinkling in the starlight. 'They call me Mors.'

'Ria Lucroy,' I replied, shaking his proffered hand.

His pale fingers were adorned with rings, their metal cold against my skin. When I pulled away, I saw that his palm was streaked with blood. I touched a hand to my neck, feeling the small wound left by Cullen's man.

'Are you all right?' Mors asked, his brows drawn low in concern.

I glanced down at the bead of crimson on my fingers and wiped it off on my skirts. 'Fine,' I said, shaking my head.' I'd seen worse today. Felt worse, as pirates thudded to their knees, their blood spattering hot across my arms, my face, my skirts.

I looked around us, watching in fascination as the crew began a dissonant sea shanty, their feet thumping against the planks as the crowd began to drink and dance, still mottled with the ichor of their enemies. Several women moved among the crew, some in pirate garb, others wearing loudly coloured clothes and gaudy jewellery, singing and dancing with smiles that outshone the moon. A tug of desire made me itch to join them, to know that kind of untamed joy. But I knew what a mask it was. No matter how human their laughter sounded, I'd just watched them rob lives from the world a hundredfold. How could they move so lightly with such a weight on their shoulders?

I looked back at Mors to ask him something, but he was staring intently down at the sea. I followed his gaze and gasped.

Something writhed in the black water. It looked like a giant serpent or eel, silk-smooth and silver-green in the moonlight. It wound in on itself, contorting like a sailor's knot around a body that floated near the surface.

'What the hell is that?' I breathed, my insides squirming.

Mors shook his head with a half-smile. 'There are too

many creatures in these parts to give them all names. But don't be afraid, lass — the dwellers of the deep are our friends. So long as we watch over her waters, the sea would never harm us. Not physically.'

Dwellers of the deep. Aberdeen had warned me of such beasts, but I'd never seen anything larger than a seal in the flesh. Magic hid in Bray, hardly touched us in Northbay. Here, it reigned.

Mors' smile fell as he added, 'It is unusual for them to breach like this.'

'Must've been attracted by all the blood,' I mused, unable to look away as the bobbing corpse sank slowly into the monster's serpentine embrace.

'Maybe,' Mors agreed darkly, though something in his expression told me he wasn't quite convinced.

I watched the creature for a moment longer, the rippling current washing over its slick green scales. Plumes of blood leached like ink into the water, a story written into the sea. I wondered where I would end up; if the salt would ever remember me.

'Come,' Mors said, guiding me away to an alcove beneath the forecastle steps where we perched atop casks of rum. I watched him for a moment, still trying to shake the image of that sea monster from my mind. The old man lounged contentedly against a crate, fingers drumming along to the tune of the crew's caterwauling. It was loud, and the day had been long, but I hadn't forgotten what I needed to know.

Now was my chance.

'Bane,' I began, waiting for Mors to look at me before I continued. 'What does he want with me? How could I possibly be worth risking an entire crew?'

Mors sighed, an apprehensive smile creeping over his lips. 'You must have a lot of questions.' I nodded, saying nothing, and after a moment, he went on. 'Oren has a bloodier past than people know. His reign is stoked by many fires and he hides them well, but there are some he's burned who refuse to live quietly with the scars. Your parents chose to escape; Bane chose to fight. He'll send as many crews as it takes to get his hands on you.'

'To what end?' I pressed. 'To kill me, just to punish his enemy?'

Mors shook his head. 'You don't realise what a powerful tool you would make.'

A *tool*. I couldn't help but scowl.

'You being here, out of Oren's reach, makes him vulnerable without even knowing. His lack of lineage is something of an embarrassment, a weak spot every noble under the sun would seek to exploit. What Bane would do with you, I can't say for certain, but having you on his side could give his crusade for the throne an actual stake. A powerful one.'

'Great,' I mumbled. 'So this is what it's like, being a princess? A tool?'

Mors exhaled shortly, a sad little laugh. 'Aye, lass. That's exactly why your mother left the capital. She didn't want this for her children.'

His words turned bitter at the end and I had to resist the urge to reach out and touch his shoulder, to comfort him. It wasn't what she'd wanted, but Mors had drawn me into it regardless.

He should *feel guilty*, I told myself. He'd done all this, just for a chance to make a traitor bleed?

'You can at least rest easy knowing we need you alive until Bane comes to collect you himself,' Mors said.

I pursed my lips, fazed by his conviction. 'Didn't exactly feel that way when Golde was trying to kill me.' Golde, who'd saved me from the same fate minutes ago.

'Ah.' Mors chuckled. 'She's always hungry for blood, but

she's a damned good first mate.'

I followed his gaze across the deck to where the black-haired woman stood, head bent in conversation with the King.

Makes sense, I thought sullenly, watching them converse. Golde's gleaming eyes scanned the deck, always watching for signs of danger. I couldn't fathom how anyone could be so faithful to such a monster. It was no wonder they'd paved the seas with so much blood; between the two of them, I'd never seen such a penchant for chaos.

'I can't comprehend what a man like you is doing here,' I said, gesturing around us.

Mors paused, as if measuring his next words carefully. 'We're all part of something greater than you could imagine, lass.' He spoke quietly, his eyes never straying from his king. 'I could never leave his side, no matter what he did.'

'You aren't going to tell me he's a good man at heart, are you?'

'At heart? No.' Mors turned to face me, his wizened eyes grave. 'I doubt even he understands the depths of what he's capable of. Good or bad.'

'I daresay one outweighs the other,' I muttered.

Mors sighed. 'Aye. Well, keep your wits about you. You'll be just fine.'

I fought the urge to look up again, to let my eyes find the shadow of the King across the deck. Mors could defend him all he liked; I knew what he was.

'Ah, the guest o' honour!'

I looked up to see Aron swaggering over with a tankard of ale in his hand, smiling sloppily down at us. I laughed as he slumped on to the crate beside me. Cuts and grazes laced his face and arms, and his shirt was filthier than usual, his musky scent alloyed with sweat, liquor and blood.

'I trust you're enjoying yourself,' I remarked, watching in amusement as he gulped down the rest of his drink, unfazed by his injuries.

The pirate grinned roguishly at me over the rim of his mug. 'Only three thin's a pirate needs, lass,' he said. 'Rum, war and a warm bed.'

I felt my cheeks redden, which made Aron laugh. He leaned back, wiping a drop of liquid from his moustache. 'Ah, ye'll understand one day.'

I shook my head awkwardly. *One day* implied I even had a future to look forward to, let alone one worth living. One full of laughter and warmth and . . . something hot and unfamiliar curled around my stomach and squeezed. I shook it off. I'd never understand.

'I wanted to thank you, actually,' I said, after a moment. 'You saved my life, the day we met.'

'Hmm?' Aron's gaze was trained on something in the distance, a figure moving among the crowd. I couldn't pinpoint the object of his distraction amid the rabble, but it wasn't hard to decipher longing on the face of a drunk man.

Who are they? I wanted to nudge him and ask, but I bit my tongue. I didn't need to be any more invested.

Drink flowed freely as the clouds slipped across the night sky, fading into a cool morning fog. Curiosity kept me on deck for several hours, observing the pirates' lively celebrations from afar. It shouldn't have surprised me how human they seemed; how they smiled at me like old friends and laughed like they had no reason not to.

Every so often, the King would turn his dark hood in my direction, though he never approached. I was glad of the distance, though it didn't stop the unnerving sensation of his shadows calling out to me from across the deck.

I headed for the forecastle steps, suddenly desperate to escape the noise. My head pounded, still spinning from my brush with death and the chaos around it.

Damned pirates, I thought. They'd cost me a step towards freedom today. Their pride would mean more time before Bane came – more time trapped on this gods-forsaken ship.

Exhaustion crawled through my bones, but the horrors of battle still raced through my mind, a carousel of death that spun on and on, the scent of it hanging like smoke in the air. I'd seen dead bodies before, but never like that. I'd never watched life bleed from someone's eyes, never seen a monster snake through the waves to feast on still-warm flesh. I wouldn't have been able to sleep if I'd tried.

My skin prickled and I glanced back at the main deck, seeing the King standing at the bottom of the stairs. I could almost feel his gaze following me as I slipped past the crowd and through the forecastle doors. I didn't look back, but I could hear his footsteps like echoes of my own as he followed. I didn't have it in me to protest so I said nothing as his dark presence swallowed up the hall behind me.

The chaos melted away the moment I stepped into the grand library. The King's reaching shadow mingled with mine as he trailed after me and I had to fight the urge to turn around and slam the doors in his face.

What does he want?

A halo of dust descended as we entered, spiralling in the dawn light that leaked through the high windows and spilled across the book-laden table. I sought refuge in a row of bookshelves as the King strode the length of the room, taking in the gleaming wood and sparkling chandelier.

'You found my library,' he observed.

A penetrating insight, I thought churlishly. I watched him through the gap in the shelves, studying the outline of his powerful shoulders as he walked.

'I haven't been in here for years,' he mused, pacing around the table.

'I imagine you don't find much time for reading between murdering and pillaging,' I murmured, half hoping he wouldn't hear.

'You underestimate me.'

I jumped at the proximity of his voice as the King came to a halt beside me. He smelled of sweat and blood, the visible stretches of his skin smeared with crimson. My stomach flipped.

'I don't think I do,' I fired back, my eyes lifting to the curve of his lips. Being literate didn't make him any less a monster.

'You're hurt,' he said.

I raised a hand to the skin above my collarbone, tracing the thin wound. A reminder of the price my blood unwittingly called for. 'I'm fine,' some part of me answered. Caught in the uncanny ring of his shadows, it was becoming increasingly harder to think.

The King extended an arm, reaching for a book on the shelf above my head and bringing it down between us. 'Read this.'

I lifted it from his calloused hand, his heavy cloak brushing my forearm. I flinched, heat sprawling across my skin where the dark material had touched me. Then he was gone, leaving me clutching the thick green volume tight in my clammy hands, its spine streaked with blood. Fresh, from his hands.

I looked down at the embossed cover, its worn leather smooth and comforting. Curious, I traced the frayed spine, trying to picture the Heartless King seated at the table before me, reading the very same book. The image dissipated before I could grasp it.

I returned slowly to my chamber, exhaustion creeping up behind my eyes. I shed my clothes and buried myself deep into the warmth of my bed, although I knew sleep was a long way off.

I stared up at the briar that bloomed in the canopy of my bed frame. There were no thoughts, no feelings or logic that could justify the destruction that had unfolded that night.

He could give me books all he liked, but I'd seen the Heartless King for what he was, seen first-hand the horrors he was capable of. I'd even, for a moment, been senseless enough to admire it. The way he'd fought had entranced me. When I closed my eyes, I could still see the fluidity of his movements, the devastating grace that raged in him like the sea.

I wondered if I, too, could kill a man with a mere twist of my hand, whether I'd have become a monster like him. Perhaps he killed simply because it came naturally to him, like breathing or walking, or like the tides rolling into shore.

Damned pirates, I thought again, cursing myself for entertaining such thoughts. There was nothing I could do but pray that despite the blood seeping into the planks above, word would still reach Bane the way it had Cullen. That he'd come for me, and whatever scheme the Heartless King's crew had in store could be put to rest. Then . . . I didn't know what would happen then. But maybe, just maybe, I could be free.

I reached for the book the King had given me and pulled it open with a reluctant sigh. The story drew me in, easing the buzzing thoughts that swarmed my brain, its pages turning into the small hours of the morning.

The sun was fully risen by the time I found sleep, my mind finally clear of the sight of glassy eyes turned up to the indifferent sky, and the cold sting of a blade pressed to my singing pulse.

9

The Heartless King and I ate in near silence each night, that infinite swath of mahogany between us, a banquet piled high to fill the void of conversation. The King gave infuriatingly vague answers that led me nowhere, but he no longer tried to stop me from leaving the moment I'd finished eating.

Ten days swept past with little useful information before I found a welcome surprise sitting atop my breakfast tray on a cool, cloudless morning. It was a messily scrawled note that read, *Find me on deck — Aron.*

A lightness carried my steps out into the crisp autumn air. I'd been too afraid to venture there during the day, but the pirates who idled around seemed unperturbed by my presence. Their King, thankfully, was nowhere in sight.

I spotted Aron leaning against the mizzenmast, cleaning his nails with the point of a dagger. 'Mornin', lass,' he called when he saw me approaching.

'To what do I owe the pleasure?' I asked, measuring his easy demeanour.

'Thought ye might be lonely.' He grinned. 'His Majesty's not always the best o' company.'

I couldn't help but smile back. If he was here to complain about the King, I was more than happy to oblige. 'Not the best, no,' I agreed. 'So you're here to entertain me?'

Aron laughed, sheathing his dagger in the baldric slung across his chest. 'I am curious to know what ye've been up to wi'out me.'

I shrugged. 'I've been spending most of my time in the library.'

The pirate raised a dark brow. 'Ye like readin'?'

'I love it,' I admitted. 'And the library here . . . it's exquisite.'

'Aye, well, I'm glad ye're keeping yerself busy, lass.' His smile slid into a sly grin. 'As I said, there ain't much to do 'round here but drinkin' and fightin' and, well . . .'

I cleared my throat, knowing exactly what the third option was. 'Yes, well, I do appreciate some company every now and then.'

'Count on me, lass. I'll be here whenever ye need.'

'Thank you.' Strangely, I meant it. 'It seems you and Mors are the only decent men around here.'

Aron snickered. 'Well, if it's books ye're after, Mors can surely help ye better than meself. Assumin' ye don't wanna ask His Majesty, o' course?'

Didn't need to ask, I thought darkly. I'd been so enraptured by the story the King had handed me I'd read it twice already – so different from anything I'd read before, so excruciatingly poetic.

'No, I don't,' I huffed. My uneasy breath faded across the water, shadows climbing the sunlit planks.

Aron glanced edgily over his shoulder. 'Wanted to give ye somethin', actually,' he said. The pirate unsheathed a dagger from his baldric and held it out to me. Its iron hilt was cast into the shape of a rose, ornate etchings swirling down the grip.

I took it hesitantly, the cold metal heavy and unfamiliar in my palm. 'It's beautiful.'

'Gods know where ye might end up,' Aron said, scratching his head. 'But I'll rest easier knowin' ye can protect yerself.'

I wasn't sure if I should be flattered or afraid. *Protect myself from what?* If these pirates weren't my enemies, then . . . I glanced down at the blade, at the blooming iron flower. 'I'm not sure I'd even know how to use it,' I admitted.

Aron grinned. 'Figured as much.'

He grabbed my fingers, pulling them apart and turning the dagger upside down in my hand. I gripped its hilt as he rotated my forearm, pointing the tip of the blade outwards, at him.

'Like this,' he said, manoeuvring my arm in a stabbing motion.

My stomach clenched. I doubted I was strong enough to cause much damage, but the thought of actually wielding something so dangerous made my heart pound.

Aron took a step back, eyes gleaming. 'C'mon, then.'

I swallowed when I realised what he wanted. He spread his arms wide, smirking in anticipation. I glowered at him, making a feeble lurch forward and bringing my weapon arm down like he'd shown me.

Aron laughed. 'Harder'n that, lass.'

I struck out again, my temper rising, but he dodged my attack as easily as swatting a fly.

'Better,' he encouraged, smirk growing.

When I lunged again, he reached out and pushed me, sending me stumbling. I recovered, darting forward faster, harder. With a rough swipe, he blocked my swinging arm and my dagger clattered to the ground. I picked it up with a scowl, raising it again.

My next attack was vicious, fuelled by irritation. Aron's

widening grin only spurred me on as my swings grew bolder, fiercer, until we were almost fighting – him to deflect my blows and me to wipe that damned look off his face.

With nothing to defend himself, I soon had Aron backed up against the quarterdeck, shoving him roughly into the wall, raising my blade to his throat.

'How's that?' I growled, wiping a trickle of sweat from my forehead with my free wrist.

Laughter rang out and I glanced behind us to see a dozen or so of the crew gathered around, watching on in amusement.

Aron straightened, looking impressed. 'Not bad, fer a princess,' he conceded with a wink. He shouldered past me, cursing good-naturedly at the pirates who mocked him from the sidelines. Then he reached for his cutlass, drawing the sword from its scabbard at his waist. He raised an eyebrow at me and grinned.

'Think ye're ready fer this?'

The dining hall shone with faded splendour. The King stood once more by the flames of the hearth, his shadows splayed across the walls. I crept towards him, drawn by an invisible string that wouldn't heed my growling instincts. *Not afraid*, I tried to remind myself. I was half sure he was only a man; it was easy to forget, when simply being around him made me feel so hollow.

I came up beside him, the light of the fire playing across my exposed shoulders. I'd spent the entire day on deck with Aron and the crew and I was covered in grime, sweat and bruises – tendrils of dark, carving me out before the flames.

I peered up at the King, still anxious to catch a glimpse of what lay beyond his hood, but the shadows went deep as ever, impervious even to the dancing blaze. His gaze fell to my bare skin, a tangible whisper of something invisible that swept along the curve of my collarbones. I would've sworn I could smell him beyond the smoke from the fire — but the scent was so like the sea, I couldn't be sure.

When he finally spoke, his words were stilted. Measured, yet somehow uncertain. 'You never told me your name.'

I blinked. *You never asked*. Why would he? No man bothered to name his pawns.

'Ria,' I said warily, even more on edge than before. 'Well — Aurelia is my given name, but I prefer Ria.'

'That's not at all the same.' His voice was gravelly, irritated.

I shrugged. 'I didn't like the name given to me, so I gave myself a new one. Suppose we're similar in that way, you and I.'

'Oh?' The King tilted his head and I swallowed.

I knew I was treading on thin ice; a dangerous game in the presence of fire. But I lifted my chin, feeling the amber light dance in my eyes. 'You're just a man who calls himself *king*.'

He let out an amused breath. 'You know nothing about me, blackbird.'

I scowled. 'What did you call me?'

His lips twitched as he reached out to twist a strand of my hair between his fingers. My heart thudded at the proximity of his large, ruinous hand. He draped the curl gently behind my shoulder, but my body stayed tense long after his arm returned to his side.

'They say when a blackbird is seen so far out at sea, it means war is coming.'

Fear churned through my veins. 'And is it?'

He hesitated before answering me. 'There's always war coming. Only fools call it peace.'

I shivered at the timbre of his words, full of foreboding. He could call me what he liked, but he wasn't about to blame me for the violent crusades of men.

'Well, I *have* a name,' I said.

'Aye,' the King agreed, his tone laced with amusement once more. 'Aurelia.'

I didn't miss the trace of distaste on his harsh tongue. It sounded different on his lips, nothing like the reproval it always was with Aberdeen. Still, I'd never liked it. Now at least I understood why. It was a princess's name, not mine.

'Are you finished making a mockery of me, *Your Majesty*?'

A low chuckle fell from his lips as he turned from the fire and took his seat at the table. I followed grudgingly, frowning at his back.

Tonight, even the expansive table between us felt insufficient. A rope-thin peace stretched between us as I dug into a plateful of roast lamb and honey-drizzled carrots. The soft meat fell apart on my tongue, the scent of rosemary and wine jus making me salivate so much I forgot all about my reluctance to let him see me enjoying the meal.

'So, did you read the book?'

It took me a moment to realise what he was talking about. I'd almost forgotten about the book in the chaos of the last two weeks. Almost forgotten whose bloodstained hand had lifted it from the shelf and given it to me. A slew of images flashed through my mind, the same ones that had haunted my restless slumber. All that destruction, and he wanted to talk about books?

I bit my cheek. 'Yes,' I said shortly, piling more food on to my plate.

The King leaned forward, the table creaking beneath his weight. 'Well?'

'It was fine.'

He sat back again, arms folded smugly. I could sense the amusement coiling around him like smoke. 'I knew you'd like it.'

I rolled my eyes, settling my attention on the plate in front of me. The King continued to watch me in silence, that unmoving hood fixed on my face. My blood simmered under his gaze, irked by the unfairness of it all. He could stare all he wanted, and I'd never get so much as a glimpse of what he was thinking.

I slammed down my cutlery with a metallic clang and glared right back at him. 'What is it you want from me?'

All trace of amusement vanished from his voice. 'Is that your question for tonight?'

I hesitated. There was still so much I didn't understand, and the recent battle had only confused me more. It was a tempting question, but one I knew would get me nowhere, so I shook my head.

'No,' I huffed, chewing on my bottom lip as I sifted through the endless things I still didn't understand. 'I want to know what will happen to me – once Bane arrives,' I said. 'If you kill him, will you still sell me to his followers?'

The sea knocked against the hull of the ship as the King mulled over his answer. 'No,' he said at last.

'Then what?' I pressed, leaning forward. 'And why did you kill Cullen's crew? Now who knows how long it'll take before Bane gets here.'

'You seem to have forgotten our deal, blackbird.'

I scowled. Our arrangement hadn't proven nearly as useful as I'd anticipated. One-word answers were doing very little to chip away at the vault of secrets I knew the King and his crew guarded. 'You didn't give me a proper answer,' I said.

He shrugged, slouching back in his chair. 'Blame that on your uninspired line of questioning.'

'I almost died the day Cullen came,' I retorted. 'Your crew seem convinced that I'm safe here, but you're apparently determined to make me think the opposite. Why won't you just tell me what you're planning? Cullen's crew were the surest means of summoning Bane, yet you killed them all.'

The glow of the hearth receded, tendrils of shadow reaching for us both. The King said nothing, and I knew it would take more than that to break his stoic exterior.

'If not to sell me, then what's the point?' I prodded. 'Are you not trying to fatten me up like cattle, ready to ransom me off to the highest bidder? I'd have thought King Oren's pockets would run deepest, but who knows – I hear pirates live like kings these days anyway.'

The chandelier flickered.

'I'm not going to *sell* you,' he ground out. My heart fluttered in fear, realising too late that it mightn't have been wise to provoke him. 'I'd kill a person before I robbed them of their humanity. I wouldn't have done you the dishonour.'

I paled, a familiar feeling settling in my chest, trickling through the cavity of my ribs. *Don't you dare feel guilty*, I wanted to growl at myself. What did a pirate know about honour?

'Excuse me for doubting your righteous moral code,' I muttered.

'Unlike Bane, or your precious uncle, my people value the lives of others. Up until the moment they raise their weapons against us.'

'I think you'll find King Oren treats his subjects a little fairer than you,' I scoffed. King Oren had a kingdom, after all. A court and a crown and a palace. What did pirates have, beyond vengeance, and the sea?

A muscle tensed in the King's jaw, barely visible through the mantle of his beard. 'Just because a man wears silk gloves doesn't mean his hands are clean.'

I barked a bitter laugh. 'I can't imagine a pirate knows much about *clean hands.*'

He exhaled sharply. 'Maybe not. But your people weep in hunger's name, not mine.'

'Blame hunger all you want,' I snapped, heat rising in my cheeks. 'Crop yields have been dwindling for years, yet here we sit gorging ourselves on food that just magically appears. *You* could ease the suffering of thousands if only you relented your rule over the seas. Tell the people they won't be harmed just for fishing!'

The King was quiet for a moment, letting my outburst echo through the hall. 'Is this what you came for, to lecture me?'

I gritted my teeth, realising nothing I said would ever pierce that veil of night-dark indifference. Nothing I did would change him. 'I came for my answer.'

'Well, you have it.'

I didn't and he knew it. I crossed my arms tightly over my chest, fixing him with a waiting glare.

The King sat back slowly in his chair, releasing a sigh. 'I'm not going to sell you. I'm not going to do anything. You'll have your life back the moment I have my steel in that bastard's throat.'

A glint of hope flickered in my chest. I knew by now *that bastard* meant Bane. Knew it was his life for mine. Yet I couldn't find it in me to feel guilty, somehow. 'You seem so certain he'll come.'

'Aye,' the King said. 'If Oren had killed my family the way he did Bane's . . . nothing would be able to stand in my way. Bane's a fool for going for the throne, but he's too far gone to ever give up now.'

So Oren had Bane's family killed. I suppressed a shudder. It didn't matter what darkness drove Bane — not when it was driving him to use me, to paint his rebellion in the colour of my blood.

'All this because he betrayed you?' I asked quietly. 'You'd really go to war?'

'One question,' the King reminded me, a tired smile playing at his lips over the rim of his goblet.

I glowered at him across the table, but the feeling in my chest was stirring, growing so strong I could almost taste it. *You'll have your life back.*

Monster or not, Bane's death would set me free.

10

Pirates lazed in the morning breeze, soaking up the weak grey sun. I sat perched on the balustrade of the forecastle deck, the stretch of wood wide enough for me to lounge back with a book spread open in my lap.

I was far enough from the crew to catch the echoes of their chatter as they brailed sails and coiled the lines languidly. Like all vessels, Father's ships had required constant maintenance and I'd never seen his crews sit idle, but it seemed the *Blood Rose* ran on something more than mortal hands. The pirates spent most of their daylight hours lying about, whittling figurines from wood, playing cards and singing shanties that made my ears burn.

My book lay neglected in my lap as I stared out at the water and listened to their tales from afar. Most were too exaggerated to be true – I hoped, anyway, for the sake of all involved. I was almost jealous of the way they sauntered through each day, rowdy and jostling, always finding something new to fight over.

The waves rolled past, the rhythm of their lapping against the hull soothing me like a lullaby. Deeper ripples swept across the surface and I sat up straighter. Whorls of seawater were transforming into shapes before my eyes, like bodies gliding through the current. I leaned over the side, peering down at the water. There they were again — faces of azure smiled up at me, their human-like features forming in the ripples of the tide. They twined around one another, arching over the surface and disappearing below.

I wondered if these were monsters of some kind, too, like the serpent I'd seen after the battle, or if they were nothing more than water. Wondered if they could be as benign as they appeared or if I was a fool for thinking I could trust anything about this place.

A shout of laughter snatched my attention and I glanced back at the crew. One figure drew my gaze, the wind blowing through his white hair, a smile stretching into the hollows of his cheeks. I watched Mors laugh alongside his crew mates, perplexed as always by his carefree demeanour, his elegant posture and hearty shouts as he argued good-naturedly with his companions.

His gaze met mine and he pulled away from the group, heading up the steps towards me. I glanced back down at the water, but the surface was as flat and still as ever.

'I was hoping to run into you,' Mors said, pausing to lean against the railing in front of me.

He held something in his hands and I smiled when I realised what it was. I closed the book in my lap and set it down, my eyes glued to the thick brown pages of the one he extended towards me.

'I brought you this,' he said.

I took the book from his leathery grasp, gazing down at its ancient pages, its ridged spine comfortingly heavy as I inspected the cover. *Tales of the Sinking Cities*, read the title.

'Aron tells me you like to read.'

I nodded, delighted by how quickly Aron and Mors had found the way to my heart. *He's not the first aboard this ship to give you books*, a dark voice reminded me.

'Thank you,' I said earnestly, leafing open the first page to find an inscription sprawled out in faded ink. *I find these stories bring hope, even when such a thing feels hopeless*. I traced my finger over the elegant script, a small smile tugging at my lips.

'It was a gift from...someone I loved,' Mors said softly. 'She found it in an ancient library back home. It inspired my love for adventure.'

I peered up at him, trying to picture Mors as a young man, golden hair thrown back from his face as he stood proud at the bow of some ship, determination bared at the unending sea. Had he ever thought he'd end up here?

I hugged the book to my chest. 'Thank you, really.'

'I know what it feels like to be lost, lass.'

His words made me pause. I didn't feel lost so much as . . . adrift.

'How did you come to be here?' I asked, my curiosity getting the better of me.

Mors squinted out over the water: a ghost of that younger man, his eyes and ambitions dimmed. 'I left King Oren's court twenty years ago – the night I helped your parents escape. After that, I travelled for many years, searching for something I wasn't even sure was real.'

I leant closer, his words stirring something wistful within me. 'Did you find it?'

'Almost.'

The reluctance in his voice had a heartbeat of its own, pulsing out across the waves; a whisper of whatever he ran from, or towards. Mors glanced down at me and smiled ruefully, and I knew exactly who had stopped him.

'What was he like back then?' I asked, trying to picture the Heartless King a decade or two younger – a child – but the image was impossible to conjure.

'Very much the same.'

I shivered, arms tightening around the book at my chest. Before I could press him for more answers, the old man dipped his head. 'I'll leave you to your reading, lass.' He must've taken my frown for disappointment, because he added, 'I believe I'll see you at dinner.'

My eyebrows shot up, hope swelling in my chest. Knowing I wouldn't have to spend another evening alone with the Heartless King was almost as good as Mors' gift.

As he retreated, I glanced back down at the book in my hands, admiring the image emblazoned on its dark-blue cover. A young boy held a great sword to the sky, a crown nested in his curls. I settled myself back on the railing and leafed open the book, wishing there was something I could do to lift the weight from that little boy's hands.

That day, I read stories of a forgotten kingdom – palaces of gleaming white marble with twisting, pearl-studded steeples and rooms that rang with the sound of the sea. I closed my eyes, imagining how the wind and tides would've cleaved their way into the hearts of those cities and their people. As I traced the worn pages of the book, a memory emerged; a familiar feeling of crumbling parchment beneath my fingertips. A map. One so ancient I couldn't make out the names scattered across its surface.

I shook my head, trying to smother the seed of hope before it could bloom. No wonder Mors had been drawn to the seas. The stories were entwined with an intoxicating hint of magic. I knew if I wasn't careful, I, too, might find myself chasing something I'd never find.

Each page pulled me in deeper, spinning tales from sea foam and salt, from wooden hulls to sandcastle spires. They told of the great King Nereus and his beloved daughter. Of the water spirits that played in the shallows of their tide-bound kingdom. I read of Arenes, a glistening seaside city, its shores pebbled with activity, where marketplaces lined the docks and the people mingled with the waves.

Most of all, I read of the sea. Of the goddess who watched fiercely over everything her tides touched, from the voyagers who journeyed her waters to the creatures that dwelled beneath. To these people, she had a name. Nerida.

I thought back to the brutal battle I'd witnessed, to the sea serpent devouring the fallen – wondering if these two worlds could ever have existed together. If the expanse beneath me could be the same one from which Nerida had once rippled forth to bring a kingdom into being. And if so, whether there was anyone but Mors and I left who knew her name.

Curlicues of ink and colour framed each page, the vellum worn thin and gold leaf details flaking. The book wasn't just old, it was well loved.

Daylight waned and the crew trickled inside, leaving me all but alone on a twilight-stained deck, the sun winking a slow farewell over lapsing waves.

I drank in the stories of the Sinking Cities; and I knew, the moment it began, that the last – and longest – tale of the book would be my favourite. The sound of the tide crashing against city walls curled around me, echoing through a rough-hewn marble palace that carried rivers in its cobbled veins. The story told of a young prince, of his love for Arenes and its surrounding isles. A love that would endure long after their kingdom sank below the waves.

Dusk turned to night. With a sigh, I gathered my skirts and

returned to my room. The rest of the story called to me, dimming what little desire I had to see the King. I didn't bother to wonder what reason he could have for inviting company, but I was eager to see Mors again, at least.

The book will be here when I get back, I told myself firmly.

Soon I was tugging myself free of my clothes in my warmly lit chamber and dragging my fingers through the salt-tangled ravels of my hair, wishing I had a mirror. I gave up quickly, sweeping my unruly curls into a knot at the top of my head and letting loose ringlets fall about my face.

I dressed in pale blue overskirts and tied a soft navy corset under my bust, wondering what my sisters would've said if they could see me now. Aberdeen would've cringed at the grime that darkened my skin, the smell of dust and ink and roses that clung to me. Felicie might've said I looked like myself again.

Sighing, I headed for the door. I was late and my mind was cluttered, so I didn't notice as I hurried out into the hall and—

'Watch it,' Golde hissed.

I stumbled back in alarm. 'Sorry,' I mumbled, smoothing down my skirts in an attempt to regain my composure.

Aron sauntered up the stairs a moment later, greeting us with an easy smile. 'Play nice,' he warned Golde, winking at me as he passed.

'I am,' Golde snapped, following Aron into the dining hall. 'Ain't like I stabbed her,' she muttered, letting the doors swing shut behind her, almost hitting me in the face. I pushed my way indignantly into the room, my gaze immediately drawn to the shadow by the fireplace.

The Heartless King wasn't alone, his head dipped low as he conversed with a woman, one vaguely familiar but whose name I didn't know. She turned when we entered, breezing straight over to me with a smile.

'Ye must be Ria,' she grinned, long black braids dancing about her shoulders. 'So glad I finally get to meet ye.'

Before I could reply, the woman yanked me into a tight hug, soft curves encircling me with warmth. It'd been so long since I'd felt such a comforting touch that once my shock faded, I almost hugged her back.

'Lass, meet Una,' Aron remarked, walking past us to take his seat at the table.

When she finally pulled away, Una was still beaming at me. She was gorgeous – charcoal hair, ebony skin, rosewood eyes. Her skirts were stitched in multicoloured cloth and her ears pierced with rows of small gold hoops that twinkled in the firelight.

'Nice to meet you, too,' I said, eyeing her sceptically. There didn't seem to be a cold bone in her body, yet she stood among those closest to the Heartless King. It felt wrong not to be afraid.

'I hope ye've not been too lonely, lass,' Una said, pulling out the chair beside Aron's and offering it to me.

I slid into it reluctantly, knowing full well that the seat to my right belonged to the King. I said nothing, but the thought of sitting so close to him for a whole evening set my teeth on edge. I was at least glad to see Mors already seated across from me, warmth lighting his ringed eyes.

'I've managed,' I told Una, offering the white-haired man a smile.

Golde threw herself down beside Mors as the King's shadow fell over the table. I kept my gaze fixed on my plate as he took his seat, his proximity curling around the edges of my consciousness.

Our meals were often shrouded in an ominous disquiet, but framed by the easy chatter of those who stood by him, whose lives were woven into the deadly fabric of his own, it made me even uneasier. It wasn't supposed to feel like this – warm, almost familiar. Especially when Una leaned around Aron and asked me with sparkling eyes, 'Tell me Ria, has our Sebastien been his usual merry self the last couple o' weeks?'

It took a moment for the name to settle on my ears. *Sebastien*. So that was what they'd called the man before he named himself King.

I lifted my eyes slowly from my plate as I spoke. 'If you consider quiet rage to be good spirits,' I replied drily, feeling his gaze upon me. It had been a long month.

Aside from a low chuckle from Aron, the crew's eyes darted to their King. Golde's narrowed to slits, the knife in her hand throwing candlelight at me, a reminder of the dangers that still lurked in the shadows around us. *They* were the danger – I was the prey.

'Ah.' Aron sighed, lips still turned up in a smile. 'The two o' ye should lighten up one o' these days.'

'And you should learn not to pester me,' the King muttered, the visible stretch of his jaw clenched tight.

Aron only shook his head and chuckled again. They really didn't fear him, I realised incredulously. Whether it made them foolish or brave I couldn't decide, but the King appeared oddly tolerant of Aron's pestering – for a man I knew could rip him limb from limb.

The evening wore on and, slowly, the tension in my chest began to dissolve. The cool undercurrent of my unease was warmed by something more than the crackling hearth. I drank in the crew's banter, Aron and Una's easy laughter and Mors' sly grins. Even Golde's sourness seemed tempered by their mirth, though her surly façade rarely slipped.

It reminded me of Aberdeen, that cold mask of indifference.

But walls went two ways. I'd spent enough time being shunned by my eldest sister to know that letting nothing out also meant letting no one in.

The first mate sat slumped in her chair, grinding a hole into the table with the point of her dagger and shooting me periodic glances that were every bit as sharp as her blades. I didn't know what the first mate's problem with me was – until Aron made a joke about my situation.

'The real tragedy in all this is Ria bein' forced to spend time with this chum-smellin' beast,' he quipped, reaching around me to clap a hand on the Heartless King's shoulder.

I sucked in a breath, waiting for his reaction. When Sebastien spoke, his voice was a growl, laced with warning. 'Told you, she's *your* damn prisoner.'

Golde looked up then, raven hair slicing shadows down her cheeks. 'Funny thin' fer a prisoner to be invited to dinner.'

Malice glinted in her dark brown eyes, making anger swell in my chest despite the chills that spiked down my arms. I hadn't done a thing to the woman, and I couldn't understand the waves of hatred that rolled off her wiry form.

I tipped my chin higher, knowing weakness would get me nowhere. 'Perhaps it's because the company he usually keeps is so poor.'

Aron and Una burst out laughing, their delight ringing through the air louder than Golde's outrage could. Even Mors broke a smirk at his own expense. I thought I caught a glimpse of an appreciative smile beneath the King's hood, but he turned his face, leaving me sure it'd simply been a trick of the light.

Una looked over at me, her hazel eyes gleaming. 'Think we'll be gettin' on just fine, lass.' She beamed again. 'Though I don't s'pose ye've had any effect on His Majesty, eh? His ol' mug ain't changed in three hundred years.'

My heart clenched in my chest and I chanced a glance up at the King's shadowed hood. I was *almost* certain Una was exaggerating. The King said nothing, fingers tightening on the arms of his chair as the uneasy silence pulsed around us.

Golde hunched forward in her seat, a strange quirk to her lips. 'Ignore her. Whatever Una lacks in pretty much everythin', she seems to make up fer wi' her tongue.'

Una tipped her head back and laughed. 'Ye *wish* ye knew what me tongue can do.'

Golde snickered begrudgingly, for once looking more chagrined than murderous. Aron, on the other hand, averted his gaze, suddenly engrossed with the food on his plate. I glanced between him and Una, curious.

Aron gave nothing away, but he pulled my gaze often that night, his jokes and outlandish comments providing a constant source of amusement. I wouldn't have called him handsome, but there was something undeniably appealing in the way he threw his head back, peals of unrestrained laughter washing over the room. His eyes shone, more gold than grey in the light of the chandelier, wrinkled by years of smiling and sun. I could tell I wasn't the only one drawn to them – Una's gaze flashed towards him frequently, as if on instinct, reeled in by the ring of his laugh.

Eventually, Golde withdrew to the fireplace to stir the flames with her sabre, leaving the seat to the right of the King empty. Una was quick to fill it, seeming determined to lift his spirits – why she bothered, I had no idea.

'Tell us, Ria,' Una said, placing a hand on the King's forearm as she spoke. 'What's it like, bein' a princess?'

Her tone was bright and expectant, but my gaze was caught on her hand. Something inexplicably sharp cut through me at the sight.

How could she touch him so casually?

The King shrugged off Una's touch as the table fell silent, waiting for my answer.

'I wouldn't know,' I told them. I was no princess. And even if I was, I could hardly say what it meant. 'My father hid us – me, my whole life. From King Oren, I suppose.'

Una furrowed her brows. 'Ye didn't know who ye are?'

'Not until recently.' I shifted in my throne-like chair, glancing around the table, my eyes landing on Mors. 'My father's a merchant, we grew up in Bray,' I explained. 'We did better than most, but we moved further north when I was fourteen. In hindsight, I guess poverty wasn't the only thing we were running from.'

Mors' eyes darkened from across the table.

'What happened?' Una asked. 'Ye didn't go hungry, did ye?'

My gaze cut sharply to her. I tried to decipher her expression, searching for a sign of some ill motive, but I saw only concern. Did she really not know?

'Of course we went hungry,' I said, trying to keep the bite from my tone. 'For weeks at a time. Every winter, or whenever our father's trade ran dry. Do you honestly not know how bad things are?'

I turned to glare at the King. He knew how much the people suffered – knew, and would do nothing to help. When he made no reply, I pressed on.

'If you just stopped killing . . . People are starving for fear of your wrath. They only turn against you because they have no place else to go. You could ease so much suffering if—'

'Only a fool'd believe we can help hungry people.' Golde turned from the hearth to glower at me over her shoulder, firelight dancing in her dark eyes.

'*I* believe it,' I insisted.

The first mate gave me a pointed look. 'Exactly.'

I scowled. Weak, foolish – she thought me all the same things Father had.

'What Golde is tryin' to say is that things've been this way fer a long time,' Aron put in, his tone almost sympathetic. 'We never killed anyone just fer fishin'. It's their own fear that keeps 'em away.'

'What about the dozens of ships that wash ashore each year?' I challenged, voice rising. How could they be so callous? 'What about my father's crew?'

Una shook her head, tight braids hanging across her face. 'Lass, it ain't so simple. Raidin's our way o' life. But we only take when there's somethin' to give. It ain't murder, just business.'

I narrowed my eyes, knowing I was fighting a losing battle – uphill, unarmed and alone. How could they justify such a thing, these pirates I'd almost started to believe had hearts? I clenched my jaw and sat back in my chair, arms crossed. 'Tell that to the families I've watched bury *your* victims.'

'Your father's crew raised their swords against us,' the King spoke at last. 'You can't blame me for their deaths when they knew the fate they were asking for.'

I suppressed a snort of contempt. 'I'll blame whoever cut holes in their chests. And you, for sanctioning it.'

'Please,' he said shortly. 'I have a fleet of twelve ships sailing under my name. You expect me to answer to all of them?'

Anger tightened like ropes around my lungs. *Yes.* 'You could tell them to stop killing. You could do anything to help, yet you don't.'

'Why should I?'

I opened my mouth to respond, but Aron beat me to it. 'We'd only fight Oren's soldiers if we could, but we've got a fleet to feed. All regular ships, mind — that's a lot o' bellies to fill wi'out magic o' any kind.'

'We only kill when they fight,' the King added. 'And anyone who fights is a fool, so I hardly see how the world is worse off without them.'

Blood roared in my ears, and I hated how shrill my voice became when I spoke. Hated him more, for causing it — for a lot of things. 'You don't see anything wrong with that?'

I could've sworn his lips turned upwards as he said, 'We're pirates, blackbird.'

Una's eyebrows shot up and Aron ducked his head to cover a smirk. I didn't know if they understood the meaning behind his nickname for me — if they, too, believed me the unwitting herald of this war against Bane — but it made me feel oddly exposed.

Una laid a palm flat on the table, reaching for me. I stared at her hand, outrage still roiling in my stomach.

'I can understand why ye're angry, lass,' she said softly. 'This world ain't easy.'

I looked away. 'The *world* isn't what forced me away from my family.'

The King sat motionless, as if unfazed by my fury, and I wished more than ever that I could see his expression.

'Your family,' he observed. 'The father who gave you up to m— to us.'

'You don't know what you're talking about,' I gritted out, not caring that my temper had slipped in a room full of people. Hearing him speak of my family arrowed longing right through my lungs. Because of him — because of all of them — I might never see my beloved father again. Might never feel his arms around me, or hear Felicie's laugh.

'Just because you can't understand love doesn't mean I don't feel it,' I said. 'I love my father more than anything. I sacrificed myself because you made me think we'd all die if I didn't.'

'Sacrifice,' the King echoed. He mulled over his next words for a long time. 'You left behind a dying land drenched in fear and a family that would've let you starve. Here you're safe, with a belly full of food and a library full of books.'

Safe. I almost laughed. But he wasn't wrong. If someone had asked me a month ago what I wanted, I'd have said those very things. Food, books, *life*.

'What I want means nothing when I can't share it with my family,' I said. 'Surely you can understand that, at least.'

Even the Heartless King must've had parents. Must have loved someone, once. But the crew's averted gazes told me I'd assumed wrong.

'Ask every person at this table whether they'd have done the same as you,' the King said. 'How much love they felt from those who raised them.'

My eyes shifted between them, a guilty flush creeping heat up my neck, into my cheeks. Only Mors met my gaze, his own clouded with a mixture of pain and sympathy.

'We all lost our mothers young,' Aron said quietly. 'To sickness, to war, to our fathers.'

A wave of foreboding washed over me. Not everyone in my family had always been warm or affectionate, but they'd never hurt me with more than words. Which, however sharp, were parchment-cuts compared to the wound of losing a mother. I knew that much, at least.

'So did I,' I murmured, feeling responsible for the sombre mood that had settled over the table. I turned to the King, wondering why I felt the need to redeem myself to a monster like him. Still, I asked, 'Don't you ever miss your father, even a little?'

The silence that followed echoed louder than sea-braced cliffs. Even so, it couldn't have prepared me for what he said next.

'I killed my father.'

11

The King's confession struck me like a hand across the cheek. I took in the crew's downcast eyes, feeling the grim silence settle around them. *They knew*. Of course they did.

My skin crawled. Maybe it was naïve of me – few people had fathers as loving as mine. But murder . . . I couldn't fathom the darkness that could've driven him to that.

He – *Sebastien* – was watching me. The hairs on the back of my neck stood on end, his shadows slipping like silk over my skin. If he was waiting for a reaction, he'd get none. I had nothing to say.

I let the crew's voices wash over me as they tentatively picked up the conversation. But the world around me was an echo as I lifted my gaze slowly up to the King, wondering if there were eyes beneath that hood at all. If he really was shadow, all the way through.

'Scared of me now, are you?' he murmured.

My glare hardened. *You wish*. But he was right, I was terrified.

Terrified of how blurred the lines were becoming between what I could and couldn't forgive. Between what I could trust and what would kill me the moment I turned my back. It would be too easy not to hate him if I let myself forget how much of the seas were blood because of him.

I stood abruptly, tossed down my napkin and stalked from the room, dodging the crews' quizzical glances.

Anger flooded through me, a churning river that rushed the air from my lungs. The glow of the crew's warmth had seeped into me, their infectious laughter tricking me into forgetting the darkness concealed in these gilded halls.

I burst into my room and slumped down at the vanity table. The useless one without a mirror. Why were there no gods-damned mirrors? I tugged my hair free from its bun, growling in frustration. This entire *ship* was damned, and everyone in it.

A part of me couldn't help but wonder why killing his own father felt so much worse than every other life he'd taken. What had I expected? Half his victims had probably been fathers to *someone*, and the crew had still tried to justify their deaths.

Floorboards creaked out in the hall and I turned, temper already rising again at the thought that the King had dared to follow me. But a gentle knock dispelled my dread as the door inched open to reveal Una, hovering in the threshold.

'Can I come in?'

I nodded, taking a deep breath to quell the rage kindling in my chest. 'Sorry for leaving like that,' I said. 'I'm just . . . I don't know. I miss my family, I suppose.'

'Lass.' Una waved me off, perching on the edge of the bed across from me. 'We're pirates. Ye can forget about manners. Just wanted to make sure ye're all right.'

I blinked at her blithe tone. 'I guess I just couldn't sit there any longer and pretend he isn't a monster.'

Una crossed her arms. 'Who asked ye to pretend?'

I tilted my head, perplexed. She knew what he was. They all did – so why were they so loyal to him?

'How could you ever trust a man who would turn on his own family?' I asked at last.

'He's more'n just a man, lass.'

I'll say. 'He isn't even a real king,' I scoffed. 'What right does he have to your loyalty?'

Una held my gaze for a long time, brown eyes dipped in a candlelight glow. 'Not all families are tied by blood,' she said eventually. 'Ye might've been lucky, but the rest o' us had to make our own. Aron, Golde, Mors, even Sebastien . . . they took me in when I had no place to turn. It ain't what he is, but what he's done. Fer me, fer his people. I'm sorry ye're caught up in all this, but ye'll understand everythin' in time.'

I frowned. *In time.* I wanted to know now.

'And what exactly am I caught up in? Why does Bane's death mean so much to you all?'

Una sighed. 'Ye heard 'bout the mutiny?'

The King had mentioned it on the night of our first dinner. I gave a half-hearted nod, hoping Una would say more.

'Bane was born noble, but he ended up on the streets young, like me. Lost his whole family to Oren, before Aron brought us both in, gave us a home here. We loved Bane fer what he was – a little twisted, but so charmin', so . . .' Una shrugged, averting her gaze. 'He was ruthless, and his noble blood made him greedy. He wanted more. Wanted revenge fer what Oren'd done. When he realised Sebastien was never goin' after the throne, he turned half our fleet against us. Lost nine ships and a lot o' lives in the process.'

Una settled back into the mattress, tucking her feet beneath her colourful skirts, a sad furrow to her thick brows.

'I'd kill anyone who came fer me family,' she said fiercely. 'But fer it to be someone we considered a brother . . .' She dipped her head, withdrawing behind the curtain of her braids. 'Ye can't imagine that kind o' betrayal.'

I sank into my chair, feeling my wary bones soften a little. 'I'm sorry,' I told her, and I meant it. 'For everything he put you through. But I don't understand this – this hunger for blood. Isn't that what led Bane to betray you in the first place? Choosing vengeance over all else?'

'*Bane* chose vengeance,' Una said grimly. 'He didn't just break our code, he spat on everythin' we'd built together. Ye migh' think us all monsters, lass, but wi'out loyalty, we've got nothin'. Ye think Sebastien betrayed his family, but that ain't what his father was. Nobody's born a killer. They're made, in brutal ways.'

I bit the inside of my cheek. This war might've had monsters on both sides, but I knew enough to see that Una wasn't one of them.

'I won't waste my breath trying to argue for Bane's life,' I said. 'I'm just trying to work out how I fit into it all.'

Una chewed her bottom lip. 'Ever since Bane struck out on his own, he's been gatherin' followers, money, allies. He could use ye to gain power, maybe even try to put ye on the throne, if he could be sure he'd have a place beside ye. I dunno, politics ain't me thing. But I know it wouldn't end pretty.'

Spiders of fear scuttled down my arms. 'And I'm supposed to just sit back and wait for him to find me here?'

'I'm hopin' it won't come to that, lass. But if we don't end it, he'll never stop,' Una said. 'Ye see that, righ'? Maybe we were wrong to get ye involved, but . . . Mors never would've put ye in danger if he thought Bane'd get his hands on ye fer a second. And if that ol' sea dog's got faith, then so do I.'

'How reassuring.'

Una's grin was a fleeting thing. 'I mean it. Sebastien ain't gonna let Bane out o' here alive, even if we all go down wi' him.' She met my eyes, then added hurriedly, 'Except fer you, o' course. Ye'll be just fine.'

I resisted the urge to scowl. 'How can I trust any of you when you call the Heartless King your *family*?'

'Trust me or don't, lassie. Either way, I plan on bein' yer friend. Ye're just gonna have to put up wi' it.'

Friend. I stared at the pirate lounging on my bed, her hazel eyes bright, trying to ignore the voice in the back of my mind that asked why she would want this – why she was so determined for me to like her, to feel safe. I shook the thought off, tucking a strand of hair behind my ear.

'I'm sorry if I was harsh on you earlier,' I said. 'I don't . . . I'm still trying to wrap my head around all this.'

Una pointed at herself with a laugh. 'Pirate, remember? Stop apologisin'.'

I gave a meek smile in return.

Her full lips stretched into a wry smile, eyes gleaming. 'Aron tells me ye've been dinin' with His Majesty every night,' she said conspiratorially.

'Not every night,' I said quickly. 'He promised me answers in exchange for each meal. Though I hardly know why.'

'Ah, even grumpy ol' bastards get lonely out here on the water.' Una sighed. 'What good's havin' fangs if ye don't get to bare 'em every now and then, eh?'

Right. Because he wanted me to fear him. Tonight had proven that I was a fool for ever forgetting to fear the extent of his heartlessness. He only wanted to toy with me, his prey.

But *prey* implied there was something to be gained, an objective of some kind.

A hunger.

I was no closer to knowing what that could be than the day I'd set foot on the *Blood Rose*. So many nights we'd dined together, yet he remained elusive, hiding behind something I couldn't see — something I wasn't sure even his most trusted companions were allowed to see.

What could be so terrible he had to hide from the world?

I could scarcely picture a face as ugly as his soul — gnarled flesh, twisted features, cold, gleaming eyes. Dead as his enemies. Whatever the conflicting legends said, the King fought like a man in his prime. Spoke like one, too. But the stories of his reign had existed for too long for that to be entirely true.

What had Una said at dinner? *Three hundred years . . .*

*

The young prince stared down at his hands, fronds of bronze flesh not yet scarred by life's callouses. They dripped blood to the marble beneath; a portrait of his future painted in rivers of red.

The old king's blood seeped into the cracks, filling jagged crevices with dark, hot crimson. It ran like veins through the palace, a swirling mosaic of red and white. The prince's home was flooded with the smell of death and the colour of his violent new dawn.

His father's sword lay where it had fallen beside his mother's body, her blood mingling with her husband's until they were indistinguishable, made one even in death.

The princeling sank to his knees, tears falling thick from his seascape eyes. He had failed — failed to separate them, failed to save her. He had failed his people, too. Doomed them to the hands of a boy with a monster's blood running through his veins, dripping from his fingertips.

His blood-spattered face ashen, he looked up at the vaulted arches of the throne room, watching the black sea swirl outside the windows, slinking ever closer . . .

My head snapped up, jerking me awake. Rain lashed against the windows, streaking the library with silver-blue light.

I blinked the drowsiness from my eyes and wiped a smudge of saliva from the corner of my mouth. I didn't know when I'd drifted off, nor how long I'd slept for, but moonlight danced across the painted ceiling and the room was darker than usual. It took me a moment to realise why, glancing up at the unlit chandelier and—

'Good evening.'

I jumped, my head whipping towards the opposite end of the table where a hulking figure sat fused with the shadows.

Sebastien.

It would take some time to reconcile such a beast with such a human name.

Murderer, my instincts growled. There was an even darker truth to that title now.

'You never came to dinner.' The King's cloaked shoulders shifted as he leaned forward in his seat, closing the book he'd been reading with a *snap*.

'I wasn't hun—' I glanced down at the dark blue cover in his hands and gasped. 'Where'd you get that?'

'Could ask you the same question.' There was a soft menace in his voice that hadn't been there before.

The hairs on my arms prickled as I looked down at my empty hands, shuddering at the thought of him lifting Mors' book from them while I slept. *Bastard.*

'Give it back.' I strode around the table towards him, hands clenching into fists. I'd been so close to the end. I needed to know what happened.

Sebastien stood and I backed away instinctively. 'I asked you where you found it,' he repeated.

'I found it here,' I told him, gesturing at the room full of books, unsure why the truth felt so dangerous.

'Don't lie to me.'

'Why does it matter?'

The King stepped closer and the briars twisted through the chandelier trembled overhead. It reminded me of the windows that had shattered from the force of his rage on the day we met, as if the ship's heart beat in synchrony with his own. Not that he had one.

'Don't let Mors fill your head with foolish hopes,' he said. 'He's wasted his own life chasing sea mist.'

'It's just a *book*,' I said. 'What, now I'm not even allowed to imagine there might be a better world out there?'

'I'll save you the trouble. There isn't.'

My temper ignited. What right did he have to take anything more from me?

'Just give it back,' I snapped.

'There are thousands of books in here. Are you still not satisfied?' Sebastien's voice lowered, jagged with restrained frustration.

'So this is about your *pride*?' I cried, his composure only infuriating me more.

A blunt laugh. 'I'm trying to warn you. Your imagination will be the death of you.'

I faltered. He was right – living in a world that didn't exist would get me nowhere in the real one. But I wasn't about to admit that. I straightened my spine, pushing my shoulders back.

'I'd rather die of my own imagination than at the filthy hands of a pirate,' I said, following him towards the door as he shoved *Tales of the Sinking Cities* into the inside pocket of his cloak.

He turned to face me in the doorway. 'You'll thank me later.'

I glowered up at him. 'I promise you, I won't.'

My heart hammered in my chest, half from anger, half from something else. Something unrecognisable. I didn't concede.

The King's chest rose and fell sharply, rhythmic as the rain that battered the ship's hull. Then he moved, making my lungs seize in my chest.

I watched warily as Sebastien extended a hand slowly, almost hesitantly, and grazed a knuckle down my neck, tracing the faint wound left by Cullen's man. A strange shudder fell through me at his touch. It wasn't cold, like I'd expected. It was scorching. Pure heat.

He dropped his hand, his voice depthless. Hypnotic. 'We'll see.'

Sebastien smirked as he stepped out into the hall, hooded figure melding into the darkness beyond. The gesture, twisted as it was, was unnervingly human.

'You're sick,' I snarled, unsure why my blood was suddenly blistering with heat.

He paused, turning to look back at me. 'Sicknesses can be cured, blackbird. What I am is forever.'

I slammed the door in his face with a hiss.

12

For six nights, I didn't dine with the King.

I spent my days on deck with the crew, listening to their shanties and letting them laugh at my terrible singing whenever I joined in. They taught me the rules to card games we never managed to finish without an argument breaking out, and, all the while, I couldn't shake the stories of the Sinking Cities from the back of my mind.

I tried distracting myself with other books, but on every page I found myself searching for some mention of those forgotten isles, some reference to crumbling citadels of tide-swallowed stone. I found none.

A storm rolled in that lasted for three days and I spent the entirety of it immersed in worlds far from my own, far from the truth of whatever was coming. I scoured history books, poems, novels so ancient and close to dust the words were practically fading under my fingertips. Nothing.

I wouldn't be able to rest until I knew the fate of that fabled kingdom, of that little prince. The King's actions had only made me hungrier for the truth. I didn't know what would happen to me, to Bane, to any of us, but *that* story had an ending. If I couldn't control mine, I could at least take comfort in someone else's.

So, when the rain finally let up, I took my chance.

I ventured outdoors and found myself a place on the sterncastle deck, positioned carefully out of the crew's way as they bustled about, chipping rust and soaking up the sunlight. They chattered as they worked, their voices a symphony against the surging waves.

I propped myself against the ship's wheel – which I'd never actually seen manned – and listened through the din for signs of movement in the navigation room below.

Days of frustration and longing held my patience firm as I waited for the King to emerge. The afternoon sun sank slowly into dusk and I was almost ready to give up when the muffled sounds of an argument reached me from the room beneath.

I crept closer to the edge of the railing, ears focused intently on the two voices. Neither was hard to recognise and I didn't have to listen long to realise the cause of Mors and the King's argument.

'. . . know it was you . . . playing at?'

'She deserves . . .'

'Don't tell me what she deserves, you're the one—'

'Evenin', lassie.'

I gasped and whirled around, coming face to face with Aron – dangling upside down. He dropped lithely from the ratlines, flipping to his feet with a grin that split his craggy face.

'Up to somethin', I hope?'

'N-no,' I stammered, scrambling upright. 'Just reading.'

We both glanced down at my empty hands and I cursed myself silently. *Could've said anything, fool.*

'Ye sure?' Aron waggled his brows. 'Perhaps I can be o' service?'

I regarded him for a moment, assessing the gleam in those storm-grey eyes, always eager for mischief. 'He took something from me.'

'Oh?'

'Yes, and I want it back. It's just a book, but—'

'Want me to distract him for ye?'

I blinked at his willingness, nodding before he could retract the offer. 'Thank you.'

'Anytime, lass.'

Aron slid down the banister to the quarterdeck and disappeared from sight. A door opened below and angry voices leaked out once more. Sebastien's growl was easily distinguishable as Aron said something about *fresh air*. There was a moment of huffed protests before Mors and the King emerged, Aron trailing after them.

I watched from behind the wooden balusters as the three men descended to the main deck. Once they were out of earshot, I darted down the steps and through the doors. I wouldn't have long.

I crept through the navigation room, recalling the fear that had gripped me the last time I'd stood here. But the windows were no longer broken, the lamps were lit, and there was no time to stop as I reached the door at the end and swung it open.

The King's bedchamber was dark. Thick curtains hung across the sterncastle windows and a single candelabra illuminated the opulent clutter. Musty volumes, scattered parchment and ancient-looking ornaments littered a sturdy writing desk. Ink bottles, daggers and discarded clothing were strewn across every available surface, dust cloying at the edges of it all. It was every bit the chamber of a king, but one a little too lived-in to feel luxurious.

I moved further inside, surprised by how normal it appeared. No human skeletons in the corners, no cauldron filled with blood. Aside from the stale darkness, it was almost . . . inviting.

Rich velvet drapes surrounded the towering four-poster bed. The dark crimson sheets were rumpled, slept in, an unwelcome reminder that this was the Heartless King's one splinter of privacy in the world, and I was invading it.

The bedsheets brought a flash of colour to mind – a flood of red, a story. It would be my own blood in a minute, if I didn't get moving.

I sifted quickly through the nightstands and beneath the mattress before turning back to the desk. As I rounded the bed, my foot snagged on an trailing sheet and I went tumbling to the ground. My hand shot out to grab hold of something – and I yanked on a swath of fabric draped over the desk. It swept to the floor beside me, sending a glimmer of light sparking through the room.

Candlelight gleamed in the surface of a mirror. I picked myself up, drawn to the glint of the looking glass. It'd been weeks since I'd seen one – seen myself. I was almost afraid to look.

I turned slowly, my petticoats stirring dust, and met my own gaze in the mirror. I blinked. It was the same face I'd always seen. The same sweeping jaw, gossamer lips, delicate nose. So why did I feel so different?

My once-gaunt features were full of life again, but it was in my eyes that I found the answer. Their honey-dipped warmth glowed bright in the winking light of the Heartless King's chamber. They'd seen so much death – so much more life, too.

And I looked older, dressed in pirate garb. Wilder. The leather corset laced over my loose blouse was more of a comfort than a restraint, and my lips quirked at the dirty hems of my skirts, imagining all the ways Aberdeen would've berated me for them.

The shadows around me shifted in the mirror, making my lungs constrict. Inconspicuous as nightfall, the Heartless King emerged over my shoulder.

I spun around, heart wedged in my throat. I'd become so accustomed to his presence I hadn't sensed him until it was too late.

Sebastien stepped closer, waves of darkness rolling from his cloaked form.

Panic fluttered in my chest. Risking my life for a book – how fitting.

'I want it back,' I blurted, before he could speak. As if I could distract him from the fact that he'd caught me snooping.

The King stayed silent for a moment, the candelabra beside me flickering between us. *Gods, he's really going to kill me.*

'The book you stole?' I prompted. 'The one—'

'I know what you meant.' Shadows leaped over the walls as he strode closer still. 'I burned it.'

My heart plummeted. *No.* 'How could you?'

'You know as well as I do why Mors gave you that book.'

His answer surprised me. I hadn't expected him to have read it, much less to acknowledge the parallel the story bore to his past. Unless . . .

'I just want to know how it ends,' I said.

'Everybody dies,' Sebastien grunted. He stepped past me, grabbing the heavy fabric at my feet and draping it back over the mirror in a swift motion, his hood never once turning toward the mirror's reflective surface.

'Do they?'

The words slipped out before I could stop them, before I even knew where they'd come from. It hadn't been until that moment that I'd suspected there could be any truth in those stories. That the end I was searching for could be standing right in front of me, cloaked in darkness.

The King turned slowly back to look at me. 'You want to start asking questions? You can tell me what the hell you're doing in my room.'

I opened my mouth to respond, then closed it again, making a mental note to curse Aron out for failing me so miserably.

'Tell me you didn't burn it,' I said quietly, unable to even summon my anger. Mors had entrusted me with those stories, with the magic in them. I'd felt it: the swell of adventure that had called to me my whole life, the same feeling that had sent him out on to the waves, captured right between those pages. Now it was gone.

'You don't need a book to explain what I am, blackbird. I might have magic, but I'm still a monster.'

Chills crept down my spine. On his lips, the word *magic* sounded so much deadlier than anything I knew.

When we were young and the world outside was dark, my sisters and I had whispered stories under the bedcovers about witches who shifted shapes and cast spells, about creatures that roamed the deep and crumbled from cliffsides. But Sebastien wasn't like those things.

I'd seen potions and enchantments advertised on the streets of Bray, but I'd never truly believed magic was more than the call of the sea until I'd seen it – shattered windows and roses blooming without soil and monsters roiling in the waves. Here, with him, magic was something different. Something deep and dark. Monstrous, maybe. But even the admission on his lips felt like a step in the right direction. Towards what, I wasn't sure.

'How does it work?' I asked. 'The shadows, the magic? Explain it to me.'

I listened to the swell of his indrawn breath like it was a tide. The room grew warmer, darker, as I waited for it to break.

'Call it a gift,' the King said at last, but the word came out bitter.

'Nerida blessed me with this . . . this power. It keeps me young, or whatever it is I am.'

Nerida. The goddess. Hearing her name aloud made my heart beat faster. 'Why you?'

He grunted. 'Maybe I deserved it.'

I scoffed. 'Because you're so benevolent?'

'No,' he said, sounding irritated. 'Because I messed up. I was supposed to prove her wrong and . . . it doesn't matter. I don't expect you to believe me when I say this curse was made to punish me more than anyone else.'

'Curse?' I echoed.

'Think about how cold and empty the night is; imagine living with a piece of that inside you.'

I hardly knew what he was saying, and I knew it was wrong to feel anything but hate for him, but fool that I was, I said, 'Empty? Have you never seen the stars?'

The shadows in the room swelled. 'Stars can't reach you down here, blackbird. You think something in that damn book is going to save you from what's coming?'

'And what *is* coming?' I hissed, suddenly regretting my softness. 'Because I'm having an awfully hard time getting an answer out of anyone.'

'Have you considered that we might not know?'

His grumbled reply made me pause. Because perhaps a part of me had believed Una when she'd said I'd be all right. Maybe some part of me had trusted in some part of them; that after all the dust settled and the blood dried, I, of all people, would still be standing.

'You'd really die for this?' I whispered. 'Let your crew die for it, too?'

His answer was hardly more than a growl. Fierce, fraught, bordering on afraid. 'I don't *know.*'

'For a king, you don't seem to know much.'

'I know I've never been pestered this much in my own gods-damned chamber before. Are you really still here?'

'If it weren't for you, I wouldn't be here at all,' I said, glowering at him. *I should be home, with my family.*

He turned, moving towards the window. 'I told you, it wasn't my idea.'

'Well you certainly seem to have come around on the whole *baiting Bane to his death* thing,' I snapped.

'What else am I supposed to do?' the King enquired. 'Conjure up a feast to lure him in?'

'You didn't seem too worried about luring anyone when you slaughtered Cullen's entire crew, stopping word from actually reaching Bane that I'm here!' I cried. 'Surely you have a brain as well as a sword.'

'Let's say I don't.'

'You're impossible.' I clenched my jaw, clutching at the last shreds of my patience. 'Don't deny that in the right hands, your magic could do far more good than bad.'

'And I suppose you'd *only* use it for good.'

'Obviously,' I ground out, irked by his derisive tone.

Sebastien snorted. 'Then perhaps you know a spell to make yourself disappear.' He turned away again, the tension in the air dissipating.

'I'd sooner use it on you,' I retorted, scowling at his back.

Book or not, I'll find what you're hiding, I thought, heading for the door before the tides of his temper could turn again.

His final words followed me out into the hall. 'Goodnight, blackbird.'

*

My feet glanced off the flagstones as I ran.

A moonlit sea flowed between the palace's sprawling, briny walls, licking at my toes. Silver light soaked the world — the spires, the stars, the sand. A tapestry of marble rose from the rocky shore, etched in centuries of history and salt. Ivory towers and yawning arches speared the black sky, their faded glory crumbling beneath the weight of time.

I slowed my pace, letting the water lapse around my ankles as the fresh air filled my lungs, weaving through my hair. I gazed around in wonder, watching the moonlight drape the wet marble like silk. Then I looked down, and froze in horror.

Rivulets of crimson streamed through the cracks in the ground, cascading through the veins of the city.

Blood. There was so much blood.

My heart accelerated, adrenaline pounding through me until all I could see was red, red, red.

Thick, hot rivers of blood sloshed around my calves as I whirled around, searching for the source. It came from everywhere, all at once. I tried to run but the rising liquid was too thick, wrapping around my ankles like boneless hands, tugging me backwards.

Then it was gone. Torn from me in a gust of wind — the blood, the palace, the night.

I gasped, lurching awake in bed. Moonlight streamed through the windows, dim compared to the starry glow of my dream. I could still feel it, sitting heavy in my chest. There was an emptiness where the darkness had been wrenched from me. A piece of night. Snatched away, as if it wasn't meant for my eyes.

But I'd seen it. Seen its beauty, its glory; seen a world of crimson tides and star-soaked sky that I wasn't ready to let go of just yet.

13

Dust circled the sunlit row of bookshelves in which the King found me several days later. I was skimming through volume after volume, scouring the pages of any book old enough to hold mention of the Sinking Cities. Still nothing.

Goosebumps prickled across my bare shoulders, but I was too absorbed in my task to notice his entrance until the doors snapped shut behind him. I kept my eyes fixed on the page in front of me. Unless he was here to apologise, I had nothing to say.

What kind of tyrant burned books?

Still bent over the novel in my hands, I moved to the table, its polished surface scattered with more volumes, their pages curled and yellowed with age. Sebastien paced to the other side of the table, studying the array of books piled around me.

I kept my gaze glued to the page as he settled into the chair opposite and pulled open an ancient tome I had yet to read.

When I finally looked up, I noticed his thick beard was gone, revealing the strong curve of his jaw beneath the hood. I read on with a furrowed brow, trying in vain not to be distracted by his nonchalant presence. I'd spent days searching for another glimpse of that faraway, forgotten land, desperate to answer the gnawing feeling my dreams had planted in my mind. But with him here, I was suddenly finding it hard to focus.

I sighed and glanced up. 'Where are we going?'

The King didn't bother to look at me as he turned the page. 'To our deaths.'

I rolled my eyes. 'You know what I mean. You obviously don't know where Bane is, so where are you travelling to? Surely you don't just swan across the seas, killing all those you encounter.'

'*Surely*.'

Growling in annoyance, I forced my attention back to the book I was reading, trying to shake off his grating presence. The few things I did know made little sense, like shreds of a torn map I couldn't piece together. I couldn't tell the sea from the land and the north from the west. How was I ever supposed to find my way home?

'Just give me the book back,' I said in exasperation. Failing to concentrate, once again.

'I told you, I burned it.'

'Fine. At least tell me why.'

'It's personal.'

I sat back with a triumphant smile. 'It is about you, then.'

'Didn't say that,' he muttered.

My smile turned smug. If irritating him was all it took, finding answers was about to get much easier. But even if it was true – even if that story *was*, somehow, about him, it explained nothing about why the Sinking Cities were never mentioned anywhere else, why

I'd never heard of them before. An entire kingdom, erased by history. *How?*

It had been two weeks since our last dinner together and I was starving for answers. Starving, but stubborn. I refocused on my book.

Later, when I turned its final page with a defeated sigh, I looked up to find Sebastien sprawled in his chair, thick leather boots resting on the table and a book propped open in his lap, a slight frown to his lips as he read. I tucked my hands beneath me, resisting the urge to reach across and yank back his hood.

Dusk filtered in through the high windows, a precarious peace softening the air between us.

The King glanced up and tossed his novel on to the table. 'Hungry?'

I nodded, my stomach rumbling as I stood and followed him to the door. He stepped back and I hurried out into the hall, an unwarranted blush creeping into my cheeks as I brushed up against his chest.

When I pushed through the heavy doors into the fire-lit dining room, I paused. Rather than the usual buffet of rich, appetising dishes, there were just two place settings laid at one end of the table.

I gazed longingly down the stretch of wood as I slipped into my new place beside the King. Gold plates harbouring aromatic meats and vegetables suffused the air with the scent of rosemary and lamb. I reached for my already brimming goblet of wine and drank eagerly, letting the heady crimson liquid fill my belly with the courage I needed.

'You never answered my last question,' I said.

The King tilted his head, shadows lengthening down the column of his neck.

'Where we're going,' I prompted, setting down my chalice.

Another long pause. He trailed a finger down the gold stem of his goblet, the dip of his throat just visible as he swallowed. 'Home,' he said at last.

'To the Sinking Cities.'

It was a wild guess, perhaps, but I felt it strike its mark. Sebastien lifted his head slowly and my heart skittered at his silence. *It's . . . real?*

'I see you're as smart as you are irritatingly curious.'

'I read a lot,' I said, smiling at his intended insult. A giddy warmth bubbled up in my chest, my blood scorching with adrenaline. *It's real.*

'I've noticed.' His voice scarcely grazed my consciousness, my mind blistering with a thousand questions, a thousand new possibilities, most of them beginning with *how* and *why*.

It's real, it's real, it's real.

That meant . . . the Heartless King wasn't just a pirate. He'd had a kingdom, once. Something real and worthwhile and *his*. So where was it now? And why was he so desperate to hide every part of himself?

I took another sip of wine, studying the slant of his broad shoulders over the rim of my goblet as I tried to order my thoughts. If those cities really had been erased from history, there was no way they could still exist. It would've taken an age for a kingdom to fade from the annals. Centuries, even. So how could he possibly go home?

'Is revenge all that's keeping you here?' I cleared my throat, sure he could hear the pounding of my heart. 'Or by *home*, did you mean . . . *below*? Where your cities are?' I shuddered at the thought. That perhaps he'd meant what he said earlier. That they sailed for only one thing . . . *To our deaths.*

A heavy sigh fell from beneath the king's hood and I cursed at myself for being too eager. I was rolling my eyes before he even spoke. '*One* question.'

I gritted my teeth, formulating a different approach as I cut into a fillet of roasted salmon, trying to appear casual. 'If that kingdom really is your home . . .' I ventured, 'I don't suppose you'd want to lead Bane's army there.'

The fish fell away from my knife, revealing a rich pink centre. Sebastien laughed. It was a sound I'd never imagined he could make, rumbling from deep within his chest. Loud and . . . warm. Not the kind of warmth that melted ice, but the kind that burned.

He shook his head, the twist of his smirk visible beneath that depthless hood. 'You amaze me.'

I widened my eyes in feigned ignorance. 'I only meant that perhaps—'

'I know exactly what you meant. You forget that it's your *uncle's* kingdom Bane wants to destroy, not mine.' He spoke as though he had any kingdom left to protect.

I sipped my wine, feeling the King's shrouded stare on my face. 'He must be either very foolish or very dangerous to think he has any chance against King Oren.'

Sebastien shrugged. 'Maybe he's both. Either way, he's dead the second I get my hands on him.'

'And after that, you'll go home?'

He was silent for a while, watching me. 'I won't stop *you* from going home, if that's what you choose.'

I narrowed my eyes. *If that's what you choose.*

'You think I have a choice?' I asked, ignoring the way he'd deflected my question. 'You think I'll be free, once Bane's dead? A life for a life – and then what? I have nowhere to go but home,

131

to hide, and that's only if King Oren never catches wind of my existence in the first place and forces me to join his court.'

A frown tugged at the King's lips. 'You always call him *King* Oren. As though you revere him, a man you don't even know.'

He was right. I didn't know my uncle, only that Father had spent our whole lives trying to shelter me and Felicie from him. He wouldn't have done so without reason, wouldn't have taken Aberdeen from her mother unless it was absolutely necessary.

Mors' words rang through my mind. *His reign is stoked by many fires and he hides them well.* Good men didn't inspire the kind of bloodlust Bane seemed to hold for King Oren, and I shuddered to imagine what he'd done to earn it.

I didn't revere him – it was more than that. I feared him; feared what having his blood in my veins might mean if he ever found out about us. I had to ensure it never came to that.

Sebastien's tone lightened, gruff but teasing, as though he could sense my unease. 'You never call me King.'

I rolled my eyes. 'I'll call you *King* once you've earned the title,' I retorted. He might've been one, once, but I doubted he'd earned a thing in his life, beyond bloodshed and terror.

Sebastien leaned back, spreading his hands. 'Enlighten me. How does one earn such a title?'

I ignored his mocking tone. 'A good king knows the value of mercy. You should show it to those who cross your waters.'

'And Oren?' he countered. 'How do you know he's merciful?'

'King Oren's people don't whisper his name in fear,' I insisted. 'Not like they do yours. They don't cower in their homes, hungry and cold, because the sound of *his* ships along the coast makes them too afraid to even touch the shore. Oren's name never sounded like a death sentence.'

The King leaned forwards, shadows winding around my

shoulders. 'That's what you expected, coming here?' he asked. 'A death sentence?'

I swallowed. 'Yes.'

I watched him exhale, listened to the heaviness that bled from within him. 'People die,' he said, his voice low. He sounded weary, almost defeated. 'Life is cruel and harsh, and innocent people suffer. That's the way it is. If you want to saddle all the pain in the world on my shoulders, fine. But there are worse mercies than death. Men like Bane would burn the whole continent down – you included – just to see the pain in Oren's eyes as it crumbled.'

My ears felt hot and my fingers clenched around my fork. Like I didn't have enough to be afraid of. My elation at discovering the truth about the Sinking Cities was crushed beneath the weight of everything real.

'It's been a pleasure, as usual,' I snapped, shoving my chair back and heading for the door.

To my chagrin, he followed, reaching out to hold the door open as I stalked out into the hall, hating how easily his long legs kept up with my angry strides.

'Bane wants peace,' Sebastien said, walking in a steady rhythm beside me. 'He thinks he can get it by burning Oren's kingdom to the ground and building a new one in the ashes. It won't work. At the end of it all, he'll just be another tyrant in a wooden chair, while the world weeps cinders around him.'

'He wants to be king,' I echoed. 'So he'd have to kill me, to get to the throne?'

'Marrying you would be more effective.'

My feet faltered. I tried to swallow, my throat suddenly drier than stone. 'That's it, then?' I asked. 'I'm supposed to sit back and wait for some man I've never met to lay claim to me, just so he can use me against my own people and burn my homeland to the ground?'

We reached my room and Sebastien pushed his way inside, turning on me the moment I crossed the threshold behind him.

'Nobody's *claiming* you,' he growled. 'Bane's dead the moment I see him, and you'll be free to go back to that damned life and suffocate.'

I faltered, my anger quashed by his quiet intensity. 'Why do you *care*?'

'My crew seem to think it matters whether you're miserable or not,' he snapped back.

'Your crew, huh?' I stepped forward, closer than I meant to, my chin tilted up in challenge.

His breath fanned against my face when he spoke. 'Believe me, I don't care what you do after this. But you're a fool if you think you'll ever do more than survive, back in that place you came from.'

'What choice do I have?' I snarled. 'I didn't ask to be a princess, to have to hide, but I'll do whatever it takes to save my sister.'

I gasped, my hand flying to my mouth before I could stop the words from escaping. *Fool.*

'I—' I stammered, but it was too late. *My sister* ... what else could I have meant? I glanced up at the King, afraid to find out what my slip-up would cost me.

A huff of laughter fell from beneath his hood. 'You don't think Mors tells me everything?'

That old bastard, I cursed. All this time, he'd known. 'You know that I'm not ... that my sister ... ?'

'If you really thought you could fool me, then you aren't as intelligent as I thought,' the King mused.

'So, what,' I spluttered, 'you've just been letting me pretend this entire time?'

His lips twisted. 'Seemed like the polite thing to do.'

I wanted to slap the smirk off his face. 'So, what now?' I asked, my irritation melding into a thousand new worries. *This is what I get for trusting a pirate.*

'You're still a princess. Good enough for me.' Sebastien – *the King* – shrugged. 'So long as nobody ever knows of your sister, this can all end with Bane's blood beneath my boots.'

Blood. Had these brutes never heard of gold? It seemed death was the only currency they had any interest in, and the wager just happened to be staked on my shoulders.

I swallowed. 'Like I said . . . I'd do anything to protect her.'

The King stared down at me for a long moment, the silence weaving its net around us. 'Aye, I know.'

I stood close enough to feel his words breeze against my cheek, yet I could still see nothing beyond his square jaw and almond lips. My eyes caught on their slope.

Tentatively, I lifted a hand, compelled to reach past the shadows, to draw back his hood. My fingers whispered over hard, stubbled flesh, cheekbones, tangled hair. Proof that there was a man under there, after all.

His hand closed around my wrist, stilling it. Stopping me from revealing too much. His fingers were long, calloused, the graze of his warm skin tugging at some unfamiliar heat within me. *It's the wine*, I told myself, shaking it off.

He let go quickly, as though he didn't like to touch me. But his other hand reached out, tipping up my chin. Forcing me to look into his darkness.

'Don't waste your time searching for something that isn't there.'

I jerked back, unsure why his touch made the rest of the world feel so hollow. He'd told me, that very night, that the kingdom I dreamed of was real. That there was truth in the stories that had given me hope when all he'd ever given was darkness. Yet here he was, sending shivers of heat across my skin with a simple graze of his hands.

'Then let me see you,' I said, trying to sound resolute. 'Save us both some time.'

I didn't care what he hid from, didn't care that I'd never be able to mend whatever was broken in him. I just wanted to *know* . . .

His hand found my chin again, his thumb tracing the curve of my bottom lip. My knees nearly buckled beneath the weight of his touch, the shadows he seared into my skin. He stood motionless, his entire being transfixed on some part of me even I couldn't see.

This should feel wrong, I thought, but my mind barely registered it. All I could feel was his thumb on my lip, that splinter of skin where our bodies were connected.

'You don't want that,' Sebastien muttered, pulling away slowly. 'You won't find what you're looking for.'

I hadn't realised my heart was racing until it slowed, until cold air replaced where his hand had been. I swallowed thickly. What *was* I looking for?

Before I could reach out to stop him, before the world around us could crumble any further, the King vanished from the room, leaving me bewildered, angry. Torn.

No. I cut my thoughts off sharply, letting out a huff. I'd let my guard down, let him get too close. Most of all, I'd been disappointed when he pulled away.

What was wrong with me?

I changed into my nightdress and climbed into bed, determined to forget the King's shadows, his touch, his voice in my ear.

I gazed up at the rose-wreathed bed frame, pondering what my sisters would say if they could see me now, stretched out among soft furs, bathing in the luxury of the Heartless King's warship.

Aberdeen would've envied the finery: washing in rosewater, dressing in silk and dining like a queen each night. Felicie would've danced alongside the crew and glowed at Mors and Aron's kindness. Neither of my sisters would've been foolish enough to bargain with the King, I knew that much.

A tangle of emotions clutched at my chest at the thought of Felicie here in my place. *It was supposed to be her.*

I couldn't name the dull, sinking feeling that filled me as I pictured myself back in Father's study, reading of adventure while my sister lived it. Or worse, if it had been Father who'd left the bay that night instead. There would have been no way out for any of us then.

If the King was telling the truth, I'd be freed by Bane's death. But now that hope felt hollow – nothing compared to what the stories of the Sinking Cities had stirred in me. The calling of the sea.

Returning to Northbay felt more like fate than a future. The cottage had always been a hideout, not a home. Sebastien was right – I'd suffocate. And for Felicie, I would. I'd make it through this and prove I could protect her, once and for all.

I thought of Sebastien's calloused hand on my wrist, his shadows coiling like flames in the base of my stomach.

Gods. I pressed my face into the pillows with a groan. *Where do I go from here?*

14

The crew moved about in an unusual clamour, loading heavy crates and locked chests on to the deck from below. Their spirits were high, their voices loud and bracing against the breeze, and the shanties they sang grew progressively lewder as the day wore on.

Aron took me up to the crow's nest, showing me how to climb the shrouds without burning my fingers on the ropes. I pulled myself on to the wooden lookout with a satisfied grunt, turning in a circle to admire the expanse of ocean, the endless, undulating blue—

I gasped. 'There's someone out there,' I said, grabbing Aron's arm and pointing to an oncoming ship, its bow angled straight for us.

The pirate laughed. 'Aye, lass. Ye think we haven't noticed?'

I smiled sheepishly over my racing heart. 'Right,' I said, trying to sound calm. Was this it? Had Bane come for me? 'And who is it, exactly?'

Aron's smile slipped for a moment before he replied, 'An old friend.'

His answer wasn't entirely reassuring, and the sharp edge of wariness didn't leave me as I asked, 'One you aren't planning to kill?'

He grinned. 'O' course. We've just got some, er, affairs to sort.'

I heard Golde's shout from the quarterdeck as she gave orders to strike the sails and drop anchor.

'C'mon.' Aron beckoned, swinging back over the lookout railing. 'Ye'd best stay out o' the way fer today. Not always the friendliest o' friends, this bunch.'

Apprehensive, I descended the ratlines behind him, the crew's shanty encircling us, rhythmic as the waves.

Glory her, glory her,
From crumblin' cliffs to Eir

Their excitement at the new ship's arrival only increased my trepidation. I'd grown used to the King's crew over the weeks, felt at ease with most of them, although *friends* might have been a stretch.

I trailed after Aron at a distance as he wove through the crowd to where the smaller ship had anchored beside the *Blood Rose*. I caught sight of the pennant flying at the ship's mainmast, a human skull wreathed with roses – the Heartless King's insignia.

Jolly drownin' melancholy
And drinkin' when we're lowly

There came an echoing cry from the other deck:

Salted tongues and gold and folly
And ruttin' 'til we're holy

Their laughter was like rolling thunder, my cheeks warming as it infused the sky.

The newcomers began to board, swinging across the divide where they were met with hearty embraces.

I hadn't realised quite how *old* Aron's friend was, however, until they lowered the gangway to the other ship and a woman emerged slowly over the side.

She couldn't have been much younger than seventy, stooped over an ivory cane that looked unsettlingly like bone, tattered tricorn hat perched over her long copper hair to symbolise her status. Dull thuds punctuated her every second step, courtesy of the wooden stump protruding from her left trouser leg. Her eyes, too hooded to make out the colour, were ringed like the hollows of an ancient tree.

I shifted into the crowd, watching with interest as the pirates around me tipped their hats and lowered their heads, the rumbling call for *mercy* on their lips. It took me a moment to realise what they meant; it wasn't a prayer, but a name.

A strange quiet fell over the deck as Aron, Golde and Mors emerged at the front of the crowd to welcome their guest.

'Mersey.' It was Golde who spoke first, and I'd never heard something so like a plea on her lips. The first mate's head was bowed, her eyes downcast, but I was too far away to read the emotion in her usually indifferent gaze.

'Hello, Golde.' The captain uttered the words like a benediction, her harsh features softening.

Aron said something in a low voice that made the old woman laugh. I retreated further as they strode past, watching them disappear into the navigation room.

The two crews grew loud and blithe once more. Remembering Aron's warning, I returned to the forecastle before I could attract any attention, wondering what *affairs* the two crews had to discuss. Given Mersey's age, I couldn't help but suspect it had something to do with the King's secrets. Perhaps she knew more about the Sinking Cities, or was old enough to understand what Una had meant about *three hundred years*.

If the King really had burned Mors' book, I'd need to find my information elsewhere. It would be foolish to show my face in a room full of pirates I didn't know, but if I wanted answers . . . I did know one person I could ask.

*

The dining hall burned with life. Oil lamps saturated the room with an orange glow, made more vibrant by the grating melody of shouts and song. The air hung thick with abrasive laughter, the voices of Sebastien's crew mingling with the newcomers'. Walking in alone, I felt the knots of my resolve slip, just a little.

A single empty chair sat to the King's left, telling me my company wasn't entirely unexpected, at least. He looked up when I entered, his hood following me as I took my seat beside him.

I averted my gaze, ears growing hot as I fiddled with the flowing sleeves of my olive-green overdress. I'd managed to avoid the King since our last dinner, and his closeness stirred the feeling of foreboding in the pit of my stomach.

He looked away without a word. It was Aron who glanced sideways at me as a lull fell across the table, his eyes gleaming with a look that said, *I told you not to come.*

Mersey wiped her mouth with the back of her hand, setting

her goblet down on the table and fixing me with a stare. 'The princess, I take it,' she remarked. Her voice was raspy, yet unnervingly steady for someone so old and battle-worn.

I shifted in my seat, biting back a retort. Mersey looked as though she'd waded through a sea of blood and dirt to get here, yet she spoke as though *princess* was the foulest thing to be.

'Surprised Bane hasn't shown his face already,' she added, her eyes still locked on mine. Both sides of the table muttered curses at his name.

'He'll come,' Aron said quietly.

I glanced sharply at him. He didn't sound too eager, for someone supposedly hell-bent on revenge.

'Well, if you're not plannin' on selling her back to him, I know me crew'd be happy to take her off your hands.' Mersey turned her gaze to Sebastien. 'Pretty thing like that. Unless, o' course—'

'Enough, Mer.' It was Golde who cut her off, the quiet menace in her voice carrying through the hushed room.

Mersey smirked, her eyes gleaming. 'Relax, Goldie. You know pretty's not me type.'

A muscle clenched in Golde's jaw and the two women stared each other down, staunch gazes cutting through the simmering tension. I tried to decipher their steely expressions, but both were as guarded as each other.

Guarding what? I wondered.

'She's here 'til Bane's dead,' Aron said into the taut silence.

Another wave of anger rolled down the table at the mention of their enemy. Whether Mersey really was a friend, it was clear the two crews stood on the same side against traitors. But the old captain's eyes were still caught in Golde's. 'Huh,' she said. Her tone was veiled, almost threatening. 'Pretty sure I can get word of your location to him before the week's out, if you want.'

'We got it covered.' Una's tone was almost defensive.

My eyes flicked up to the King, wondering why he said nothing. If what Mersey said was true, he could have his revenge soon. And me – I could slip away before King Oren ever caught wind of my whereabouts. I could go home.

But once again, Sebastien's crew seemed in no hurry. If they were as hungry for vengeance as they claimed, then why weren't they leaping at Mersey's offer? Why had they killed Cullen's crew – was their bloodlust really so insurmountable?

Still, I said nothing. Because I knew that the day Bane came would be the day the world around me shattered. When what little security I had on the *Blood Rose* would crumble and I'd be left to face my future, alone.

Mersey lounged back, wooden leg propped up on a stool beside her, long hair the colour of dying autumn leaves splayed around her shoulders. 'No sign o' the bastard, then?' she grunted.

I didn't like the impatience that snapped at her words, like a hound awaiting a meal.

'He sent Cullen 'bout five weeks ago,' Aron answered. 'Shouldn't be too long.'

'Cullen.' Mersey's first mate scoffed, tipping back in his chair. 'Hated the bilge-sucker. Should've taken more'n his teeth when I had the chance.'

'Aye. If you need backup . . .' Mersey raised her whisper-thin brows at the King.

'We'll handle it,' he replied bluntly.

'I heard he's got more'n a thousand. Peasants, farmers – all the hungry ones are joining him these days.'

'He's no fool,' Golde countered. 'Won't risk losin' more'n a couple o' crews.'

Mersey shrugged, looking unconvinced. 'They might be halfway dead already, but they outnumber you. I ain't gonna let you face him alone.'

'Ye said ye weren't gonna drag the fleet into a losin' battle,' Aron muttered. 'It ain't worth it.'

'The *fleet*,' Mersey hissed. 'That doesn't mean I'm letting you . . . Gods – you're so determined to be reckless. Don't tell me you honestly think—'

'Seven hundred we took out, the year Oren succeeded,' Golde interrupted, eyes brimming with a violent nostalgia. 'Remember?'

A small smile slipped across Mersey's furrowed lips, her anger seeming to evaporate when her eyes met Golde's. 'Aye, I remember.'

My stomach lurched. *Seven hundred*. I didn't know why I was surprised. It was who they were: thieves, pillagers, murderers. I released a long, slow breath, trying to chase away the nauseating feeling. Why did I keep letting myself forget the things they'd done?

As if he sensed my unease, Aron leaned in to speak low in my ear. 'It's our way o' life, lass,' he said. 'The seas ain't safe fer anyone, and those who face us know what's comin'. Doesn't stop 'em.'

I folded my arms over my chest, frowning at his casual tone. It didn't change the facts, didn't lessen the grief of the families their victims left behind.

'When ye have something worth defending,' he added, even quieter, 'see if ye wouldn't kill to protect it.'

Aron turned his back to respond to someone on his other side and I sat back, heart thudding. It wasn't his ominous tone but Golde's words that had me on edge. *The year Oren succeeded*. Golde barely looked twenty; King Oren had ruled for thirty years at least.

'We'll handle Bane,' Sebastien said, drawing my attention

back to the conversation at hand. His voice fell sharp through the heavy quiet, leaving no room to argue. 'The rest of his followers are yours.'

The man at Mersey's side fixed his dull gaze on me. 'Then why not just take her wi' us?' he sneered, addressing everyone but me. 'Ye don't need her if Bane's comin' anyway. Just kill him 'fore he gets the chance to check.'

Sebastien leaned forward to rest his arms on the table, the hall darkening as he spoke. 'Think you deserve a reward, Col?'

'Just sayin', Yer Majesty.' Col scratched the side of his shaved head, his smirk slipping. 'Might give us more reason to fight, knowin' we got a *princess*—'

'You fly my pennant, you fight for me.' Sebastien's words were slow, deadly as the waves. The entire table fell silent and I sat up straighter, the hairs on my arms prickling. 'You want to take that flag down? Be my guest. Then you fight against me, and you know what I do to my enemies.'

Col shifted in his seat, opening his mouth as if to object. I almost wished he'd say something more – something to draw out the real monster hiding beneath that hood.

'Got it, Your Majesty,' Mersey interceded. I didn't miss the bite to her tone as she said the words. 'But I can't promise how many'll follow your orders forever. Careful what you leave behind.'

Leave behind? Where was he going?

I shrank back in my chair, pretending to fixate on my plate while my mind raced. I'd heard the answer before: *home*. But it still made little sense – what home did they have beyond the hull of this ship? If the Sinking Cities had truly been swallowed by the waves, if their kingdom had sunk below, what could there be left to return to?

'Enough talkin',' Golde grunted, snatching a bottle of rum

from the centre of the table. 'Ye'll do as we say, long as we're here. Col, open yer mouth again and I'll be happy to shut it for ye. Permanently.'

Col slouched back, arms crossed over his barrel chest, quiet at last. I glared at him from across the table, almost reassured by the anger that seeped from the King's shadowy figure beside me.

The discord eased as the pirates settled back into their conversations, emptying bottle after bottle between them. I drank nothing myself, knowing I'd be a fool to let my guard down around any of them. I'd *been* a fool to ever think I could.

I gazed around the table as they laughed and drank, their faces cleaved by fire and shadow, so strange yet so human. The same, yet different all at once from the ruthless mercenaries I'd watched cut down their enemies in battle. Perhaps Aron was right. How else could they preserve this life of theirs when its very nature went against everything the outside world stood for?

I felt a hand on my arm and looked up to see Una standing over my chair. She jerked her head towards the blazing hearth at the other end of the room. I followed, wondering whether it was really she who wanted my company, or the others who didn't.

'Don't listen to anythin' that bastard Col says,' Una assured me as we settled into a pair of armchairs before the mantelpiece. 'Ye don't need to worry 'bout them.'

'Why exactly are they here, then?' I asked.

'Oh, just visitin',' Una said dismissively. But she was a bad liar — I could read it in her wrinkled brow.

'Captain Mersey used to be part of your crew, didn't she?' I guessed. 'Aron said she was an old friend.'

'Something like that, aye.' Una swept her long braids over one shoulder, the sadness in her eyes illuminated by the fire. 'She's been captain o' Sebastien's fleet since before I was even born.'

'Why did she leave?'

Una shook her head. 'Too painful.'

I followed her gaze back to the table behind us. To Golde, her head bent in sullen silence. To Mersey who, despite her lively crew, didn't seem to be able to muster so much as a smile. I'd sensed the tension between them, the undercurrent of something buried deep beneath spite and weak indifference.

'Fifty years ago they met,' Una said softly.

My eyes darted to Golde, taking in her youthful skin and fathomless eyes. *Fifty years.* I held my breath, knowing Una was telling me more than she should. More than anyone else seemed willing to.

'I wasn't alive then, o' course.' Una's words were barely audible over the crackling flames. 'But Aron was here. He told me 'bout the way Golde and Mersey fell in love – the way ye can only once in a lifetime. However long that migh' be. Ye don't let go o' that kinda love, ye know? No matter how hard ye try.'

I looked down at the fire, my eyes hot. I didn't know – didn't think I ever would.

My gaze was drawn back to the table as Aron's laughter rang out. I'd been fooled, I realised, by their smiles. It was no wonder they fought so wildly, so recklessly. Their real wounds ran centuries deep, more piercing than any they could earn in battle.

I shivered, turning back to the hearth to watch the pirouetting flames: a pantomime of fire, playing out memories over the coals. I saw my family, gathered around in the living room. Heard my father, reading stories over the hiss of cinders. I could've loved that life, that peaceful existence. Maybe someday I would. But to lose it, time and time again? To outlive each person, each place, I ever dared to love? Maybe Sebastien had been right. Maybe it was a curse.

'And you?' I asked quietly. 'What's your place in all this?'

'Same as theirs,' Una murmured. ''Til the very end.'

The shadows in the grate twisted, turning to figures that danced beneath swirling ash. Pirates, made of the night. Words I'd overheard and almost forgotten washed up on the shores of my mind, reminding me that the secrets went far deeper than I could grasp. *Less than three months . . . doomed . . . Something greater than you could imagine . . . Three hundred years.*

When I looked up, Aron was there, pulling Una away, their figures nothing more than receding silhouettes. I blinked a few times, letting my eyes readjust to the room. The glow of the embers was warm on my face, battling with the caress of darkness, the King's creeping shadows.

I could feel him watching me as I rose to my feet, sparing a glance back at the table. Screeches of laughter punctured the air as drunken pirates fell over themselves, slapping the table, shoving one another from their seats. The din receded as Sebastien stood and headed towards me.

'I suppose you have a question for me.' He paused at my shoulder, overshadowing the flames.

I didn't need time to think. Everything new I'd learned, every bit of it bleeding a thousand new questions, it was all tied to one dark truth, one impossible fact.

'Tell me how old you are,' I said.

'Twenty-one,' the King responded, something like amusement lighting his words.

I gritted my teeth. *We're playing games, then?* 'Let me rephrase that,' I glowered. 'How many years have you been alive?'

'I already answered—'

'I wasn't asking before. Answer me.'

Shadows swelled as Sebastien inhaled. 'I won't lie to you.'

I recognised his words for what they were – a warning. 'Good.'

The sigh that fell from his lips made my stomach flip, because I knew what was coming. Knew, yet I needed to hear it from him.

'I've been alive for almost three hundred and twenty-one years,' he said. 'Is that what you wanted to hear?'

I nodded, my heart racing too fast to respond, to breathe. I stared into the flames, wishing their heat could ease the goosebumps from my arms.

I could practically feel Sebastien's gaze slide across my shoulders as he stepped closer. 'Three hundred years I've been without a heart.' Coals burned in his words, too. 'Three hundred years I've roamed the seas, spilling blood and inspiring the legends that make your people cower from the coasts.'

Biting chills crept through my veins, chasing back the warmth of the hearth. *Three hundred years without a heart*. Did he mean . . . ? My lungs faltered at the thought that his moniker might mean something more. More than just cruel; more than just a man with a little magic.

'Why are you telling me this?' I whispered, unable to look at him.

His cloak brushed against my skirts as he leant closer. 'Because I'm a monster,' he said, his voice rough in my ear. 'And you're naïve enough to believe that I'm more – that I could change.'

'I'm eighteen years old,' I managed. 'If you can't understand *hope*, maybe you should bother someone as old and cynical as yourself.'

His breath of laughter grazed my shoulder. 'Hard to find anyone my own age these days.'

My urge to laugh was swallowed by the pit of dread churning in my stomach. *I should be running*, I thought. *I should've run a long time ago*. But my feet were fixed to the floor, eyes entranced by the flames, my body thrumming like the air between us. I wanted him to touch me again.

149

'The sea — she did this to you?' I breathed. *Why, when...* *How?* The questions felt endless, their answers barbed like thorns. I didn't know if I could handle the truth of it all, but not knowing was worse.

When he answered, the amusement had vanished from his tone. '*I* did this to myself. Aron and Golde followed, but I never asked them to. It was me who wrought these shackles of eternity around our wrists.'

'How could you choose such a thing?' I asked, knowing an endless life didn't mean a good one. Golde and Mersey's hearts no doubt bore the scars to prove it. Maybe Aron's, too.

'We're all ruins, blackbird,' he said softly. Firelight flickered against the line of his jaw, playing into the shadows of his hood. 'We don't get to choose the things that destroy us.'

15

By the time the sun crested the horizon the next morning, most of the pirates had already said their farewells and returned to their duties. But as the gangway was lowered for Mersey, a note of finality rang through the sky. I moved among the crowd, trying to stay within earshot while keeping myself hidden.

'Forgot to mention,' Mersey was saying to Golde and the King as I crept closer. 'Saw masts a few leagues off. Only a couple o' days out if these winds keep up. Left them alone so as not to keep you waiting, but you might wanna expect company.'

'Thanks,' Golde said, her voice unusually soft.

Mersey turned to the King, her cane tapping the planks. If he said something to her, I didn't hear it. But the ancient – younger – pirate looked up at him and said quietly, 'Prove me wrong.'

Chills spiked down my back at her words. I could feel the decades sitting heavy in the air between them. What they'd been

151

through together, what it had made them, I could scarcely fathom. But as they bowed their heads in farewell, I knew this day was, in some strange way, an end.

Sebastien gave the captain a curt nod and backed away, leaving his first mate alone to say her goodbyes. There was a ripple in the crowd, a shifting of gazes and bodies as they retreated. I hung back, curious, my heart pulsing quietly as I sheltered in the alcove of the stairs.

Mersey leant forward, her back hunched, and whispered something in Golde's ear, a withered hand lingering on the first mate's cheek. They stayed like that for a long time, cloaked in a haze of longing and an unforgiving sorrow. I caught only snatches of their words — words that tugged at something I never thought I'd feel for that ruthless, black-haired pirate.

'As much as always,' Mersey was saying. 'More.'

'It hurts...' Golde's murmured reply reached me in shreds. '...even when ye're gone.'

Their heads bent lower, making their mouths impossible to read. Mersey reached for Golde's hand and my heart clenched at the sight. *Gods.* How must it feel, to hold love that tightly and still be forced to watch it slip away, piece by piece?

Golde nodded at something the old captain was saying, dark hair falling across her face.

I inched as close as I could without being seen, my back pressed up against the wood.

'I'm old too, Goldie.'

'Old enough to come home?'

The first mate's plea lingered heavy in the air. With it, a cloud of guilt sank over my shoulders. This moment was theirs; it was too private, too much, even for me. But before I could slip away, it was over.

'Almost,' Mersey said. Then, with shuffling, half-wooden steps, she turned and left – half a century of history crumbling in her wake.

*

A week later, I emerged into the cool grey afternoon, finding an unsettling stillness hanging over the crew. Two dark blots loomed on the cloud-streaked horizon. The winds had slowed, but it seemed company had finally found us.

The King stood port side of the quarterdeck, watching the oncoming tall ships with Aron and Golde a few paces behind him. Poised, dangerous, their faces were hard as granite. Una and Mors walked amongst the rest of the crew below, weaving through the eight dozen or so bodies that lined the decks, steel blades hanging at their sides.

Mors pushed through the crowd when he saw me, reaching out to guide me back the way I'd come.

'Keep below today, lass,' he warned, white brows dipping over his eyes.

I glanced over his shoulder at the ships approaching across the water and headed straight for the quarterdeck. 'Who is it?'

Mors shook his head, following close at my heels. 'Doesn't matter, just get inside.'

Fear feathered through me, but I swallowed it quickly. I wouldn't cower below when there was a battle being fought on deck. Not if I was the cause.

'*Who is it?*' I asked again, planting my feet at the top of the stairs. I squinted at the horizon, trying to make out the colours of the approaching vessels, but it was useless.

Aron turned to look at me, his eyes telling me everything I needed to know. 'Bane.'

I tried to steady my breathing, my heartbeat swelling in my ears. He was here.

'What now?' I asked, barely hearing myself over the pounding of my blood.

'Now those traitors die on the planks where they betrayed us,' Golde growled, her eyes fixed on the encroaching ships.

Now they die, because of me. Because Bane thought my blood a currency he could use to buy his revenge against Oren. Or worse – buy *me.*

I looked over at the King. 'I'm staying on deck,' I said, wondering if he even cared.

He barely spared me a glance before he grunted, 'Let her.'

The lines that rayed from Mors' eyes deepened with worry, but he stepped back. 'Stand with them,' he said, jerking his chin at the trio near the side of the ship. 'And *stay* there.'

I moved reluctantly towards them, manoeuvring myself into the King's shadow. I knew from experience that, come a battle, it would be the safest place to stand.

The crew stood on high alert as Bane's ships neared. I couldn't help glancing over my shoulder at Golde every few seconds, unnerved at having her keen blade beyond my line of sight. She'd saved my life once, almost defended me in front of Mersey's crew, yet I still wasn't sure where we stood. Wasn't convinced she wouldn't turn that sabre on me, given half a chance.

'Don't worry 'bout her, lass,' Aron said. 'Someone stands behind ye, it means they've got yer back.'

I nodded, not quite believing him – but it was a comfort to know I had at least one ally on that deck. I dug my nails into my palms to keep my focus on what lay ahead. The rose-hilted dagger Aron had given me pressed uncomfortably against the base of my ribs, but the cold metal was oddly reassuring. I'd taken to keeping it on me everywhere I went since the day he'd given it to me, but today I was overly conscious of its steely presence. I sent a silent prayer to the sea that I wouldn't have to use it.

I watched the nearer of the two ships as the crew onboard furled her emerald sails. Above them flapped a pennant I'd seen only once before: a fury-eyed mermaid clutching a blade not unlike my own.

This was it. The man who'd marked me as his prey, the one who lusted for something in my blood the way the crew lusted for his. He'd come this far. What did he have to lose?

'They're boarding,' Aron remarked, as the vessel glided slowly alongside the *Blood Rose*'s port, the second ship close behind.

Golde's eyes narrowed. 'Let 'em.'

Like the pack of beasts they were, the pirates of the *Blood Rose* tipped their heads back and howled to the swarm of dark clouds above. Chills ripped down my arms. I imagined how it must sound to Bane's crew, hearing the promise of destruction roll across the waves towards them; a cry sharpened by freedom and salt. Still, they approached.

The *Blood Rose*'s crew waited with impatient hands, blades gleaming like fangs bared in anticipation of flesh. Soon enough, irons flew over the side of the deck. They let them come, hunger mounting tangibly in the air. Like drool, it trickled through me; a cold, lifeless dread.

Bane's crew boarded, but they didn't draw their weapons – not yet, as if they knew exactly what fate it would afford them. My mind swam as the two sides of the ship came to a standstill. Bane's crew was an odd mix of pirates and peasants, some poised like they lived for battle; others – the leaner, hungriest-looking ones – like they weren't ready to die for it. For me.

Like the first crack of thunder before a storm, a single set of footsteps echoed over the planks, each a bright flash of something impending. Nausea swirled in my stomach as the newcomers parted for their captain. Then there he stood, at the bottom of the stairs.

Bane.

A thicket of light brown hair framed his features, and from beneath the collar of his calico shirt crept the furrowed red of old burn marks. War was etched into the harsh lines of his sun-beaten face, but when he smiled, it transformed.

He dragged a hand through his shaggy hair and grinned. 'Long time no see.'

An ominous silence settled over the ship before Sebastien lifted his head and spoke. 'Quite an audience to bring to your own death,' he remarked.

Bane showed no hint of fear, but the long, scarred fingers of his right hand never strayed from the hilt of his cutlass. His nails were painted black with kohl, bitten to stubs.

'Not really how I see things going today, love,' he quipped. 'Bit old to be taking on the likes of us, aren't you?'

Behind me, Golde let out a hiss. 'I'm gonna feed that bastard his own tongue,' she muttered to Aron.

I could sense Sebastien's irritation, too. I knew that if Bane had come alone, he'd be bleeding out on the planks already. But with the second ship anchored close by, the *Blood Rose*'s crew were outnumbered almost two to one. A battle would mean heavy losses on both sides.

Bane's gaze slid over to me. 'Let her come forward.'

Dread climbed the back of my throat as I took a hesitant step; then, when Sebastien made no move to stop me, another. I hovered for a moment at the top of the stairs, caught between the Heartless King and this vengeful traitor, unsure which side of the battlefield was mine.

Bane's eyes raked down my face. His gaze was startlingly green, sharp as talon-tips as it pried into my skin.

I shifted on my feet, stirred by a sudden urge to flee. I had expected to fear him as much as I did his designs on my future, yet . . . what scared me most was how human he seemed. Not like the Heartless King – not a fabled shadow, or a beast.

Bane's expression was unflinching, but it wasn't unkind. Perhaps that was what unsettled me most.

If I truly wanted to escape the *Blood Rose*, this was my chance. I could take the risk, pray that whatever Bane was planning involved keeping me alive, perhaps even setting me free someday. But it was a steep risk – a terrifying one.

The skies darkened with an impending storm. My skin prickled as the waters grew ominously still. Bane's burning gaze was still fixed on my face.

Behind me, Sebastien's sword grated in its scabbard. 'If you think she's yours to take, come and get her.'

Bane advanced towards the stairs, his footsteps sharp as my rabid heartbeat.

'Don't come any closer,' I choked out, fear constricting my voice. Who I feared for most, I wasn't sure. But another step and I knew that the volatile peace would snap, that no one would be safe. Not Aron, who'd fought for me. Not Mors, who'd known my parents in a way I never had. Not Una, who'd shown me nothing but warmth. Golde, perhaps, I could live without.

I could feel the King watching me, waiting to see what I'd do. He wasn't going to stop me. Not yet. Perhaps he was curious which ship I thought had a better chance of taking me towards a future worth living.

I couldn't choose which world I'd rather be trapped in, not when all I wanted was to be free. Bane wasn't there to save me, but he was there. A chance — I just didn't know what it might cost to take.

'Don't think ye're gettin' outta here alive,' Golde gritted out, impatience getting the best of her.

Bane smirked. 'Don't think you can stop me, love. I've been doing quite well for myself, if you hadn't heard.'

Golde drew her sabre. The sound was like lightning in an empty sky. 'Ye're a traitor,' she spat. 'And ye'll die like one.'

'I've only ever had one goal,' Bane said, his tone suddenly serious. 'And I never turned my back on that. I've promised a better life to those who side with me, and I plan to give it to them. We've taken more from Oren than he's ever given us, and we'll keep going 'til he has nothing left.'

His eyes flickered over to me again. My heart dropped into my stomach, a cold sweat erupting over my skin. He didn't look so harmless now.

'Give me the girl,' he said.

'She ain't goin' anywhere,' Aron growled.

I wanted to believe him, I realised. Wanted this world over Bane's. But it had to end one way or another. And when the ash settled and the blood dried, there'd only be one side left standing. The question was, which?

I took a deep breath. 'I—'

A deafening roar drowned me out.

A sudden tempest of water swirled into the sky above the *Blood Rose*. From the crest of a soaring wave, a colossal form reared its serpentine head. A deluge flooded over the ship, drenching those closest to the edge.

Swords screeched in their scabbards as the beast towered over us. It was like nothing I'd ever seen, its skin slick and its limbs snake-like, each as large as the creature I'd seen the night of that first battle and edged with spikes. Scales clung to its angular skull, bones protruding sharply from the sides of its reptilian head as it stared down at us through yellow, slitted eyes.

Tentacles as thick as masts snaked out from the creature's slippery hide as more seawater surged over the deck. I choked back a scream as it slammed into the planks, splintering the wood right in front of my feet.

I stumbled back into Sebastien's chest and he pulled me behind him, striding forward with his broadsword raised. Which of his foes he was shielding me from, I didn't know – I'd lost sight of Bane amid the chaos of both crews. I could only watch in horror as the monster opened its cavernous jaw and unleashed a jet of fire.

My cry of warning died in my throat. Sebastien darted back, narrowly missing the flames as they engulfed the mizzenmast. Pirates surged into action, their figures flickering through the blaze as they advanced from every angle, but they were too slow. The monster turned its face and seared them from the deck, leaving nothing but scorch marks behind.

I whirled around in panic, heart slamming against my ribs. This was *wrong*. Mors had assured me the creatures of the deep were harmless, that they wouldn't hurt those who ruled the surface. But this one seemed to have every intention of taking us under.

Golde seemed to be wondering the same thing. 'The hell's goin' on?' she roared over the chaos. 'Why's it attackin' us?'

The King shook his head in dismay, wiping ash from his face as he raised his sword. He pushed forward again, blade slicing through the air as he lunged from the quarterdeck, slashing the nearest tentacle clean off. Steaming black liquid sprayed from the open wound, sending him staggering back once more.

The two crews were impossible to distinguish as they barrelled forward, blades brandished, war cries burning in their throats. Leading the charge on the main deck, Bane bellowed for his crew to retreat as he swung an assault against the monster's hide.

The crackle of burning flesh stoked the chaos and I gagged at the stench of smouldering blood. Pirates collapsed on both sides, their screams paring the air. They convulsed, writhing as they burned, their bodies blackening to coals.

Bane continued to bark orders over the spitting flames, darting between clusters of the injured and dying.

'Abandon ship!' he boomed.

Bane's command rang through me. *Last chance*, I realised, watching as his crew hurled themselves over the divide between the ships, racing for safety. Even the *Blood Rose* couldn't survive this, and if she was going down, I wasn't going with her.

Run.

Flames roared up the masts as I hurtled down the stairs, bolting for the opposite side of the deck where Bane stood, watching me run. Around me, pirates cried out for release as the monster flailed above them, its limbs tearing through the ratlines.

Fire swept across the ship, blocking my path. I staggered back as pirates barrelled past me, their swords raised at the creature above. Bane's crew were retreating, but his face swam before me through the dazzling inferno.

'C'mon,' he hollered. 'Keep running!'

My feet clung to the planks, like I'd melted to the spot. Because suddenly I was afraid of the fire dancing in Bane's eyes. Not the flames – the fury.

When he saw that I wouldn't move, he made to dart forward, to reach through the blaze and grab me. The flames leaped higher, chasing him back. Bane cursed, staggering after his crew towards the edge of the deck, away from me.

'We don't have to be enemies, love,' he called. 'You'd be smart to side with me. You'd have *power*.'

I backed away, the spitting cinders swallowing the gap between us.

'The winter solstice,' Bane yelled. 'Tell them – Whale Rock, I'll be waiting. If they don't hand you over, they're dead.'

My heart plummeted, senses overcome by smoke.

Whale Rock? I could do nothing but stare through the haze as the last of Bane's crew swung from ropes and dove recklessly on to the decks of their ships, desperate to escape the devastation.

With the wind on their side, the two frigates retreated quickly across the horizon. But the battle erupting around me had only just begun.

16

The two monsters were locked in battle. Sebastien, with his broadsword gleaming, his movements as graceful and deadly as I remembered; and the writhing sea creature – exhaling fire and spilling venom from its wounds. Despite the King's ruthless power, the monster was something otherworldly. With every blow Sebastien landed in its scaly hide, bubbling liquid seethed across the planks, chasing him back.

The creature's powerful tendrils lashed out wildly, each strike landing closer and closer to its target, throwing back the bodies of the few pirates still standing. I fought the urge to scramble below deck, knowing I'd have no chance of surviving if I became trapped on a sinking ship.

Then Aron was there, grabbing my arm and tugging me with him. The main yardarm came crashing down right where I'd stood, splintering against the planks before it went up in flames.

'Take cover, lass!'

I scrambled back, finding shelter behind the steps that led to the quarterdeck as another stream of fire erupted from the monster's mouth. Half a dozen pirates charged forward with their weapons aloft, cries burning in their throats.

I scanned the ship frantically for a glimpse of Una or Mors, but they were nowhere in sight. An ash-tasting dread settled in my stomach. *Gods, let them be safe.*

The King, Aron and Golde fought in a seamless rhythm, bound together by lifetimes of experience. But their tireless assaults did little more than flood the ship with searing black fluid.

A great serpentine limb swept across the deck and struck Sebastien, sending him crashing into the steps beside me. I gasped as the planks splintered with the force of his landing, but he picked himself up from the rubble a moment later, wiping a trickle of blood from his chin.

The monster was relentless, raging, sending another vicious blow that caught Aron by the ankle and whipped him through the air. I cried out as he slammed to the deck, motionless.

Aron. I sprinted from my refuge, feet skittering over scorched wood.

The mizzenmast toppled, crashing down between us, barring my path. I scrambled back again, trembling fingers gripping the banister behind me. I glanced up at the storm clouds gathering above, knowing there was nothing I could do to help him. *Don't be dead.*

I glanced over at Sebastien, his hood fixed on where Aron had fallen, chest heaving as he caught his breath. He turned to face me, reaching out to snag my wrist and push me further back into the sheltered doorway. I felt his gaze like a shadow as it flickered over my body.

His voice rasped like fire. 'Are you hurt?'

I shook my head, gasping for air from the ash-choked sky. Words formed on his lips, but his head snapped around at the sound of striking metal.

Golde's grunts punctured the chaos, her sabre glinting – a shard of steel tempered by the inferno around her. She swung again and again, landing well-aimed blows that spurted black blood into the grey sky. The creature's branching limbs thrashed through the air, tearing through the *Blood Rose*'s crimson sails and wrenching gallant yards from their posts.

A few members of the crew still scrambled about below, coughing and spluttering as they dragged bodies from the wreckage and battled the flames with splintered barrels of ale. My nails dug sharply into my palms as Golde made a daring leap from the deck and landed on one of the monster's slippery tentacles, darting between the boughs of its sweeping limbs, blade hurtling towards its neck.

The creature reacted just in time. Another tentacle sliced through the air, its tip edged with spikes, and slashed through Golde's weapon arm. I winced at the sound of her strangled cry. Somehow, she managed to keep her footing as her sword plunged to the ocean below.

Golde straightened slowly, a dagger now clutched in her right hand, eyes bright with fury. She ran nimbly up the swaying, sinuous branches of the creature's body towards its fire-breathing head. The monster reared, corded limbs whisking her through the air as if she were nothing more than an insect. She slammed into the starboard railing and slumped to the deck, blood soaking through her sleeve.

Sebastien cursed. His broadsword smouldered with inhuman blood as he rounded on me once more. He placed a firm hand on my stomach and pushed me further into the alcove.

Behind us, the deck was unnervingly quiet. Dread seeped into me, thick as blood. My fingers curled around Sebastien's cloak as I searched for the words to tell him not to go back. To stay with me.

'Don't move,' he warned in my ear, sending chills down my arms. But when he turned, the monster was upon us.

Its jaw stretched wide, revealing rows upon rows of dagger-like teeth and the roiling stench of the deep. Fire rumbled in its throat and Sebastien seized me, shoving me into the wall behind. His arms caged me in, shielding me from the blaze that erupted from the beast's mouth.

His roar of agony ripped through me. Flames tore apart the world around us as his back took the full force of the monster's scorching assault. His cloak enveloped me, shadows closing around us as the world was overcome by blackness and blistering heat. I could see nothing, feel nothing beyond the rough hairs of his jaw grazing my cheek and the heaving of his chest against mine. And the fire, burning through us both.

The surge of flames subsided and Sebastien staggered back, his jaw taut and pale as he drew in a breath that rattled like steel over coals. He turned back to the monster with rigid shoulders, broadsword held loosely in his hand.

I gasped. The hem of his tattered cloak still smouldered, falling to shreds around him to reveal the raw, ravaged skin beneath. Blood oozed from his wounds as he limped towards the creature again.

'Don't—' I cried, a moment too late.

I dove sideways as the monster's next attack swept towards us. A spike-tipped tentacle whizzed past my ear, striking the King square in the chest and sweeping him from the *Blood Rose*'s deck.

I cowered back against the railing as his dark form was swallowed by the sea, leaving me alone among the ruins.

Swift and ferocious as the ocean, the monster beat down on the ship, shattering wood and spraying scalding ink across its surface.

The masts splintered and I cowered back, surrounded by fire and the shrivelled remains of the pirates who'd been brave enough to face it.

No one left to save me now, I thought, trying to swallow the flood of panic in my chest as I gazed around the last of the crew, their shouts hoarse as they worked to shift flaming debris over the sides of the ship, dousing flames with buckets of bilge. They toiled tirelessly to salvage what they could, but it would mean nothing if the monster managed to bring us all asunder.

I peered up at the creature from my hiding place, watching it tear through the *Blood Rose*'s proud opulence. Thin, membranous skin stretched out from either side of its face, shielding the joint between its bony skull and great, craning neck.

There.

I'd seen what Golde was aiming for, knew what needed to be done. But if even she'd failed . . . A brain full of books and a little iron dagger – what chance did I have?

I scanned the destruction around me, the litany of bodies, Aron and Golde among them. My mind raced, struggling to stay afloat in the flood of doubt and terror that seized me. I was no warrior; the idea of hurting anything was like acid on my tongue, churning my stomach until I thought I might vomit. I tried to swallow my panic, knowing I didn't have a choice. I couldn't afford to fail.

I waited with bated breath until the creature aimed its next blow. Then, ignoring the way my body baulked, I darted into the open, arm reaching out to snag the hilt of a discarded cutlass as I went. It slid awkwardly into my grasp, the metal cold and unfamiliar between my sweat-slippery fingers. Barely remembering to breathe, I raced for the opposite edge of the deck and launched myself over the rail, into the breeze.

For a split second, the world was nothing but wind, the air thick with coiling smoke. I soared through it like an arrow – realising my mistake just in time. My feet thudded against the slimy, ocean-slick skin of the creature's craning neck, boots scrabbling for purchase, but the rose-hilted dagger was already in my hand.

I jolted forward, sinking the iron blade into the monster's back. It shrieked, rearing. My stomach swooped as the surface beneath me dropped away for a moment, clinging as hard as I could with my sweaty palm to the iron grip of my dagger. It held firm, and when the creature rose up once more, I moved—

I had no time to steady myself, no time to think or breathe or prepare for what I was about to do. I plunged my sword into the monster's rubbery flesh, right at the base of its neck.

With a sickening squelch, the blow pierced its throat, driven by more force than I'd known I possessed. Inky liquid flooded from the wound as I wrenched the blade free and scrambled back, tumbling down the creature's bony snout.

It let out a sky-piercing shriek as I plummeted to the deck, the cold, hard wood jolting through me and knocking the air from my lungs. I crawled for cover, gasping raggedly as the monster keened another shrill, earth-shattering note. Its giant maw slammed on to the deck, snapping the yards from their masts as it collapsed, oozing blood that reeked of rust and rotting flesh. Then it toppled backwards and slipped into the sea with a final, dark ripple.

Dead.

I heaved myself to my feet, choking on embers and disbelief, my heart pounding louder than the fire, the chaos, the echo of screams. I'd killed it – *killed.* I wanted to collapse at the thought. Wanted to leave my shaking, bloodstained hands behind and curl up someplace warm and cry.

I wondered if the King had ever felt that way when he struck life from the world – so consumed with disgust and relief that his body no longer felt like his own. Or, more likely, if he felt nothing at all.

I blinked. *Sebastien.*

I picked myself up and raced to the starboard edge, adrenaline roaring through me once more. I couldn't give up, not just yet. Not when he was out there, drifting like a shadow over the water, bleeding crimson to the waves. The blood, for once, his own.

Rain began to patter down, quelling the fires that raged on the main deck and sending spirals of smoke into the air. There was movement among the crew, the stirring of broken bones. Many, I knew, would never wake. The survivors watched me from the rubble, eyes wide. It would've been easy enough to winch a tender down to the water; they were in no position to stop me from rowing myself away, as far as I could, for as long as it took. I'd find Bane's crew and let them steer me somewhere closer to home. No – not home. Someplace else. The capital, perhaps. A different world; a different king.

What are you waiting for? my mind asked, but my feet didn't turn. They didn't carry me to the waiting keel, didn't point in the direction of my past.

I took a deep breath, facing the water. Sebastien was out there, dying. I could feel the diminishing ebb of his powers like the ocean's own fading pulse. The downpour drummed steadily across the surface of the sea.

A voice broke through the din, its sharp edge grated with pain. 'Ye'll drown, lass.'

Golde limped closer, clutching her injured arm. A gaping wound marred the skin from her wrist to her elbow, bright crimson trickling through her fingertips.

I blinked, rain rolling from my lashes to my cheeks. I hadn't realised what I was planning to do until I heard the disbelief in her voice. Only a fool would attempt it, I knew that much.

I grabbed hold of a thick length of rope still bound to a fallen shroud and gave it an experimental tug. 'He's dying out there.'

Golde flicked her gaze to the water. 'If he's s'posed to come back, he will,' she said, staggering closer.

I secured the rope around my waist with a grim smile, trying to ignore her eyes burning into my back. My mind screamed that she was right, but there was no time to listen. Where was her loyalty now?

I clambered on to the wooden banister and stared out at the depthless sea. Then, with a great, resounding breath, I dove.

The ocean enveloped me, cold and unforgiving as the sky above. Desperation filled my lungs like seawater as I swam, thinking only of the king whose death-bound body had shielded me from fire. Enough monsters had died for one day. I wouldn't be the cause of another.

I'd learned to swim in the rivers and brooks that wound through the rolling landscape of the north, and I'd learned well, but fighting against the tide was like trying to swim upstream. With my petticoats weighing me down, I struggled against the current, the rope dragging through the waves behind me.

The salt stung my eyes, the rain making it almost impossible to see, but I could sense Sebastien nearby. Something drew me to him, like the ocean pulling me through its veins towards its own pulsing heartbeat.

Finally, when my muscles burned from the exertion, my frigid fingertips grazed the torn folds of his coat. I tugged the King towards me, tasting the tang of his blood in the sea on my trembling lips, sharp as steel.

Kicking to keep afloat, I untied the rope from my waist and wound it hurriedly around his unconscious body. I knew I'd glimpsed only a fraction of the creatures that lurked in these waters, and I had no desire to encounter any more. Feeling somewhat lighter, and fuelled by my desire to get back to the safety of the ship, I gripped the rope between my frozen hands and began the gruelling return to the *Blood Rose*.

My legs dragged as I pulled myself along its length, the sea stealing the fight from my body. Just when the last of my strength leached from my bones, the rumble of voices sounded through the rain. An icy relief washed over me, pushing me through that final, agonising distance.

A rope ladder tumbled down the hull and I grabbed hold with numb fingers. Hands lifted me from the sea, pulling me aboard, drenched from head to toe and shivering like morning grass.

I stumbled through the small crowd, my skirts sopping and clinging to my body, barely registering the planks beneath me. Pirates shambled to the rail, nursing their injuries and wincing with every step, their clothes wet and ragged. I watched on, dread trickling cold as the seawater down my spine, as they dredged their king from the depths. The sight of Sebastien's rope-bound body being hauled aboard chilled me to the core.

The deck was already slick with rain, but it was he who brought the ocean flooding, sodden and black-cloaked as its sunless depths. Through the blur of frantic activity and the shouts of his crew, I saw only him.

It took half a dozen pirates to carry him, blood and water dripping in their wake. The last shreds of his hooded cloak fell away as they settled him on the dark red canvas of a fallen sail.

Voices called out to me, hands grasping my shoulders, trying to pull me away, but I heard nothing, felt nothing. More voices – louder, brasher – argued over my head as I slipped between them, falling to my knees at the King's side.

Droplets cascaded over his features, down sloping cheekbones to full lips rimed with salt. I pushed the hair back from his forehead, seeing him at last for what he really was. A man. Sebastien – cruel and heartless, but made of flesh, not stone.

There were no gills, no horns, no scales. His brows were strong, furrowed. Dark as the curls clinging to his temples. A single raindrop rolled down the rugged line of his nose.

My frigid hands grasped his shoulders, trying to pull him back to consciousness, to me. Finally, Sebastien's chest rose and, with a great, shuddering breath, his eyes flew open.

The world around us stilled, then disappeared all together, as my gaze met that of the Heartless King.

17

His eyes were black as starless nights.

Nestled beneath thick brows, even in his lessened state, Sebastien's gaze shone with a dark power that made my skin crawl. His eyes were glassy, fluttering shut again a moment later. He hadn't seen me, but it was too late. I'd seen him.

The chaos around us returned and the crew reached for their king, pushing me out of the way as they lifted the sail beneath him and carried his body from the storm.

Rain battered the deck, washing away remnants of detritus and gore. I stumbled along behind the crew as they carried Sebastien through the doors of the navigation room, filthy shirts plastered to their skin. I watched from the doorway as they laid him to rest on the great bed, seeping blood and salt into the furs.

A firm grasp on my wrist tugged me back to reality. Golde's face swam before me, sharp cheekbones cutting through the fog of my vision.

'Get outta here, lass. Ye've done enough.'

I looked down, eyes fixing on a spot of red on the top of her boot, watching it grow. Dark liquid dripped steadily from Golde's wounded arm, but when I glanced up to point it out, she was already gone, bent over the King's bedside.

I swayed on my feet, wondering how the moments had slipped away, why each blink seemed to eclipse more than just a heartbeat.

You always think you can fix things, but you can't. The scathing voice in the back of my mind sounded unsettlingly like Aberdeen's. I shook my head, but I couldn't escape the buzzing words that clawed at my skull.

What did I care if Sebastien pulled through? He'd saved me and I'd done all I could to return the favour. I didn't owe him more than that, surely. But I knew the lump that sat heavy in my throat wouldn't dissolve until I saw him wake again.

The bustling room shifted and I caught sight of Aron standing by the bed. A breath of relief escaped me as our gazes met. He looked tired, wet, with a jagged wound running down his cheek, but he was alive.

I shoved my way across the room until his arms closed around me, pulling me tight against him. He let me stay there for a long time before pulling back with a reassuring smile, but his expression quickly slipped into one of concern. It took me a moment to realise that he was talking, but the words never reached my ears.

The room was suddenly crowded, filled with voices, jarring and anxious. I heard my name, felt hands reaching for me, trying to tear my attention in different directions. When I looked up again, Una and Mors were there, too, their expressions ridged with worry.

Something cracked inside me at the sight of them and a surge of questions flooded my mind. They filled my lungs and chased the air from them, making my breaths come sharp and quick.

You left me, I wanted to cry, my eyes burning with relief. *I thought you were gone.*

But it was as though my mind shouted the words from a clifftop, into the wind, and my mouth never caught hold of them. I couldn't force them out, couldn't move.

Mors wrapped a blanket around my shoulders, leading me towards the door.

I'm fine, I tried to say, but all that came out was a croak.

'Ye're a'ight, lassie,' echoed Una's gentle voice.

'I didn't know what to do,' I finally muttered. I could still feel the ghost of Golde's grip on my arm.

'You did all you could,' Mors said softly, hands warm on my back, guiding me away. I wondered if he knew what I'd really done. My hands now knew the feeling of flesh, torn through. Knew the shudder of bone against steel in a way I'd never wanted them to.

I shrugged Mors off and turned back towards the bed, deaf to the crew's protests. I needed to make sure he was all right; needed to know that what I'd done wasn't for nothing. The voices dissolved into murmurs as I leaned over Sebastien's body. Perhaps it was because he'd so recently been pulled from its clutches, but there was something in him – from the sands of his skin to the shadows that played across his face – that still reminded me of the sea.

His broad chest was caked with blood and salt, and as I pulled back the last shreds of his once-white shirt, I saw the deep gash that ran the length of his torso. It tore through the hard muscle of his abdomen, reaching from his ribs to the ridge of his shoulder.

I knew, somewhere in the vaults of my mind, that the bleeding needed to be stopped and the wound cleaned before it started to fester. But before I could move or ask for alcohol and cloth, the raw skin surrounding the wound began to constrict. My breath hitched as tendons of flesh wound forth, weaving the skin back together before my very eyes. I leant in, watching as Sebastien's chest mended itself in a slow ripple, leaving nothing but a trickle of blood behind.

Mystified, I laid a hand on his rough, oaken skin. It burned feverishly beneath my fingertips, a reminder that he'd been wounded in more ways than one. His back was likely in far worse condition.

Unable to help my curiosity, I skimmed my fingers down the planes of his powerful torso. I could smell the brine entangled in the dark curls of his hair, could smell the ocean in him. Under all the blood and sweat and ash, it was there – the wind, the tides, the sand. Sebastien didn't flinch as my hands glided over his remaining wounds, those left to heal on their own. Many were fresh, still beaded with crimson. Others dissolved beneath my touch.

His skin warmed me, easing the iciness from my fingertips as rain lashed against the cabin windows. I stared down at my hands, pale against his bronze skin, and my stomach turned hollow.

The room seemed to be shrinking, growing fainter as the memory of what I'd done encroached. It crept up from inside me, pulling my body back in time. I couldn't feel Sebastien's skin beneath my palm any more, only the smooth lick of steel, my fingers wrapped tight around dagger and sword. My nostrils filled with the scent of hot blood, of sea rot and smoke.

I shuddered, spinning back into the dark room.

When I looked up, Sebastien's black eyes were open. Watching me, glittering.

'Your hands are cold.'

I snatched them back, cheeks suddenly hot as I realised how close I stood, my knees pressed into the mattress, seeking his warmth. I cleared my throat and stepped back from the bed, immediately colder.

'You're alive,' I remarked quietly, not knowing how to act. How to treat the monster who'd saved my life. Whose life I'd saved in return.

I'd watched them raise him from the sea like a fallen god: his wings waterlogged, a crown of tangled rope. Something in the sight had made my eyes burn. Not for his heart, but . . .

Maybe it was the hands that had pulled him from the darkness, the souls that followed him and the bodies that fought and fell for him. Something about it had made me wish, for an instant, that he wasn't as irredeemably cursed as he claimed.

'Come away, lass.'

Mors was beside me again, his wrinkled hand on my shoulder and, this time, I let my feet follow him, slipping past pirates who juggled armfuls of bandages and liquor bottles, their faces eddying around my vision.

Soon I was trailing after Una's colourful skirts, letting her lead me back to my cold, empty chamber. I wavered on my feet, my mind swimming in a river of fatigue. I was all too happy to let Una steer me towards the bed, pulling back the crisp sheets. My fingers fumbled with my corset strings for a moment before the thought struck me.

'You left,' I said, remembering the stillness of the *Blood Rose* as I'd stood, alone, among the wreckage.

'Didn't leave, lass,' Una said, nudging my hands aside to take over. 'Had somethin' important to do.'

I was too tired for subtleties. 'What?'

The pirate sighed, her exhalation warm on my bare shoulder as I shrugged out of my damp petticoats. 'Gatherin' things,' Una answered. 'Ledgers, books, documents and such. Things that ought not to be lost when . . . if somethin' were to happen.'

I understood, somehow. Knowledge was one of the few things

that couldn't be rebuilt.

Una pulled a dry nightgown over my head and I collapsed into bed, my eyes closing before I hit the pillow. But even after the door clicked shut and I pulled the furs around myself, I couldn't find rest. Words echoed through my weary mind, circling in a sleepless cloud over my head.

. . . the sea is growing impatient . . . won't be long . . .

To our deaths . . .

After hours of delirium, sleep finally found me. But it wasn't peace that awaited me behind the shroud of darkness. It was the clash of battle, loud and violent as the destruction I'd witnessed that day. Bane's promise echoed through the din. *If they don't hand you over, they're dead.*

Rest came in scraps, for every time I managed to break free from the chaos, an inhuman scream would throw me back to the waking world.

Daylight sank in, cold and harsh, and my limbs ached as I pulled myself upright. The room around me felt oddly distant and when my eyes fell to my shaking hands, I understood what had changed.

The memory of what I'd done dripped through my fingers like blood. The sea monster's beastly form reared in my mind's eye and I shuddered, visions of smoke and brandished swords flitting before me.

I slunk outside in search of an escape from my mind, drinking in the fresh air and daylight. But the sight that met me was no respite from my brutal dreams.

The deck was a ruin of its previous glory. A line of figures lay beside the railing, wrapped in white shrouds. A handful of pirates moved about, dragging charred remains from the wreckage and crouching over the fallen. They walked with heavy steps and downcast eyes, stooped beneath the weight of their grief.

The ship was undergoing her own slow reparation process. Scorched rose briars wound steadily back up splintered masts which seemed to be piecing themselves back together as I picked my way across the deck, marvelling at the devastation wreaked by a single creature.

I ambled through the navigation room and inched open the door at the end.

Sebastien lay at the centre of the four-poster, his chest bound with thick white bandages. I stepped cautiously into the bedchamber, surprised to find it otherwise empty. Wet footprints encircled the bed, an echo of the previous day's flurry of activity.

I crept forward, peering through the hanging drapes at the face he'd concealed for so long. His burnished gold skin looked pale and I wondered when light had last caressed the skin of his brow and the curls of his ebony hair. I reached out to lay a hand on his forearm and a jolt pierced through my body. His skin burned.

Sebastien's eyes blinked open, sliding over to me. 'Can I help you?'

'I think you might have a fever.'

He stared at me with derision in his moonless gaze. 'I was scorched by fire, remember?'

I remembered.

He seemed awfully calm for a man who'd almost been scoured from the world. A man who'd thrown his body between the flames and . . . me.

I swallowed thickly. 'Is there anything I can do?'

'You can start by making better decisions,' he muttered, his voice gravelly. 'I don't know how you're alive right now, but you shouldn't be.'

I arched a brow at him, tucking my trembling fingers behind my back, wishing I could hold them still. 'Are you saying I shouldn't have saved you?'

There was a hard smile on his lips when he answered, 'Can't blame a man for wanting an easy way out.'

My eyes narrowed. A way out of what? Living? I stepped back from the bed. I wouldn't try to help him if he didn't care to help himself.

But long fingers snared around my forearm, pulling me back. Sebastien moved towards me with a grunt of pain, face twisting as he drew himself up, his gaze fixed intently on mine. 'Golde told me what you did,' he said.

I snatched my arm from his grasp. 'If I'd known you had a death wish, believe me, I wouldn't have bothered.'

'That's not what I meant.' Sebastien sounded almost as tired as I felt. Burned and drowned, we'd both emerged from the same kind of hell. He tried again, softer. 'You shouldn't have risked yourself like that.'

'You did the same for me,' I pointed out. Memories of fire flashed around me, his sturdy arms, his chest against mine.

'Drowning would've been no way to thank me.' Sebastien winced again, shifting to the edge of the mattress, agony flashing in his eyes.

'Don't—' I began, but he was already swinging his legs over the side of the bed, sitting up in front of me.

I watched him, my eyes drawn to his, measuring their intensity. It was strange, seeing his whole face in the light. His features were strong, stubbled, but *young*. The darkness of his gaze was unsettling, but not . . . monstrous.

Before I could even begin to fathom their depths, his eyes dropped to my hands. I tucked them back into my skirts, clenching my fists to hide how they shook. I hadn't been able to hold them

179

steady since they'd touched the hilt of that sword. Even in my dreams, they'd quaked amid the clash of battle.

'You look terrible,' Sebastien said gently.

My scoff drowned in my throat. He was right. I'd barely slept, barely been able to shake the heaviness from my bones.

'Thanks,' I replied, a smile tugging at the corner of my lips.

When I looked up, my stomach flipped.

His gaze was trained on my mouth, the ghost of an answering smirk painting his own. He held out his palms and I stared at them for a long moment, bewildered.

'Give me your hands,' he said, fingers beckoning mine.

My breathing shallowed, unnerved by how readily my feet took me forward, to him. I slid my hands tentatively into his and inhaled sharply, standing rigid between his legs, unsure how to respond to his touch when it no longer made me shudder in fear.

A look of deep concentration etched Sebastien's brow as he folded his hands around mine. I couldn't tear my eyes away from his face. Couldn't stop drinking in the rugged planes of his sun-sculpted features. Couldn't believe that, after all this time, he was just a man.

'Killing a monster doesn't make you one,' he said eventually, his thumbs tracing the paths of my veins. He didn't look up, voice so low that I had to lean closer to hear. 'Taking a life to save others – that doesn't make you . . . like me.'

When I looked down, my fingers no longer trembled. Shrouded in his, they didn't seem so unforgivable. The world outside wasn't so terrifying, not with the Heartless King's calloused hands wrapped around mine. Hands that had bled bodies of life, sending shivers through me as they circled my skin. I stared down at them, lost in the sensation.

'It scares me,' I murmured. 'I never wanted to kill anything.

To know how it feels . . . how easy it is.'

'Death is always the easy part,' he replied, fingers whispering along the veins of my pulse. My blood sang for it, his touch. 'Living with it . . . that takes time. But you'll learn. You saved a lot more lives than you took yesterday.'

He raised his gaze to mine slowly, his eyes so soft I could feel myself melting into them. Two months ago, I'd quaked at the mere thought of him, more a myth than a man. Yet as his hands slid slowly up to my jaw, I couldn't resist. I leaned in.

My heart raced, lips quivering as my fingers curled around his broad, burning shoulders. The taste of desire on his breath was like wine, like quicksand, and I was sinking. His thumb traced a path over my bottom lip, catching my shallow breaths. Every shadow in the room stilled as I shifted closer.

My eyes fluttered closed as he tilted his head, stubble grazing my cheek as his mouth reached for mine.

The door swung open.

18

I spun around in alarm as Aron's head poked inside, his face still grimy and spattered with blood from yesterday's battle, as though he'd worked through the night on deck.

'Have ye seen—?' He broke off as his eyes landed on us, my body wedged between Sebastien's thighs, his hand on my chin. Aron's face split into a wicked grin. 'Ria. I was just lookin' for ye.'

Searing shame flooded through me as I glanced up at Sebastien, seeing the embers of lust that still burned in his gaze.

'I'll be out in a moment,' I whispered.

'Take yer time.' Aron winked, darting out and pulling the door shut behind him. A faint laugh rang out, then silence.

I bit my lip. Sebastien's gaze didn't stray from my face. It took me a moment to gather the strength to step back, to withdraw my hands from around his shoulders.

A muscle pulsed in his jaw as he let his hand fall, eyes shifting as they studied me.

'You were right,' I managed, when I'd mustered a voice strong enough to carry the weight of my words. I looked down as I backed away, unable to meet his gaze. 'I'm not like you. I can't . . . do this. I can't spill blood without it tainting my own. I can't pretend that this – that *you* don't terrify me.'

'You scare me, too, blackbird.'

The raw truth in his words cut deep. I shook my head, struggling to swallow. Something thick and foreign was threading its way through me, twining through my bones. It was that feeling I was afraid of most – feeling it for him.

I hurried from the room without a backward glance. What could he possibly fear from me? I didn't want to know the answer. Because the idea that I could mean anything to him . . . *that* was something to be afraid of.

Aron was waiting in the navigation room, leaning against the wall with a smirk plastered across his face.

'You can stop that right now,' I snapped, relieved when the door shut behind me and I could breathe normally again. 'Nothing happened.'

Aron held his hands up defensively and chuckled. 'Didn't say anythin', lass.'

I rolled my eyes, following him out into the crisp morning air. The storm clouds crowding the horizon had lifted. The fallen yards had already been replaced, and the sails miraculously mended; but those white cerements remained – a line of bodies awaiting their seaborne burials.

'What did you want, Aron?' I asked, trying to soften my steely tone.

I should be thanking him. That thought presented a far more unwelcome question. How far would things have gone if he hadn't interrupted?

183

Aron held out a small vial, the amber liquid inside gleaming in the rising sunlight. 'Got this fer His Majesty,' he explained. 'Mors reckons it works wonders fer burns.'

I eyed the bottle archly. 'And what exactly do you expect *me* to do with it?'

He at least had the tact to look sheepish. 'Thought ye migh' be able to apply it to his back . . .'

'I'm supposed to be his prisoner, not his nurse.'

'I know,' Aron assured me. The rings under his eyes ran deep. It seemed he'd had even less rest than I had. 'I'm sorry to ask – ye've done more'n enough – but . . .' He glanced behind us at the crew shifting debris and muttering prayers over their fallen crew mates. I could see the fractured sorrow in his gaze, in the dip of his heavy brow. 'Could ye do me a favour, just fer today?'

I snatched the vial from his outstretched hand with a huff. 'Just today,' I agreed. 'And only because you're asking.'

'Owe ye, lass. Ten times over.' Aron shoved his hands into his pockets, studying the toes of his boots for a moment with a quiet intensity. Then he backed away with a wink, heading for the side of the deck where the rest of the crew had gathered, anguish seeping from their slumped shoulders into the sunlit sky.

I returned reluctantly to Sebastien's room, finding him right where I'd left him, arms braced against his knees, head bent in thought. I gritted my teeth, fighting the urge to slip straight back into his embrace. A single touch – a momentary lapse – and my body was practically begging for more.

The smell of salt and blood followed me as I crossed to the windows and threw open the thick curtains. Daylight sliced through the latticed windows, filling the chamber. Perhaps light, if nothing else, could guard me from the pull of his shadows.

'The hell are you doing?' Sebastien snapped, shielding his

eyes as he glared at me over his shoulder.

'It was too dark in here,' I replied shortly, bustling over to the nightstand and soaking a strip of cloth in the bowl of water that rested atop a stack of books. 'Take your bandages off, I'm going to clean your wound.'

'I'm fine.'

'Just do as I say so I can leave.' I kept my tone clipped and cautious, but my cheeks felt hot, my breath a little short. 'I've seen the promise of death that fever brings. You're just too stubborn to admit you aren't invincible.'

He seemed to sense my impatience, reaching back to unwind the long strip of bloodied bandage from his torso with a heavy sigh. I tried to avert my eyes, but I couldn't tear them away from his muscles, rippling beneath the light.

I'd never seen a desert but I'd read of them. I imagined his skin was like that – deep gold dunes, sands shifting with the wind, ridges draped in heat.

Sebastien pulled the final piece of cloth away and a small gasp fell from my lips. His flesh had been stripped away, scourged by flames. But the skin had hardened and begun to scab over, as if the wound had been inflicted several days ago.

I settled on to the mattress behind him, using the wet cloth to wipe away the dried blood as gently as I could. I uncorked the vial and tipped a little ointment over the wound. Sebastien's entire body tensed as the amber liquid trickled over his raw flesh.

'Sorry,' I mumbled, spreading it lightly over his skin with my fingertips.

The muscles of his shoulders corded tight as I worked, tensing with my every touch like it was torture. I tried to be gentle. He was hot, his damaged skin smouldering like dying coals.

'You've seen fevers?' he asked through gritted teeth. 'When?'

It took me a moment to remember what he was talking about, surprised he'd even been listening.

'My sister, Felicie,' I explained as I traced the jagged edge of his wound. 'She's always been prone to sickness – bad lungs, I think. I took care of her often, especially when our father was away on business.'

Her last fever had been one of the worst, seven long nights of blue lips and sweat-drenched sheets. Eighteen years, and it was the first time I'd seen fear in Aberdeen's eyes.

'You'd really do anything for her?' Sebastien mused.

'I'm here, aren't I?'

'Still, *anything* is a bold claim.'

I clenched my teeth, reminding myself who I was talking to. 'Our mother died giving birth to me,' I told him, unsure why I bothered. He'd never understand. 'If it wasn't for me, my sisters would've had her to take care of them instead.'

A dark thought snaked through the back of my skull, but it took me a moment to place. It was the mention of mothers that nagged at me. Not mine, but his.

I wrapped Sebastien's wound in fresh bandages and sat back, wiping my hands on my skirts. He released a ragged breath, relief purling across his broad shoulders.

My eyes trailed his exposed skin, the lump in my throat growing as I remembered the story. I hadn't thought about what the truth in those tales meant for Sebastien. For the little prince, once so full of hope, so full of love.

'What was it like?' I asked quietly. 'Having a mother?'

I expected him to pull away, tell me to leave, but Sebastien didn't move. I listened to his breathing: waiting, hoping.

'It was . . .' he began, his voice ragged, unsteady. 'It was like knowing you'd always be loved. No matter what you did, who you became.'

My eyes burned at the bitterness in his voice. He might not believe it any more – might think himself too far gone to ever be loved again – but it was clear how much he'd loved his mother. Centuries ago, when he'd been capable of such a thing.

His head dipped lower, tendons in his neck going taut. A constellation of white scars fanned like sun rays from his freckled spine, old wounds that had seeded themselves into the fabric of his flesh long ago, branded by something dark and ancient. I swallowed. According to the book, he'd been just eleven years old when he'd watched his father butcher the woman he loved most in the world on the throne-room floor. Eleven years old, when he'd picked up that sword.

'Are you—' I stumbled over my words. 'Do you ever regret what you did? Killing him?'

I half expected him to close up again, to snap and recoil from my curiosity, but Sebastien merely shook his head. 'I regret a lot of things, blackbird. I regret tainting the waters of my homeland. I regret failing my people, then and now. But I've never regretted *that*. Nerida thought us both traitors for the blood we spilled that day, but to me, it was always going to end that way. I only wish I'd done it sooner.'

'Nerida?' I echoed.

'I told you the gods provide me things,' he said, sounding almost amused. 'And what god would be petty enough to curse a pirate but the sea?'

My lips parted, a breath escaping me. His apparent immortality, his powers, his ship . . . all things I had considered gifts. 'She really cursed you?' I ventured. 'Is that why that monster attacked us? Because the sea hates you?'

Sebastien laughed harshly. 'She doesn't hate me, no. And as for that monster . . . I don't know.'

He fell into a contemplative silence. I traced my eyes over the crest of his shoulder blades. He'd always been this looming shadow, this inscrutable power shrouded in darkness. But here he sat, drowned in sunlight, exposed to my hungry gaze. Shadows lingered in the slope of his neck, in the rough-hewn lines of his arms, in the curls of hair that brushed the tops of his shoulders. I resisted the urge to reach out and run my fingers through it, wondering if it would feel as sun-soaked and briny as it smelled.

I leaned forward, my hair tickling the rugged landscape of his back, wanting to touch him but not knowing how. Sebastien exhaled, leaning back ever so slightly, relaxing into me until my forehead brushed the top of his spine.

Then he tensed, arching away from me, hands combing through his hair just as I'd longed to do. I flexed my fists, wondering what it would feel like to have those fingers in my hair. To feel him—

'Get out of here, blackbird,' he said, breaking my trance.

I sank back on my haunches, lungs tight. I knew I'd already stayed far longer than I should have, yet I couldn't help asking, 'Why?'

'Because,' Sebastien rumbled, his voice twisting knots in my stomach, curling my toes, 'it's going to become increasingly harder not to kiss you if you keep climbing into my bed.'

*

Rain dripped from my lashes to the banister of the forecastle. The clouds hung low and heavy as the crew moved through the drizzle towards the funeral shrouds that lined the centre of the deck. I watched from above as they shuffled forward in pairs, carrying their fallen crew-mates and tossing them overboard. Each dull splash plummeted through me like the stones that weighed their bodies down. The death-stitched hammocks outnumbered the living. Pirates, who'd seemed invincible in battle, torn apart by the sea.

I brushed back my water-flecked hair, trying to chase away the guilt that had settled in the hollow of my stomach and wouldn't budge. None of them would've been on deck that day if it weren't for me – for the fact that Bane seemed determined to take me from them.

Bane. He wanted to meet on the winter solstice, just two weeks away. The gods only knew what kind of army he'd bring this time, and the *Blood Rose*'s crew was in no position to face them.

I hadn't yet mentioned Bane's ultimatum to anyone. Because the sooner they knew, the sooner the King and his crew would have to decide the kind of end they wanted for this war. The sooner it would all be over, one way or another.

Aron and Mors moved side by side across the deck below, heaving a canvas-bound corpse on to their shoulders. Their footsteps echoed like punches to my gut. I'd scarcely spoken to any of them in days, leaving them to heal their wounds in peace.

Out of respect, I told myself. *Nothing more.*

'Good morning.'

I blinked. I hadn't noticed Sebastien approaching until he was beside me, staring down at the rites unfolding below.

I glanced sideways at him. Colour warmed his cheeks, his jaw shadowed by a layer of fine, dark growth. He wore a clean grey shirt beneath a heavy coat, thick and leathery like his old cloak, only there was no hood. Something in him must have burned with it, the something that told him to hide.

'You look . . . better,' I deadpanned.

His gaze slid over me, eyeing my clothes: the soiled hems of my olive-green skirts, the tattered brocade jacket I'd taken to wearing with the sleeves rolled up. I didn't care that it was too big for me, it was comfortable and warm, and the pockets ran deep enough to carry books.

Sebastien's gaze landed on mine. 'So do you.'

I touched a hand to the tangle of my hair, frizzy from the rain, feeling my cheeks warm. My eyes darted back to the deck below, fingers tracing the grain of the wooden banister.

'I'm sorry,' I said. 'You know, for your losses.'

I wondered how it would've felt to see so many of his crew die. Wondering whether loss meant anything, without a heart to feel love.

Sebastien grunted in reply. He moved closer, leaning down to brace his forearms on the railing, his shoulder brushing mine. We stood side by side, watching the cerements plunge overboard, both outsiders to the crew's grief.

'I saw you, you know,' he said after a while. 'During the attack. You were about to leave with him – with Bane.'

'I was *about* to escape certain death,' I amended. Only I'd frozen. I'd been so afraid of the anger in a man's eyes I'd stood fixed on a burning ship, ready to go down with it.

Sebastien's black eyes met mine, curious. 'So if he came back tomorrow, would you go?'

Of course not. I turned to face him properly. 'Why is it you get to ask pointless hypothetical questions while I hardly ever get a straight answer from you?'

'Fair point,' he conceded.

The light rain let up and the crew carted out barrels of rum, the sombre air lifting with their spirits. It was time to honour the dead the way only pirates knew how.

I took a deep breath. 'I know where Bane will be,' I said, knowing I couldn't avoid telling him forever. Knowing I might be damning us all as I did. 'He told me. He wants you to meet him – I'm guessing he'll have an army lying in wait. Didn't seem like he planned to give up on me any time soon.'

Sebastien nodded slowly. 'I see.'

'Whale Rock,' I told him. 'He said he'd be waiting on the winter solstice. That you should hand me over or he'll kill you.'

'I see,' he said again, sounding amused.

'Whale Rock – where is that?' I asked, watching him mull over the new information. 'I've never heard of it.'

'An island, just off the coast,' Sebastien explained. 'Few days south of Bray. No one's lived there in years, but we've got . . . history with that place. Let's just say they were never much fond of pirates.'

His tone was short, making me think there was more to it, but I had bigger things to worry about.

'You aren't planning to go, are you?' I prodded.

'Of course we're going.'

I gaped at him. 'Even if he has you outnumbered, ten to one?'

'You've seen me take on ten men,' Sebastien said wryly. 'You think I'm scared?'

I rolled my eyes. '*You* might not be, but how do you expect your crew to survive?'

He shrugged. 'It'll be their choice. Though I already know what every person on this ship will decide.'

I scowled. *Pirates.* They'd choose vengeance over anything, even their lives. 'But you have a fleet. You could bring Mersey's crew, at least.'

Sebastien's smirk twisted and I had to force my gaze from his lips. 'You giving me war counsel now, blackbird?'

'I'm just saying—'

'Your concern is flattering, but if Bane's death is the last thing

I ever give my crew, I'll be satisfied. I won't drag any more lives into it.'

I clenched my jaw tight. So he was admitting they might not win. He'd lead them all into a losing battle and be the only one to come out unscathed. 'And me?' I asked. 'I know it's selfish to wonder, when my life might be the only one he spares, but . . .'

'I won't let him take you,' Sebastien said, as if he could read my thoughts.

I snorted. 'Nerida may have bestowed her magic upon you, but you can hardly stop an army.'

He shrugged, shoulder nudging mine as he leaned further over the railing, staring down at the crew as they danced and drank. 'You don't think I'd at least try?'

I hesitated. 'Why would you bother?'

Sebastien turned slowly to face me again. 'That's a good question.'

His tone was flat, but when I met his gaze, there was something almost uncertain in it, something curious.

He thought I'd been trying to escape. I almost wished I had. When the world had caught fire, I should have fled, because how terrifying, to trust that this place could ever offer me freedom? To trust the Heartless King . . .

I had to. If I was ever going to make it home, I had to trust that Sebastien would get me there. That, for whatever reason, he'd keep his word and protect me.

'Tell me something,' I ventured softly.

Once again, I expected him to protest, but his quizzical expression faded as he tilted his head. 'What do you want to know?'

For once, my mind didn't churn with a thousand questions. I didn't want to know about Bane, or the Sinking Cities, or the past. This was part of no bargain. This was Sebastien, offering a piece of himself to me.

My gaze traced the path of his neck up to his black, whirlpool eyes. 'The hood,' I began, my words catching. 'Why did you wear it? What good did it ever do to hide?'

The ridge of his throat shifted as he swallowed. I didn't know if he was going to answer – didn't think he knew, either – but I held my breath, waiting.

He looked away, squinting over my shoulder at the blurred grey line of the horizon. It was almost impossible to distinguish where the sea ended and the sky began.

'Easier, isn't it?' he said, words stirring from the gravel of his voice. 'Not to be seen. Really could've been a monster under that cloak – no one would've known the difference.'

I hadn't been expecting such raw honesty. I curled my hands around the railing, forcing myself not to reach out and touch him. What he'd said was real, but it didn't make him any less the beast he'd tried to hide.

His eyes shifted from the watercolour horizon to me, to my hands. 'Or,' he went on, dipping his head closer, 'maybe I just look good in black.'

A ribbon of laughter burst out of me before I could snatch it back. I flushed, biting my lip to hide a smile.

Sebastien inched closer and my eyes fell to his chest, his loose shirt revealing a glimpse of the bandages beneath. A reminder that he walked with the burden of his actions. That he was, in fact, human. The soft grey material was streaked with splashes of rain, light as the cloudy sky against his bronze skin.

He cleared his throat and my eyes flickered up, blush deepening. *Subtle.*

'Will I see you at dinner?'

I held his inky, expectant gaze, my pulse quickening at the thought. It'd been two weeks since we'd dined alone together and so much had changed. He'd sworn he wouldn't, but *he* had changed. That, or I really was as naïve as he thought. He'd been hiding, yes, but now he wasn't. Now he was sharing himself with me, promising me protection. As though he almost . . . *cared*.

I stepped back. Killing a monster was hard enough, but caring for one . . . I already had people – good people – to care about, to protect. I couldn't let the Heartless King get in the way of that.

'I don't—' I began quietly. 'I don't think that's a good idea.'

Sebastien's brows drew together over his smouldering gaze, but he watched me go in silence as I hurried back towards the forecastle, eager to put as much distance between us as I could.

Inside, two figures stood further along the hall, something tender in the way their heads were bent close, despite the space between their bodies.

Aron and Una looked up, springing apart when they saw me approaching. I opened my mouth to greet them, but Una hurried past without a word, tears gleaming in her eyes.

Aron offered me an apologetic smile. 'Later, lass,' he mumbled, retreating and disappearing down the stairs.

A sadness swirled in their wake, one I almost understood. I touched a hand to my lips, wondering just how many lives had been torn apart by the broken world of the *Blood Rose*.

Enough, I told myself firmly. I didn't need to add mine to the list.

19

The second I woke, I knew something was wrong.

It was the sound of rain, trickling down the window panes, spilling from the sill to the floor below. Water was coming in – but the dark sky outside was cloudless, serene. It wasn't raining.

I'm dreaming, I thought, watching a sheet of water flood down the glass. *It's just another nightmare.*

Only it wasn't.

The puddle forming on the floor swelled, shifting, rising from the ground and taking shape. A creature slipped into being, limbs forming as liquid turned to bone. Water draped its skeleton like a veil of skin, transparent and shimmering blue in the moonlight.

I scrambled back against my headboard in horror as the creature drew itself up, long claw-like fingers unfurling.

'What——?' I choked out, my mouth agape as it slithered towards the end of my bed. 'Who are you?'

The creature slunk closer, its gaunt face and moon-bright eyes sending chills racing through me. Whatever it was, it wore an expression I knew well. Hunger.

'What do you want?' I whispered, fear wrapped tight around my throat.

It spoke in a hiss, revealing rows of needle-sharp teeth and a flickering, forked tongue. '*Vengeance.*'

Water dripped to the floorboards as it moved, the gills on its neck pulsing like my racing heart. I inched slowly to the edge of the bed, fingers reaching for the side of the mattress, my muscles clenched, ready to bolt for the door.

Let this be a dream, I prayed. But my trembling hands felt the wood of the bedpost, felt the smooth silk of the bedsheets, felt the air as it ripped in and out of my lungs. I wasn't dreaming.

A shrill hiss licked from the creature's mouth. 'You *killed*,' it said, seaweed hair slick to its bony skull. 'You killed my *sssibling*, and now you think you can take him? *Murderer.*'

Him? Ice-cold dread swept down my spine.

The creature lunged.

I screamed, tumbling from the bed and racing for the door, but I was too slow. Pain tore through my shoulder, claws of pure fire raking through my skin before I could reach the doorknob. Skeletal fingers wrapped around my arm and threw me backwards.

Pain erupted from the base of my skull as my head cracked against the bedpost. I slammed into the wood with a cry, stumbling back and scrambling for the nightstand. My fingers scrabbled with the drawer's latch as the creature advanced, the smell of chum and rotting fish churning my stomach.

This couldn't be how I died. Not here. Not alone.

But there was no way out. No way to live – unless . . .

My fumbling fingers yanked open the nightstand drawer,

wrapping around the little dagger inside. I turned just in time. Wet, clammy fingers seized my neck, shoving me back into the wall. My head spun, blackness splitting my vision in two, stars blooming before me.

'*Die*,' it snarled, rancid breath ice-cold on my face.

The rose-shaped hilt of the dagger was slippery in my palm, but I clutched it tight.

I have to, I thought, tears stinging my eyes. My lungs constricted, pulsing with my last snatch of air. *Now.*

I drew back my arm, chest burning like I was caught in a blaze of fire once more and squeezed my eyes shut.

Bones crunched. There was a sickening *snap*, and the iron grip around my neck vanished. My eyes flew wide.

Sebastien was there, the creature's limp body slipping between his hands, dissolving into a puddle at our feet.

I gasped in relief, struggling for breath that burned my throat, the world shifting in and out of focus. His arm shot out, steadying me as I took great, dizzying gulps of air.

'What *was* that?' I rasped.

'I don't know,' he said darkly. His eyes were trained on my face, scanning. His brows furrowed. 'You're hurt.'

I glanced over my shoulder and winced as something hot sliced down my arm, seeing the tracks of crimson that tore through my shirt. I leaned back against the bedpost, my chest heaving. The pain throbbed in time with my racing heart but the tightness in my lungs eased.

Sebastien stepped closer. His gaze searched mine in a way that only made my breathing more erratic. I reached for his arm, still catching my breath, unable to find the words to thank him.

I held his gaze, my heart slowing and speeding up all at once. There was a current pulsing in the air between us, a tide that tugged him that final step, chest brushing up against mine.

Something metal clattered to the floor. My dagger, the one I'd been holding, ready to use.

'Are you all right?' Sebastien asked quietly, his voice like sandstone, scraping against every part of me. My spine tingled.

'I'm not sure,' I whispered, finding it hard to swallow. Finding it hard to do anything, really, but curl my hand tighter around his forearm.

His rough fingers slid along the sensitive flesh of my wrist, sending goosebumps prickling over my skin. *I am now*, I thought. The more he touched me, the more the rest of the world seemed to right itself.

The coarse texture of his bandages brushed against my blouse. The smell of him – salt and sand and steel – was intoxicating. Sebastien lifted his free hand, fingers gliding along my jaw, slipping into my hair.

Something hot fluttered in my belly and I angled myself closer, feeling my quickening pulse in every part of my body.

'Kiss me,' I breathed.

'Why would you want that?' he murmured, eyes never leaving my mouth.

I shook my head. I had no answer to give, except that I wanted it. *Gods*, I wanted it. 'Just this once.'

His head tipped forward, warm lips closing over my cold ones. So gentle, so fleeting, it tugged my heartstrings along with him when he pulled back.

A sigh escaped me, but I didn't open my eyes. Didn't want it to be over.

'Again.'

I tasted my whisper on his tongue as he complied, lips recapturing mine. His fingers slid around the back of my neck and I caved, melting into his cruel, capable hands.

His kiss was soft, tongue like silk as it slipped past my lips, dipping into my mouth. He caught my bottom lip gently between his teeth, drawing my mouth open wider before he took it again, tongue searing hot and salted.

Oh.

Shivers cascaded down my body and I tilted my head back, letting him in deeper, letting his arms hold me as my knees went weak. The bedpost was firm against my back, the only thing stopping me from crumbling completely as the rest of the world slipped away.

Again, again, again.

I grew hungrier, biting his lip, trying to draw out the power I could feel him withholding. His shadows were thick in my chest, my heart racing with the thrill of power that shot through me.

He tasted of salt. Of the sun. Of a warm, calm sea, settling my nerves and setting them alight again as his tongue grazed over mine.

Sebastien pulled back, panting, and our eyes locked. I couldn't tell where his pupils ended and his irises began – it was all so dark, all so consuming. Glinting like coals, like the promise of fire.

Again, I wanted to say, craving the taste of him, of relief. But I couldn't find my voice over the heat creeping through me. Sharp pangs rippled from my shoulder to the rest of my body, making my head spin. Not just from his body against mine – there was pain there, a lick of flame.

I glanced over my shoulder. Blood trailed down my arm, dripping to the floor that seemed to be getting further and further away.

Warm fingers closed around my arm and a voice rang in my ear. 'Ria, can you hear me?'

I swayed on my feet. My mind whirled, spiralling into the numbing heat. I knew that voice – missed it most at night. But the burning in my shoulder drowned it out. I could feel it, the fire, leaching through my veins with every pump of my heart.

It's killing me. The realisation crept in hot as the creature's venom, dark as the shadows that swarmed around me.

'Don't say that,' came that voice. That tide-crashing, sand-coarse voice. The world swept away from beneath me, my head falling back into a nest of warmth, the smell of my cliffs curling in my nostrils.

'It hurts.' The words tumbled clumsily from my mouth, muddled by the swimming walls and dimming moonlight.

'Aye, blackbird, I know.'

The world was a blur but he stood steady, leaning over me on the bed, his words undercut by the tearing of material.

I heard thunder in the distance. Quiet, hurried thunder, then voices that made my eyes ache to reopen. Cold air breezed against my shoulder, tempering the fire that scorched me from within. I tried to call out, to say their names, but the darkness ripped the words from my throat, drowning out the world once and for all.

Only one thought stuck, a stubborn star in the all-consuming night.

Again.

A searing pain in my shoulder tore me from the dark. I lurched awake, a sharp ache lacing my movements as I lifted my head from the pillow. I lay flat on my stomach, the chamber filled with late afternoon light and murmured conversation.

Golde sat perched on the rim of the claw-footed tub, talking to Aron and Una, who lounged in chairs by the window. My gaze drifted to the end of the bed, finding Sebastien hovering there, his eyes fixed on me. A once-white tunic hung loosely over his bandaged chest. Both were streaked with blood.

My blood, I realised. My heart skipped.

'All done,' said Mors.

The old man was seated on the mattress behind me, a needle in hand. I angled my head to catch a glimpse of the three long claw-marks marring my shoulder blade, the skin knitted back together by rows of tiny, neat stitches.

'How'd you do that?' I asked groggily.

'Have to make myself useful somehow,' Mors smiled, patting my leg. 'The ship may mend herself, but sailors don't. Perhaps I could teach you sometime.'

My heart clenched at the kindness in his voice. *Sometime* felt faraway, but the thought of spending it with Mors was a comfort to my aching bones. 'I'd like that.'

He tucked a leather pouch into his trousers and rose from the bed as Una moved closer, helping me sit up and pull a clean shirt down over my head.

'What about the venom?' I asked. 'It burned . . . I thought it was going to kill me.'

Mors shrugged. 'There wasn't a body left for me to examine, but it seems the venom wasn't potent enough to kill, only weaken.'

Weak. I resisted the urge to scowl.

'It's because I killed that creature,' I whispered. The crew exchanged glances around me, looking unconvinced. 'It wanted revenge.'

I looked down at my hands, pain throbbing in my head and my shoulder. *Clean.* My hands were as clean as they were ever going to be. He'd saved me again – not just from the monster, but from its blood.

Una settled down beside me, resting a comforting hand on my arm. 'Ye're safe now, lass,' she said, but her brows were drawn low.

I gave her a dubious smile, glancing around at the crew. They all wore equally troubled expressions.

'Knew she'd never play fair,' Golde grumbled, scowling out at the dreary horizon.

'Who?' I asked. *And what does she mean, play?*

Aron shook his head. 'Nothin', lass. No one.'

I shot him a disgruntled look. I was tired of living in the dark, especially if my life was somehow at stake.

'Will one of you tell me what's going on?' I demanded.

Four pairs of eyes slid over to their king. I glared up at Sebastien, standing stoically at the end of my bed.

'It's the sea, isn't it?' I said. 'She's angry at you, right? Now she's trying to kill us – kill me.'

I could feel them shifting under the weight of my words, but I looked only at Sebastien, daring him to deny it. I watched him, waiting for his guard to waver, but it never did.

'When you betray a god,' he said finally, 'you lose. We've spent the last three centuries learning that lesson.'

My stomach turned. What kind of god was the sea, if her actions had done nothing but spill chaos across the continent for three hundred years? *Petty*, Sebastien had said. I was beginning to think he was right.

'That's the reason you're trapped here, isn't it?' I asked. 'She – Nerida – took your kingdom.'

'Aye.'

I held his gaze for as long as I could, unnerved by the weight of it, of everything around us. I'd never asked for this. Not for the blood pulsing in my veins, nor staining my hands. Not to be an enemy of the sea I'd only ever loved, nor filled with this unfathomable desire for the man who reigned it.

So Nerida had frozen time and woven her magic into the timber of the *Blood Rose*. Into Sebastien. For all the longing she'd etched into my soul, now it was her – that very sea – turning against us.

I thought of the spirits I'd spotted in the waves that day on deck, their human-like features soft, friendly – the same ones I was almost certain had pulled *Leviathan* from the bay. They were different from the beasts that had attacked us. Not the same as the sea they came from, the one that seemed to want me dead.

If all this was true, then there was nowhere to hide. No way I'd be safe again if I'd unwittingly made an enemy of the very thing keeping us afloat.

I swallowed. Great. Just one more thing to fear – a god.

The crew filtered out, leaving me to recover, but Una lingered behind, her hand still warm on my forearm. I watched Sebastien duck out into the hall, not sparing me so much as a glance. Disappointment sank into my aching bones, making my stomach flutter uneasily.

'What'd ye do to him?' Una asked as the door shut behind them. When she looked at me, her eyes sparkled.

I blinked. 'What do you mean?'

'He's different,' she said, raising a thick brow.

I didn't need to ask who she meant. I snorted. 'He is not. You said it yourself, he hasn't changed in three hundred years.'

Una shook her head with a frown. 'Ye didn't know him before. The last few weeks . . .' She chewed her bottom lip. 'It's like he's wakin' up.'

I hugged the sheets to my chest. *Kiss me* – my own words echoed through my mind. Heat crept across my cheekbones as I remembered his breath on my lips, his fist in my hair, the trace of salt on his tongue.

'I didn't do anything,' I lied, hoping my racing heart didn't give me away.

Una smirked, stretching out on the bed beside me and tucking a pillow beneath her head. 'If ye say so. But I've never seen him show his face in the open, in front of the crew. It ain't like he's in short supply o' cloaks.'

I rolled my eyes. There was a small, quiet part of me that felt pleased, but another voice spoke in the back of my mind, one slick and sharp as steel. *You think you can take him.* Who else could the creature have meant?

Maybe the crew was right. Maybe it wasn't just about revenge.

'Do you really think the sea sent those monsters?' I asked.

'Aye.' Una drummed her fingers on the mattress. 'The sea . . . she's restless, angry. Feels us gettin' closer.'

I turned to look at her, dark braids splayed out across the pale silk, hazel eyes soft beneath her pinched brows. 'Closer to what?' I pressed, feeling my chest tighten.

Una rolled on to her back beside me, staring up at the winding rose vines overhead as she mulled over her answer. 'The end,' she said eventually, waving a hand at the room around us. 'To all this. Time moves on. At some point, so must we.'

I reached down and grabbed her wrist, making her look at me. 'Don't be cryptic. Just tell me what you know,' I begged.

The corners of her frown twisted, tugged by something wistful, something weary. She slid her wrist from my grasp, fingers threading through mine. 'He'd kill me if I did,' she joked softly. 'S'taken me eight years to know as much as I do. He trusts ye, just give him time.'

Eight years.

'I don't have that kind of time,' I told her. I had just over a week until the solstice. Just over a week to work out what the hell I was going to do. Hand myself over and try to negotiate peace? Or watch more blood be spilled over me, and pray it would set me free? It wasn't a choice, really.

Una's frown deepened. 'Aye . . . Whale Rock. Sebastien told us. S'pose time is movin' quicker than I'd have liked. Won't stop us fightin', though.'

'What if you didn't have to fight?' I ventured. 'What if I went willingly? If we could just convince the crew to let Bane go, you could all live. This could end *peacefully*.'

Una's soft features hardened. 'That ain't how this works. Bane was our brother. He *turned on us*.' Her voice broke, splintered by the depth of his betrayal. 'He chose a family that was already dead over the family we gave him. Swindled us fer money, ships, *politics*. We'll protect ye as best we can, but there's no sense in tryin' to save anybody. Wouldn't be a pirate if I didn't die fightin' fer the people I love.'

I gripped her hand tighter. 'Don't die for this,' I pleaded.

But I could see it in her eyes, the kind of iron will that couldn't be shaken.

Home, Sebastien had said they were going. Now they were changing course for a place that hated them. They'd die on strange tides if it meant killing a man they'd once loved.

I sighed, knowing it was no use arguing. If I was going to try to save them, I'd have to do it on my own.

Una leaned over to kiss my temple, her calloused hand squeezing mine before she let go. My limbs felt like lead and I could only watch with a sinking heart as she padded towards the door.

She gave me one last sad smile and slipped out into the hall. 'Get some rest.'

I sagged back into the bed and buried my way beneath the furs, seeking warmth but finding none. My shoulder ached, the back of my skull throbbed, and my mind churned with questions.

I rolled over, wincing at the pain that spiked through my

stitches. The room was gloomy, filled with cloudy evening light. The windows stood solid as they always had, but I felt so much more exposed. If that creature could get in without breaking them . . . the gods only knew what might come next.

20

Rain drizzled down the windows for hours. The sound of it filling my chamber was enough to jolt me awake every time sleep closed in. My heart hammered in my chest, eyes darting to the glass.

It's nothing, I kept telling myself, but the shadows were playing tricks on me and I didn't trust the panes to keep out the darkness any longer.

I rolled on to my back, wincing at the pain that nipped my shoulder, and tossed the sheets aside. The sound of the storm flooded my mind with memories of the previous night. A hiss, a flash of searing pain, claws wrapped around my throat. The clatter of my dagger on wood. Then Sebastien, his hands, his lips. His arms, lifting me from the dark.

I turned over, burying my face into the pillow, and groaned. Then I clambered out of bed, draped a soft grey fur around my shoulders and headed for the door.

My body steered me where my mind told me not to go: out into the cold, my bare feet splashing across the deck as I hurried up the steps, slipping into the warmth of the navigation room.

Honey-gold light trickled from beneath the doorway at the other end of the cabin. I halted before it, my hand raised to knock, my mind and body locked in a raging sword fight.

Don't go in there, the logical part of me cried. But I didn't want to be logical. Didn't want to be alone in that room. Didn't want to be anywhere, really, but with him.

The door swung open.

'Oh.'

Sebastien stood in the doorway, his dark hair tousled, dressed in a nightshirt and pants. My hand fell limply to my side as we stared at each other, silent but for the rain drumming against the windows behind me.

'I was just . . .' I faltered, flushing at how foolish I looked, standing damp and barefoot on his threshold in the middle of the night. 'I wanted to—'

'I was coming to see you,' he cut me off. 'I wanted to talk to you this morning, I . . . I'm sorry.'

My stomach flipped.

A cold draft whispered in behind me and I shivered. Sebastien glanced over at the windows, the storm-thick night, and stepped back to let me pass.

'I couldn't sleep,' I whispered, suddenly all too aware that I was *here*, in his bedchamber, wearing nothing but my nightgown. Because I was scared of nightmares and the rain.

'How's your shoulder?' he asked, shutting the door behind us. Moonlight trickled through the windows, but the sound of the rain was muffled here, the shadows wrapped reassuringly around the walls.

I shrugged, then winced. 'It's fine.'

His lips twisted. 'Couldn't sleep either,' he said, clearing his throat. 'I wanted to see — wanted to make sure you were all right.'

I swallowed, remembering the last time I'd seen him, spattered with my blood. Una's voice crept into my mind but I pushed it away. He was different in this light — cold and blue yet softened by the rain. He stood as imposing as ever, but half-dressed, almost . . . uncertain.

Sebastien raked a hand through his hair, pushing it behind his shoulders, the light of the moon caught in his endless eyes. I could feel my heart in my throat, making it hard to breathe.

I shouldn't be here. I knew that already, but here I was. Searching for something I couldn't name, a feeling he'd stirred in me, something halfway between shadow and fire.

I moved slowly towards the desk, my fingers reaching for the swath of dark green velvet that covered it. I watched his reflection in the windows as he stilled, tensing as though he was watching my every move.

Curious, my hand curled around the material and tugged. The fabric fell away to reveal the mirror beneath, sending candlelight bouncing back to stroke my face.

He was on me in a flash, grabbing my arm and spinning me from the gilt looking-glass. 'What are you doing?'

I stared up at him. What would I have done, I wondered, if my own gaze had been black, rather than gold? Would I, too, have hidden from my own emptiness?

'What are you so afraid of?' I whispered.

I measured the waning anger in that coal-black gaze, wondering what I looked like through eyes that dark. If the shadows blinded him, the way they did me. But they couldn't have: he was looking at me like he could see all the way through to my soul.

'You tell me you can't change, but you saved my life,' I pointed out. 'Twice.'

His voice was quiet. 'You saved yourself.'

Almost. But he'd saved me in more ways than one last night. I sighed, my temper shifting like sand. 'Answer my question. What are you so afraid of?'

His hand slid across my uninjured shoulder, moving to rest at the base of my neck. My mouth went dry as his thumb whispered up the column of my throat. Goosebumps bloomed outward from his touch.

'I told you,' he said at last. 'You.'

'Don't mock me.'

But it wasn't derision I saw in his eyes, nor the cold gleam of the moon. There was something hot, something dangerous, simmering in them. A fire that coursed through him. Blood pounding, scorching, in rhythm with my own.

I knew the answer. *This* was what scared him. Letting me see it.

His grip tightened and I inhaled. My heart thrilled, afraid he'd kiss me – terrified he wouldn't. I leaned in. He must've seen the trust in my eyes, felt the danger stirring in the murkiness between us, because when my parted lips grazed expectantly against his, Sebastien pulled back.

'Ria—'

I closed the gap, grabbing the back of his neck and pulling the Heartless King's mouth down to mine. Heat flared in my stomach as he melted into the kiss, teeth grazing my tongue. My fists curled around the collar of his shirt, tugging him closer.

His fingers wound into my hair in response, stubble scraping my cheeks, my chin, reigniting the flames he'd lit inside me last night.

I pulled back for a second, panting, and when I looked up, my breathing faltered. Faltered, because for a moment, I'd expected the

210

man whose kiss I craved like the sea to be full of something other than darkness.

I held his gaze, my chest rising and falling rapidly against his.

Sebastien's grip softened at my hesitation. 'Still want me?' he whispered.

My breath quickened. 'Yes.' *So badly*.

'Good.' He closed the gap, crashing our mouths together. There was a groan on my lips, but I didn't know if it was his or mine.

Sebastien's hands slid down to grip my thighs and I gasped as he lifted me on to the desk, pushing me backwards. I slammed into the mirror, feeling its surface fracture behind me. Pain bloomed in my shoulder as the impact tore through my wound.

Sebastien swore. 'Blackbird,' he muttered, pulling his hand away from my back, palm flecked with scarlet. He cursed again. 'I'm sorry.'

I wasn't. I craned my neck to peer at my blood-spattered reflection in the mirror, seeing the bright red seeping through my chemise where some of my stitches had reopened. But the pain was fleeting, mingling with the heat already knotted in my veins. He'd set something alight in me and I wasn't ready to let it burn out.

'Since when were you afraid of spilling a little blood?' I challenged.

Fire spiked my stomach as his lips curved into a wry smile. Sebastien raised his hand to my neck, smearing it with crimson before he leaned in again. 'You are a wicked thing, Ria Lucroy,' he said against my lips.

The sound of my name on his tongue was like a branding iron, so hot and sharp I knew it would never sound the same again. I grinned. His hands slid into my hair, tilting my head back to kiss my open mouth with a ferocity I'd only ever witnessed in battle.

I arched into him, my legs tightening around his waist. I'd seen his body — a tapestry of blood and magic and scars. The beauty of it couldn't compare with how good it felt, pressed against my own, his shadows filling the air as I inhaled.

My whole body softened into him. Relief. Amid monsters and curses and betrayal, it was *this* I hadn't been able to stop thinking about all day.

Sebastien pulled back from the desk, carrying me with him over to the bed. A flash of white crossed my vision as he tossed his shirt to the floor before the heat of his body closed around me again. I dragged my fingernails down his powerful biceps, earning a growl that rumbled through me like wildfire.

'You'll be the death of me,' I breathed. *A thousand times over.*

'Aye, I know,' he replied, lips never leaving mine.

A twist of flames speared through me as his mouth moved to the sensitive skin below my ear, teeth dragging over my pulse. My head rolled back, eyes sliding open — and suddenly I wished they hadn't.

As I gazed up at the roses wreathed through the bed's canopy, the leaves shifted. A thicket of verdant eyes blinked open, glaring down at me. They were cold, bright, sending a river of shame rushing through me, extinguishing the heat of Sebastien's touch. *If my family could see me now . . .*

I tensed and he glanced down at me, eyes clouding over. 'What's wrong?'

I wormed out from beneath him, cheeks blistering. 'I didn't come here to warm your bed,' I snapped, scrambling to my feet. *Liar.*

Laughter gleamed in Sebastien's eyes. 'If I wanted a warm bed, there are easier ways than having you bleed all over it.'

I glanced at my back in the mirror, seeing the rills of blood that trickled beneath my nightdress. It served me right, I thought, panic bubbling in my throat.

'Relax,' he said. 'I can help.'

'How?' I sounded shrill, even to my own ears, uncertainty seeping into my buzzing veins. There was a lot of blood.

The dark sea of his voice was calm, edged with irritation. 'Lie down.'

I didn't move.

Sebastien gestured to the sheets with a sigh. 'Just let me look.'

Hesitantly, I crawled back on to the bed and sat cross-legged in front of him. *When did I start believing him capable of fixing anything?* I wondered, terrified by the thought.

I tensed as the bed sank and his knees settled on either side of me.

'Lift your arms,' he murmured.

I complied, wincing at the ache in my shoulder blade. His hands skimmed up my sides, gathering the material of my shift and slipping it over my head. I pulled my hair over my shoulders to cover my chest, unsettled by how easy it felt to be so exposed in front of him.

As if he's ever wrought anything more than ruin, I thought ruefully – but his hands said otherwise. They were impossibly gentle as they skated over my shoulder, reminding me of the way he'd soothed the tremors from my fingers. His words lived inside me still. *Killing a monster doesn't make you one.* Yet he'd still been there, quick to steal the creature's life before I could. Why would a man who felt nothing do what he'd done for me? How could a man without a heart—

The mattress moved again and Sebastien lay down, winding a hand around my waist to pull me with him, his bare chest firm against my back.

'What are you—?'

213

'Just go to sleep.'

Heat clung to me, the air still buzzing with something hot, alive. The throbbing in my shoulder faded with every breath I took in his arms.

What am I doing?

I was too tired to wonder for long. I settled my head between the broad planes of his chest, my hair spilling dark and silken across his torso. As we fell through the haze of night, I listened. The world was silent, my breathing soft as I waited for the sound of a heartbeat murmuring beneath me.

I listened, yet . . . the silence echoed on.

21

I woke drenched in sweat.

The room was still dark, pre-dawn light running silver among the shadows. I was hot, too hot, and I peeled myself from Sebastien's scorching embrace. His skin was slick, burning.

I gathered a sheet around my body as I slid from the bed, the pearly silk flecked with red. I hugged it to my chest as my feet met the cool floor, and caught sight of myself in the mirror opposite.

My reflection wavered in its distorted surface as I approached. A smear of crimson marked my neck and my stomach tightened at the memory of Sebastien's hand there, his lips soon after. A shiver slipped through me. I really did look wicked.

I turned before the mirror, realising what he'd done. My shoulder was pale in the light, caked with dried blood, but the skin was smooth, unmarked. I stepped closer, eyes widening at the splintered image. All traces of my wounds – of Mors' stitches – were gone.

He'd healed me.

'Little blackbird, so entranced by her own reflection.'

I spun around to see Sebastien watching me, his head propped up among the cushions. Despite the lift of amusement on his lips, his skin was ashen, a sheen of sweat visible above his brow. Perspiration clung to his hair, beaded across his broad chest.

'You look like death,' I remarked, clutching the sheet tighter around me. I knew I should've thanked him, but acknowledging what he'd done made it hard to be angry. And if I couldn't blame *him* for what had happened . . .

'Then why don't you make yourself useful and fetch me a wet cloth?' he croaked, the harsh edge in his voice falling short.

I scowled. 'To smother you with,' I muttered. But his pallid expression worried me. I didn't take the threat of fever lightly.

I took a clean rag from the nightstand and rinsed it in the small basin of water, my hands sending a swirl of red into the bowl.

'I didn't know you could heal others,' I remarked, wringing out and passing him the damp cloth. He took it with a grunt. 'All this time, you could've used your powers to do good.'

Sebastien shrugged, wiping his forehead with the cool fabric. 'And why would I do that?'

Why do it for me? I wanted to ask, pulling a chair from the window to his bedside with a huff. I'd seen fevers leach the life from Felicie's eyes one too many times, and I was beginning to suspect even the Heartless King couldn't fight off death forever. 'You're telling me that in three hundred years, you've never once used your powers to help someone?'

'I did once,' he remarked, bringing the cloth down across his chest. 'And I never intended to do it again. So try to keep out of trouble, will you?'

You're the trouble, I thought churlishly, as he settled back into the cushions with a groan.

Sebastien's features blanched as he drew short breaths, chest rising and falling sharply. I watched him, remembering how invincible he'd seemed just last night. My mind couldn't help wandering there, remembering other things . . . His lips, the graze of his teeth. The drag of his hands in my hair, the smell of sweat and salt as his powerful arms bound me to him like ropes.

I leaned forward, elbows braced on the side of the mattress, missing his warmth, knowing I shouldn't. His breathing had shallowed, the colour all but drained from his skin. He looked like stone, the immortalised effigy of some war god whose battles still raged beneath the waves. Ancient, young, inhuman.

'Are you still alive?' I whispered.

One eye blinked open. 'If I'd known how much you'd pester me, I would've killed you the moment we met.'

I flashed him a mock smile. 'Glad to see the fever hasn't weakened your humour.'

Sebastien huffed a laugh in response, his arm reaching out across the bed towards me, fingers stretched open, inviting. 'Come back.'

'Why?' I asked, incredulous.

He arched an eyebrow, a lazy smirk tugging at his lips. 'You look cold,' he offered, voice hoarse.

My arms tightened around myself, resisting the pull of his tides, the growing ache in my stomach. I tore my eyes away.

'I'm fine,' I said stiffly, drawing back.

It wouldn't be long before daylight crept through the stillness, and I slunk back to my bedroom to bathe, torn chemise clutched tight around my wintry body. I'd return to check on him soon – but watching over Sebastien felt safer once he was sleeping.

The bath was already waiting for me, filling the room with steam and the scent of rosewater. Dried blood still caked my skin and the scent of *him* clung to me like a shadow.

I let my ruined nightdress fall to the floor, stepping gingerly into the scalding water. I sat for a long time, letting it swirl and eddy around the island of my body, a stretch of sand in a reddening sea.

I should probably have scrubbed myself clean, scouring the smears of blood from my back, my neck, my chest. Everywhere those murderous hands had been. Perhaps then I'd forget how good it had felt to give in.

But I didn't want to forget.

As I relaxed, thoughts began to filter through the haze, gathering around me like fish caught in the woven net of my mind. Things I couldn't avoid any longer.

He's heartless. I'd known it all along, had it ingrained in me like a story etched in wood. I'd been *raised* to fear him. And yet—

I want him. No matter how badly I wanted to pretend I didn't. His kiss lingered on my lips, in the knots of my stomach. Something had changed between us, blurring the lines between what I knew and what I knew I couldn't have.

It would've been so easy to die hating him. To curse his cruel hands until my last breath. But those hands . . . Heat crept over my cheeks as I thought of what his hands had done. They'd tugged me into a new world, one that wasn't shattered by sea monsters and swords and life debts. A world I wasn't ready to let go of just yet.

It doesn't erase the things he's done. No – but it made it hard to think of him without aching.

I pulled myself out of the tub, water cascading from my body, knowing I shouldn't dwell on such a dangerous precipice. I had to think of my family, had to remember that there was more to this world than the *Blood Rose* and her inhabitants.

Still, whether I wanted him or not, I couldn't leave Sebastien to face a fever on his own.

When I sidled back into the navigation room sometime around midday, Mors was pouring over a large tome at the round table, his gold-ringed fingers skimming across its ancient pages. He glanced up, eyes warming when he saw me in the doorway.

'Good afternoon,' he greeted, closing the book.

I hesitated. 'I just came to check on the King,' I said, forgetting I shouldn't have known about his worsened state in the first place.

Luckily, Mors said nothing of it. 'I saw him just an hour ago. It is strange how long he's taking to heal. Though I suppose . . .' He shook his head, offering me a smile. 'He seems to be doing well.'

I glanced at the door at the end of the room. 'Oh, good.'

'How's your shoulder?'

'Fine, thank you,' I said, my words a little too rushed to be natural. A familiar heat crept from the tips of my ears to the apples of my cheeks, and I prayed he wouldn't ask to look at his now-vanished needlework.

Oblivious to my unease, Mors nodded. 'Glad to hear it.'

I hovered halfway between the door and him, wondering whether I should go, but there were so many questions still unanswered that I couldn't help myself from slipping into the seat opposite him.

'You really don't know what that creature was?' I asked, the tang of its rotten breath still thick in my nose.

Mors' smile turned sympathetic. He tapped the cover of the book in front of him. 'I was just doing some research. Unfortunately, sightings of such creatures are rare, and we know only a fraction of those who dwell in the deep.' He shrugged. 'We've come across monsters like it before, but never ones so resolved to kill. The important thing is that you're safe now.'

'You think any of us are safe?' I asked. How could he say that, when my would-be assassin had slipped through the very walls of the ship they called home? A ship they were steering straight into the jaws of battle?

'I can have someone stand guard outside your door, if it would make you feel better,' Mors offered, and his eyes were so earnest that I almost said yes.

'No – thank you, that's not necessary.' I shook my head in a manner I could only hope appeared casual, though I knew my traitorous face too well. How would I explain the next time I slunk out of my chambers in the middle of the night?

There won't be a next time, I scolded myself.

A dip of concern wrinkled Mors' white brows. 'You can trust me, lass. If something is bothering you—'

'It's all the things I don't know that bother me,' I said, interrupting him before he could speculate any further. 'I've been kept in the dark since I got here. If you'd all just be honest with me, maybe I could help.'

The old man's expression eased into a smile. 'You have so much of your parents in you.'

I wanted to curse him out for changing the subject, for evading my curiosity yet again, but my parents were the one thing I'd have given anything to hear more about.

I leaned forward. 'Tell me about them,' I pleaded. 'Even Father feels like a stranger to me now. I want to know what they were like, back when you knew them.'

'Two decades ago, they were my best friends,' Mors said. There was something almost bitter in his voice as he spoke. Something like regret. 'Your father married young, at King Oren's behest, to a woman named Adalina. They were never unhappy, but he only ever loved your mother. When Oren found out Estelle

220

was pregnant by him, I arranged for your parents' escape to the north. He lost all his heirs in one that day.'

'Why did they leave?' I asked. What could a princess have to fear from her own brother?

'That court is no place for anyone – especially not a child.' Mors shook his head. 'Estelle didn't want it for her daughter, and neither did Adalina. She gave Aberdeen to your father in the hopes she'd have a normal life. I admit, I half hoped I'd never find out what became of you all. I took twenty years of silence as a good sign.'

Poor Aberdeen, I thought, picturing a dark-haired little girl being whisked from her home, from her mother, all for a *normal* life. As much as I'd resented it, that was all she'd ever tried to do for me. Protect me.

It was strange hearing Aberdeen's name on Mors' lips. He seemed to know more about my family than I ever had. Father certainly hadn't given much away about his first wife, or the reasons he'd left her.

'How could Aberdeen's mother just give her up like that?' I asked, a note of sadness sitting in my chest as I thought of my eldest sister. She'd been starved of a mother figure as much as I had, and I couldn't imagine the pain of being deserted that way. Was a *normal life* really worth it?

Mors shook his head, gaze full of sympathy. 'It broke her heart to do. But she trusted your father – they were friends more than they ever were husband and wife. She knew how he loved your mother. Neither of them were capable of hiding that, even from Oren.'

'Is his court really so bad?' I ventured. If protecting Felicie meant I'd wind up there one day, then I wanted to know what I faced. What I was trading this life for next.

Mors' lips thinned. 'It's why we left. Your parents, Bane, me.

After a while in that place, you begin to miss . . .' He trailed off, all the futures he could've had reflected in his honey-coloured eyes.

'What?' I urged, leaning closer.

'Living.'

I met Mors' gaze across the table. *Living*. My heart ached a little at that – to know my mother had longed for the same things I did. Knowing she'd risked everything for a life of her own, only to die before she could truly live it. I thought of Felicie, of her fever-stricken form curled over on a flimsy mattress. Had it been worth it, in the end?

'And you?' I asked Mors. 'If my parents were your closest friends, why didn't you go with them?'

'Sometimes I wish I had.' He stared into the distance for a long moment before he glanced back at me with a wan smile. 'But this is the life for me, lass. I couldn't turn my back on it now.'

'This life,' I mused. 'Chasing revenge.'

'Justice,' Mors corrected. 'Bane knew the gravity of his actions when he turned against us. He chose this path for all of us.'

I frowned. Sebastien had said a similar thing about my father's crew. About fishermen, merchants, fathers and sisters and sons. 'You really think more bloodshed is the answer?'

'If it were up to me, lass, there would be another way. But I know better than to bring the politics of court to the seas.'

His words irked me. 'You're the one who started all this,' I said, recalling the last story Father had ever told me. 'You exposed my father in front of the crew. How could you, if you knew it meant condemning his child?'

Mors bowed his head, hiding the shame that filled his eyes. 'I wouldn't blame you if you hated me, lass. I wish there was a way to explain – to make you understand that I will love your parents until my dying breath. Truly, I believed it was for the greater good . . .'

'You chose this life for yourself,' I said. 'What right did you have to choose it for me?'

'It killed me to do,' he murmured, hands brushing over the book in front of him. 'But your being here might save more lives than one.'

My frown deepened. There it was again – *the greater good.* I could only assume it had something to do with the sea, with this curse Sebastien had mentioned. Perhaps that was why these pirates were so willing to throw themselves into this vendetta of theirs. Perhaps Nerida demanded it. I didn't know. All I knew was that I didn't want them to die. That if it came down to it, I might do something foolish again.

'What about Bane?' I asked, steering my mind from those murky waters. 'What did Oren do to his family?'

We don't have to be enemies, love.

I knew I could never trust him, knew I'd probably be better off dead than siding with a traitor like him, but if joining him could spare the crew . . .

Mors shook his head, frowning. 'I wasn't there to witness it, but I've heard the stories. Of what my . . . of the things Oren did. A whole noble house burned to the ground for a slight against his name. Six sons, all killed in the blaze. They found Bane, the seventh, just standing in the ashes.'

'And you'd kill him for wanting revenge?' I asked.

Mors fidgeted with the gold rings banding his pale fingers. 'People don't become pirates because their lives were easy,' he said eventually. 'Everyone here has been through things, been burned by those they trusted. That's why loyalty means everything. If you can't trust your crew, then none of this means anything. Bane choosing his tortured past over the home he found here was like spitting on every single thing we stand for.' He sighed heavily, sounding exhausted. 'Ensuring that those who turned against us that day pay for what they did is the one thing keeping this ship together right now. Truly, lass' – he looked up, meeting my eyes – 'I am sorry I brought you into this. I let my loyalties blind me; I forgot where I came from.'

I wanted to be angry, but . . . I pictured the world without Mors' actions. Father would be dead. I'd still be meandering over the cliffs of Northbay, picking through the scraps of the life we had there. Hungry, lonely, longing for the sea. I never would've ventured beyond the bay, never would've met the man in front of me. That last thought stung more than I'd expected.

'You were lucky then, I suppose,' I said.

Mors tilted his head, white hair brushing his narrow shoulders. 'Lucky?'

'You found your calling. Adventure.'

'Adventure calls to us all,' Mors said. 'I simply chose to follow.'

Chose. I almost laughed. I'd forfeited my right to choose the moment *Leviathan* pulled out of the bay. I'd chosen my sisters, chosen the unknown, chosen life over death. It was a privilege to call survival a *choice*.

I gazed down at the map unfurled between us, admiring the way the land spilled into the sea, the isles that rose from her waters. Mors was right. Adventure called to me; it always had. I could only hope for a day I, too, would be free enough to follow.

Mors rose from his seat and rounded the table, laying a hand on my shoulder. The simplicity of his touch made my eyes burn, so warm and reassuring that I felt somehow closer to home.

'You remind me so much of your mother sometimes,' he said softly.

I knew that I looked like her, but the gentle conviction with which Mors spoke made me wonder just how close they'd been. Made me think the connection I felt to him went more than skin-deep.

I stood to meet his embrace, letting his arms fold around me, letting the smell of parchment and ink drive away my doubts. *He lost all his heirs in one that day.*

'She was your sister too, wasn't she?' I murmured into the crook of his shoulder, my eyes welling with tears. 'You're Oren's missing brother.'

Mors stroked my hair. When he pulled back, his eyes were glistening. Gold, too. 'I wanted to tell you. But I was afraid what you'd think of me. That you might despise me.'

'Despise you?' I echoed.

Mors wiped a tear from my cheek with his thumb. 'Helping your mother escape made me an outlaw. I couldn't go back – couldn't claim my place as Oren's heir, even if I tried. I'm useless to Bane, and he knows it. As much as I want to, I can't save you from him now.'

I shook my head and sniffed. 'I never would've asked you to do that.'

Mors looped his arms around me and once more I let myself rest against my uncle's chest, soaking in a feeling I thought I'd never have again. Comfort – home.

22

My breath billowed as I burst out into the cold, a crimson blur against the startlingly white world. Had it not been for the gentle, swirling downfall of snow, I'd have thought I'd stepped into a painting. It was so soft, so serene, a shifting mosaic of sea foam and sapphire blue.

I watched the flakes spiral downward, smiling as they nested among the curls of my hair and the fur trimming of my cloak. Pirates dotted the deck, huddled around barrels of rum, playing cards and cursing the frigid air.

Aron's voice was loud and bracing against the crisp air as he, Mors and Una sauntered towards me, their boots crunching through the fine layer of frost.

'First snow,' Una remarked dully, squinting up at the bright grey sky.

'No reason not to enjoy it, eh?' Aron chirped, kicking snow at her skirts.

'Ye're dead,' she growled, lunging at him. Aron dodged her attack, bolting behind the mast as she sent handfuls of snow flying. Their laughter rang out as they darted across the deck, launching snowballs through the air.

'Hello,' Mors said warmly.

I took in the guarded look in his eyes despite the smile on his lips. There was something wary there, something trenchant that made me wonder how much more he was keeping from me.

My uncle. There was something hollow in the word when it belonged to King Oren, too. The revelation paled in comparison to how much Mors meant to me already. King Oren could never be my family.

'Good afternoon,' I said, a mirroring smile creeping over my lips. I opened my mouth to say more when the navigation room doors swung open and Golde and Sebastien emerged.

My head snapped towards the quarterdeck. Three days it had been, and still my entire body tensed at the sight of him. Three days since I'd woken in his arms, in his bed – since he'd drained himself to heal me.

I tore my eyes back to the water, my heart beating faster as Sebastien and his first mate's footsteps descended the stairs. There was something sour about the mood they brought with them, casting a gloom over the main deck, dampening the noise of Aron and Una's snow fight.

Before I could gather my thoughts, Sebastien was there, his dark gaze slipping curiously between Mors and me.

'Give us a minute,' he said, jerking his chin at Mors. My uncle glanced at me, questioning.

'I'm fine,' I said, waving him off reassuringly.

Mors turned slowly and headed towards Golde, saying something to her in a low voice. I watched them go, before dragging my gaze reluctantly back to Sebastien.

He waited until I did, eyebrow quirked slightly. The dark growth along his jaw was getting longer and I itched to run my fingers through it, to feel the coarse hair beneath my palms.

I glanced away. 'How're you feeling?' I asked.

He stepped closer, still watching me with the same expression, halfway between grave and bemused. 'Better now. I see Mors finally told you the truth.'

I bristled. So he'd known. Of course he had. There were no secrets in this place, only between the crew and me. 'No thanks to you,' I muttered. *You could've told me.*

'Aren't you happy?'

'Of course I am,' I sighed. 'In this sea of strangers, I found a part of my family, yet—'

'*Strangers,*' Sebastien echoed. 'Is that what we are to you?'

He fell back a step and I cursed my body for arching with him, mourning the space between us. 'I didn't mean it like that.'

Two and a half months ago, that was exactly what we'd been. Strangers. Yet there I stood, all logic stifled beneath an ocean of shadows. Mors, my uncle. Una, my friend. Aron – less of a stranger than anyone I'd ever met. They were pirates, yes, their lives steeped in blood and chaos, but also loyalty, love, joy . . .

Before I could say anything more, something cold and hard struck my shoulder. I yelped and spun around to see Aron duck behind a stack of barrels. I cursed, stifling a laugh as I bent down to scoop icy slush into my hands and launch it in his direction.

Sebastien shook his head in exasperation, but Mors was quick to my side, sending a lump of snow hurtling straight for Aron's stomach. Only then did Una swing down from the rigging, pelting snow over our heads.

I squealed, my cries turning into laughter as our battle

continued, stretching on until sunset gleamed against the verglas, turning the deck gold. The crew's spirits only heightened as the moon emerged and we tumbled inside, shaking snow from our hair and tracking wet footprints through the halls.

Una pulled me into a chair by the hearth in the dining room, insisting she needed to *do something* about my hair.

'Ye look far too much like a princess still,' she said, skilled fingers working quickly to weave small braids into my curls. The crew gathered around the table behind us, far enough away that their conversation became indistinguishable from the crackling flames.

'So,' she began, her fingers twining through my hair in a steady rhythm. A single word and my skin already singed with embarrassment. 'Sebastien . . . ?'

'It's nothing,' I muttered, knowing full well she wouldn't let me leave it at that.

Una's fingers stilled in my hair. 'Told ye – I've lived here almost a decade and the man's never once shown his face to the crew,' she said. 'It ain't nothin', lass. Not to me.'

I bit my lip.

You scare me, too, blackbird. He'd said that – that he was afraid of me. I shook my head. 'I mean it. You know who he is, what he's like.'

Una tied off the braid she was working on with a length of string and perched on the arm of the chair, her citrus and wood smell filling my nostrils. 'Nothin' good's ever easy,' she said, nudging my shoulder.

Good? What good could come from a place like this? From a man like him? I wrapped my arms around myself with a shrug. 'He's a monster,' I whispered, my last defence in a battle I'd stumbled into unarmed.

'A monster he migh' be,' she said, a wicked gleam in her gaze. 'But he's a man in the ways that count, if ye know what I—'

'I know what you mean,' I snapped, cheeks flaming. 'But haven't you seen his eyes? You can't explain away a darkness like that.'

'The colour don't mean nothin', lass,' Una insisted. 'It's what ye see in 'em that matters.'

I threw a glance behind me, catching Sebastien's gaze for a moment, those glittering depths spearing through me like iron. My mind filled with visions of him, of his lips, his hands, his voice.

I looked away. 'It can't – I can't.'

Una's brows inched slowly higher. 'Ye're a bad liar, even to yerself.'

'Who made you the expert?' I asked begrudgingly.

Una shook her head with a half-smile. 'I've been wi' a lotta people, lass. I know how they work.'

Her eyes drifted past me, to the crew gathered around the table. I followed her gaze, to see Aron grinning at something Mors had said.

'What about him?' I asked.

Una shook her head, braids falling across her face, eyes dropping to her lap. 'Not him. No – never him.'

I softened, resisting the urge to reach out and hug her. I remembered the way she'd spoken about Golde and Mersey, about how time had torn them apart.

'I don't want it to be like that,' I said quietly.

'Like what?'

'Impossible.'

'It wouldn't be,' she said, the reflection of the embers burning in her gaze.

'How could you possibly know?' I whispered back, admiring the slope of her features in the flickering light.

She pursed her full lips. 'I know love,' she said after a while. 'I know Aron loves me. Maybe not the way I want – but he gave me a home here, kept me safe. From a bad place, bad people. When Sebastien learned how they'd treated me . . . he went back there and tore that place to the ground. Barely a soul alive who's ever hurt someone Sebastien loved. Except Bane.'

I suppressed a shudder. 'You think that's love?'

Una shrugged. 'He's not so monstrous, really. Fer a pirate.'

I stared into the flames again, something nagging at the back of my mind. 'Whale Rock,' I said slowly. 'That's where you came from?'

Una nodded, her eyes downcast. *No one's lived there in years.* I shivered, not wanting to imagine all the ways the Heartless King had turned that place to ruin.

I'd see it for myself soon enough. The *Blood Rose* was set on her course, the crew determined to sail into a battle we all knew they wouldn't come out of unscathed. As for me . . . I was trying my hardest not to think about what I'd do next. What kind of choice I might have to make.

Before my worries could take root, Aron approached, bending over me to twirl a tendril of my hair around his finger. 'Looks good, lass,' he said with a wink.

Una shoved his shoulder. 'Don't ye be winkin' at her like that,' she scolded.

Aron grinned, deceptively playful, given the way he stilled at her touch. We walked to the table together and I slid into the seat beside Sebastien, fighting the urge to look at him.

'Nobody talk to me 'til I've eaten,' Golde grumbled, reaching forward to pile an obscene amount of food on to her plate. She appeared in even worse spirits than usual and I could only assume it had something to do with whatever she'd spent the day discussing with Sebastien. She shovelled forkfuls into her mouth, barely pausing to swallow.

'*Pirates*,' Mors muttered, echoing my thoughts with a smile.

Aron pulled a bottle from the centre of the table and uncorked it. The green glass sparked light through the dining hall, dark liquid sloshing as he filled his goblet to the brim. Una took it from him and did the same, mischief gleaming in their eyes.

'Trick is to be drunk 'fore the cold can get ye,' Aron explained, taking a long swig.

'Cheers to that,' Una echoed, passing me a full chalice before she poured another for herself.

I sniffed the rum hesitantly, its rich, spiced aroma filling my nostrils. I glanced up at Sebastien, watching the dip of his Adam's apple as he drained his goblet in a single gulp and slammed it back on to the table.

He stared at me from beneath his lashes, drawing me into his gaze. The clamour of the crew faded until I could hear nothing but the blood in my ears and see nothing but him. The rum burned my throat as it slid down – but even more scorching was the look on Sebastien's face as he watched me. He raised a hand, dragging a thumb across his lower lip to catch a bead of liquor, eyes drinking in my reaction.

My stomach tightened. I tore my gaze from his before my desire could light my eyes for the whole table to see, biting my lip to chase away a wry smile.

I ate in silence, listening to the brewing argument between Aron, Una and Golde over which of them could stomach the most drink. Drink which, steadily, they were going through by the bottle.

'The last time ye had a dozen drinks, ye were sick all o'er me!' Aron roared.

'Ye're one to talk, ye flea-bitten swine,' Una yelled back, pelting a boiled potato at his head. 'Who was it that had the whole crew swabbin' the decks when he couldn't keep down a bottle o' rum?'

Aron laughed uproariously. 'Oh, we'll see tonight, lassie. Ye won't survive the swim and I won't save ye when ye're drownin'.'

Una scoffed. 'We'll see who's *drownin'* when I'm holdin' yer head underwater.'

'Ye'll be out cold 'fore ye get the chance,' he said, shaking his head dismissively.

Golde snorted. 'Aye. Don't ye think we've a *fair* bit more experience than ye, lassie?'

Una crossed her arms over her chest, muttering something beneath her breath about *damned* and *ancient bastards*.

'Fancy joinin' us, lass?' Aron asked, turning his attention to me.

I choked. 'To swim?' I looked around the table at the crew's amused faces. 'In the ocean? At this time of year?'

'They do it every winter,' Mors explained with a roll of his eyes. 'No one's drowned yet, but – well, we can always hope.'

'So, ye up fer it?' Aron pressed.

Una shot him a glare. 'She's a *princess*, Aron.'

'Aye, a princess who could outswim all yer lily-livered arses,' Golde remarked, her voice low in the dim light.

I glanced over at her, meeting those dark, angular eyes. 'I doubt anyone would call me a princess now,' I said, taking another sip of rum, relishing its heat. I didn't need Aberdeen here to tell me that *princesses* didn't drink with pirates and sleep in the bed of their king.

Aron's eyes twinkled. 'No reason ye can't join us, then.'

'Leave it,' Sebastien growled, cutting through their lively chatter. They were the first words he'd spoken all night, and I shot him an indignant glare, hating the way my heart jumped at the sound of his voice.

'You know, I think I will,' I said, turning back to Aron.

Sebastien eyed the goblet in my hand with a smirk. 'I think you've had enough of that,' he observed.

'I thought pirates were *supposed* to get drunk,' I retorted, taking another sip.

He looked unimpressed. 'Is that so?'

Aron snickered. 'Aye, she's one o' us now.'

Sebastien arched a brow at me. 'Think you're a pirate, do you?'

I glanced across the table and grinned at Aron over the rim of my cup. 'A wise man once told me that a pirate needs only three things,' I replied wilfully. 'Rum, war and – well, I've practically had them all.'

Una spat out her drink with a loud snort. Aron thumped her on the back, the pride in his smile making my heart swell. Even Mors shook his head with a chuckle, cheeks flushing as he glanced down at his plate.

'Aye.' Sebastien shot me a wry look, inclining his head. 'Drink, then.'

23

S tumbling out into the frost, I understood why the crew had been so eager to fill their bellies with rum. I thanked the gods for its buzzing heat as the icy moonlight caught me in its fist, turning my skin inwards, my breath misting the air.

The effects of the alcohol caught up with me quickly, tripping up my footsteps as I walked. Sebastien's hand shot out to steady me, his long strides keeping pace beside me. I tried to brush him off but my steps steered me closer to his side, absorbing the warmth from his body.

Aron and Una wandered a few steps ahead, howling with laughter at something the rest of us had missed.

We stopped beneath the mainmast, the crew tossing their weapons into a pile and kicking off their shoes. Golde cried the order to *heave to* and drop anchor before she darted up the ratlines in a flash, disappearing into the darkness.

Una grinned, nudging my ribs. 'Watch this.'

We turned our gazes up as the first mate's dark silhouette appeared against the crimson mainsail. She straightened, unwavering, and launched herself backwards into the breeze. I watched in amazement as Golde arced over our heads and plunged into the waters below. Moments later, a black shape re-emerged, inky hair wavering around her like seaweed.

Pirates dove off from all sides of the deck, their splashes puncturing the air. Others, the old and injured, gathered to stand watch, Mors among them.

Una went next, a beam plastered on her face as she ran full tilt towards the gangway, bare feet thumping against the wood. She vaulted into the air, her whoop of delight warming the frost.

My laughter followed her as I slipped off my outer layers and leather boots, feet meeting the biting cold planks.

'Blackbird.' Sebastien's hand was warm on my waist, pulling me towards him, away from the water's call. 'You're drunk,' he said, voice flat as the sea.

I leaned into his chest, looking up at him with a pout painting my lips. 'And you're no fun.'

A muscle feathered in his jaw, but I turned away before he could say anything more. Aron was waiting a few steps ahead, his eyes silver in the moonlight.

'C'mon,' he called, hand extended.

I followed, excitement bubbling in my chest. I longed to feel the air sweep around me, to glide through it as Golde had; to fly.

'Climb them ratlines, lass. Like I showed ye,' Aron instructed, guiding me as I pulled myself up the shrouds, the ropes coarse beneath my icy toes. He followed close behind, arm extended to catch me if I lost my footing.

I could sense Sebastien watching from below, the sounds of the crew fading behind us as we climbed higher and higher. It felt much further than it had looked from the deck and my arms were tiring.

'Almost there,' Aron encouraged, grasping hold of the yardarm and hoisting himself on to it. He reached for my hands as I clambered up after him and rose unsteadily to my feet, relying on Aron's wiry arms to keep me from falling. The sky yawned around us, endless and speckled with stars. I couldn't tell where it ended and where the sea began.

I resisted the urge to jump then, to leap into the abyss, and took the length of rope that Aron pulled towards us, a loose brace hanging from the spar above.

The pirate wound an arm around my waist, pulling me tight against him. 'D'ye trust me, lass?'

I looked up at his bearded face, the scar that ran down his cheek, the smell of rum and sweat and salt that clung to him. I nodded.

He grinned again. 'Hold tight and don't let go 'til I say.'

My hands tightened around the rope. Before I knew what was happening, Aron pitched us from the yard and into the sky. We swung out, the night sweeping through my lungs.

'Now,' he yelled, when the darkness was all around us, the sea stretching below.

I let go.

A scream leaped from my throat as I hurtled towards the waves, clutching my knees to my chest just in time as I plunged into the glacial water.

For a few glorious moments, the sea was all around me. I looked up, seeing the faded moonlight against the surface, the silhouetted figures of the crew, a world filled with laughter and starlight.

We see you.

I whipped around. There was a voice, one separate and the same from the sea. I saw nothing but darkness, until the water rippled around me, taking shape – bodies, faces, morphing from a twist in the current. Laughter sounded, a tinkling somehow unmuffled by the chasmic, choking water. I met the gaze of another, so human yet made from nothing but waves, its gentle face purling ever-closer as it swam towards me.

We see you, they said again, speaking as one. *We watch you.*

They smiled, and the tug of the deep in my chest grew stronger than ever.

Who are you? I tried to say, but the ocean swallowed my words. The spirits continued to circle me, their eyes bright, beckoning me to play.

My lungs burned. I fought the urge to open my lips, to gulp down a mouthful of the sea I knew would drown me, every part of me arching inwards, craving air.

I broke through the surface, gasping. Ice-needles pricked my face, the taste of salt sharp on my lips.

The three pirates lazed across the waves ahead of me, oblivious to the movement below the surface. I glanced wildly around me at the calm, endless sea. No sign that anything was stirring, that anything made a home in it but us.

I watched the crew, resisting the urge to dive below again. Una scooped water in her palms and tossed it upwards, scattering droplets of moonlight across the surface. A vicious water fight ensued, the horizon erupting with their cries and splashing limbs. Una screeched, clambering on to Aron's back in an attempt to submerge him, their laughter loud enough to fill the sky.

I smiled, watching from a safe distance, my hands raking through the water, relishing the feeling of the ocean between my fingertips, smoother than silk. I'd never seen the crew look so happy, so relaxed. Glowing, beneath the stars.

I glanced up at the hull of the *Blood Rose*, the colossal figurehead towering above, her arms outstretched, drooping rose tresses pouring from her hands. I could scarcely see Sebastien from so far below, but I could *feel* him, his power, like a beacon of shadow.

'C'mon!'

Una's yell tore my attention away. The crew's heads were tipped towards their king as he emerged by the railing above. I squinted, watching as he shed his coat and boots and stepped up on to the balustrade.

He dove gracefully, gliding into the water with the ease of a fish. The sea rippled, welcoming him into its fold.

I had to remind myself to breathe every few moments as I waited for him to resurface. I wondered what he saw down there; whether the waves showed themselves to him like they did me. Whether they loved or feared him, or both.

He appeared right in front of me, water cascading down his face and shoulders as he emerged, rising god-like from the ocean depths. I exhaled, my breath blooming in a cloud of frost.

Sebastien moved as fluidly in the water as he did on land, gliding closer with his gaze locked on mine. His shadows curled around me, anchoring me amid the vast ocean. Darkness swirled in his eyes, discomfiting in the way they always seemed to see something I couldn't.

'Look up,' he said.

I did, and my breath caught in my throat. Stars domed the sky, a sea of their own. I tipped my head back, treading water as I gazed up in wonder at the infinity of the night. A glimmer of light streaked across the darkness, a flash of dying worlds.

I gasped. 'Did you see that?'

Sebastien's lips curved slowly into a smile. 'They say if you see a star fall, the gods will grant you a wish.'

My mind ticked over the possibilities, the endless things I could ask for, given a little magic of my own. To see my family again, to feed them, to protect the crew from Bane's army . . . All those things, all those fates strung in the balance.

I pushed away from him and submerged myself once more, welcoming the stillness, the silence. Wishing the world would go away, just for a moment.

The heat in Sebastien's eyes still pulsed through me as I swam, a reminder of the few things I didn't want to forget. There was nothing but ocean between us, his shadows winding like vines through my body.

When I re-emerged, the crew called for us to return to the ship and I swam slowly, reluctantly, to meet them. Water flowed like wings from my back as I rose from the sea, climbing into the tender they'd winched down from the deck. The others tumbled in after me, a mess of drenched clothes and frostbitten flesh.

Una squashed in beside me, wrapping her arms around my shivering body. We clutched at one another for warmth as the small boat was hauled up the *Blood Rose*'s hull, the air turning to ice in our lungs. Golde cursed furiously, gathering her weapons and shoes as soon as we reached the deck and racing indoors.

'See ye later, lass,' Una said to me with chattering teeth. 'Stay warm.' She placed a sloppy kiss against my cheek and disappeared with a wave, Aron close at her heels.

The deck was near-empty by the time the doors shut behind them. I turned to find Sebastien's gaze locked on mine. I wrapped my arms around myself, rubbing my shoulders to create friction. My dress was plastered to me, seeping icy water into my bones.

'So,' he said quietly, inclining his head to indicate I should follow him to the quarterdeck. 'What did you wish for?'

I chewed my trembling lips, too cold to think. 'I *wished* I hadn't been foolish enough to go into that godsforsaken water,' I grumbled, hurrying after him.

He turned a few steps from the sterncastle, advancing on me until I backed up against the mizzenmast. He raised an arm over my head, chest brushing up against mine. I made a sound of protest, but he was the only warm thing in the world and my greedy hands tugged him closer.

'You going to give me a proper answer?' he asked, a gentle menace in his voice that made my toes curl against the frozen wood.

I watched the water droplets trail over the hollows of his throat, lost for words. When I didn't reply, he leaned in, thumb tugging at my bottom lip, brushing heat along its curve. My lips parted, breath clouding the air between us. His gaze travelled down my neck, sending chills rippling across my collarbones.

'What're you doing?' I whispered.

His eyes flickered back to mine, so dark they made my lungs seize, the frozen air knocked from them.

'Nothing,' he murmured, so close I could taste his answer. My traitorous body pressed against him, his chest warm through the wetness of his shirt.

My mouth fell open at the brush of his tongue, my frustration melting into a pool of desire that nested at my very core. His mouth grazed mine, lips soft and warm and inviting ... I placed a hand on his chest, my mind swimming with rum and desire and the echo of the sea, fighting my own body for control, for the strength to resist him.

Nothing, I'd told Una. As if kissing him wasn't like standing at the precipice of a cliff. As if his lips didn't make me feel like I was falling – through shadows, through oceans, through time.

Sebastien's forehead brushed mine. 'You can't hide from this, blackbird,' he said. 'Believe me, I've tried.'

'Maybe you should try harder,' I breathed.

His smirk was fleeting, the weight of his gaze growing heavier. We both knew I didn't want that.

Gods, this was getting dangerous.

He sighed, dropping his arm from above my head. I swallowed, missing his touch the moment it was gone. Sebastien backed away and pulled open the doors to the navigation room. Light flooded out, illuminating him as he stood there, watching me with an unreadable expression.

'Coming?'

I sighed. *Obviously*.

I brushed past him and hurried inside, the ice of the outside world releasing its hold on me. The room was warmly lit with oil lamps that eased the chill from my skin. I strode towards the table, circling it slowly. Beneath the clutter, that ancient map was still spread across the surface. I traced a finger down to the forgotten isles clustered at the mouth of the Channel.

'That's it, isn't it?' I asked quietly. 'Your home.'

Sebastien approached me from behind. 'Aye,' he said, pushing my wet hair aside and kissing the top of my shoulder. My heart skipped, as it did at every mention of the Sinking Cities, every crumb of new information I gleaned – every time he touched me, too.

I studied the map for a moment longer, trying to ignore the heat of his fingers as they trailed down my arms, wondering how it had all slipped away. His kingdom, his people . . . what had become of them? Centuries had passed and still he roamed the seas. Why? What had the sea gained by taking it away?

I turned to face Sebastien, leaning back against the table. 'Do you miss it?'

He didn't meet my gaze, eyes focused on his hands as they traced the curve of my bodice. 'Every day.'

Every day, for *three hundred years*.

I caved, leaning in to cup his face in my hands. His lips were there to meet me and I tasted the centuries of longing twined in his fervent kiss.

I didn't let go until it felt as though my lungs might burst, burying my face in the curve of his neck. It was still damp from the sea and I inhaled, breathing in rainstorms and wind and salt.

'You smell like poetry,' I whispered.

Sebastien laughed. 'You're definitely drunk.'

I wasn't drunk. At least, I didn't think so. If I was, I wouldn't have felt everything so vividly. Wouldn't have noticed the slight crook in his nose, the pool of shadows between his collarbones, the way the sunspots on his chest seemed to spell my name.

'I wished I could be happy like this again.'

The words escaped me before I could stop them, before I could stop my soul from baring itself to the Heartless King. The rum urged them from my lips, telling me his skin was a safe place to bury secrets.

Maybe I am drunk.

His hand found my chin, lifting my gaze back to his. For a long moment, he seemed to mull over his words, sifting through those too dangerous to say aloud.

'You will be,' he said finally. 'I promised you freedom. The moment this is all over, you'll be home.'

Disappointment settled heavily in my chest. I shook my head, forehead pressed to his sturdy chest. 'You're so convinced I'm going to make it through this at all.'

His rough hands slid back down my arms, sending shivers up my spine. 'You're stronger than you realise.'

I fought the urge to laugh. Strong? I was soft, gentle. *Weak.* Even Father had known I couldn't handle the truth about my own identity.

Sebastien threaded his fingers through mine. 'These hands,' he murmured. 'You think you're weak, but these hands killed a monster most would cower before. These hands pulled me from the depths of the sea when they should've let me drown. You don't think there's strength in that?'

I looked up at him, finding admiration in his eyes where I'd only ever expected to see darkness. Before I could reply, Sebastien's gaze shifted to something caught in my hair. He reached up to draw it out, bringing it between us. A single, withered petal.

I glanced up at the vines wreathed through the limbs of the chandelier over our heads. The wine-red rosebuds were browning, the leaves gnarled.

I opened my mouth to ask him what was happening to them, when something flashed across his gaze, something almost like pain, and my lips fell closed again. He was always hurting – always. For once, I didn't want to press.

Sebastien opened his fingers, letting the petal flutter to the ground between us. His hands moved to my hips, pulling me closer, and I reached out to slip a hand beneath the shirt plastered to his skin. I trailed my fingertips down the sinewy planes of his stomach, feeling a shudder pass through him.

I'd read enough books to know that killing a monster was far easier than taming one. But as my fingers circled lower, Sebastien's eyes slid shut and a soft groan fell from his lips. It was hypnotising, watching him melt for me.

His mouth parted, hands skimming up my sides. I tilted my chin to meet him, lips hovering a hair's breadth from his, our breaths mingling.

'Tell the fleet to stop killing.'

Sebastien's eyes blinked open, diluted with longing. 'What?'

'Send word that you won't harm those who resort to the seas, no matter who raises their swords against you,' I said softly. 'Teach them mercy.'

I felt the huff of his laugh against my cheek, his hands tightening on my hips. 'Aye, all right.'

I inhaled sharply. 'Do you mean it?'

Sebastien nodded, fingers gliding up my spine, into my hair, pulling my mouth to his. 'Whatever you want, blackbird. It's done.'

His words unfurled in my stomach, his voice rich as velvet, harsh as a cliff face. He was crumbling, I realised. From my touch.

His head dropped low, our noses bumping as I brushed my lips lightly over his. A heady meld of lust and power swirled in the pit of my stomach as I peeled my chemise over my head, letting his hands chase away the frost.

His eyes widened, throat moving as he swallowed. He kissed my forehead, the bridge of my nose, the corner of my mouth.

I ran a hand back up the exposed skin of his stomach and he looked down at me, tilting his head.

'I want to look at you,' I whispered, trying to stifle the heat rising in my cheeks. I wanted to see him the way I had once, his back drenched in light, shadows speared by the sun's glow. I wanted to see all of him.

His lips twitched, apparently satisfied, before he began to undress with slow, fluid motions. I glanced away as he shed the last of his clothes, my cheeks burning hotter.

'Look.'

I did, letting my eyes linger on his silhouette in the candlelight. And I thought: no wonder so many had bowed before him. He truly was a thing of glory. Staggering, brutal glory.

His breaths were shallow in my ear as I trailed a hand down his great, marbled chest, hunger growing inside me with every passing moment.

'Gods, Ria, not like that.'

I glanced up at him, confusion lacing with my desire.

He grasped me lightly by the chin, stepping even closer and kicking aside his discarded clothes. 'Unless you want me to finish before we've even begun,' he murmured, 'I suggest you don't look at me like that.'

I bit my lip. 'Like what?'

Sebastien's hooded gaze searched mine. His eyes were the exact shade of the night, an ocean encompassed in their depths. 'Like . . . I might be the most beautiful thing you've ever seen.'

'You might be,' I whispered.

His breathing shifted – quickened. He took my hand, sliding it up over his chest to the place his heart should've been. His skin was warm and supple despite the hard muscle beneath, but there was no sound, no gentle rhythm against my fingertips.

'Wish you could feel what you do to me,' he rasped, before capturing my mouth in a kiss that burned like fire.

I tugged his lower lip between my teeth, a groan melting from his tongue. His satisfaction hummed, making his chest vibrate under my touch.

He pulled back a fraction, looking down at me with the eyes of an abyss. The coal in them flashed bright, but his voice was hoarse when he spoke. 'Tell me you want me.'

I grinned. 'Why don't you make me?'

24

When I woke, my entire body ached.

I groaned loudly, burying my face in the pillows, pushing Sebastien's hands from my waist. My mouth was dry, lips cracked, and my head throbbed with the ferocity of a thunderstorm. I thought I might die of thirst, but the pounding in my head told me not to move. Not until the world stopped spinning.

Sebastien stirred, but still I didn't budge, the weight of the skies pressing down around my skull. After a few moments, he nudged my ribs and I pulled myself upright, stomach lurching.

He sat beside me, holding out a wooden cup. 'Drink.'

I took it and drank eagerly, the water trickling down my chin, but I didn't care.

'Better?' he asked, watching with a smirk as I wiped my mouth with the back of my hand, passing him back the empty mug.

'Marginally,' I grunted.

Sebastien chuckled. The rawness of his laughter resonated in my chest, making me forget, momentarily, my discomfort. I stretched out my tired limbs as he set the cup down and lay back, fingertips whispering down the ridge of my spine. It was still early — too early to be awake. The room was streaked with soft blue light, the first herald of dawn, and already the sun felt too bright, too intrusive.

I sank back into him, nestling my face in the bridge of his shoulder. My fingers skimmed over his torso, my body sluggish, limbs heavy from exertion, threaded with an unfamiliar ache.

Outside, snow fell. Frost licked the windows and the fleecy clouds gathering at the sea's end promised something even colder to come. My eyes travelled to the roses wreathed through the canopy as a petal parted from its stem and drifted, red as blood, on to the mattress beside me.

Something in my stomach grew heavy at the sight. Why were they dying?

Sebastien shifted beneath me and I looked up to find his gaze trained on my face, burning away the last embers of sleep.

'What're you thinking about?' he asked, voice sweeping through the quiet room.

'Just . . . everything,' I mumbled.

His arms tightened around me. 'That isn't a proper answer.'

I tipped my head up and shot him a triumphant smile. 'Well, now you know how it feels.'

I felt his answering laugh in every part of me. I pressed my face back against his rumbling chest, unable to shake my smile. We lay in silence for a long time, cocooned in warmth beneath the slowly descending petals.

I skimmed a hand up his chest, coming to rest over his ribcage. My fingertips drummed against his skin. There it was — the root of every reason we could never work.

'Is it really gone?' I whispered. 'Are you really . . .' I couldn't bring myself to say the word. *Heartless* had always been an epithet, a title. I'd never imagined it could be true.

Sebastien exhaled, then nodded.

My own heart thudded immeasurably louder. 'How? Did someone . . . cut it out?'

Hair fell across his face. 'Aye,' he said, a new kind of darkness shadowing his eyes. 'I did.'

A chill swept through me, ominous and cold as the frost outside. I tried to picture it, to imagine the Heartless King – then, just a king – on his knees before some monstrous god, a blade in his hand as he carved open his own chest.

'What could possibly be worth your heart?' I asked, my fingernails digging into his skin, into that hollow place, unable to fathom his emptiness.

I felt his lips in my hair, his breath coiling in the shell of my ear as he said, 'There are some things we'd sacrifice anything for.'

I shivered. I knew the feeling; the determination, the courage I'd never possessed before, rearing its head in a moment of need. He was right. I'd risked everything, and I'd do it again.

'Tell me,' I said.

'You can't fix me,' Sebastien grumbled in reply.

'I know.'

His gaze burned deep into mine – he knew what I was asking, which part of him I longed to understand. He took a long, heavy breath and I waited, settling my head against his chest, my heart fluttering wildly. Finally, he spoke.

'When it's quiet at night . . . when the halls are empty and the torches lie dying in their brackets, I think about how my hands were shaking.'

I didn't dare look at him, didn't do a thing but listen. To his words and to the silence that echoed all the way inside him.

'I remember everything about that day. How the wind whipped around me, how the ship rocked, how the blade was cold against my skin. The planks were hard beneath me, unforgiving, as I knelt before Nerida, ready to die.'

He paused, gathering himself.

'At first, it felt like water, like the sea flooding out of me. But it was a hot, red sea, and it spilled across the planks, staining them crimson, giving the *Rose* her new name. With each twist of the knife, I felt it pierce my soul, cutting me open in more ways than one.

'My bones shivered when I broke through, when I tore my chest apart and reached in – my hand dripping with blood as I pulled out my throbbing heart, clutched between my fingers.'

Sunrise bled through the glass, trickling over the hollow cage of his chest. I didn't dare move, didn't breathe.

'I tossed it before me, before the sea, knowing it was no longer mine. Knowing that with every pulse, I was dying, thinking I'd made a worthy sacrifice.'

There was a twist of spite in his voice as he spoke. 'When I woke, I was even darker and more powerful than before. It broke Aron and Golde to see what I'd done – what I'd become – but I never regretted it. Never.'

I bit my tongue, stemming a flood of questions. What magic was *worthy* of this – of an eternity without a heart? I thought of Golde and Mersey, of Aron and his quiet, lonely fear. Which was the true curse? To live alone in shadows, or to love and lose it, five lifetimes over?

'And was it? A worthy sacrifice?' I asked, almost afraid to hear the answer.

'Aye,' Sebastien murmured. 'I was a monster before that day, don't forget.'

I glanced down at his hand on my stomach. I hadn't forgotten.

250

I knew there was no way to forgive the things he'd done, knew he was driven by a darkness I couldn't understand. Knew, and yet . . .

His hand wove into my hair and I let him pull me to him, our bodies moving against one another. I kissed him languidly, relishing in the slow torture of his touch, his long fingers sending shivers from my scalp to the bottom of my spine.

'How does it end?' I whispered when we broke apart.

Sebastien sighed, his breath grazing my lips before he pulled away. He fell back into the cushions, staring up at the ceiling. 'Nerida gets my kingdom,' he said quietly. 'She gets me. Everything I have. She wins.'

The defeat in his voice made my throat close up. 'You called it a curse. Can't you break it?'

He furrowed his brow, looking . . . crestfallen. 'I don't know, blackbird. You've taught me to hope when I've spent the last three centuries doing the opposite. But that . . . that's all it is. Hope.'

My instincts rose up in protest, but the pained look in his eyes told me not to pry any further. Not today.

I thought of the book Mors had given me, the stories of the Sinking Cities, the magic swirling within its pages. I could understand someone giving their heart for a place like that. What I didn't understand was why he didn't return, why he'd stopped fighting, why he spoke as if he'd already lost.

I curled into Sebastien's side, feeling powerless. I didn't know if he'd ever tell me the full story, but there wasn't long left until the solstice – mere days before I'd need to make a decision I couldn't come back from. I was so close to understanding, to getting the answers I'd sought for so long. I could feel myself circling the elusive truth. I just wasn't sure I could grasp it in time.

*

I stirred back awake in the wintry daylight, my head still fuzzy, mouth dry. I reached out into the furs, searching for warmth but finding none. I sat up, glancing around the chamber in confusion. I was alone.

I could hear Sebastien – all of them, voices leaking from beneath the navigation-room door. Their grumbling piled over the top of one another as I stretched, my muscles soft with a satisfying ache.

Dragging myself out of bed, I pulled Sebastien's coat from the back of an armchair and shrugged it on, rolling the thick cuffs past my fingertips. It sat heavy on my shoulders, its weight comforting as I wrapped it tight around myself.

'How long?' Sebastien's voice was muffled, but laced with an urgency I didn't understand.

'Two days,' came Golde's reply. 'The bastard knows.'

Their voices rose all at once, words pouring over one another in outrage. When I heard my name, and Bane's, I padded into the navigation room, too curious to care about my state of undress.

All five of them fell silent the moment I entered. They surrounded the large table, the mood unexpectedly grave. Sebastien sat with his head bowed, facing away from me. But it was clear from everyone else's faces that something was wrong.

Mors' eyes widened when he saw me and I flushed, not missing the meaningful look exchanged between Aron and Una.

'What's happened?' I asked, glancing between them.

Aron was hunched forward, his face crumpled in defeat. Golde sat cross-legged on the table, scratching at its surface with her dagger.

'I won't ruin her like this.' Sebastien's growl shot through me like ice. He didn't so much as acknowledge my presence.

'What's going on?' I asked, more firmly.

Finally, he turned and looked at me. The man he'd been

that morning was gone, shielded behind stony eyes. 'I'm sending you home.'

'Home?' I repeated, the word foreign on my tongue.

Una's hazel eyes glistened with pity. 'We know where Bane'll be now,' she mumbled. 'Probably best if ye . . . don't come.'

The air pulled taut, straining like the breath in my lungs.

Home. The word on Sebastien's lips conjured a far different image from the one I knew he meant. There was no cottage or cliffside that could live up to that. But my family . . .

I stared at Sebastien, wishing he'd look at me again. I could hardly reconcile his rigid posture with the man who'd kissed me back to sleep at dawn.

'Why don't ye let her choose?' Aron grumbled.

'I don't want her here,' Sebastien snapped.

I flinched. Didn't want me walking into battle with him, or didn't want me at all? Those were two very different things.

He stood and stalked towards the doors, throwing them open. Snow billowed in with the breeze. Still he wouldn't meet my gaze.

'Course ye don't,' Golde snarled after him. 'Mer always said ye were a coward.'

I stared in disbelief as Sebastien stormed outside, slamming the doors behind him. A puff of snow spiralled to the ground in his wake and, for once, I felt a chill in the sea air as it swept through me.

My stomach knotted around itself, twisted by anger and betrayal and a sharp, stinging hurt. *I don't want her here.* His words were as bitter as the icy wind, tearing to shreds the memories clutched to my chest. After everything . . .

The crew were all watching me, their eyes bright with expectation, and something that looked awfully, dangerously, like hope.

'I suppose I have you lot to thank for this,' I said, trying not to sound accusatory.

The pirates in front of me baulked.

'Thank us, lass?' Una asked.

'I assume this was your idea. Trying to keep me away from Bane never seemed like much of a priority; now all of a sudden he wants me gone?' Why else would Sebastien even suggest letting me go? Unless he really didn't want me any more.

'Honoured ye think us so noble,' Aron replied, scoffing at the thought. 'But I'd not be parted with ye if I had the choice.'

He hooked an arm around my shoulders, pulling me into his side. I leaned against him, grateful for the sturdiness of his presence when it felt like the world was crumbling around us.

'It's not over,' he said. 'Just go talk to him.'

I disentangled myself. 'Why bother? You heard him. He doesn't want me here.'

Why did they care so much? From the beginning, they'd all seemed so determined to plant seeds of hope in me. But why? And why choose me, of all places, to sow them?

'He don't mean what he's sayin',' Aron prompted. 'Don't let fear get the best o' ye.'

'You're one to talk,' I said, glancing from him to Una. Hating how defensive I sounded.

His jaw clenched, voice so quiet I almost missed it. 'Don't go there,' he warned.

'Well, don't be such a hypocrite.'

Storm clouds brewed in Aron's grey eyes. My second warning. 'I've been livin' three hundred years, lass,' he said. 'I'll take yer advice once ye can say the same.'

I huffed. 'You can't expect me to stay where I'm not wanted.'

I looked between the four of them, their faces pained, Golde's shoulders slumped. Sebastien wasn't the only one who'd shown me how to be happy in a place like this, how to live. Just the thought of leaving them all opened an ache in my chest that threatened to consume me.

I released a sigh. I wasn't going anywhere without at least trying to understand why.

'Fine.'

When I stepped out to face the cold, I saw him. Sebastien sat on the snow-covered steps, staring out at the empty deck. I stood in the doorway for a moment, watching snowflakes drift across his broad shoulders.

He sat with his legs set apart, arms braced against his knees, so deep in thought that he didn't glance up until I stood in front of him. But the warmth I'd come to expect from his presence was missing. He remained stiff, unresponsive.

We stewed in silence for a moment longer, two stark figures in a dome of white. But my need for warmth wore down my patience and I moved closer, nudging my way between his legs to fix him with a waiting stare.

Sebastien gave in a fraction, reaching out to graze his fingers down my sides over the folds of his cloak. So lightly, as though he didn't dare touch me properly. It only made me colder.

I lifted my chin, gaze sharpening. 'What changed?'

'Nothing's changed.' His reply was icy as the frost. He faced the horizon, eyes fixed on something that wasn't there. Goosebumps prickled down my arms.

'You're pushing me away.'

Snow swirled in Sebastien's gaze, a dark mirror to the world around us. 'We can't pretend that this won't break us any more,' he said. 'Can't have a princess thinking she'd have a better life with pirates.'

'Don't call me that.'

He exhaled. 'You don't want the title, so go home,' he said dismissively. 'Before it's too late and you end up a pawn to a man who cares about you even less than I do.'

'You're unbelievable,' I snapped, fighting the urge to laugh and cry all at once. His words stung too much to admit. I thought about the cottage, about my sisters' empty stomachs and our father's empty coffers. I couldn't turn my back on them. But I couldn't pretend a future there could ever make me happy, not now that I knew what it actually meant.

'We'll reach Whale Rock in two days,' he said. 'Bane will be waiting with an army, like you said. I can only protect you from him for so long. It's better if you're gone before things . . . get worse.'

I opened my mouth, then closed it again. 'If this is your way of trying to save me,' I said after a moment, 'why don't you just say that?'

'What does it matter?' Sebastien snapped. 'Do you want to see your family again or not?'

'Of course I do!'

'Then *go*. This might be your last chance.'

Any sane person would've left the moment he suggested it. Turned and run. But it had become glaringly obvious over the past few months that I hardly qualified as *sane*.

'How many more need to die before you let go of this damned vendetta?' I pressed. 'You'd really give up everything just to kill a man who betrayed your trust?'

'Can't let go,' he muttered. 'Not even for you.'

I took a deep, steadying breath. Nothing was going to convince him – any of them. For whatever reason, they were sailing into this battle like they had nothing to lose. But if I could find Bane first, try to negotiate with him, maybe I could save them. Save *someone* . . . I shook my head, chasing back those thoughts. I wasn't going to sacrifice myself for a secret they didn't trust me to keep.

'Does this have something to do with the curse?' I prompted. 'You think the sea might attack again?'

Sebastien clenched his jaw, looking away. 'I've already told you too much. We don't need you any more. Why isn't that reason enough?'

It was the word *we* that cut deepest. I fought to blink back the burning behind my eyes before it could take hold.

Sebastien glanced up at me, catching sight of my expression. 'I'm letting you go before Bane can get his hands on you. He'll be dead by the time you're with your family again and King Oren will never hear so much as a word of any of this. Isn't that what you want – to be free?'

'Yes, but . . .' *Not like this.* I swallowed, glancing down at my freezing hands. *Not when you're in danger.* 'Going back there just doesn't feel like freedom any more.'

'You won't go hungry again, if that's what you're worried about.' Sebastien's voice was almost unguarded again, almost warm. 'I'll give you food, clothes, gold. Whatever you need.'

I leaned into him with a sigh, letting his familiar smell wash over me, warm like sun-baked sand and salted as the breeze. *Why?* I wanted to cry. *Why is this so easy for you?*

He was offering me everything I'd wanted, ten weeks ago: a safeguard against the winter, a way to protect my family. A chance to save them. But given a real wish, and the chance to be selfish, we both knew what I'd ask for.

'Don't do this,' I pleaded. 'Not with me.'

His fingers gripped my chin and pulled my face slowly to his. He kissed me, fiercely – so hungrily that I almost believed he wanted it. Wanted me. And I melted into him, my eyes squeezed shut, desperate to cling to the moment a little while longer. But it was only a moment, and Sebastien tore himself away.

'You're killing me,' he panted, his voice a broken whisper. He ran a hand through his hair, eyes full of anguish.

I traced the line of his stubbled jaw, trying to swallow the lump caught in my throat. 'We're already ruins, remember?'

He shook his head, brow creasing. 'Not you, blackbird,' he said. 'Not yet. And I won't be the one who destroys you.'

I stepped back, cold air cleaving between us. 'Coward,' I hissed, hating the way my eyes burned for him. I knew exactly what he was afraid of – knew he could taste it on my tongue. It scared me, too. 'You can lie to yourself all you want but I don't need protecting. Not from you.'

He looked away. I recoiled, hurt more by his silence than his excuses.

'Fine,' I bit out. 'If you want me gone so badly, have a tender ready and I'll leave tonight. Just know, I'd have fought for you. I'd have given myself over if it meant saving the crew. So don't pretend you're doing this for me.'

I turned on my heel and stormed from the deck, cursing every one of those cruel pirates and my foolish heart for letting them in. How naïve I'd been, to think that the Heartless King, whose destruction threatened the very bounds of my world, wouldn't destroy me, too.

25

The dark sky loomed beyond the windows. Just that morning, it had been a different world entirely – one made bright by something more than the sun. Sebastien had been different, too. Tender, vulnerable. But with the daybreak, the harsh edges of what he was had crept back in.

I slipped his coat to the floor and stepped out of it, into the porcelain tub. Rose petals drifted across the hot water, thoughts swirling through my mind as my fingers traced lazily over the surface. I sank deeper into its warmth, watching the light dance across the ceiling.

It would be my last taste of luxury, one final indulgence before I returned to whatever life awaited me at the cottage. I tried not to imagine what I'd find; whether there would be any money left, any food. Anyone. We'd been getting by a month at a time, stringing out what little we had to last as long as possible . . . *At least we'll be able to face it together.*

I rested my head back against the rim of the tub, limbs softening in the water. The roses that adorned the corners of the room were the colour of wine, their thorns gnarled and uninviting. I wasn't sure when they'd begun to wither — whether anyone else had noticed.

I watched the water evaporate from my arms, steam pouring like shadows from my skin. Sadness tugged at the edges of my mind, but I resisted, refusing to think of everything I was on the brink of losing. If Sebastien wouldn't fight for whatever this was, for what we'd found in each other, then he'd lose me.

I swallowed the lump that rose in my throat at the thought.

Countless lives already lined the sea floor, a blanket woven from corpses, stitched by the very hands that had set my body alight with desire. That I ached for, even now. He had to know it; had to see that I craved him as much as I ever had the sea.

But I'd served my purpose. I'd brought them Bane on a silver platter. Maybe that was all they'd ever wanted. Maybe this *greater good* Mors had spoken of really was just revenge and I'd tricked myself into believing it could all mean something more.

A ribbon of light unfurled from the doorway and he appeared, filling the threshold.

I watched Sebastien's reflection in the window. His presence was like a shift in the wind, his looming silhouette growing as he neared. Even through his echo in the glass, I could see the way his gaze drank in the sight of me, stretched out beneath the water.

I turned around as he knelt by the bath, bringing his face level with mine. He rested his arm on the lip of the tub, the reflection of the water rippling in his eyes.

Steam coiled through the air between us as he reached into the bath and drew out my hand. I watched warily, my frown slipping when he turned my palm outwards and placed a kiss at its centre, so soft it reopened the ache in my chest – speared through it like an arrow. His eyes flickered up to mine and my stomach fluttered.

'I can't love you, blackbird,' Sebastien said huskily. 'Not the way you deserve.'

My heart clenched. Who had mentioned *love*? He was the Heartless King, he was . . . I'd known all along what he was. And yet, when he leaned in, my lips were there to meet his, my eyes closed in blind trust of him. Of his murderous hands and cruel tongue.

His kiss was painfully gentle. I curled my palm into a fist beneath the water, feeling the ghost of his lips against it, as if I could cling on to that snatch of affection. As if it could be enough. The ache in my chest grew and grew.

I sat up to face him properly, water trickling over my shoulders. 'All I ever asked from you was the truth.'

'I know,' he said, catching a droplet that rolled down my chin with his thumb.

'If you want me to go, I'll go,' I whispered. 'Just not like this. Not without knowing why.'

He took a deep breath and let it go, sending a billow of steam towards me. 'Then give me tonight. One more chance . . . I'll explain everything.'

My heart skipped a beat. 'Everything?'

Sebastien's voice was thick. 'No more secrets.'

He slid a hand behind my head, fingers brushing the damp curls at the nape of my neck, and I pressed my forehead to his. Eventually, I nodded, the water rippling with my movement. If this was his way of fighting for me, I'd give it to him. One last chance.

'No more secrets,' I agreed.

Sebastien offered me something too grim to be a smile.

I watched from beneath my wet lashes as he retreated, turning back in the doorway.

'Meet me on deck in an hour.'

The grand doors towered before me, ornate wood carved with swirling rose briars and jagged thorns. It wasn't fear pushing the air from my lungs but a breathless expectancy, the promise of what lay beyond.

Of the truth, at last.

I opened the doors and stepped out into the cool evening air. The dying sun glowed, casting light over everything: the towering masts, the blood-red sails, *him*.

Sebastien stood at the centre of the snow-powdered deck, tall and proud, dressed in a fine white shirt and dark trousers, drenched in the last light of the day. A smile twisted at the corners of my mouth. He looked, I thought, like a king.

His lips parted at the sight of me. I knew what it was – knew why the coal of his eyes had never burned quite so hot, why he was staring at me as though I could eclipse the horizon itself.

I looked like a pirate.

The dark, untamed waves of my hair tumbled down my bare shoulders, over my soft blouse. From the brown leather of my corset spilled layers of fine-spun crimson, skirts of ruby silk that whispered over the steps as I descended, footsteps echoing like shadows in my wake.

But it wasn't my clothes that Sebastien gazed at with all the intensity of the sun. He was looking at *me*, his eyes devouring the light of my own in their reflection, pulling me in – a surging maelstrom of darkness. He must've told the crew to keep below, for there wasn't another soul in sight. Just us, and the waking stars, and the sea.

I crossed the planks towards him, irked by the lingering bloodstains on the wood. They'd disappeared far more quickly after the battle with Cullen's crew.

When I reached Sebastien beneath the branching limbs of the mainmast, my heart sank into the pit of my stomach. The truth of what this was shone clear as the night in his eyes, in the skies of pain that swirled within them. This wasn't just about answers; this was a farewell.

'You can't stay here,' he murmured, answering my unspoken ache. His eyes were still glued to my face, still filled with wonder. 'Even if we had a chance of killing Bane and his army . . . If Oren ever heard you were here, you'd never be free.'

I exhaled slowly. Was it really King Oren he was afraid of? Or me?

My eyes burned at the idea of leaving, of him thinking it was what I wanted. I'd tried to tell him the truth, tried to show him that this life was the only kind of freedom I wanted. But I couldn't say more without betraying everything I'd left behind. Without failing my sisters, who I'd sworn I could protect.

The star-sown blanket of night unfolded above us. Dying petals descended around us, as though the *Blood Rose* wept in tears of crimson.

He reached for me and I folded, my arms circling him as he pulled me into a strong embrace. When he kissed me, it felt like my very soul splintered. It tore me, all the way through.

Sebastien broke away first, pressing his forehead against mine as I gasped for air, struggling to remember that there was more to living than the feeling of his body against mine.

He was right. We'd destroy each other.

'I'm sorry,' he said.

'What for?' I murmured.

Sebastien laughed humourlessly. 'For everything. For making you a prisoner, for keeping you here so long. I was being selfish, I thought . . .'

I waited for him to finish, but he never did. He tilted his head to admire me and I could've sworn, for a moment, his eyes were more stars than night sky.

Sebastien shook his head. 'I should've let you go the moment you told me about Whale Rock.'

'Maybe,' I admitted. It would've made this easier. But I didn't have the strength to be angry. Not when all the secrets, all the frustration, all the fighting, had led us here.

'I want . . .' Sebastien began, his head bowed to mine. 'Gods, Ria, I wish—'

'What?' I took his hand and pressed it to my chest, wishing my heart could beat enough for the both of us.

He swallowed. 'Never mind. What do *you* want?'

Tears slipped down my cheeks. The moon, the stars, the sea; it all paled in comparison to him. I remembered our deal. *No more secrets.* No matter the cost.

'I want to stay.'

My voice broke, and with it, a thousand promises – to my family, my future, myself.

There was a long pause, a stretch of silence and the solitary thunder of my heart.

'Don't say that,' Sebastien murmured, stroking my cheeks with his battle-hardened thumbs. 'Don't ask to stay, because I'm selfish enough to let you.'

'It's not your choice,' I told him. 'This is my home.'

It was greedy, I knew, to want this life when I had another. When I already had a family, one who no doubt mourned me and suffered somewhere far away. It was the life I'd been given, the only one I deserved.

Sebastien gestured around us. 'This isn't home. This is a prison.'

I understood what he meant, what this ship was to him. Beautiful, but bound to the waves. It was all he'd ever wanted, to go home.

'Tell me,' I said, stepping closer. 'Tell me what happened to your kingdom, your people. Why did the sea take them?'

Sebastien drew in a great breath, steeling himself. Whatever he was about to say, I knew it would answer everything. *Everything*. My hands curled tight around his shirt collar, ready to pull the answers out of him.

'I was eleven years old,' he said slowly. 'My father was a brutal man. He . . . I watched him hurt my mother for the last time that day. I was too late to save her – so I killed him. I thought it was vengeance, but all I did was make myself an echo of him, make the seas redder.

'Nerida felt betrayed by the way we'd turned on one another. She was always distrustful of mankind, but our people were sworn to keep her safe. We proved her right not to believe in us.'

Sebastien broke off, his words bitter. He laid a hand at the base of my neck, fingers trembling against my skin. He sighed, and went on. 'In one fell swoop, I became a killer and a king. The sea wanted to take it all back, to drown my kingdom, deny us a place in her world. I swore I could change things, that I'd become the king my people deserved. Nerida gave me a decade to prove her wrong, to show that she hadn't been a fool to entrust us with her tides. But I failed – or so she said. I gave up my heart for another chance to save my people, but . . . it doesn't matter. Even if I could break the curse, I can't go home without a heart. I can't rule them like this.'

I stroked a hand over his cheek, reaching for his brow, wishing I could ease the pain from it, from him. 'But you can,' I insisted. 'You rule now – you have a fleet who follow you. A crew who loves you. You've always been a king.'

He shook his head. 'It isn't the same, blackbird. Our people are – *were* – guardians of the ocean. I became a profiteer, driven by anger and spite and the blood I knew I could never wash from my hands.' His voice broke, springing heat behind my eyes. 'I don't want them to see me like this.'

I swallowed. 'But the curse – you *can* break it? You could go home, somehow?'

The furrow between his eyebrows deepened and he averted his gaze.

'No more secrets,' I reminded him.

'Aye,' Sebastien murmured, his voice burdened by an eternity. 'I was . . . You were right. I'm a coward.'

My heart sped up. 'So, how do we do it?'

'There's nothing to be done, blackbird,' he said, his shoulders sagging. 'In order to break it, to save them . . . I'd need to do something I'm not capable of. I'd need to love.'

Love. Of course that was the answer. But without a heart . . .

I held his stare, understanding at last. Seeing Sebastien for what he was, underneath it all: a boy, with a night sky in his eyes that I ached to fill with stars. I watched him cave beneath the light of my gaze, feeling his breath against my cheek, and my reservations went with him, crumbling.

He kissed me. Kissed me with everything he had, filled with such uncontainable power that I trembled under its weight, sure my heart would've shattered had it not been held so tightly in his grasp. This man who'd torn lives from the coasts, whose murderous hands had tainted the seas red and soothed aches from my skin – all that power, and still it wasn't enough.

I pulled back a fraction, letting a sliver of moonlight carve out the space between our lips. 'Sebastien, I—'

The sound of something wet hitting the deck made me jump. I spun around as a dark figure emerged over the ship's railing, clambering aboard the snow-dusted deck, coughing and spluttering.

My eyes widened in horror — it was just a boy, no older than thirteen or fourteen. I darted past Sebastien and hurried towards the young stranger as he dragged himself to his feet. Hunger was etched in his hollow cheeks. Sopping, ill-fitting clothes clung to his dark skin and his eyes widened when they reached my face.

'It's you,' he breathed.

26

The boy staggered to his feet, scarcely more than chattering bones drenched in salt and seawater, rubbing his shoulders to bring a breath of warmth back into his body.

'Who are you?' I asked, hoarse over the thrashing of my frantic heart.

'My name is Theo,' he answered, voice trembling from the cold. 'The captain sent me to see if you were still alive.'

'Your captain?' I prompted, dread rising like bile in my throat. I looked out to sea, spotting the outline of masts on the dark horizon. *It's too soon*, I thought, trying to swallow my panic. We weren't there yet. The solstice wasn't for another two days.

'Answer quick, lad,' Sebastien growled, coming to stand over my shoulder.

Theo shivered in his sopping clothes, standing tall despite being dwarfed by the Heartless King. 'I don't know her name,' he answered, his voice admirably calm over the chattering of his teeth. 'She sent me to see if you were alive.'

She?

'Why?' I asked. The last thing we needed was a new enemy to fear. I glanced back at the masts drawing nearer on the horizon.

'You'd better talk faster than that,' Sebastien muttered.

I eyed the tension building in his shoulders and stepped between the two of them. 'What does your captain want with me?' I asked Theo, keeping my tone soft despite the pounding of my blood.

The boy shook his head. 'I don't know, I'm sorry. I'm not one of them. A pirate caught me stealing in Bray. This task is my debt.' He glanced sideways at Sebastien, wary. 'The captain told me only to return if the princess was dead. She said you would not kill an unarmed boy.'

Sebastien huffed, still glaring down at Theo. 'If we send you back, will you tell them she's dead?'

'Depends how much you'll pay me.'

I stifled a laugh at the boy's courage.

'Thin ice, lad,' Sebastien grunted, but his anger was hollow. This boy wasn't our enemy, but the ship approaching on the horizon could well be. *A pirate*, he'd said. It had to be Bane – who else?

The frigate breezed through the night towards us, sails bared like fangs.

'We aren't sending him back,' I said firmly. 'He needs warmth. And food – look at him.'

Theo offered me a grimace of a smile. 'Thank you, Your Highness.'

I frowned at the title, pity burrowing itself into my stomach. He was just another pawn caught up in these pirates' games, not so different from me.

Theo ran a hand over his shaven head, glancing between the two of us.

I looked sideways at Sebastien, but before I could say anything, the doors to the deck below burst open and the crew hurried out, their feet thundering up the steps, faces stricken.

'Yer Majesty, we just saw . . . masts on the—' Golde broke off as she caught sight of the gangly boy at my side. 'Ah.'

'Who's this?' Aron asked, jerking his chin at Theo.

'Still working that out,' Sebastien answered, turning to face the oncoming tall ship. 'Think his captain wants to bargain.'

Golde barked a laugh. 'Send me over there,' she said, fingers gliding down the curve of her blade as she watched the approaching vessel. 'I'll bargain 'em into bloody pulps.'

'I say let 'em come,' Una said. 'Little practice 'fore we meet Bane, eh?'

Sebastien nodded. 'Aye.'

This was what I'd wanted. For them to fight for me. But how many would die in the process?

'S'pose it's perfect timin',' Golde snarled, pacing away from us. 'We kill the crew, she gets a free ship to sail herself home on.'

I frowned at the first mate's back. There I was, thinking we'd made some progress.

'Sorry to inform you, but I'm not going anywhere,' I retorted.

Golde halted in her tracks. Aron and Mors both snapped to attention, their eyes widening.

'Ye're stayin'?' Una breathed.

Sebastien's arm encircled my shoulders. I looked up at him, warmth spreading through my chest at the softness of his features.

'So long as whoever this is goes quietly,' I said firmly. 'I don't want any more blood spilled on my account.'

Sebastien leant down, pressing his lips to my temple. I looked over at the crew as a flurry of emotion crossed their faces. Aron's smile was tight; Una's unrestrained. Mors settled back against the mast, a twist of pride to his lips. Was this what he'd wanted? *A strange fate to contrive for your own niece.*

'Doubt yer family'd take ye back anyway,' Golde grunted. 'Ye smell like a pirate.'

I grinned. When she looked up again, I could've sworn there was the ghost of an answering smile on the first mate's lips. She'd have missed me, and she knew it.

Theo shrank back, wrapping his long arms around his skeletal body.

'You must be freezing,' I told him. 'Let me take you inside.'

'Th-thank you,' the boy stuttered, his lips an icy shade of twilight.

'Not happening,' Sebastien cut in, his arm tightening around my shoulders.

I scowled. 'We can't let him freeze to death.'

'I'm not letting you out of my sight until I know who these bastards are and what they're planning.' He jerked his chin at Theo. 'Una, take the lad inside. Give him dry clothes and food, and bring him back when you're done. If he tries anything . . .'

Una nodded, steering the shivering boy back the way she'd come with a reassuring smile, though I knew about the dagger she kept hidden in her boot. If he *did* try anything, I didn't doubt she'd make him regret it.

Theo's posture didn't relax for a moment, but he went willingly, sparing me a nod of thanks over his shoulder.

I watched the others – Golde, Aron and Mors – their faces carved by shadows in the moonlight. I knew then I'd made the right choice. That standing beside them was the only way I wanted to go on. Aron lounged against the port side rail, his easy posture hardened by the prospect of battle. Golde resumed her pacing, the anticipation in her footsteps barely contained. The air grew colder and I pressed closer into Sebastien's side, his arms chasing the shivers from my body.

I leaned my head back against his chest, content to absorb one last moment of peace before it was torn from us. Perhaps *peace* wasn't the right word, but as the mysterious ship approached, the world around us felt calm, tranquil. There were still things to be said, still answers he'd promised, but they could wait.

'They're here,' Aron said at last.

A single galley pulled away from the unknown vessel, drawing across the waves towards us. I could make out a dozen or so bodies crammed on board, their faces obscured by the darkness. It was brave, I thought, to bring so little backup.

More of the *Blood Rose*'s crew emerged from below decks, crowding behind us with their weapons drawn, silver blades slicing moonlight through the air. If it came down to it, I knew it would be a quick fight. One that a dozen sailors had little chance of winning.

'Stay close,' Sebastien muttered as Aron and Mors lowered the rope ladders from the starboard. A more diplomatic welcome than I'd anticipated – but given the bloodthirsty crew waiting on deck, it felt a little hollow.

Shadowy figures emerged over the side of the deck. Their tattered boots met the planks, swords clanking at their sides. My stomach fluttered despite Sebastien's reassuring hand on the small of my back. It was too dark to make out the newcomers' faces and there was no way to distinguish their captain from their equally shabby attire. They weren't soldiers, but they weren't quite pirates, either.

Golde's shoulders rose like the hackles of a wild animal as she slunk towards them. The pirates around me stirred with anticipation, ruffled by the scent of coming battle. I focused on Sebastien's hand, my anchor, reminding myself that nothing could tear me from this place.

But then a voice ripped through the quiet, shattering my resolve – shattering *everything*.

'Ria!'

A figure broke free from the crowd, racing across the deck. There was a flash of raven hair and brown skin and then my sister was there, shoving her way through the crew and barrelling into me. Her chest slammed against mine, long arms pulling me into a ferocious hug, so fierce and full of relief it made my eyes burn.

Aberdeen.

The breath knocked from my lungs, half from the force of her embrace and half from the shock that she was there at all. My arms encircled her and I hugged her back, my disbelief misting the air when I exhaled.

Aberdeen squeezed tighter before she pulled back, her brows pinched. 'What the *hell* were you thinking?' A storm rolled through the pale blue of her eyes as she shook me by the shoulders. 'You should be dead a hundred times over by now. What is *wrong* with you?'

I blinked, unable to grasp what was happening. 'What . . . what are you doing here?' I stammered, when all other words seemed to fail. 'How . . . ?'

Gods. It had been another life – another world – when I'd last seen my sister, never mind that I couldn't remember the last time she'd hugged me. Yet here she was, standing before me with a voice that made everything seem all right, even when I knew it wasn't.

'Quick, we have to go,' Aberdeen said, her words rushed as her eyes darted to the crew around us. They stood with their blades drawn, eyes narrow, but any good pirate could see she was no threat to me then.

'What do you mean? What's happened?'

'I'm here to rescue you, Aurelia,' she said, as though it was obvious. Her gaze darted from me to the crew. To Sebastien. She leant in, voice a frantic whisper in my ear. 'The crew will hold them off for as long as they can. We have to go *now*.'

'Aberdeen . . .' What was I supposed to tell her – that she'd come for nothing?

'She belongs here now.'

Behind us, Aron stood with his shoulders squared, cutlass in hand, ready to fight. I searched for the words to explain to Aberdeen that he was right. That I didn't need to be rescued at all.

It might have been the moonlight, turning her blue gaze grey, but those eyes seemed to harden, like stone. 'You don't understand,' she told me, cold fingers wrapping around my wrist. There was an edge of panic in her voice, one I'd never heard before. 'We have to go . . . Felicie was taken, Father's been arrested. I came to get you. We need to go, *now*.'

My stomach plummeted, all my fears crashing down around me with the weight of the sky. 'Taken? Arrested? But – how? I don't understand.' This couldn't be happening.

Aberdeen's grip on my wrist turned vice-like, tightening until it hurt. 'I was in the village, saw the soldiers come on horseback. They took them both – there was nothing I could do. I promise I'll explain everything later, we just have to go.'

'Go?' I echoed. My knees trembled. Everything was falling apart. 'Go where?'

'To the capital,' Aberdeen insisted, trying to drag me away. 'Father never told you but your mother—'

'I know.' I cut her off, holding my ground. 'I know everything.'

There was something heavy in my throat. Something suffocating. 'They're really gone?'

Aberdeen nodded, her eyes narrowing. Probably wondering how I knew. How I'd uncovered secrets in a place like this. 'Word's everywhere,' she said. 'Father was arrested for kidnapping your mother. They want to see him hanged.'

'*What?*' My knees almost buckled and it took everything I had to stay standing. *Hanged.* The word curled around my sickened stomach, tightening like a noose.

'We have to go, Aurelia,' Aberdeen insisted. 'We have to save them.'

I nodded, finding it hard to breathe. Around us, the air buzzed with bared teeth and grating impatience. I had to go. *I wasn't ready.* I glanced at Aron, at Sebastien, at Mors, then Aberdeen, all of them watching, waiting. How could one heart be torn in so many places at once?

Golde's eyes gleamed, still fixed on the sailors who'd brought Aberdeen across the water, but Sebastien held her back, his lips pressed into a hard line.

I couldn't speak, couldn't choose. Because how could I? How could I live another life after the one I'd found here? How could I turn my back on my *father*?

Aberdeen's gaze slid over my shoulder, taking in the ragged crew who stood protectively around me, restless as the coursing tides. I could only imagine what she saw . . . bloodlust, grime, pointed swords. She drew herself up, resolute in the face of the Heartless King.

'Let my sister go,' she said firmly, a shiver of steel in the moonlight. 'Do one good deed – perhaps the gods will send you to a gentler hell.'

My mouth fell open at her boldness. Even without his cloak, Sebastien was no ordinary man. He was still swathed in legend and shadows and magic, yet my sister was staring at him like she had any right not to be afraid.

'I'm not stopping her,' Sebastien said, but I could hear the restraint in his voice.

The guilt in my stomach spread, swallowing me up. There was no one stopping me, no one standing in my way. Was I really selfish enough to let my father hang without even trying to stop it? The thought made me sick. I held Sebastien's gaze, unable to mask the anguish that raged through me like wildfire. Aberdeen had crossed oceans to find me. The gods only knew how she'd done it, but here she was. Even if I was cruel enough to turn my back on that, I couldn't do it to Father. Never to Felicie.

'All right,' I breathed, my words hitching on the panic that swelled in my chest.

'No!' Golde burst out, rushing forward, but Aron grabbed her wrist, holding her back. I met his gaze, the hurt in it piercing me like a knife through the heart.

Aberdeen shot me a sharp glance, but her iron grip on my wrist disappeared. 'Good.'

'Hold on,' Mors said, striding forward, the lines of his forehead deeper than ever.

'She's my sister,' Aberdeen said, staring down the old man until he stopped in his tracks. 'She belongs with me.'

'What d'ye know about where she belongs?' Golde snarled, shaking off Aron's hold.

Aberdeen glowered at the first mate, unruffled. 'I'm not leaving without her,' she said coolly.

The scrape of Golde's sabre in its scabbard cut through the silence. 'What makes ye think ye'll be leaving at all?'

'Golde,' Sebastien warned quietly.

My heart clenched. How could I simply walk away from him,

276

from this, knowing any day now my crew would sail straight into a war of their own? How could *this* be the end?

The battle raging in my chest made it impossible to breathe. *Don't let me go.*

Sebastien's eyes were like chasms in the world breaking apart around us. He shook his head, almost imperceptibly, telling me what I was too afraid to ask. There was no other way.

I turned back to my sister, struggling to breathe through the pure dread that choked my throat. 'How are you even here?' I asked, eyeing the crew behind her. How was this even possible?

Aberdeen blinked. 'I came to *rescue* you.'

'I know, but Father, Felicie . . .'

'I used what little gold we had to get to Bray, to buy passage to the capital to find them,' she explained brusquely. 'But the ports were riddled with pirates. And, funnily enough, it was *your* name on all their lips. I was so convinced you'd be dead, but . . . I had to be sure.'

Even with Felicie in danger, even when she should've given up on me, she hadn't. I swallowed.

'I knew you'd do anything to help me save them.' Her words were so edged they sounded almost like a warning.

'Of course I will,' I croaked, the words grating on my tongue like sand. A heavy sigh of defeat sounded behind me, but I couldn't be sure who it came from. 'Just let me say goodbye.'

Aberdeen's eyes narrowed again, darting around at the crew. 'We don't have time, Aurelia. We have to go.'

The urgency in her voice sped on my racing heart. *I'm not ready. Not yet.*

'Please,' I whispered, meeting my sister's eyes and hoping that, for once, she'd understand me. 'Just a little while. I need to get my things.'

Things – I had nothing here but them.

I could see the confusion clouding Aberdeen's eyes. How strange it must be, to find me standing firm in the circle of the crew. The old man, the unruly pirates, the savage first mate. The Heartless King himself.

I'd seen the danger in them, once. I saw it still. But there were too many memories fogging the months since we'd met that it was almost impossible to remember.

Aberdeen relented. 'One hour,' she said tersely.

One hour. After that, I didn't know what she'd do. But for Felicie's sake, I didn't want to find out.

27

I stared out from the window of my old chamber, the faint glow of candlelight leaking out into the inky night sky. The galley bobbed on the black water, pulling away from the *Blood Rose* with Aberdeen on board. She'd dragged together some kind of rescue mission from the gods only knew where, using money we didn't have, just to find me. To save me.

Now it was my turn to protect us. To venture into King Oren's outstretched arms and try to twist them in our favour – try to save Father. Even if that meant abandoning my crew, letting them sail into Bane's waiting onslaught without me.

I didn't want to imagine what he'd do when he discovered I wasn't there.

I can't leave them like this. I shook my head for the thousandth time, reminding myself I no longer had a choice.

My eyes travelled the moonlight-dappled room, from the canopy of the bed under which I'd passed so many restless nights to the window through which I'd watched the sea, trying to convince myself it wasn't my home.

Draped across the mattress was the black coat I'd taken from Sebastien's room. I lifted the heavy fabric from the bed and slid my arms through the sleeves, shrugging it on. It smelled of him – of books and firelight and the sea. The thick leather settled around me, an echo of comfort that resounded inside my empty chest.

I rolled up the sleeves as I turned for the door, the coat-tails almost brushing the floor, when I heard footsteps out in the hall. The last person I expected to see was Golde, slouching against the doorframe, dressed in her usual grubby attire, sabre hanging at her hip.

'Hello,' I said, failing to mask the surprise in my voice.

Golde ignored my greeting. 'So,' she said slowly. 'Ye're really leavin'.'

'S'pose you're happy about it,' I remarked.

The first mate shook her head. 'Just impressed ye made it this long,' she said with a smirk. 'Ye might be a fool, and vain as a peacock, and ye haven't got a clue about nothin'—'

I rolled my eyes. 'Is this going somewhere?'

Golde's sable hair gleamed in the silver light. 'I know the rest o' them talk a lot about hope. "S the only reason Mors and Una've stuck 'round so damn long . . .'

I raised a brow, unsure where she was going. 'And you?' I prompted. 'You're just here for the pillaging, then?'

'Aye.' Golde glanced away. 'But if it weren't fer hope . . . Well, I would've killed ye a long time ago, ye know.'

'Nice to hear,' I deadpanned. Like she hadn't tried.

'Not that I'd much hope fer ye anyway. Pathetic, scraggly thing ye were. But if I'd known— Why're ye smiling?' She broke off, fixing me with that familiar glare.

'No reason.' I bit down on my grin. 'I just realised this might be the first time we've spoken without you threatening me with a dagger.'

'We ain't finished yet,' Golde said, already reaching for the blade at her side.

'No, ah – I think we're done.'

'That's what I thought,' the first mate grunted, sheathing her sabre and retreating to the hall. But she hesitated a moment, fingers drumming on her sword hilt. 'Look,' she said with a sigh. 'I came to thank ye.'

'Thank me?'

'Aye.' Golde shifted on her feet, shoulders rigid with tension, jaw clenched. 'Ye reminded him how to live,' she said at last, eyes darting to the floor. 'No matter what happens, I'll always owe ye fer that.'

I glanced at the horizon beyond the windows, trying to hold back the tears that pricked at my eyes. Golde, who was hurting and hid it. Golde, who'd saved me from Cullen's men and tried to stop me from diving into the water after Sebastien. However she felt about me, Aron had been right. She had my back.

'My family needs me,' I choked out.

'Aye,' Golde said, turning back into the hall. 'They do.'

I emerged into the cool night air, each step slower and heavier than the last. When I raised my eyes, I saw them – Una, Mors, Aron and Sebastien were gathered under the moonlight, lined up at the edge of the main deck where Theo and a second sailor waited, looking nervously at their companions. Their ship hovered close by, awaiting my arrival. I was glad Aberdeen wasn't there to watch, to see me break apart my own heart, piece by piece. She'd come so far, fought so hard, and I knew she'd do it all over again for

281

Felicie. I couldn't let her go on alone.

I swallowed, dragging my feet to move where my heart couldn't. Una's cheeks were flushed and tracked with tears as she pulled me fiercely into her arms. I hugged her back, my head buried against her shoulder, inhaling her citrus scent, wishing I didn't have to let go. Wishing the day would end before it had even begun, that the nightmare would be over.

Una pulled back, her eyes soft, molten hazel. 'Won't ye stay?' she asked quietly.

'I can't,' I said, the words bleeding like a lie from my tongue. But I had to believe it. 'I need to save my family.'

Una wiped her eyes with a sniff. 'Just don't go forgettin' me, a'ight?'

I squeezed her hand tightly, trying to draw the strength I needed from her touch. My stubborn heart was still caught in her fractured smile when I pulled myself away.

I looked at Mors next, trying to blink back the tears that blurred my vision.

'You could come with me,' I said wistfully. But we both knew he couldn't. The seas were his kingdom now, and the place I had to go would kill both our souls the same.

'You could stay,' he countered, a hopeless quirk to his lips, hands reaching out to squeeze my shoulders gently, holding me at arm's length. I let my tears splash to the planks as I stared back at the man who'd been family to me when I thought I had none. 'Give my best to your father.'

'I will,' I whispered. The image of Father chained in a cell, slumped and shackled, was the only thing strong enough to drag me on.

I turned to Aron, unable to summon the words – *any* words – to tell him goodbye. So I let him pull me into his chest and wrapped my arms tight around his neck, smelling the sweat and grime that clung to him, thinking how sad it was that I'd never smell it again. I could hear the echo of his laugh in my mind, could picture his crooked smile and hear his voice as he taught me all the ways to be alive.

'You can't be afraid of her forever,' I whispered in his ear, praying to gods I wasn't sure I believed in that he would survive Bane. That he'd live a life worthy of his good, good heart. 'Tell her how you really feel.'

His arms tightened around me and I pressed a kiss to his cheek, his beard tickling my lips. Then I let go, dropping my arms to my sides, taking shallow breaths to hold back the storm inside my breaking heart.

'Be good, lass,' he said with a wink, but the levity of his tone didn't quite reach his eyes.

I didn't trust myself to speak, to open my mouth without unleashing the sobs that welled in the back of my throat. Instead, I patted the inside pocket of the coat where my dagger was hidden and nodded, mustering the strength I needed to take that final step.

The crisp winter night swallowed up my unfurling heartache as I pulled away and turned to face the Heartless King for the last time. I couldn't blink back my tears any longer as I stood before Sebastien, feeling the weight of something unbearable pressing down around us.

'Come here,' he whispered, but I was already upon him, folding into his arms.

Not ready, I thought. *I'm not ready for this to be over.*

I kept my eyes closed as his lips found mine. His kiss was long, torturous, all-consuming. My heart throbbed when we pulled apart; that distance alone was too much – I ached to think of the sea that would soon swallow it.

'Like you in my coat,' Sebastien said, breathing heavily.

Not ready, not ready, not ready.

'Good,' I replied, too tired to bear the weight of my smile. 'I'm keeping it.'

His fingers were in my hair, my gaze captured in his, but it still wasn't enough. Then he pressed his forehead against mine and suddenly it was too much – all too much to bear.

Gods, don't let me go.

Sebastien cleared his throat. 'I owe you something.' He withdrew something from his pocket, holding it out to me. A book.

I looked up at him, lips parting. 'You didn't burn it.'

I took the worn blue novel and clutched it to my chest, knowing where the truth had been hidden all along. Knowing that everything I'd ever wondered was hidden between those final yellowed pages, written centuries ago in ink that would answer my soul.

'Don't read it until you reach the capital,' Sebastien said, his hand curling around my chin. 'Promise me.'

I met his searching gaze and nodded. Nodded because, after everything, I didn't want my last words to be a lie. Then I slipped the novel into the pocket of his coat, feeling its weight against my hip. I only wished there was a part of me I could give him in return.

Long fingers curled around my lapels and Sebastien pulled me close again. 'Whatever happens,' he warned, bending down to my ear, 'don't come back.'

Silent tears tracked my cheeks, but I forced myself to think of Father, of the twined, frost-gripped ropes of the noose that awaited him. Of Felicie, trembling beside a tyrant's throne.

I don't have a choice.

'Whatever happens—' I murmured, but he shook his head, cutting me off.

'This isn't your fight any more, blackbird.' He wrapped his arms around me and pulled me against him, holding me tight, as if he could prevent anything from finding its way between us. What lies we told ourselves. He buried his face in my hair, lips grazing the shell of my ear. 'Told you this would ruin us.'

Salt tears stole down my cheeks. How many more centuries would he go on like this, believing himself incapable of breaking the curse? Of falling in love? Maybe if I'd done more — *been* more — I could've helped him see it. But I hadn't, I wasn't. I was leaving.

Sebastien pushed the hair back from my face, stroking it gently, gingerly. As if I were fragile, as if his rough hands could turn me to dust and wind and send me sweeping away. He tilted his head, a curl of his hair brushing my cheek. I stared at him, feathering a fingertip over his furrowed brow, his jaw, his strong, slightly crooked nose.

'I want to remember you,' I said, eyes tracing every detail of his face I couldn't touch.

His lips ghosted up the curve of my nose, placing a kiss to my brow. 'I'll remember you until I'm dust.'

The softness in his voice was like wrought iron around my heart, constricting until I thought I, too, might disintegrate.

When I glanced up, his eyes were black mirrors of the night. And when he kissed me, I tasted the ocean on his lips. But whether they were his tears or mine, I couldn't tell.

I disentangled myself first, when the pain in my chest felt like it might rip right through me, wiping my cheeks as I backed away, my heart beating savagely in my chest.

Don't, it begged me, as my feet pulled me to where Theo waited. I swung myself over the railing, ropes rough beneath my palms. *Don't go.*

But I'd seen what time did to lovers like us. Seen it in Golde, in Mersey, in Aron. I'd be old and grey, and Sebastien would stay just as he was. Just as I wanted him, until I'd hate him for wanting me, too.

I gripped Theo's arm for support as my foot found the first rung of the ladder and I began my descent, letting the hull eclipse my last glimpse of the crew. I didn't look back. Not once. Because if I did, I'd do something foolish, like love him and change my mind.

28

The ship rocked gently, her opalescent sails sighing with the wind. I drifted to the bow, watching the afternoon sky bleed snow, the lapping waves swallowing each swirling flake. Storm clouds loomed on the horizon, the same purple-grey as my icy fingertips.

Sailors milled about, the strangers whose hands had hauled me on board in the middle of the night. Their conversations were quiet, dull, and I ached for noise. The ship smelled of fish and sick, a reminder that not every vessel had magic to maintain it. I closed my eyes, tasting the frost on my lips, letting it numb me. I couldn't shoulder the weight of my thoughts any more. My guilt, my despair, my regret.

Time yawned ahead of me, two weeks of a journey I wanted no part of. Two weeks before my sacrifice would mean anything, before I'd be able to hold Felicie in my arms and throw myself at the feet of a king I wanted nothing to do with. Until then, all I could do was wait, and wallow.

The days were at their shortest. The *Blood Rose* would be closing in on her destination. Soon, my crew would be fighting for their lives, thinking there was something noble in deaths so raw and reckless.

I listened to the sound of the ropes creaking as the ship swayed steadily, imagining they were chains. I rubbed my wrists, reminding myself that I was the free one, that it was Father imprisoned, my sister likely bound to the throne. The waves swept below, a distant rumble of thunder rolling through me. The storm couldn't come soon enough.

'Did you hear me?'

I jumped at the sound of Aberdeen's voice. I glanced sideways at her wish a sheepish smile. She was so different now – not just in the dirty white shirt she wore tucked into navy skirts, or the way her hair had come loose from its braid, dark strands falling about her face. Her skin was darker, her features more defined. She was stronger, yet . . . softer.

'Sorry,' I murmured, suddenly aware of my dishevelled appearance, my red-rimmed eyes and tousled hair, and the coat that shrouded me, my leather shadow.

'I said I know you've been through a lot, but we'll be home soon,' she said.

'You mean the capital,' I corrected. That place would never be my home.

'Right.' Aberdeen pursed her lips. 'I don't see how you could complain about joining a court as its princess.'

I stared out at the sea. 'You know me better than that.'

Aberdeen shrugged – a gesture so profoundly unlike her it made me pause. 'All I know is you're safe now. That's what matters.'

I sighed. She'd come all this way, I reminded myself, just for me. How was she supposed to know I didn't want it?

'There's a storm coming,' my sister said after a while. 'We should head inside.'

I was too weary to resist as she led me to a cabin tucked away down the hall of the quarterdeck. It was small and cramped, two bunks shoved up against either wall and a window that let in the sound of the sea. I was grateful for the privacy at least. I couldn't have endured the noise of a berth, surrounded by strangers and voices and a crew that wasn't mine.

The spare mattress was thin and the sheets stiff, but the bed was still better than the one I'd had at the cottage. I collapsed on to my back, staring up at the timber ceiling, knowing I'd get no sleep.

Evening sank into night. Aberdeen stretched out on her own too-short bed, her back facing me, toes dangling over the edge. I stared at the space between her shoulder blades, the darkness blurring as the candle beneath the window flickered.

Rain lashed against the glass as the storm picked up, pitching the ship from side to side. Its wooden hull hurled against the tempest, but I scarcely felt it. The real storm was the one wrenching me apart from the inside. Shadows stole through the window, closing around me as I curled up in Sebastien's coat. Even now, even from here, he warmed me. Shutting my eyes tight, I buried my head in its folds, exhausted.

Sleep evaded me still. I fidgeted, trying to find comfort in the unforgiving mattress, but there was something hard wedged into my side. I fumbled through the leather and tugged out the worn copy of Mors' book.

My fingers shook as I clutched its thick yellow pages. I'd almost forgotten about it, about my hollow promise not to read it until I was weeks away from the truth it would reveal.

I'd be damned if I let him tell me what to do, especially now.

The brittle pages of Sebastien's story leafed open before me, coloured with age and inked with promises of the world I hungered for more than any other. I inched towards the solitary candle, its sputtering flame casting just enough light to read by. The words coiled around my heart, doing something to heal the wound there; a wound that ran deeper with every passing minute, with every billowing breath of the sea as it pulled me further from home.

The world around me melted away, dissolving into another . . .

The sea slipped over the stone walls of that kingdom and into its briny heart. She came as she did for every sailor, when their lungs loosed one last breath to the skies.

Long she had been nothing more than a tide. Now, she rose.

Roiling waves lapped at the rocky shores of the Sinking Cities as Nerida came to stand before their boy king. She had seen king turn on queen, son turn on father. Who was to stop it from being her tides they turned on next?

They had proven true what she had always known, that she was wise to keep her magic to herself, to safeguard it against poisoned human hearts. If the child king could not repent, his people would join her below, where they belonged.

He stood tall for one so young, blocking Nerida's path at the city gates. There, he swore to restore the balance between her waves and his people, and promised to show her she had been right to choose his kin as her guardians.

Nerida had come to reclaim them, but when she heard the pleas of those who lived to worship her waters, she relented. The little king vowed she would know only peace from that day forth.

For a time, the marble kingdom flourished. Its people were voyagers, wanderers, and their king fought and ruled alongside them, guided by the ocean that wove through his cities' cobbled hearts.

Each year, he returned home from the seas a little more a man. A decade passed and Nerida came to know him well, poised proud like the figurehead of a great ship, the wind curling around him as if he were impenetrable, unshakeable, even to her touch.

The sea knew his eyes, knew well the love that swirled within them as he gazed into her depths. And because the hearts of gods are fickle, too, she loved him back.

But ten years did little to wash the tint of betrayal from her blue waters. And so, when she came once more for his kingdom, the goddess came for him, too. For his heart.

The sea spoke to her king, to the only mortal she believed worthy. And when she professed her love to him, he knelt before her and swore that if it was his heart that she desired, she would have it – have it, in exchange for the safety of his kingdom.

Nerida accepted. Seeing how her tides hungered for his heart, but knowing he could only ever belong to his kingdom, the king unsheathed his dagger and plunged it into his chest. He tore himself open, pried out his beating mortal heart and threw it to the planks of his ship before her.

When he did, it was love – pure, crimson love – that flowed from him. It coated the deck, weaving like briars into the fabric of the ship he called home.

'I belong only to my people,' he told her, blood dripping from his chin, his hands, his broken ribs.

The goddess, enraged by his rejection, turned his people to stone. As promised, her waves would never harm them, for water could no longer breach their pebbled lips.

It was only then that the light the sea had loved in her king winked out. Still twisted with spite, she relinquished, at last, a little of her magic. To serve him in his torment. To turn him into something that could not be mended. To remind him of her love for him, each and every day.

'Live on,' she told him. 'Learn to love as you have claimed to love me, or your people shall remain stone forever. Bare your hateful soul to another and see if you will ever find one as worthy as me.'

'But I don't have a heart,' he tried to plead, feeling the rift of his new emptiness breaking open from within.

Nerida's laugh was an echo in his hollow chest. Three hundred years she gave him, to learn that he could not live without the love he had let slip through his fingers. Three hundred years of flesh before he, too, would be stone.

He woke the next dawn in a body fraught with shadow. The two most loyal to him stood by his side, watching as his new powers clawed at the mortal within.

The Sinking Cities crumbled beneath the ocean's choking waves without a king to stand in their way. Only when he found a love as true as Nerida's, without a heartbeat to guide him, would his kingdom see the light of the surface again.

And so, those cities of rust would lie in the greatest depths of that mournful sea, awaiting the return of their king . . .

The storm outside was mirrored in my unwanted dreams. I spent the pitch-black hours tossed between broken kingdoms and bloody hands. It was in a thicket of shadow that I found myself, surrounded by wind and rain and anguish.

But I wasn't alone – Sebastien was with me, his hands warm and reassuring on my cheeks. Until darkness tore its way between us. I heard his voice, a shout of pain in the wind, the fury of the tempest that roared around us, stealing the cries from my throat.

I jolted awake.

Centuries of pain sat heavy in my chest, Sebastien's cry still echoing through me. My turbulent dreams were nothing compared to what was real – what I'd turned my back on.

I reached up to touch my face, feeling the smudges of ink and tears on my cheeks. The sea was against us. I should've known from the start. Monsters conjured from nightmares, their claws hungry for my flesh. Fire from the deep. What else could've brought a civilisation to its knees but the love of a god?

Don't come back.

Sebastien's words had haunted me since I'd left. Now I understood why he'd taken that book from me – why he'd been so afraid to show me the truth. Because if I'd known, if I'd understood the extent of his pain, his sacrifice, I might never have left.

I buried my head into his coat, pressed my palms to my eyes – because even the sight of shadows was too much – and let the quiet sobs wrack me.

They need me, cried a voice in the back of my head. But my family needed me, too. I thought of Father in chains, of Felicie, and every reason I was there to begin with.

Why? I wanted to scream at the sky. *Why do I have to choose?*

Sebastien and Aron and Golde had suffered for so long, for centuries, and now . . . Now it was almost over. *Less than three months*, Aron had said, when the leaves were halfway brown and the skies still dipped in blue. Almost three months ago, he'd said that.

Now I knew what those words meant, the curse they called into being. No wonder my crew were so determined to throw themselves into the path of danger. Facing Bane was hardly a risk if eternal damnation awaited them either way. *Two days*, Golde had said. *The bastard knows.*

Bane had chosen the solstice for a reason, knowing his enemy would only have hours to live. *Coward.* But if they could break the curse . . . if I could just get to them in time—

I raced for the door, wrenching it open and hurtling out on to the deck. Finally, I understood. Everything clicked into place at the exact moment it fell apart. This vendetta against Bane wasn't the only thing they cared about. It was the only thing they could *control.*

One final attempt to feel free, before eternity swallowed them whole.

Rain and sea spray whipped against me as the ship rode through the storm. I didn't know how I could help, if any part of me was strong enough to break a centuries-old curse, to make a heartless man love me, but I had to try. I couldn't lose them. Not to Bane, not to the sea.

A single sailor stood at the helm, her weather-beaten hands clutching the wheel. She turned when I appeared behind her, struggling to catch my breath.

'Turn the ship around,' I cried, the wind whipping my hair wildly around my face. How frantic I must've looked – how desperate. 'I need you to take me back.'

The sailor's eyes widened, catching the moonlight. 'Your Highness . . .'

I shrank back from the title. It was hollow, ill-fitting. Unwanted. 'Whatever my sister told you, we have to go back,' I said. 'A detour. Whale Rock – do you know it?'

The woman nodded, looking bewildered. Still, her hands on the wheel didn't move.

I looked up at what I could see of the stars. Struggling to remember what I knew of navigation, trying to place myself amidst the endless sky, to work out which way would lead me home. But the stars pointed us wrong.

'We're heading north,' I realised aloud, my heart thudding in my chest. I looked to the sailor at the wheel. 'We're going the wrong way,' I told her slowly, still trying to piece things together. The capital was south. Father and Felicie were south. There was nothing north of here but cliffs . . .

Aberdeen would have known – would have noticed. Where was she taking me?

'Aurelia!'

My head snapped around to see my sister standing on the threshold of the quarterdeck, dark hair wild around her face, boots unlaced. Her eyes darted between the two of us, my heavy breathing, her helmswoman's hesitant posture.

For a moment, the rain drumming on wood was the only sound.

'I'm going back,' I told her quietly, resolutely.

'You are not.' Aberdeen's eyes narrowed on me. 'I told you, Father and Felicie are in danger. Why would you ever want to go back?'

I took a steadying breath, trying to calm my racing heart. Trying to make a shred of sense of all this. 'If they're really in danger,' I said slowly. 'Then why are you taking me in the opposite direction?'

'I don't know what you're talking about,' Aberdeen said, sounding flustered. 'You can't go back to that ship. To those monsters.'

My heart throbbed in my chest. Aching, begging. 'Either you tell me what's going on or I swear, I'll *swim* back.' I had to see them again – see *him* . . . If I could find a way to break the curse, maybe I could stop them from throwing themselves into battle, stop them from thinking a quick death – an easy way out – was the best they could hope for. 'I need to see them,' I said, my voice rising. 'I'm not asking for forever, I just need a little more time.'

Aberdeen swept the damp hair back from her face. 'I should've known,' she muttered, eyes darkening. 'Bane was right. They corrupted you.'

My hands curled into fists. 'Nobody *corrupted*—'

A wave of ice washed over me. A cold, deadly realisation. It sank in slowly, every part of me resisting, saying that it was impossible. I could scarcely speak over the anger that constricted my lungs, my heart, my voice.

'*Bane?*' I breathed.

She looked uncertain, for once. 'It's nothing. I heard his name mentioned in Bray, I—'

'Don't you dare lie to me, Aberdeen.'

The ship heeled, the fury in my chest rearing as I stared down my sister.

She averted her gaze, looking around like she was searching for something. An explanation, perhaps. Then she huffed an angry sigh. 'I'm only trying to protect you.'

'What. Have. You. Done?'

Her voice was almost pleading. 'When I got to Bray, I . . . I was coming to save you. Felicie and Father were never taken.'

My lips parted, a breath of disbelief escaping. *What?*

'I at least had to know if you were alive. And when I heard all those outlaws clamouring for your blood . . . I had to do something.'

'Why didn't you just *tell* me?' I demanded, my voice echoing somewhere distant, somewhere far from my body. 'I could have explained. I never would've left.'

'Exactly,' she said emphatically. 'I needed a way to get to you, and when I found Bane . . . All he wants is to bring Oren down, Aurelia. He assured me he won't hurt you, he just wants you out of the way.'

'So, what – he sent you to kidnap me in his place?'

Confusion flickered across Aberdeen's face. 'I sent myself. I promised him I would keep you safe until the battle was over.'

'And then what?' I cried, voice shrill against the vicious wind. 'Don't you realise what he wants with me? He'll use me to crown himself king! You'd rather force me into marriage than—?'

'Of course not,' she snapped, cutting me off. 'I would never honour a deal with a pirate. I'm taking us home, Aurelia. You're free.'

The words sat between us, sinking through the heavy air. 'What do you mean, free?'

She folded her arms impatiently, fixing me with a hard stare. 'Bane told me those *pirates* had some kind of hold on you, that you'd hardly come willingly. I said I could make you – and I did, didn't I?'

'You were right to lie to him, but not to me.'

'Can't you see I'm trying to save you?' Aberdeen shouted, the wind tearing the words from her lips.

I took a step towards her, letting my voice drop low. 'If Bane thinks we're on our way to a safe place, then where, exactly, is he?'

The colour faded from her dark cheeks. 'Whale Rock. He said he'd meet us in Bray, after . . . Once it's over.'

'Over?' My voice sounded a thousand leagues away. 'If he believes I'm already his, what battle is he trying to keep me safe from in the first place?'

'I may have suggested . . . I just thought—' Aberdeen swallowed, drawing herself up. 'I told him he'd have a better chance of taking down a king if he had the army of one.' Foreboding washed over me, leaving goosebumps in its wake. 'He wants to take the Heartless King's fleet.'

The world fell away. I gasped for air, but there was none. There was nothing. Only words, ringing through my mind. *Then he, too, would be stone.* If I couldn't stop this, save them . . . Every last thing loved by the people I'd left behind would be lost.

I was going to be sick.

'Ria?' Aberdeen's hand was gripping my arm, trying to pull me back to the world, the one she'd torn apart.

I tugged myself free. 'You don't know what you've done.'

Her silver-blue eyes were dark with concern. 'I'm sorry, I—'

'We have to go back. You have to take me home.'

'I *am* taking you home,' Aberdeen insisted. 'Bane won't find us there. We'll be safe, I swear.'

'No.' I shook my head. 'No. I need to get back to the *Blood Rose*, before it's too late.' *If it isn't already*, came a dark voice. Dread, thick as blood, simmered in my chest.

I could see Aberdeen's frustration in the set of her shoulders, the tautness of her jaw. But I couldn't give up. Not until I knew, not until I'd tried.

'Take me back. *Now.*' I looked over at the sailor manning the helm. 'Tell her. Turn the ship around.'

Aberdeen's expression was caught halfway between apologetic and resolute. 'Ria, I can't. We don't belong to this world – we have to go home.'

I shook my head, over and over. 'I won't,' I told her, more resolute than ever. 'I won't keep running.'

When she didn't respond, my resolve hardened, frustration heating my blood. If Golde were here, Aberdeen would be dead and I'd be halfway home already. I reached into my coat, fingers curling around the rose-shaped hilt of my dagger.

'What are you doing?' Aberdeen whispered, eyes widening as I drew the blade out.

'You'd better turn this damned ship around before we both find out exactly what I'm capable of right now,' I warned.

'You're being ridiculous—'

'You lied to me!' I cried, tremors of the heartbreak splitting open inside me tearing through my voice. '*Again*. You tricked me, because you could tell the moment you set foot on that ship that it was exactly where I belonged!'

It might have been the moon, sinking towards the sea, but I could've sworn my sister's expression softened. The wind died down, making it suddenly too quiet, too calm.

'Put that knife away.' Aberdeen sounded exhausted and imperative all at once. 'Gods, I didn't think even *you* would side with a bunch of murderers.'

I gritted my teeth, though I couldn't exactly argue with the *murderer* part. My heart was pounding in my chest, my nails digging into my palms. 'Please,' I whispered. 'Take me home.'

Aberdeen held my gaze. She knew what I needed — didn't understand it, but she knew. Hope climbed through me, through the shreds of my heart, ready to wind it back together.

At last, she nodded. 'All right.'

I exhaled, my lungs emptying like it was their first breath, like I'd been holding it for eighteen years. 'Thank you.'

Her expression was grim. 'I don't know what this could cost us. I promised Bane I'd keep you away from the battle. I can't save you again. Not if you go back there.'

'I know.'

Aberdeen rolled her eyes with a groan. 'Gods, Aurelia. I always knew you'd be the death of us.'

29

The solstice sun slunk above the waterline.

Aberdeen and I sat side by side, watching dawn dissolve. The hard ridge of the step dug into my back, the wood where we sat at the bottom of the stairs cold and unforgiving. As was the silence, stretched taut between us.

For a long time, the air was too thick to speak. The storm evaporated around us, fog oozing from the waves. I couldn't shake the dread from my bones, so I just sighed, staring out at the water.

'I am grateful,' I mustered lamely. 'That you're here. That you came for me at all.'

Aberdeen bit out a laugh. 'A lot of good it did.'

We lapsed into silence again.

With the waves rolling past and the sun pulling the shadows into its fold, winter felt like a dream – those nights with Sebastien, those days in the snow with the crew and the icy, ruthless sea. I missed Aron's laugh and Una's smile, Mors' steady arms. Golde's blade flashing in the low light. All I could feel was *missing*, so fierce it made me feel sick.

It might be over already. I swallowed thickly, trying to tame the roaring ache inside me. *I might be too late.*

They mightn't have made it past daybreak – I didn't know how curses worked. I only knew that death would be a mercy in their eyes; an end that was hot and fast and meant something. I might have chosen death, too, over the cold, endless depths of eternity.

But I had to hope. I had to be as they had always been – strong, ready to fight.

'You never told me how you got here,' I said, a feeble attempt to force my mind away from such thoughts. 'How'd you find Bane in the first place?'

'Wasn't hard,' Aberdeen replied. 'He was docked in the quay, preparing to depart. I found his crew in a tavern and managed to persuade them to take me along.'

Unease settled in the pit of my stomach. 'Persuade them? How?'

Aberdeen's tawny skin pinked, a flush creeping up her high cheekbones. 'I won a place among them. Turns out I have quite a knack for cards.'

I gaped at her. Cold, quiet Aberdeen. My proud, sleek-haired sister, playing cards with pirates. All for me.

'You gambled?' I spluttered.

'I *won*,' she amended, a small smile tugging at her lips. 'Anyhow – I found my way on to his ship. Bane told me he'd seen you; that the Heartless King's crew had their hooks in you. I didn't want to believe it – swore it couldn't be true, until I set foot on that ship. Saw it in your eyes. In his, too, if you can even call them that.'

I didn't have to ask who she meant. It hurt to hear, to know that whatever Sebastien and I had was real enough to exist outside of us, to be seen. At least once, before we lost it.'

A lump, hot like coal, formed in the centre of my chest. 'If you thought I was dead, then why did you even go to Bray?'

Aberdeen's silver-blue eyes flared like molten steel in the sunrise. 'You're my *sister*.'

I swallowed, glancing down at my hands curled in my lap. My eyes burned. Aberdeen wasn't carved from stone like I'd always thought; she was flesh and blood and heartache, too.

'I'm so sorry,' I murmured.

She grimaced at the emotion in my words. 'Don't be. I never should have let you go.'

'You couldn't have stopped me.'

'I could have tried harder.'

I offered her a small shrug. 'And then where would we be? Still hungry, still hidden from the world.'

'Guess so,' Aberdeen said, settling back against the steps.

'Though if you'd just told me the truth from the start—'

'Don't,' she cut me off, lips pursed. 'Father and I were only ever trying to protect you.'

'I never asked for protection.' A traitorous crack formed in my words. 'All I wanted was your love.'

'I always loved you,' she said quietly, gaze fixed on the horizon. 'You shut me out.'

'I shut *you* out?' I cried. 'You were always so . . . distant.'

'I was scared,' Aberdeen admitted. 'You never had a clue the danger you were in.'

I felt my cheeks burn. I'd always done whatever I could to soften the burden on my eldest sister's shoulders, but apparently it hadn't been enough. She'd been taken from one mother for Felicie's sake, then lost another because of me.

'You're sure it wasn't just because you disliked me?' I joked.

'Please.' Aberdeen rolled her eyes. 'You were unbearable.'

Indignation swelled in my chest and I opened my mouth to protest.

She laughed, finally looking at me. Dark hairs danced around her face in the breeze. 'You *were*! Running around with your head in the clouds, thinking you could save us all.'

I shook my head. 'I only ever wanted to help.'

Aberdeen gave me a sad smile. 'I know,' she conceded. 'You did more than I ever could have. I suppose you're braver than I gave you credit for.'

I wondered if she'd still call me *brave* if she knew everything I'd done.

'You still could have told me,' I pressed. 'You know I would've done anything to protect Felicie.'

'I know. And then you'd have gone and done something stupid. Like sacrificing yourself to a tyrant. Or falling in love with one.'

My heart stuttered in my chest. 'What?'

'Please,' she sneered. 'Any fool could've seen the way you looked at him.'

I flinched at the disgust in her tone. How could I ever make her understand who Sebastien really was? How all those stories of the Heartless King hid a man who'd torn out his own heart to save his people, whose body had shielded me from fire, carved me from it, brought me to life . . .

I wasn't sure if I loved him. Didn't know what that meant, to people like us. But I knew, given half a chance, I'd fight tooth and nail for that shred of happiness we'd dug out of the darkness.

I opened my mouth to explain, but I knew my words would be wasted. Bane's presence sat heavy between us, woven like roots into the foundation of this bridge we'd just begun to build. It made me nervous, the fact that my sister had bargained with someone so vengeful, so broken, even if she'd planned to betray him all along.

'Did anyone tell you Bane's story?' I asked. I thought of the burn marks I'd seen, wondering how much of him was scarred by what Oren had done. 'Why he's so determined to tear down a whole kingdom?'

Aberdeen drew her braid over one shoulder, fingers skimming down its ridges. 'I heard it,' she said. 'It isn't pretty.'

I offered a small smile. 'You know those are my favourite stories.'

'There was some deal between Bane's father and the old king,' Aberdeen began. 'Your grandfather, I suppose. Bane was born into one of the high families, with five or six brothers. Perhaps they posed a threat of imbalance at court – I'm not sure. But when Oren succeeded, things soured between them. They say soldiers raided their estate in the dead of night. By the time the sun rose, everything they had was ash and all their sons were dead, save one. Bane was just four years old.'

That part, I knew. I shivered, remembering what Mors had said. *Four years old*, and they'd found him standing there, alone amongst the ruin. My heart ached for the little boy Bane had been when his world had turned to cinders around him.

The early morning light cast strange shadows over Aberdeen's cheeks. 'Bane's been raiding Oren's ships for years, taking gold and supplies, expanding his reach. He may only have a peasant army, but they're fuelled by hunger.'

'They won't get that far on empty stomachs,' I pointed out. 'It takes more than rage to win a war.'

'That's exactly what I told Bane,' she replied. 'All men bleed the same. Even kings. I told him eliminating Oren would be easy enough, but sever a serpent's head and its venom can still kill you. If he really wants a new world, he'll need an army large enough to take this one down first. Pirates are the obvious choice.'

An icy dread slithered through me. When had we become these people? When had we learned to carry weapons and speak of serpents like we knew what it was to slay them?

'Real pirates understand loyalty,' I said. 'Bane doesn't. If we get to Whale Rock in time . . . I'll kill him before I let him hurt anyone again.'

Aberdeen clicked her tongue, sceptical as ever. 'Is it worth it?' she asked. 'All this? Do they really mean that much to you?'

I didn't hesitate. 'In every way.'

Aberdeen's lips thinned. 'Then you'd better not mess this up.'

She didn't know how right she was.

I lifted my chin, feeling three hundred years of fate descending around my shoulders. 'I won't.'

The sun sat heavy on the horizon as a wedge of land came into view. Whale Rock lanced out from the sea, a stark grey outcrop crowned with long, ivory bones. The skeleton of a great beast lay at the island's peak, ribs spread wide like jaws. As we coasted past, I saw the rubble of what looked like a village: crumbling stone structures that had been razed to the ground. Ashes. I shivered, not wanting to imagine what had happened there – what Sebastien and his crew had done.

A splotch of crimson bled through the fog. Anticipation buzzed in my chest as the scent of home curled around our ship, welcoming me.

'Sails!' called a voice from above.

Slowly, more masts emerged from the sea mist around us, their emerald sails topped by fluttering black flags. I cursed, a cold new wave of dread washing over me.

Bane.

There was blood on the breeze as the sounds of battle whispered across the water, a faint swell of salt and steel and war. Nine ships dotted the water around the *Blood Rose*, all dwarfed by her immense size, but I knew the crew onboard couldn't hold out for long against the tide of their enemies.

I hurried to the port side, Aberdeen a step behind. *Good*, was all I could think. *It isn't over yet.*

My sister's gaze was glued to the battle raging ahead. 'I can't let you go into that.'

I shook my head. 'You really can't stop me.'

She tucked a strand of her hair back into its braid. 'Aurelia. You can't fight an army.'

'I have to do something,' I said.

Aberdeen's eyes were sharp — steely with the kind of determination that had pushed her from the bounds of the continent to find me. 'If you make it . . . if you ever need me, just send word,' she said. 'I'll be there.'

A lump clotted in my throat at her words. If I made it past today, it would either be as Bane's prisoner, or . . . Or I'd have everything I'd ever wanted. I wouldn't need to be taken care of ever again.

'I want you to live, too, all right?' I said. Whether I had a future or not, I didn't want hers wasted. Nor Felicie's. There was so much more to the world than the distant threat of a throne and the dark cliffs of the bay.

'You're not going to die, are you?' my sister asked.

I choked on a laugh. 'Gods, I don't know. Probably — maybe. Hopefully not.'

Her huff sounded so much like a laugh I couldn't be sure if she was angry or amused. 'Just . . . promise me you won't die for *him*.'

I bit my lip. If I could choose — no, I'd never choose that. I didn't want to die. I wanted to sail the seas, seize the wind and make it steer me across the world; I wanted the crew by my side. But suddenly, with the clash of battle thickening on the breeze the closer we drew to the *Blood Rose*, that was beginning to feel impossible.

'I'm scared,' I whispered, so quietly I almost hoped she wouldn't hear.

Aberdeen sighed. 'I don't remember the last time I wasn't.'

I nodded, oddly calmed by her admission.

I drew Mors' book from my pocket and held it out to her. 'Here,' I said lamely. 'There's a map, and . . . if you ever want to find me – these stories, they'll explain everything. Maybe you could join me, some day.'

I loved that book, but I didn't need it any more. The *Blood Rose* was borne of the same magic that filled those pages, that had filled my heart with aching every day of my life. Those tales would do better in my sisters' hands now. Maybe it could teach them something, make them want more.

Maybe this wouldn't be the end for us, after all.

Aberdeen took the book hesitantly, fingers wary as they grasped the worn binding, skimming over the image of the little prince – my prince – on the cover.

'Are you going to be all right?' I asked.

She nodded. 'The crew will take me back to Bray. Nothing will stop me getting home.'

Ahead of us, the *Blood Rose*'s deck swarmed with bodies, too crowded to distinguish friend from foe as we anchored beside her.

My hands shook as one of the sailors tossed a grappling iron to the banisters above, gave it a tug and passed it over to me with a nod. What if I was too late?

I took the rope between my trembling fingers and glanced back at Aberdeen, unsure how to say goodbye, after everything.

'We'll find each other again,' she said, tapping the book in her hands. 'Eventually.'

I felt a rush of gratitude for her hard-cast determination. I couldn't have parted with my past without knowing it was safe in her hands. 'I love you,' I whispered. And, with a last half-hearted attempt at a smile, I jumped.

I careened through the air and collided with the hull of the *Blood Rose*, trying to dull the impact with my feet. The wind whipped around me, trying to sweep me like a leaf into its fold. Aron's voice guided me in my head as I braced my feet on either side of the rope and began to climb. My hands and feet worked more out of desperation than agility, fuelled by something in my very bones. I scaled the ship's hull, rising to meet the echoing embrace of the *Blood Rose*, terrified to discover what awaited me on the other side.

The sounds of battle erupted around me as I scrambled on to the banister at last, arms aching.

Pirates danced across the planks, blades parrying, the two crews indistinguishable. I crouched on the rail for a moment, scanning the fray. The deafening clang of metal on metal and the stench of blood were overwhelming, but my eyes were drawn immediately to the centre of the deck.

Two figures were pitched in a raging duel.

I would've recognised those broad shoulders anywhere. The shadowed movements that could cut through stone, the dark hair that whipped around him as he spun. His broadsword met the cutlass of the captain who faced him, again and again.

Sebastien and Bane fought like steel and water. Bane was nimble, dodging each assault with lithe steps, a blur of black leather. But there was nothing so impervious, so invincible, as the force that opposed him. Bane's every blow was buffeted by the storm of Sebastien's fury. It was clear as the oncoming sunset which of the two would win; the surging tides against the sinking sun.

But in an instant, something changed. The second my feet touched the planks, Sebastien's demeanour shifted.

He turned. The battle around us seemed to slow, the entire world a mere echo of the moment his gaze met mine. Black and gold, like the stars returning to the sky after an age of darkness.

For a split second, my heart swelled in my chest, full again at last. The world was frozen, ours . . . until it wasn't—

Until Bane's sword hurtled through the air, and plunged into Sebastien's chest.

30

A roar like the death of a sun tore through the sky.

I screamed, hurtling through the fray, the bloodshed, the din of battle. That cry of agony ripped through me like the wind, fracturing the world in two. The chaos blurred around me as I dodged blades and blood-spatter, racing for Sebastien as he fell to his knees, broadsword clattering to the ground.

Crimson arced through the air as Bane withdrew his blade. He grunted as blood – Sebastien's blood – scattered, painting the deck, the sails, me.

Bane's emerald eyes widened when he caught sight of me. 'Guess I overestimated that sister of yours,' he panted. 'Didn't think you'd be coming back.'

I shoved past him without a word, racing towards Sebastien. Despite the rivers of red trickling down his front, he held himself up just long enough for me to fly into his arms, pulling me tight against his blood-soaked chest.

'I told you not to come back,' he breathed, lips pressed into my hair as he cradled me against him.

I clasped my hands on either side of his face, an unfathomable relief filling me at the feeling of his body against mine. 'Should've known I wouldn't listen,' I told him, smiling through the terror that gripped me.

Dark curls hung across his face as he hunched over, gasping in pain. My skirts were already soaked scarlet, his blood spilling across the planks of the *Blood Rose* just as it had three centuries ago.

'Go home, blackbird,' he rasped, nothing but despair left in his voice.

'I am home,' I said softly, pushing the hair back from his face. My fingers smeared blood across his temple, but I didn't care. All the world could be blood and I would still be there, with him.

I grasped his chin in my hand, desperate to see his face, his eyes, to feel the breath on his lips . . . any sign that his powers would pull him through Bane's fatal blow.

He drew his eyes up to mine, slowly, as if even that caused him pain. 'Blackbird,' he whispered, the word escaping him like air, like life. But there was such death in his voice, such a tired, weary pain, that it ripped right through me, turning my hope to shreds. His eyes were darker than I'd ever seen them.

I shook my head furiously, fingers curling around his wrists. His thumb stroked my cheek, my jaw, my lips, leaving smears of blood everywhere he touched.

'You're too stubborn to die,' I told him fiercely, but the words snagged on the thorns in my throat, coming out so ragged even I didn't believe them. I pressed my forehead against his, willing life back into his paling flesh and I closed my eyes, knowing it would take something more than hope to save him. To save us all.

'Come away, love,' Bane said, his sword raised once more. 'You're too late.'

My hand sought comfort in the warmth behind Sebastien's neck. His long fingers curled into the material of my skirts, as if he could draw strength from me as his own faded.

'I'm not leaving his side,' I said.

'You're wasted on him,' Bane replied, grass-dappled eyes darting between us. 'I know about the curse. You won't win. Let me take you home.'

He grasped my forearm in an attempt to pry me away.

Sebastien's head snapped up, his eyes glittering with rage. There was life in him yet.

'Let go of her,' he snarled, each word bared like fangs, 'before I tear that hand from your body.'

His dying voice thundered across the deck with such force that the battle around us halted. Pirates from both crews turned to watch the wavering immortality of the Heartless King. Still, Bane didn't back down.

Fool, I thought.

I wrenched myself free from Bane's grip, meeting his gleaming green gaze.

'I won't leave him,' I repeated, my words firm as the planks beneath my feet. 'I won't let you take his army, either.'

Bane wiped the blood from his cutlass on his trouser leg, looking unimpressed. 'And what're you gonna do to stop me, exactly?'

My hand inched towards my dagger. *I'll kill you*, I thought, picturing all the ways I could squeeze the life from that traitor's neck.

Bane eyed my fingers as they reached for that iron rose hilt. He chuckled, shooting me a lazy grin. 'Gonna kill me, love?'

The whispers of battle around us should've made it hard to hear, but his mocking lanced right through me. I didn't want to be a killer. But how else could this end?

Bane's cutlass dangled lazily from his kohl-painted fingers, his gold rings glinting in the late afternoon light. I glanced down at Sebastien, hunched over in pain.

'Had me worried for a second.' Bane's gaze was still fixed on me. 'Thought you might've saved the day, turning up like this. Alas . . .' His eyes drifted to Sebastien, emeralds sharper than diamond. 'Too late.'

Sebastien's fingers twitched around my calf, but I couldn't look at him. *The curse*, a voice reminded me. I'd come back to break the curse. *But how?* Not like this – I needed more time.

Bane took a step forward, ignoring the hiss that fell from Sebastien's ashen lips. 'Come away,' he said. His voice was silken, almost a purr. 'I'll take you home, love. I told you, I don't want to be your enemy. We could *build* something together.'

'I'm not going anywhere with you.'

Bane's smile dropped. 'Not the monster you think I am, princess.'

'Good men don't need to say that.'

He laughed at that. 'Aye, well. Very human of me to admit, but I am sorry it's come to this.'

'No, you aren't,' I hissed. 'You only had to wait for the curse to end to claim the fleet for yourself. Instead, you started a fight you knew they wouldn't be able to finish. You came to watch them bleed because that's all you know – destruction.'

Finally, I saw the truth. It was always going to end like this: war. Sebastien had sensed it the moment we'd met.

Bane's voice was bitter, his lips curling as he spoke. 'Say what you want. He's dying and there's nothing you can do about it.'

'He isn't,' I insisted. 'He'll heal.'

Bane arched a brow. The blood pooling at Sebastien's feet was

313

spreading. A thick, dark sea that dripped through the cracks in the planks.

'Join me now and I'll let the rest of them live,' the traitor said.

Just then, Aron shoved his way through Bane's crew to join me at Sebastien's side. His face was streaked with blood, his shirt torn and hanging in pieces around his tanned skin. His gaze fell on Sebastien and I watched the colour leave him, all at once.

'Why are ye doin' this?' he snarled, a storm blazing in his eyes. His knuckles turned white around the hilt of his bloodied blade. 'The fleet'll never follow a traitor like ye.'

I was hardly listening. I had to do something, quickly, but it was becoming increasingly harder to think straight with Sebastien bleeding out at my feet.

'He started it,' Bane retorted, gaze locked on Aron's. 'It wouldn't have to *be* like this if you just let them fight for me.'

He looked at me, then. Eyes bright and wild. Full of pain and so much more – so much anger, so much desperation. 'Bet *you* could convince him, though,' he said slowly.

I ran my fingers through the ends of Sebastien's hair. I could hear his laboured breathing, feel his weight as he sagged against me. He was fading, and my heart was racing.

I don't have time for this.

Bane drummed his painted nails against the steel of his curved blade. 'I have an army of my own ready to pull this ship apart,' he said. 'But perhaps you could persuade your darling king to lend me his forces. Spare us all such a messy end. You have an uncle here, no? Wouldn't you like to save him? Side with me and I'll call it off.'

I glanced at Aron, knowing the fear in my wild eyes would tell him everything I was thinking. Even if I couldn't break the curse, if I was too late . . . I could still save some of them. Mors, Una . . .

Aron looked at Sebastien, then back at me. 'He's not dead yet,' he murmured.

My breaths turned shallow. *Think*. Not dead yet – but the end, one way or another, was coming. *What would Sebastien do?*

I didn't have to ask.

'I don't make deals with traitors,' I spat. 'Nothing could ever entice me to join you.'

Bane shrugged, gazing down the length of his cutlass, still red with Sebastien's blood. 'We're more alike than you think,' he said. 'We both belong to the sea, but our duties to family tie us to the continent. It's no way to live, caught in the Channel like this. I think we could free ourselves, if we worked together.'

'What do you know about family?' I hissed. 'You turned your back on this one.'

'I already had a family.' Bane's gaze went cold. Gone was the purring, the endearments. 'I only ever had one goal and I never turned my back on it. I came to Whale Rock as a boy, searching the lawless north for others like me. Sebastien's crew taught me what I needed to know to build a fleet of my own. To make Oren pay for what he did. I'll thank them in his blood.'

I narrowed my eyes at him. Bane really believed the continent he fought for would be a better place. But it was tainted with Sebastien's blood now. I'd die before I touched a world made in the ruin of him.

The deck quieted. I listened for Sebastien's breathing, trying to still my frantic heart long enough to hear it. It was there – fainter than the wind.

Gods. I had to save him. But how? He was the one with magic, the one who fought and healed and bound himself in sacrifice. What good was I?

I searched the chaos for my crew. Bodies were moving on all sides, cloaked in the same mixture of leather and steel and crimson

315

mist. Where was Golde? Where were Una, and Mors?

My heart raced faster.

Bane fixed me with a heavy stare. 'Oren burned them,' he said coldly. 'My family. Now I'm going to burn down every single thing he's ever built. I'll watch it all crumble, watch the shackles melt. You love this life so much. Why don't you want it for everyone? Freedom?'

I do, I wanted to say. But if freedom from Oren meant losing Sebastien, losing his whole kingdom? *No.*

'We ain't gonna make this easy fer ye,' Aron said, raising his sword.

Bane looked right past him, at Sebastien, whose breathing had grown heavy, ragged.

'Command the fleet to join me or I'll *make* you,' Bane said. 'And I really don't wanna do that, love.'

'You won't leave here alive,' Sebastien growled, looking up at Bane through the curtain of his hair with such black fury in his eyes I knew even the gods would've feared him then.

It should have sounded like an empty threat, coming from a man whose blood was draining to the seas. But as he spoke, the sound of grating steel cut through the air.

I looked up and there they were. All of them: Aron, Golde, Una, Mors. Their eyes were hungry, their faces flecked with blood, their blades throwing echoes of sunlight across the deck. The other pirates encircling us drew back, their cutlasses casting shadows like a sundial over Sebastien's kneeling form. The battle wasn't yet lost – but time was slipping away.

Sebastien grunted in pain and my heart fractured at the sound. I didn't know how long his powers would hold up against a wound so fresh and so vicious, but the sound of his struggle was enough to stoke the flames within me.

'Leave now or you won't leave at all,' I warned Bane.

A smirk flitted across Bane's face. 'Threatening me, are you? I've got enough backup to stretch this fight out as long as it takes.' He eyed the sinking sun. 'And let's face it. Won't take long.'

'You didn't need this war, Bane,' Sebastien snarled. 'You could've just taken Ria and waited. We'll be stone by sundown. But you just had to come – had to take out all that self-loathing on someone. Pretend there's something noble about everything you've done.'

Sundown. My heart quickened. It was so soon – too soon.

'Big words coming from a dead man,' Bane said, his voice low, eyes dark.

Sebastien shook his head with a sharp exhale. 'I have my crew, my people waiting back home. Must kill you to know even the Heartless King did a better job of being loved than you.'

Bane bared his teeth, clutching his cutlass tighter. 'Shut up,' he snarled, spittle arcing through the air. Fury rolled from his lithe body, driven from the depths of his darkness, that rotting thing King Oren had broken in him.

Sebastien glared up at him. 'You're a worse coward than I am,' he hissed, spitting blood at the captain's feet.

Bane was on him before I could react, kicking Sebastien square in the chest, sending him thudding on to his back.

I cried out as Bane leaned over him, hand fisted in his shirt, their faces a hair's breadth apart, cutlass raised to the Heartless King's throat.

'Killing you now would be a mercy you don't deserve,' he sneered.

I was ready to lunge forward and rip him apart, but Golde was already there, leaping over Sebastien with her daggers drawn.

Bane was too quick, darting to his feet, parrying her swing. His blows struck hard against her flashing steel, each shriek of metal

317

piercing the air. They fought brutally, savagely. But I'd never seen Golde so frenzied, or so clumsy.

Bane whipped around with a blinding force, elbow connecting hard with her face. Golde stumbled back with a strangled cry, blood flowing between her fingers as she clutched at her nose. Bane stared her down, panting. Behind him, the sun sank lower, lighting up the crimson that painted the deck.

Sundown.

Golde made another run at him. But Aron was there, crashing into her, holding her back. 'Golde . . .'

Bane spat at her feet. 'Time's up, love,' he smirked.

Golde thrashed against Aron's hold, trying to shake him off until he grabbed her jaw roughly and turned her face to the horizon. *'Look.'*

She stilled, slackening in his hold. 'No . . .'

Golde's voice was distant, an echo amongst the stars.

Rays of sunset curled like claws over the sides of the deck.

Steel clattered against wood and I turned to see Aron, his sword at his feet, eyes fixed on the skyline. The sun touched the edge of the horizon, sending a haze of orange light bleeding across the water, and I felt the enormity of time crushing around us. This was it.

'I'm sorry,' Sebastien murmured, and I could've sworn there was a tremor of something in his voice, a ripple of unchartered waters that sounded a lot like fear. 'I never wanted it to end like this.'

'No,' I whimpered, as the sky dissolved into dusk. 'No. Not now.'

Sebastien panted, struggling to pull himself upright. He lurched to his knees, his head hanging over his feet. I followed his gaze downwards and gasped.

The brown leather of Sebastien's boots was turning to stone before my eyes. The world swam in and out of focus as the tide of grey crept from the ground upwards, as time began to take back what it had given him.

'No,' I breathed again, unable to believe what I was seeing.

His fingers tightened around mine, turning colder with every passing moment.

I looked up, searching for someone – anyone – to help.

The amusement in Bane's eyes faded as Aron and Golde sank to their knees, succumbing to the curse I'd failed to break.

I choked back a sob. There weren't many people in this world whom Golde would bow before, but there she was – knees meeting hard planks when I knew her heart was somewhere far away.

I could scarcely see past my tears by the time I tore my eyes from her, back to the man at my side. His gaze was fixed on Bane, harder now than ever, more grey than black.

'We'll finish this in hell,' he said, voice so hollow it made me ache.

Bane dipped his head. Humble, for a man with the world crumbling right into his lap. 'See you there, love.'

No, no, no.

A warm, gentle hand closed around my shoulder. 'Come away, lass,' Mors said. 'Don't watch.'

But I couldn't move. It was as if I, too, were turning to stone. I wove my fingers into that familiar place at the back of Sebastien's neck, where he'd always been warm. Where I'd held him in those rare moments I'd been able to convince myself that even the tides couldn't tear us apart.

A single broken sob made me turn.

I met Una's eyes, wide and full of pain. We were the same, then, as she watched the life in Aron slip away.

Aron didn't face his king. No, as the wave of stone washed over him, he stared up at the pirate girl who'd made a home in all our hearts. I didn't want to imagine the look of terror in his eyes as they held hers for the last time.

'Lass,' he groaned, his voice rougher than stone. And then so was he – stone.

Mors pulled Una against his chest, letting his shirt soak up her tears as the last drop of colour drained from Aron's body. My hands moved blindly to Sebastien's cold face, seeing even the shadows drain from his eyes until they were flat and hard as granite.

'Don't go,' I pleaded. 'Please, stay. I need you here. I need you . . .' *I needed them all.*

My hands trembled as they stroked his hardened cheeks, knowing it was my last chance, my only chance to restore all the things that had been broken. One last chance to tell him—

'I love you,' I breathed, exhaling the words as easily as air. Not because it needed to be said but because it was the truth. Because I couldn't let him die without knowing. 'Gods, I love you.'

His hands pulled my face to his, cold lips tugging at mine, one last time. His words came out broken as he was, right down to the marrow. 'Then don't watch,' he choked.

A different kind of fear rattled through me. A bone-shaking, cold terror that rammed my heart like a pike.

'*I love you,*' I repeated helplessly. My final hope escaped me in a whisper, turning to mist, to salt and sea air, spiralling across the water and into the empty shell of his ear. I held my breath, waiting for the world to right itself. For the seas to lapse and for my king to return.

But despite that, despite my every heartbeat that begged for him, I felt his end in every part of me. His shoulders rose, taking in a breath that would never reach the skies.

The stone claimed him, immortalising that last ripple of movement forever.

No.

I hadn't been entirely sure – hadn't known what it really meant – until that exact moment. I loved him. More than I'd ever loved the sea. But still I'd lost him to it. Lost him, lost Aron, lost Golde. I'd lost.

'Told you,' Bane murmured. 'You were wasted here from the start.'

I looked up at him, trying to blink the tears from my eyes, to see anything but the broken pieces of my heart slipping away like the blood between my palms.

'No,' I whispered. *It can't end like this.*

The waves must've been listening – must've heard the broken echo of my heartbeat – because as my tears fell, they rose.

'Take her,' Bane ordered.

But as his crew swelled forth, so, too, did the sea.

31

Bane's crew charged forward, their blades drawn, attempting to pry me from the circle of statues that Sebastien, Aron and Golde had become. I thrashed against them alongside Mors and Una, their swords doing more than my elbows and dagger could. Beyond my furious cries, there echoed a great rumbling from the deep.

Water erupted around the *Blood Rose*, flooding over the sides of the ship as something colossal spiralled into the air. The swell descended, cascading across the planks and chasing Bane's crew back. Their shouts were drowned out by the waves that swept over the deck, lapsing around us and seeping into my skirts. It was no monster this time. When the deluge subsided, something far more beautiful, far more dangerous, emerged.

Nerida purled forth from her raging tides, aqueous limbs wavering as she strode into being. Rippling blue shifted to flesh. The dark sands of her skin glowed bronze beneath the setting sun, her eyes like tide pools as they came to rest upon me.

My hand fell instinctively to Sebastien's shoulder, seeking the reassurance of his warmth, but I was met with stone. I watched the sea with wary eyes, unsure whether she'd come to save or condemn us, whether I ought to bow or beg.

The goddess's wavering figure absorbed the sunlight, casting a blue glow over the planks around her.

'Gods,' Bane whispered, gaping at her. 'It's all true.'

The sea spoke, her voice dancing like thunder across the waves. 'This does not concern you, mortal.'

'I am here to claim the Heartless King's fleet,' Bane retorted, trying to sound imperious though his words faltered, warped by incredulity. 'They belong to me now.'

'You own nothing.' The dismissal was clear in her tone as she flowed past him. 'Leave, human. I don't want your traitor's blood tainting my waters.'

Bane took a step back, cutlass still clutched before him, eyes gleaming, hackles raised. I could tell he wasn't going anywhere.

Nerida didn't seem to care, turning her cerulean eyes on me. The orange rust of sunset sparked against her sloping cheekbones, making her glow from within. My breath caught at her inhuman beauty.

'So.' Her voice sent a chill through me that the water never had. 'You are the girl.'

I said nothing, wiping the tracks of salt from my cheeks, watching her shell lips and waiting for the words that would free us.

I love him, I thought. *That has to be enough.*

But the fear crashing through my heart made me doubt whether it was. Was I too late? Was my love even enough? I wished I could turn back time – reverse the sunset and force those words from my lips a moment sooner.

'In love but out of time,' Nerida murmured, reaching out to trace a finger along the curve of Sebastien's arm. There was an exaggerated pout on her lips as she drank in his stone features. 'So sad.'

I looked into her gleaming eyes, turned indigo as twilight settled over us. I could barely recognise the sea I loved in them.

I'd never truly feared the water, until now.

'Please,' I whispered, knowing I couldn't fight a tide so devastatingly cold. 'Bring him back.'

The sea shook her head, hair rippling like silk over her shoulders. 'Like his heart, he belongs to me now. I saved his people. This is his fate.'

You didn't save them, I wanted to cry. *You turned them to stone.*

Instead, I bit my tongue, hating the tears that betrayed me, that laid my mortal weakness bare before a god. The deck was silent, the pirates entranced by the scene unfurling before them. The goddess and the girl, and the man whose heart of stone belonged to us both.

I dug within myself, steeling my will into a weapon I could use. 'Give him back his heart and take mine,' I said. 'If he's stone, then so am I.'

Nerida laughed. Peals of siren song filled the air, hollow as shells. 'You thought you would be rewarded for loving a monster? Did you think you could redeem him, little girl? That your love could purge the blood he has spilt from my seas?'

The blood drained from my face, deserting me. I'd said the words, and meant them – had been so sure that the answer to everything had been stitched inside me all along.

'I know your heart, Aurelia Lucroy.' The ocean's eyes glittered, bright and infinitely cold. 'You are selfish, human, and for your greed, you have forgotten those capable of loving you truly. Your own family.'

Shame sliced through me at the thought. I'd never forget my family, but I had left them to a life none of us wanted. All for a chance to save my crew – and now I'd failed them, too.

'I said it, I *love* him—' The words came out choked, so bitter I could scarcely stomach them. 'Bring him back. All of them.'

'Foolish girl,' snarled the goddess. 'This isn't about you. The curse was his alone to break, just as his heart is mine to keep.'

I blinked, looking around me at the faces of the crew, remembering that I was swept up in something centuries old, something about so much more than a king. Mersey, Mors, Bane, Una, now me. So many of us mortals drawn into the heart of something timeless, unable to outlive it, unable to survive unbroken by it.

'Tell me how,' I pleaded. 'How do I save them?'

Those eyes of winter seas bore into mine. 'You don't.'

Nerida strode in a slow circle, pausing to trail a delicate finger over Aron's bowed granite head, the slope of his neck. My eyes burned at the thought of never seeing him smile again. A world empty of his laughter, his crinkled eyes and slouching gait . . . It would be just that – empty.

Una drew back a step, her eyes wide with fear as she gazed up at the goddess. Mors' arm tightened protectively around her shoulders.

'There is no soul more lonely than a god.' The sea moved towards Golde and my hands curled into fists as I fought the urge to shove myself between them, to stop Nerida from laying a finger on her. 'I lived for thousands of years in peace before bringing mortals under my dominion. I knew their greed, their wiles – I should have known better than to let their cities take root in my waves. To trust a *man* with my heart.'

Her gaze slid to Sebastien, full of spite – yet not entirely.

'I knew that with his people in the way, his heart would never truly be mine. I turned them to stone so that my touch would not fill their lungs, as I had promised. And in return I took his heart, for it should have been mine alone to take. I gave him three hundred years, thinking that if he could not love me enough with a heart, then he would be hopeless to love another without it.'

'You should've let him die!' I cried. 'If you truly loved him, you'd have let him die rather than watch him torture himself for centuries.'

'How could I?' mused the sea. 'How could I let him bleed to death because the very idea of being mine was so abhorrent to him? I wanted to save him, and yet . . . I hated him with all that I am.'

'You cursed him.'

'I curse him every day, human. He destroyed me, just as he will you. Even with a heart, he is too broken to love.'

'You're wrong,' I choked out, angry that a part of me would have believed her, once.

'Oh?' There was nothing gentle left about the sea's cruel, serpentine beauty. Her brow arched like the crest of a wave, her fingers curling into talons. 'I watched, year after year, as the Heartless King came to deserve his title. The powers I gave him were only an extra temptation to become the monster I knew he would. Three hundred years of blood taint my waters now, and you still believe him capable of redemption? Of love?'

I looked down at Sebastien. His final expression held nothing but anguish. *I can't love you, blackbird.* Those had been his very words. I knew it – and loved him anyway.

How was I supposed to convince a god if I couldn't even convince myself?

'That's it, then.' There was a triumphant gleam in Bane's eyes as he moved closer again. 'It's over. Come with me, Ria. This is your last chance.'

'I told you to leave, human,' Nerida snapped, her eyes still fixed on me.

Bane didn't heed her command. He strode closer, cutlass still held warily ahead, glancing between the sea and me. He was trying to help, I realised faintly. Giving me a chance to escape whatever doom was settling over this moment. There must've been some small part of him, some kernel of the boy he'd once been, that still cared for this crew. For Sebastien. Because Bane was still here, extending a hand slowly towards me. The wind tugged at his chestnut hair, his untucked shirt. I remembered his words – *we don't have to be enemies*. But that was before.

I curled my hands into fists, glaring with all the anger I had left at the traitor bastard who'd thrust his sword through Sebastien's chest.

'C'mon, love,' he coaxed. 'I'll take you home.'

Before I could speak, the goddess whirled on him. Strands of pure, crystalline water flared through the air as she spun. '*Enough*,' she snarled.

'Ria—'

My name was scarcely out of Bane's mouth before his entire body froze. His emerald eyes flew wide as Nerida raised a hand. A trail of water leaked from his eye, as though he was crying. My stomach churned. Something wasn't right.

The dread swimming in his gaze evaporated into sheer terror. His mouth gaped but all that came out was a gurgle. The goddess curled her hand into a fist and water poured from Bane's mouth, his nose, his eyes. Throttled cries punctured the air and he convulsed, his knees hitting the planks with a *crack*.

She was killing him, I realised in horror.

Water surged down his throat, ripping through his body, drowning him from the inside out. Bane thrashed, his screams caught in the flood. His hands clawed at his neck, scrabbling for air that would never come. I met his eyes, red and running with tears as salty as the sea that choked him.

So this was vengeance.

Out of the corner of my eye, I saw Una reach for Aron, but her fingers fell limply back to her side. There was no comfort, only stone.

I stifled a cry, watching as Bane writhed against the planks. Nerida tightened her fist. With one last gargle, he slumped against the wood. Dead.

I gasped in a lungful of air, realising I'd been holding my breath with him. My head spun, the planks swaying beneath me. He was dead.

Nerida's laughter scattered like pearls across the deck. Just like that, she'd killed him. This man whose name had haunted me for months, whose campaign against my uncle might have brought the continent to its knees. Dead, now. All of it.

Murmurs rumbled through the crowd of pirates gathered around us.

I glanced down at Sebastien, the stone slope of his shoulders, the stone hair that hung across his stone face, casting him into an eternity of shadows. My gaze shifted back to the sea, heart thudding in my chest.

'Please,' I said, my tongue dry as bark knowing she could end me, too, at any moment. 'If you love him, let him live.'

The laughter evaporated from her eyes. 'Why let him live, when I have so enjoyed watching him die for the last three hundred years? He doesn't love you. That makes him *mine*.'

You own nothing, I wanted to snarl. But my knees felt so close to buckling, my mind too fogged to think. Bane's glassy eyes stared at me from across the deck, a reminder of how quickly she could bring us all asunder.

'Please,' I whispered, knowing that I couldn't fight a tide so devastatingly cold. 'He loves me.'

Nerida's gaze turned to harsh, jagged glass. Her words, too, could have drawn blood. 'Prove it.'

My heart sank. He'd said it himself. He wasn't capable of love. Everything I felt for him, it meant nothing, changed nothing.

I reached out a hand and laid it on Sebastien's shoulder, feeling the sting of the rough stone against my skin. He was cold. *He's never cold.*

This wasn't working, only bringing me closer to throwing myself at the goddess's feet and weeping until I drowned us all.

I forced myself to look at Aron and Golde through the blurring threat of tears. If they were still alive, they'd have the answer – even if it was only bloodshed. But they were lost to me – lost to the battle I'd been left alone to fight once more.

Bane was right. The curse had won. How could I fight that? The evidence was right there, before my eyes. He was stone. He didn't love me. He couldn't.

I'm sorry, I thought, my hand slipping from his shoulder.

'He loves her.'

Mors stepped forward, facing Nerida with the defiance of a king. His lined face was warm in the melting dusk, his gold eyes fiercer than the sinking sun.

'He chose to let her go when he knew it would end like this,' my uncle said. 'He chose *her*, over his people – the one thing he has always put above all else. If that isn't love, then I've never loved a thing in my life.'

'Aye, it's true.' Una cut in. 'And when ye tried to take her from

329

us, he stood between yer creatures and her. He would'a burned to save her.'

Una met my eyes, her reassuring smile so full of terror and conviction at once that my doubt slipped away. It seemed so obvious, all of a sudden. The way he'd held me while he healed me. The way he'd looked at me the night I left. The way he'd let me go, rather than make me watch him destroy himself.

This, I realised, looking around me. *This is what he was trying to save me from.*

I'd let him convince me that it was impossible, but I'd felt it in my bones when he kissed me. I knew it like the tides knew the shore.

A thread of steel twined through me as I turned back to the sea. I was fighting the will of a god, but I *wasn't* doing it alone.

'They're right,' I said. 'You'd need a human heart to see it, but he loves me.'

The air turned icy. 'He never said the words.'

'That was never the bargain,' I asserted, as if I had any idea. My mind scrambled for a way to make sense of this, to save him. 'He never said it aloud because he didn't believe himself capable. How can you expect a man to know he's in love if he can't feel it?'

Nerida looked triumphant. 'Precisely, human. He could not feel it.'

I gritted my teeth, imagining I had his strength, his unquestionable power.

'Yet he loves me,' I said. 'You know it as well as I do. You felt it. Why else would you send those creatures? You thought I'd escape, given the chance, but I stayed. And when that didn't work, you tried to have me killed. Why seek to stop something you believed to be impossible?'

A ghost of amusement passed over Nerida's lips, but in its wake, her eyes burned with an unfathomable fury, glinting red as the sun's last drops of life bled out into the water.

'It's no wonder you are a princess,' she hissed. 'You act as though you have earned the world.'

She circled me, feet soundless against the planks. The waves whispered around us.

'My tides pity you,' she said at last, coming to stop in front of me. 'They say you deserve a chance at happiness. A chance at a love as pure as the one you have always shown me.'

Hope, like sunlight, began to rise in my chest, telling me I was close, so close. That perhaps I hadn't lost everything just yet.

'Is that what you desire, human?' the goddess asked. 'You wish to see his kingdom? To free his people?'

'It's all I want.'

My lungs tightened as the goddess curled her fingers into a fist once more.

A whorl of water burst from her hand, erupting over us.

A gasp fell from my lips as Aron and Golde thudded to their hands and knees, spluttering, drenched – alive.

Una was on them before I could blink, tugging them both close, ignoring Golde's protests, a mess of tears and salt water and cries of relief.

Then it was just Aron, Aron and her, arms caught around one another, sopping wet and so entwined I didn't think either of them would ever let go. I blinked back my own tears. *At last.*

'It is done,' said the sea.

When I turned, I saw him – Sebastien. Water dripped to the planks as he lifted his head, eyes immediately on mine. I collapsed into him, letting his arms cage me in against his chest.

I buried my face into his neck, feeling the warmth as it returned to his skin, his wet hair against my cheek. His large hands cupped my

331

face and he pulled back in disbelief. So much love coursed through me at the sight of him that I was afraid, for a moment, of breaking.

'Don't ever scare me like that again,' I whispered, my tears indistinguishable from the seawater that rolled down my cheeks.

Sebastien didn't reply. His muscles were taut beneath my hands and I pulled back, concern knitting my brows together.

I only needed to glance down to see the source of his pain. The blood coating our clothes still flowed from his body. His wound was as severe as ever, the colour draining from him as quickly as it had returned. One glance at his face was all it took to realise that he was still in the clutches of death.

Above us, Nerida's face had twisted into an expression of choking vengeance.

'Why isn't he healing?' I croaked.

'He won't heal,' the sea replied coolly. 'As the sun waned, so did his powers.'

Cruel shadows devoured Nerida's gaze as I realised in horror what she meant. 'No . . . you have to help him! Please – he'll die. He doesn't have a heart.'

Those eyes of cobalt glittered. The stars above seemed to wink out, one by one.

'Oh, I know.'

32

Storm clouds marbled the crimson sky as I frantically tore strips of fabric from my skirts, pressing them against Sebastien's chest to staunch the incessant flow of blood. It was Aberdeen's words that came to me then, with Sebastien slumped at my feet, hardly able to see through my tears. *All men bleed the same. Even kings.*

'Your kingdom will be awaiting your return,' Nerida said with a smirk.

Blood trickled through my fingers as I pressed desperately against Sebastien's gaping wound. Golde stood the closest to me, her face stricken. How similar this must've looked to that moment, three hundred years ago, when the world had first shattered at her feet.

'Why are you doing this?' I cried, gazing up at the sea I had spent eighteen years aching for.

The swirling pools of the goddess's eyes were tainted by such cruelty that they were scarcely blue. 'You wanted a man and I gave you one,' she replied icily. 'Now you will learn how easily they die.'

'Don't do this,' I whispered, tasting salt on my tongue. '*Please.*'

'You really thought I would let you have him?' Nerida scoffed.

I understood then how Sebastien must've felt, all those centuries ago. Kneeling before the sea with his beating heart laid bare. I was the same, at the mercy of that great, cruel god, with nowhere to hide and nothing left to sacrifice. My own heart should've been frantic in my chest, but it wasn't. It was on its knees, bleeding out and turning cold before her once more.

Nerida turned away from us, a satisfied smirk on her lips. I felt my soul fracture more with each of her ebbing footsteps.

'So you're just going to let him die?' I cried out, voice jagged with pain. 'I thought you loved him.'

The sea's laugh rumbled as black clouds unfurled over the sky, obscuring the stars. 'I will love him again,' she assured me. 'When he joins me beneath, as all pirates do.'

Her words sank in, slipping through the valley of my chest, into that empty place where my heart used to be. *He's going to die.*

A cry fell from my lips as Sebastien collapsed into me, his breathing ragged. I helped him to lie down, desperate to ease his pain but so afraid to see him yet another step closer to death.

'Ria,' he murmured, his hand finding mine against his blood-soaked chest, trying to pull my attention towards him.

But I couldn't look. Couldn't bear to see him like that.

I glanced around desperately, seeing the anxious faces of our crew, but only the sea could return what she'd taken. And she was leaving. Her elegant form strode across the deck, her human features fading as she prepared to rejoin her world below the waves.

'Please,' I cried after her. 'I've spent my whole life loving you.

Don't turn your back on me now!'

Nerida's face rippled between flesh and crystal waves, causing the pirates closest to her to stagger back in fear.

'You're right,' she said, tilting her head as if in thought. 'I think I shall watch.'

Before I could say anything, before I could plead one last time, Sebastien squeezed my hand, his grasp frighteningly weak. 'Ria,' he said again, and my name was like blood on his lips.

'Don't,' I whimpered. 'Please don't go.'

His hand stroked my hair gently as my tears joined the river of blood that flowed from him. Something flared in his gaze. Trepidation. We both knew what was happening, how little he had left. But he just gazed at me, like that was enough.

And it almost was — almost ripped me in two, just looking at him.

I curled my fingers around his wrist, feeling under his ruined white shirt for the thrum of a pulse that wasn't there.

Sebastien pulled me closer, my cheek against his lips. 'I love you,' he whispered into my skin. Chills rippled over my shoulders, down my arms, into my bones. 'Think I was born loving you, blackbird. Even when I couldn't, I just did.'

My heart broke open, too full to hold the words he bled to me. I was sobbing when I reached for him, my heart so broken with love I was afraid it might fail me all together.

'I love you,' he repeated. 'And I'll love you again. Even when I'm gone. Tomorrow, and the day after that, and every day that comes. Again and again and again. I'll love you until I'm dust, and then some.'

I couldn't speak through the tears that rolled down my cheeks so I just let him pull me down to him, into him, kissing him like my heart could fuse with the emptiness of him and fill it.

'No!' a voice barked, so powerful that the planks beneath us

335

trembled. My head snapped up.

Nerida's eyes were alight with anger, but she wasn't addressing anyone on deck.

Great columns of water rose from the sea, swirling in the air as they transformed into figures, slipping over the sides of the ship. I recognised them – the spirits of the ocean, their gentle features made of rippling, gossamer water, hair like rolling sea foam. They were the waves, come to life.

They wound gracefully through the air, seascape eyes telling me not to be afraid. I recognised them well – they'd brought me here, watched over me, called to me my entire life.

'Save him,' I whispered, knowing that these were my friends, that I hadn't loved them in vain. 'Please.'

'Stay back,' Nerida commanded, danger coursing through the current of her voice.

'Do you truly love him, little one?' asked a spirit, the cerulean waters of its face shaped like an old woman's, the gentle smile reflected upon them as soft as the waking moonlight.

I nodded frantically, my tears spelling out the truth. 'I do.'

'I forbid it!' Anger radiated from the goddess like rays of sun amid the night sky.

But her waves didn't listen.

'We reward those who love us,' said another, its voice a melody of the sea breeze, whispering shells, crashing tides. 'You have loved us well, Ria Lucroy. Now we repay it.'

The spirit raised a hand just as Nerida had done. The air grew restless as the sound of magic hummed through it. Something was stirring.

I lifted my chin, wariness clouding my gaze despite the hope swimming in my every breath, unsure which way the tides were about to turn. A small eddy appeared in the air between us, winding and churning into shape. I tried to make out what it was as it swam towards me – something made of dark, swirling blue.

A heart.

It drifted through the air, pulsing sapphire, and sank into Sebastien's motionless chest, seeping through his skin and stitching it back together.

A moment passed, an endless, liquid heartbeat. He didn't stir. Panicked by his stillness, I searched his features for any sign of life, for breath or warmth, but found none, his eyes shut to the world.

'You faithless *snakes*,' shrieked the sea, her rage shaking the stars, hair whirling around her in a halo of shattered moonlight. 'How dare you betray me?'

The waters grew disturbed, restless, but the spirits of the waves spoke as one. 'This heart is a gift,' they said, still facing me despite Nerida's fury. 'So that your people may find home once more. So that you will be loved as you have loved. We will be watching you.'

'Thank you,' I choked out, but I couldn't feel relief. Sebastien still hadn't woken, and I'd been tricked one too many times to trust their kindness.

'Heed my words, human,' Nerida snarled at me, words stifled by an inhuman rage. 'I swear upon all that lives below, you will regret this night. Someday, your wretched hearts will betray you. Then we will see how you beg at my feet, how you will curse this day and beseech me to take back your king.'

Great black clouds spilled across the sky and a torrent of rain poured down upon us, wiping all trace of the sea and her spirits from the deck, though the echo of her threats remained.

Sebastien released a shuddering breath and his eyes flew open. I gasped in relief, scrambling to kneel over him, clutching his chest, his arms, making sure he was healed, that he was real. But as I peered down at him, I could see instantly that something was different. It wasn't his heartbeat, thrumming like the rain upon the decks, but his eyes . . .

Something fathomless swam within. They were dark as ever, as the deepest depths of the ocean, yet there was light in them, too. They were no longer black, but the inky blue of the sea that had brought us together and torn us apart all at once.

He reached up to stroke my face, pulling me down to him; to a kiss that tugged the broken strings of my heart back together.

'Thought I told you to stop saving my damn life,' he breathed.

I laughed against his lips, kissing him, again, again, again.

'Ria . . .' He exhaled my name like a prayer, gripping me tighter, as though he was afraid I'd slip away. The taste of salt and blood mingled on our clumsy lips – his soft and warm against my fearful, frigid ones. His next words came gravelly from his throat. 'You were so brave.'

'I thought I'd lost you,' I whispered back. 'I couldn't – I just can't . . .' My voice broke at the thought, remembering how it had felt to watch him die. Twice.

'You'll never lose me,' he swore, with enough conviction for the both of us. 'You're in my bones, blackbird. My everything.'

I was crying again, but I didn't care. He sat up and I wrapped my arms tight around his neck, revelling in the warmth of his chest against mine.

Footsteps surrounded us and I looked up to see our crew edging tentatively closer. I let out a sigh at the sight of them all. There they stood, covered in salt water and blood, drowning beneath the rain yet somehow more alive than ever.

The downpour scoured away the pool of blood at our boots, as if the pain of it all could simply be swept out to sea. Golde wiped a trickle of blood from her nose, her chest rising and falling sharply.

Mors looked at me with glowing eyes, filled with a pride that made my heart swell. Aron shifted on his feet, his eyes landing anywhere but on the woman beside him, her colourful skirts dark and heavy with rain, her fingers laced tightly through his.

I smiled.

Sebastien clambered to his feet, tugging me with him. I watched as his gaze swept the deck. The remnants of Bane's crew were huddled by the starboard edge, clustered behind the body of their captain. I reached for Sebastien's hand. Just days ago, killing Bane had seemed the only thing he cared about. One traitor's blood on his hands, worth all this pain.

'Does it matter?' I asked quietly. 'Are you angry you didn't kill him yourself?'

The answer was written in Sebastien's stern brow and stiff shoulders as he took in Bane's dead body, tossed to the side as though he'd been insignificant all along. He *was* angry. But the moment he met my gaze, it dissolved.

'No,' he answered, lips sliding into a smile.

Elation bubbled up in my chest, the horrors of the last few hours finally fading. We were free.

Hours later, we stood at the bow of the ship to watch the sun re-emerge, seeping light through the heavy storm clouds. It was a dawn I thought we'd never see. Along with the sorrow, the guilt, the regret, I was brimming with relief.

Golde stood nearby, leaning out over the rolling water with one arm looped through the ratlines. I wondered what it felt like, being mortal again after so long. Knowing the future was both boundless and finite all at once. She'd see her kingdom again. That had to ease a little of the ache. But from the way the first mate's eyes clung to the horizon, I knew there was something else out there, some part of her still missing. Someone.

Sebastien wrapped an arm around my shoulders and dropped his forehead to mine, his sigh grazing my cheek. I smiled, leaning into his chest and looking out at the sea. Waves swept past, basking in the palette of rippling, liquid daybreak as the soft glow of sunrise soaked into our skin.

'Where do we go from here?' I asked. Then I looked up, reading the answer in Sebastien's gaze as he grinned.

Adventure was calling, and it sounded like *home*.

Acknowledgements

My love for this book got me through my final year of high school, a university degree, a global pandemic and all the bits in between. The girl I was five years ago probably wouldn't recognise me now, but I honestly don't know where or who I would be without these characters, and without the people who helped me along the way.

First and foremost, my unstoppable agent, Lucy Irvine, who saw all the things I love about this book and helped me bring them to life. Thank you for being the person I needed in my corner, even from the other side of the world. And the rest of the team at Peters, Fraser and Dunlop, for all their hard work.

Naomi Greenwood, my incredible editor, who loves this love story almost as much as I do. Thank you for your passion, vision and belief in my stories, and in me. It truly means the world.

My parents, who provided me with food and endless cups of tea and a home in which to be an absolute book-hoarding menace. Who supported me as much as I ever let them, and then some.

I don't say it enough, but thank you. My grandmothers, who have always been some of my most stalwart supporters. Princess, who was the very best dog, and saw me through it all. My brother . . . you know who you are.

Jimena — who was the first person to believe in this book, who read it in all its messiness and loved it anyway, and who I will never truly forgive for watching *Outlander* without me.

Isobel Kanaley, Hannah Kroeger, Kyle Rampal and Flinders Twartz, who made even the darkest times some of the brightest; I'm so lucky to have you guys. But also Kalina Kenney, Remy Miletto, Veronica Whitaker, Abi Ma and Amy Galliford. Thank you for the laughs, the uplifting and the occasional reason to leave my house. I love you all.

Tiffany Wang. I didn't even know you when I wrote this book. Like, at all. I just want the proof in print that I knew you before you got famous. (Thanks for the support, BTW.)

Sydney Langford, Birdie Schae, Grace Varley, Gabrielle, Briana and all my endlessly kind and funny and talented Twitter friends who made this journey so much less lonely, I love you!

To the amazingly helpful Sophie Snow and Tara Freitag, who (somehow) put up with the melted Swiss cheese of a plot that this book once was, thank you for all your insights.

To the incredible team at Hachette Children's Group whose magic brought this book to life, I will never be able to thank you enough. Kaltoun Yusuf, Laura Pritchard, Jen Alliston, Bec Gillies, Emily Thomas, Sarah Farmer, Inka Roszkowska and Binita Naik. And, of course Olga Skomorokhova, for her stunning illustrations!

I can't forget the awesome Sales and Rights teams, led by Nicola Goode and Tracy Phillips, as well as everyone working in the Australia and New Zealand offices, including Cassy Nacard, Georgie Carroll, Tracy Yong, Alison Shucksmith, Tania Mackenzie-Cooke and Sacha Beguely.

I would also like to acknowledge the traditional custodians of the land on which I live and write, the Gadigal people of the Eora Nation. I pay my respects to their Elders, past and present, and recognise the enduring connections that First Peoples have to the land and waters. Sovereignty was never ceded.

Lastly, of course, I must thank you, the reader. (Unless you're one of the people I already mentioned, in which case you're probably reading this for free.) I hope, more than anything, that this book gave you a little magic to hold on to — I know it did for me, and I'm still holding on.

© Captured By Belle

Sarah Street is a YA fantasy author,
born and raised on Gadigal land in Sydney, Australia.
She has a BA in English and Criminology and spends
her days amid a hoard of books, playing Hozier songs
to her houseplants and deciding what great
body of water to write about next.

Follow Sarah on Twitter @**sarahastreet**

sarahstreetauthor.com